WICKED LITTLE
GAMES

DEE PALMER

Warning: ADULT CONTENT 18+ Also this book is a DUET...read into that what you will, but you don't have long to wait until the next book....only 8 weeks!

For free stories sign up to my Newsletter on the contact page at http://deepalmerwriter.com/ (Promise No Spam)
or click here

http://eepurl.com/biZ6g1

OTHER BOOKS BY DEE

DEDICATION

For the lovely ladies and gents that opened up their homes to me on my adventure of a lifetime: Amanda & Kyle, Patty & Scott, Katie & Louis, Jane & John, Maggie and to Paula & Sean, Lynn, Shannon & Bruce for keeping me company.

And for my Husband…it's lucky you love me!

PART 1

CHAPTER ONE

Tia

"Y**ou're the Devil**," I whisper. It's barely audible above my own ragged breaths, but he heard me, loud and clear. Striding forward, I match each of his steps with a retreating step of my own. This was a dance we had enjoyed in the past, but not today. I'm grateful when my back finally hits the door of his office; my legs had begun to tremble, and I feared I was about to hit the deck. My hands press against the solid wood for support, and fixing my eyes on his, I start to shake my head.

A futile non-verbal request for him to stop.

He steps so close my breath catches, and I actually stop breathing for a moment. Closing my eyes, I drop my chin to my chest.

Please don't do this.

His knuckle brushes my jaw, and he tips my whole face up with his fingertip but makes no other movement, no sound at all. He simply waits. When the silence becomes too much, I open my eyes and meet his gaze.

"I told you I was." His lips form the perfect smile, and his eyes seem to darken to an impossible shade of midnight blue.

It's strange; I always thought the devil would have darker

colouring, inky black hair, a deep tan maybe, and eyes you would easily lose your soul to. Not him. Although the eyes are spot on, everything else was way off; he couldn't look less like the Lucifer of the movies. He is tall, towering over me now, broad, strong shoulders, but slim, fit, stunning actually. His rough blond hair falls over his eyes, and on any other day, that would be a crime. No, he looks more like an angel than the devil I know him to be. He looks like a Nordic God.

The pain ripping me apart from the inside out escapes in a sob that I can't contain and takes us both by surprise. My hand flies to my mouth, too late to hide the heartbreak. He laughs, a hollow sound that chills my blood, and even the tender way he tucks my hair away from my face feels too raw.

Please don't do this.

"Oh, Princess, you always did know how to make me laugh," he states with a wry smile that makes my stomach turn.

"My pain amuses you?" I manage to form actual words when I feel utterly speechless and broken.

"No, your naiveté amuses me." He sighs. "I told you I was the Devil, Tia, and yet you are surprised when I drag you to Hell." He draws his bottom lip in slowly between his teeth, and even now I can feel my body betray me. My fingers twitch, restless to touch him just one more time. My heart clenches, and there is an unwelcome spark of heat right between my legs. He inhales deeply through his nose and flashes a knowing grin, which adds mortification to my devastation.

He's acutely aware of how he affects me; he always has been.

He chuckles and leans closer. His mouth is just below my ear before he speaks. "Your pain is just a pleasant bonus, princess."

"Oh, God." I gasp, my fist clutching at the unbearable pain cleaving through my heart.

"Now, princess, do you really think He will save a little sinner like you? Besides, He really can't help you now, not when your soul is already mine." His lips press a kiss on the crook of my neck, and I whimper. They always feel like heaven on my skin, and now it's no different, except everything is different.

"What do you want?" I've lost so much. My tone fails to hide my absolute desolation.

"Everything."

"I gave you everything...I gave you my heart, damn it. I have nothing left." The tears I have managed to hold at bay fall, bursting unbidden from my eyes as I hold his unwavering gaze.

"Now we both know that's not true." He sucks some air through his pursed lips, shaking his head lightly as if he is reprimanding a small child.

"I don't understand." I sniff, dragging the back of my hand unceremoniously along the underside of my nose and roughly drying my cheeks in an attempt to regain some composure.

"I think it's cute that you believe your heart holds any interest to someone like me. What am I saying? There is no one like me," he taunts, then tilts his head to one side as if thinking how best to deliver his next line. "You promised me forever, princess, and there's only one thing that is truly forever." His eyes narrow, and the cruel smile that has been an almost permanent fixture since he brought me here, vanishes. His expression is chillingly vacant and so changed, I barely recognise this monster before me. "I've come for your soul, Tia." He pulls back just enough to slide his hand into his back pocket, retrieving a long slim dagger. He flips it with ease, catching it and wrapping his fingers around the handle like it was moulded only to fit his hand. The tip of the blade is reflected in his eyes, and the sharp edge shines brightly, even in the dim light of the fading evening.

"I don't understand. I didn't do anything wrong. I love you," I plead, my hand resting on his chest where his heart should be.

"I think, with that statement, you've answered your own question, haven't you, princess?" His tone drops, and his expression is *now deadly serious. He waits again for realisation of what he's asking to slowly sink in. It doesn't take long. No.*

"I can't do this." I mouth the words because I can't bring myself to say them out loud. It doesn't matter. Whether he's lip reading or mind reading, he knows me, and he knows this is no longer a choice I have to make.

"I know, princess...I know." His voice is softly soothing, coaxing me, and I comply. His words are like a balm, hypnotic, and I find I am no longer able to resist or fight him. He places the blade in my hand, cupping his larger hands over the top and gripping tight. He twists the blade until it is pointed just below my rib cage and angled upward, perfectly aimed for maximum impact. I'm shaking my head because I know I can't do what he's asking me to do. Then he hugs me...he steps his strong body into mine and presses us both hard against the door.

"Ah! Oh...oh...please...please." The dagger burns like a thousand blades as it pierces my skin. A tidal wave of pain tears through my body, and I continue to cry out.

It hurts so much.

"I do love it when you beg." He jolts the blade deeper, and I can feel it slicing through my flesh. The pain is unbearable. I can't breathe. Every nerve is screaming in agony as I feel my lungs burn with the blood now filling them from inside. I start to choke. Even at this time, I take comfort from the knowledge that this flesh and blood pain is fleeting and is only a fraction of the devastation my heart feels.

It will all be over soon.

"Why are you smiling?" My vision is a little blurry, but I can see the confusion on his face.

"Because, at least this pain will end," I answer, slumping against him with weakness. My words are faint. He tilts my head up; it's too heavy for me to hold and flops to one side, but he is careful to ensure I am looking into his eyes when he speaks. He

wants to make sure I truly understand my fate.

"Princess, trust me, this is just the beginning."

"Tia! Tia! For fuck's sake, wake up!" The booming, deep, throaty voice penetrates my darkness, and from the edge of worry in the tone, he's had trouble waking me this time. My eyes spring open but are still filled with tears. I blink rapidly to clear them, enough to focus on the face before me. Long, silky black hair frames his handsome face. Deep, dark eyes that have shone with wickedness and lust now look troubled. He drags his hand through his hair, which is long enough to fall neatly back away from his face without tucking it behind his ears. This face has a shadow of stubble that is a few days past a shave but not quite a beard. He's naked, that's not a surprise. It's his house, and he's never been the shy sort of guy, which is something of a paradox considering his heartbreaking agoraphobia. Although I don't know why; the two aren't linked in any way. It just seems strange how someone so confident, rational, and intelligent can let this disease rule his life, but then that's the very nub of a phobia; it isn't rational.

His chest is heaving, and I guess that is from the long run from his room to mine. I can't help but admire the work he puts into maintaining such a muscular body. *It's impressive what a decent set of weights and a treadmill can achieve.* Smooth, olive skin over taut muscles, which flex and ripple as he continues to draw in heavy breaths. He's such a beautiful person, inside and out. Still, I have just one friend in this world, and I'm not going to ruin what we have by doing something as ugly as fucking. *Sex ruins everything.*

"Logan, I'm fine." I shuffle up my bed and try to disentangle my legs from the bed sheets. My lower body resembles an Egyptian mummy where I must've been twisting and turning for some time. I'm soaked through, too. My t-shirt is almost completely see-through, and it hasn't gone unnoticed. "Ahem, my eyes are up here." I snap my fingers in front of my breasts to get his attention and point to my face.

"Yes, but your perky nipples are right there, and I don't care what nightmare you were having, those babies are a fucking dream come true." He grins and lets out a loud laugh when my cheeks burn from his wayward attention. He can be such an arse sometimes, but he does have a way of distracting me. I pull the sheet up high to my neck and roll my eyes when his bottom lip pushes out in a brattish pout. He holds the sulky look for a moment before his dark chocolate brown eyes lose their playful crinkle, as his face softens and is once again etched with worry.

"I'm fine. I'm sorry I woke you." I sigh and reach from under the sheet to hold his hand. He squeezes and wraps his other hand over mine. He is soft-spoken at the best of times when it's just us, but I find myself tilting forward to hear him now.

"Tia, you could've woken the dead with that cry. It's only that we live in such an old and extremely well soundproofed little home that I don't have the neighbours banging on my door." He fails to mask his real concern with talk of noise pollution, but I'm happy to play along.

"Logan, this is a mansion, and our nearest neighbour is a good half a mile away," I retort.

"They still might've heard you, T." He pulls my fingers to his mouth and presses my hand to his cheek. The chill and cold sweat from my nightmare begins to lose its grip with every kind gesture this man bestows without hesitation, and it just warms my soul.

"I'm sorry. I wish they'd stop, too. I hate that I wake you every night."

"I don't give a fuck about that. It's not like I work; I can sleep all day if I want, but you work, and I know you haven't had a full night sleep since you started that job. Is this worth it, Tia? You don't need to do this." His tone is almost pleading, but he already saved me once. I'm not going to sponge off him any more than I need to. Besides, it's not just about the money.

"I want to work; I *need* to work. You have given me more than I can ever repay. I need to contribute something to this weird relationship," I argue.

"I love our weird relationship, and you saved me just as much. Besides, you know I have zero interest in money. I have money. I have lots of money. We could take this to the next level if that helps. I could probably learn to fancy you enough to stop with the hookers," he teases, tilting his head and flashing a roguish smile that would have the girls falling at his feet if he'd let them.

"Oh, Logan, you say the sweetest things; you're such a romantic." I mock fan myself at his crudeness.

"Aren't I though?"

"You know you're like a brother to me, right?" I clench my jaw to try and hide the lie, his eyes narrow, looking closely for any sign of truth. It has to be like this. I can't lose him; I won't. He sniffs and sucks in a slow breath before shrugging off my comment.

"Since this isn't *Game of Thrones*, and the sister thing is a hard limit for me, *and* there is no fucking way I see you as a relative in *any* respect, I'm ignoring that comment and keeping us fucking firmly on the table."

"Logan!" I slap him with the back of my hand on his taut tummy, which tenses on impact to rock-hard undulating muscle, and I have to fight everything in me not to turn my hand and just caress his skin, his body. To let my fingers explore where my cowardly heart fears to go.

"Look T, I don't mind coming down the hall every night, bollock naked to rescue your arse from whatever demon hell you're dreaming, but they seem to be getting worse. Are they always the same?" I close my eyes, trying not to recall the dream, but the images are ingrained, and I nod my head.

"Always the same, the location might vary but the actual death is always the same, and it's always...*him.*" With effort, I swallow the dry lump in my throat, my chest still aching from the dagger. The pain felt is so genuine it carried over into my reality.

"You die in your dreams?" His back straightens, but I ease him down, squeezing his hand and hopefully returning some of the comfort he gives me.

"Yes, but don't panic; it usually just means a big change ahead, and I think that's pretty spot on, don't you?" I let out a humourless laugh, which makes his brows pull together in a deep frown.

"Why the devil?" he asks, his voice thick with concern. "I mean, why is he the devil in your dreams do you think?"

"Because he turned out to the devil in real life. Only the devil could do what he did." My words drift from my lips with no emotion, not anymore. "They're just dreams, albeit they're dragging residual feelings from the very depths of my sub-conscious, and I'd much rather my subconscious left me well enough alone." I force a tight smile. "Still, I'm sure they'll stop one day."

"If you survive that long...no sleep and you haven't been eating my gourmet cooking for weeks. You look like shit."

"There you go again, you sweet talker."

"I'm serious." He narrows his eyes, and for once, he does look serious, deadly serious. I try to smile, but it's having little influence. He's really mad at me this time.

"I know, Logan." I let out a long breath and hold his gaze. "Look, there's not much I can do about the lack of sleep and broken nights. I'm not taking tablets, so I'll just have to deal. I will make an effort though, with the food if that pleases you?"

"It would. It's pretty much the only thing I do, apart from the hookers, that gives me joy, and when you don't eat what I lovingly prepare, I feel like I've failed," he states quietly, and his honesty takes me back. He's such a closed book most of the time that, when he does share like this, I feel hugely honoured and like a complete shit at the same time.

"Oh Logan, god, not at all. I'm so sorry. I love your cooking. I love our mealtimes. Actually, I live for our mealtimes, but I've just not felt that hungry recently." I shuffle closer to him and hold my hand to his cheek, stroking the stubble with my thumb. He leans into my palm. Not a second passes before his head snaps up, his eyes wide with shock.

"You're not pregnant, are you?"

"You have to have sex for that to happen," I lament.

"Not necessarily." His eyes dart suspiciously between my belly and my face.

"I'm not pregnant." Pulling my hands from his, I wrap my arms around my tummy. I'm not protecting anything in there, just my pride at his accusatory glare.

"Good, because I still get first dibs on your womb if you want offspring. That was the deal when I invited you to move in."

"Fuck off was it the deal!" I snap, and he wisely leans out of my reach before I can nut punch him. "And you didn't invite me…you found me living in your basement. Three months *after* I had already moved in."

"My little thief." He never fails to get my heart hammering with the possessive way he says the word 'my'. I love that more than I should. "I knew you were there after a week of having to double order in on bread and cheese. I thought for a moment I had an enormous mouse that liked his cheese in a sandwich." He grins and wiggles his thick brows.

"What? You've never told me that. Why the hell didn't you call me out sooner?" My jaw drops, and he has the good grace to look at least a little sheepish. He offers up a slight shrug in his non-existent defence. "You let me freeze my arse off in the basement for eleven more weeks. Why?"

"I needed to be sure."

"Of what?"

"I needed to be sure you weren't a wicked lie." His voice drops to a whisper, and the sadness in his eyes breaks my fucking heart. We all have demons, but for the most part, they don't come out to play. I don't think that's the case with Logan, but I know so little about him. He has to be the most private person I've ever met, and as much as I've tried, he won't let me in. Whatever haunts him, he keeps it locked inside, and since I am not sleeping on the street because he took pity on me, I am not going to pry.

We all have secrets.

"Oh, Logan, come here." I open my arms wide, and his face lights up.

"Yes…boobs. I get the boob hug." He grins like a schoolboy about to cop his first feel.

"How can you be super scary intimidating one minute, and the next, you're a complete dork?" He climbs into my hold, and his strong arms thread behind me, but we're at a funny angle so we can't get close.

"Just lucky, I guess. And if it gets me close to these girls, I'll happily play the dork." He shifts and lifts me across his lap. My cotton girl boxer shorts are the only thing preventing his swelling cock from nestling where no man has ever been.

"Don't be an arse." I slap the back of his head, which makes him laugh. He holds me tight, and it feels unbearably good. I hope it does for him, too. I feel like I am always taking from him, and he asks so little in return, just my company.

"And it's always him?" he asks after several long minutes. I had closed my eyes and almost drifted off. I draw in a steady breath and nod.

"Yep, I haven't seen him in so long, and yet it's definitely him that destroys me every night."

"Something about first loves, eh?" he muses with a bitterness I happen to share.

"They're just dreams," I reply flatly.

"That may be true, my little thief." He kisses the top of my head, and I smile at my nickname. "But these dreams are also a warning. It's your subconscious speaking a truth you might not see, or might not see until it's too late. Listen to them, and learn from them. Ignore them, and you may as well hand me that dagger." He looks down at me as I look up. I know he cares for me. I wish I wasn't such a coward.

"You'd never hurt me." I feel safe in his arms. I know him. More importantly, I trust him.

"No, Tia, I wouldn't, but since I can't *ever* leave this house, I might not be around to save you, either." He points this out with a mix of sadness and resignation that hits me hard. The last thing this man needs is my shit on top of his own.

"I'll be fine," I say with enough conviction he actually smiles before giving me yet another lifeline.

"You want me to stay and sleep with you?"

"Do you mind?"

"You know I don't, so long as you don't mind my erection digging into your side for the rest of the night." He states this as a matter of fact.

"The only time I mind your erection is when I know it's been balls deep in some hired-in skank." I screw my face up at the thought.

"Well, my balls have been nowhere near any body part except my right hand for a while, so you're safe." He waves his hand, and somehow that image hasn't helped my face lose any of its distaste.

"Delightful,"

"Well, if you would let me fuck you, I wouldn't need the hookers or my right hand," he teases.

"You'd stop masturbating if we fucked?" My tone is rightly incredulous.

"No, but I'd have your right hand to do that for me if we were together." He looks at me with a mix of arrogance and lust.

"You know, I used to wonder why you only ever paid for sex. I mean you're very easy on the eye. I guessed you could get any girl you wanted, but now...now I'm not so sure."

"Ah, you love my innate charm and straight talking." His eyes dip to his solid erection, and I can't help but do the same. It's massive, kind of hard to ignore. My cheeks flash with heat, and I can feel the liquid pooling between my legs. This is a dangerous game we play, but I need him so much I can't fuck it up. I let out a light laugh before blowing out some of the heat he is generating in my body.

"Foul mouthed and filthy minded, you mean." I push him playfully on his shoulder, like you would a mate, a buddy, not someone you want but can't have, *ever.*

"That, too. Just so you know, the minute you stop referring to me as your brother, I am in there." He wiggles his finger in the general direction of my crotch, and I brush off his comment, like I have a million times before. I don't think of him as my brother, not in the least; it's just easier. I'm a fucked up mess of feelings at the best of times, but I won't let sex change us, and I can't risk losing him. "Now scoot over, and let me start the fondling process." He slides in behind me and pulls me to his body. He moulds perfectly, his large frame completely encasing mine. His hand reaches up to squeeze one of my breasts.

"Hug, not fondle." I pull his hand away and entwine my fingers so I can hold him safely at my waist.

"Potato, po-tah-to." He rolls his hips so his cock is wedged right up against my arse. *It's going to be a long night.* His breathing quickly becomes shallow, but I know he's still awake, so I ask something that plagues me.

"Why don't you try having a real relationship, Logan? You deserve better than this." I mean it when I say the words, but it doesn't stop the painful twist in my gut all the same. No, not my gut, maybe just a little higher. He lets out a sleepy groan and pulls me tighter to his warm body. There's not a millimetre of space between us.

"Girlfriends tend to want to go on dates, T," he reasons

"I guess," I sigh. I don't really believe that's his only option for normality, but I do understand his situation is complicated. Before I can contradict him, he whispers into my ear.

"Besides, there's nothing better than this."

CHAPTER TWO

Tia

I can hear Logan stirring from his slumber. He can sleep like the dead, and often, when he's wrapped around me like he was last night, I can barely breathe. It feels good, though, so I'd never complain. He makes me feel safe, and for someone like me, that is worth its weight in gold. Or more importantly, worth me keeping my legs together and fighting the feelings I have for him. *Logan deserves better than me.* I doubt he feels the same, anyway. Needing someone for company is one thing, but loving them is entirely different, and even that counts for shit in my experience so I'd rather close that door and just have whatever it is we have. It works, and that's all that matters.

"Come back to bed, Dodge." He lets out a rough throaty yawn that morphs into a sexy deep moan and satisfied sigh. He mixes up the nicknames he calls me depending on his mood. He called me the not-so Artful Dodger the night he caught me thieving from his fridge all those months ago and it's stuck, along with T, little thief, and trouble, but I'll answer to anything if it's said with that deep sexy drawl.

Stop it, Tia. Just stop.

The bed creaks with the weight of his movement, as he stretches and pulls himself up. He drags his hand over his sleepy dark features, his long mane falling over his face, his thick brow furrowed as his eyes finally fix on mine, and he releases that brilliant heart-stealing smile. The drapes may still be drawn, but I doubt the sunrise would rival that view for shine.

"Oh, someone's been busy." His eyes flit from mine to the easel over my shoulder. I have been engrossed for hours choosing this distraction over sleep in the end. I find it's the only thing that really calms me. It's the only time when there is no pain, no memories. There's nothing but me and my canvas, whatever that might be. This week it's a watercolour, and I have been working on this picture for a few days. I really wanted to get it finished today before work, and I have been putting the finishing touches since the early hours. I find it hard to admit a piece is finished when I've put so much of myself into it; it's like I can't let go.

Stupid, I know, and this one is slightly different, so I don't have the same attachment, but the feeling is still there, just diluted. A little like the pastel layers of watercolour paint on this hand-pressed paper. For me, portraits are too personal, especially from a live model so I always shy away and explain that portraits aren't my thing. However, I wanted to give my boss, Maria, something for taking a chance on me. I managed to get a few pictures from her Facebook page and opted for a watercolour of her only grandchild.

I think it's finished. I rinse my brush vigorously in the jar of water before drying it carefully on the cloth in my lap. Looking over at Logan, I can see him appraising my work. The level of concentration always fascinates me. He never just glances; he studies. He takes his time, and he takes it all in.

He sees everything.

My own demons and my nightmares I think I'm so smart at

hiding, well, they never go unnoticed, not by him.

He flips onto his tummy and drags himself to the end of the bed. He lays his arms flat along the wrought iron frame and drops his chin to rest his head, never taking his eyes from the painting. Several minutes pass, and I silently study him as he literally watches paint dry. I bite my lips to stop from smirking.

"Don't smirk, this is serious stuff." He flashes a quick glance my way, and his tone only pitches with a mild warning. I hold my hands up in mock surrender.

"Oh, I know…deadly serious. My work doesn't leave this room without your seal of approval." I'm grinning now and even risk a playful shake of my head.

"Damn straight it doesn't," he retorts and arches his brow high as if I've said something ridiculous. This whole situation is ridiculous. It's not like I've sold anything.

"So do you like it?" I ask after another pause for observation and requisite silence. He holds up his finger to stop me, and I am about to lose my shit if he makes me wait any longer when his face changes from stern to warm and then fills with overt pride. That look just about makes my heart burst.

"Really, you like it?" I repeat.

"It's…it's not your normal depressing abstract shit, so, yes, I love it."

"Hey, I like my abstract shit." I fold my arms defensively over my chest, and he is instantly leaping over the bar on the bed and is seated beside me, naked. He sits cross-legged and lifts me into his arms.

"Um, naked, Logan," I cry out.

"Um, always naked, Tia," he teases, his arms squeezing, but he refrains from pulling me down into what I know is a semi-erection just waiting to rise. He continues to speak as if this isn't the most awkward thing ever. Maybe for him, it really isn't.

"I love your abstracts, you know that, but you can't deny they are some seriously fucked-up shit, dark and full of your pain." I stiffen in his hold. "Hey, it's okay, T; it's how you cope. I get that. We all have our outlets." His voice softens, and his breath is warm against my neck. "Anyway, as I was saying, the portrait is different. This, well, it feels full of hope."

"Hope?" I twist in his arms and look up, but he doesn't look down. He's just staring at the little girl on the easel.

"Yeah, it's a child before the world got involved and fucked her up. So that moment you captured on her face right there is pure undiluted hope." I follow his gaze, and his bright smile fades. I feel the wave of sadness at his beautiful words.

"God, you're wasted here, Logan." I grab his chin. His stubble prickles my fingers, and when I tip his chin so he meets my gaze, we are face-to-face in a curtain of his dark, glossy hair. I swallow the dryness and try to ignore the building tension. I can't fathom the reason for it, but I feel it as clear as I feel him growing hard beneath my bottom. I power on, ignoring the sensual nudging below. "You should be a poet or a writer, Logan. Not a computer geek with an over-active right hand." I try to joke, but it falls flat with the intensity of his gaze.

"We've talked about how you might replace my right hand…" I slap my hands over my ears and wriggle from his lap, grateful he helps me off, or I would probably injure his now solid, and, honestly, this close up, enormous erection. I have to force my eyes skyward.

"Yes, we have, so let's not. Besides, there's only so much teasing I can take before I might start to believe you," I joke.

"Who said I was teasing?" He doesn't sound like he's joking.

"Logan," I warn.

"Tia." He mimics my tone, but he still looks anything but playful. He looks incendiary.

"How about some breakfast?" I deflect and am grateful

enough to let out a huge relieved breath when he answers.

"You're cooking?" He stands, his erection defying gravity and straining to reach his belly button. I spin on the spot. Man, I can't stop looking. I wasn't always like this, and in fairness to him, he's always wandered around the house naked at night, sometimes during the day, but always at night.

"If you like." I hand him one of his t-shirts I stole from the laundry, but he just chuckles and holds it in his hand.

"Only if I want to spend the rest of the day in the toilet, Dodge. I think I'll take a rain-check." He chuckles and makes his way to the door. I still haven't turned round, pretending to gather my clothes and tidy. I am the least tidy person, and I know he must be grinning his arse off. Only I won't turn round to check. I can just sense the amusement.

"I'm not that bad, I'm just not as good as you."

"I'll cook, but I need to deal with this first." I turn because I'm an idiot and actually thought he might be referring to something other than his cock.

"What the hell, Logan!"

"Price of being nestled up against your fine arse all night. So you can watch or join in." I'm transfixed at the sight of him palming himself, stroking up and down, and I know I shouldn't, but it's hypnotic and really hot. I never thought that could look hot, never felt anything like I feel now, watching him. My face is on fire, blood's rushing in my ears, and I can feel a liquid heat between my legs that I barely recognise. I physically shake myself, and after my momentary lack of sanity, I slap one hand over my eyes and manoeuvre Logan toward the open door with the other.

"Or the third alternative, you can go back to your own room, you complete animal."

"Fine, fine...but just so you know, we're inevitable, Tia," he calls out as he pads down the hall. I shut the door and slide to the floor, my heart thumping so loud I can no longer hear his heavy footsteps. I exhale and drop my head to my hands.

I wish that were true.

I don't bother to get dressed, just pull on some old pj bottoms and an oversized hoodie that also belongs to Logan. I pull the collar up to my nose and take a deep sniff, and it smells just like him despite being fresh out of the laundry. A rich scent of manliness with a hint of thick forest after a downpour. Ironic that his aroma is the very essence of nature when he never steps a single foot outside. As tragic as I find this crippling phobia, he brushes it off with the same dismissive statement whenever anyone asks.

'The world's a fucked up place, so why the hell would I want to go outside when everything I need can be delivered right to my door?'

I've been living here for just under two years, and I have to say, he has a point. I only feel safe and happy when that front door closes behind me.

The kitchen is the warmest room in the house courtesy of the Aga kicking out a gentle heat 24/7. Faint and delicious smells linger until they are replaced with Logan's current cooking project. This morning it's bacon. My mouth waters, and my tummy rumbles in anticipation. I silently pad the length of the kitchen in my bare feet and take my seat at the table where Logan has already poured me a piping hot cup of tea. The steam is rising in gentle plumes, and I dump a large heaped spoon of sugar before I blow to cool it enough to take a sip. He's facing the cooker and most likely didn't hear me enter from the other end of the forty-foot long room. His naked arse cheeks seem to be taunting me. The tight round muscles flex and move when he jiggles to the angry Irish folk music blaring through the speakers. He does have a white tie knotted in the middle of his back, the ends of the apron dangling perilously close to the crack in his arse. I smile at his only concession to clothing in the kitchen. Safety first when there's bacon frying. It's not that he's *always* naked; he's just *mostly always* naked.

"It's lucky I'm not working until tonight. What's the ETA on those scrambled eggs?" I've finished my tea and skimmed the newspaper for anything remotely upbeat but settle on the crossword, which I've nearly finished.

"You're funny." He doesn't bother to turn but steps to the side so I can see him gently folding a golden-looking mound of what I assume are eggs. "This masterpiece needs none of your impatience and all of my attention."

"It does smell good, but what's with the glass bowl. We have pans, you know." Giving up on the last impossible clues on the last remaining words of the crossword, I fold the paper and walk over to the Aga. I nudge his side when he doesn't respond.

"Peasant," he quips, lightly shaking his head with fake disapproval. "This is a bain-marie, the bowl rests in the simmering water, heating the glass gently and the eggs cook from that heat. It's why they taste so damn good, and I've never heard you complain before."

"I'm not really complaining now. I've just never seen you cook eggs like this before."

"You're normally still asleep while I'm cooking breakfast. My princess likes to have her breakfast in bed, remember?" he teases, but the smile I was wearing slips from my face. "What? What's wrong?" He moves the pan from the heat and turns to me, lifting my fallen face high so our eyes are locked.

"It's…" I hesitate, but I know there is no point saying it's nothing when he knows damn well I'd be lying. "Can you not call me princess?"

"Why?"

"I love all the nicknames you've given me, even when you call me fuckwit, but not…just not princess, please."

"Of course. Care to tell me…oh…" His jaw clenches, and the stubble darkens when the muscles twitching pull the hairs closer together. His dark brow thickens with anger. "*He* used to call you that." He spits the words like he was the one abandoned, left broken, and completely heartbroken.

"It's silly, I know." I try to shrug it off, and his eyes dip to keep the contact, and he strokes his knuckles along my jawline.

"It is, but not for the reason you think." His deep voice softens, and I shake my head, blinking back the pain of the betrayal I feel every damn time *he* crosses my mind. "Tia, listen to me." Logan's face is so close all I can see is his impossibly large chocolate eyes, swirling with tiny specks of gold and onyx, framed by the longest lashes this side of false. "He's a cunt and a coward. If you give him this power over you, even with just a word, then he's winning. It's just a word, Tia. It lost all it's meaning the day he left you to rot in jail."

"You're right; I'm sorry." The tears that threatened vanish, and I draw in a steadying breath. Logan pulls me hard against his solid chest. His strong arms envelop me as his body moulds protectively around my much smaller frame. I take every bit of comfort from him.

"Don't apologise; you've done nothing wrong." He pulls back and holds my gaze with a look that speaks volumes, his words meaning so much more than this little exchange.

I did nothing wrong.

"Come on, fuckwit." He raises a playful brow, and I let out an unladylike snort at the welcome change of atmosphere.

He turns the heat off and removes the plates from the warming oven. Carefully placing the buttered toast, strips of pale pink smoked salmon in elaborate curls, he ladles the eggs into a soft mound in the centre of the plate. The bacon has its own side dish because it would spoil the aesthetics of the dish, but breakfast isn't breakfast without bacon. I'm about to take the plate from the side when his disapproving growl makes me stop. My fingertips were poised to lift, but are left hovering comically in mid-air. He holds his finger up in warning, but really, that growl had me frozen to the spot. The finishing touch, he sprinkles with some finely chopped chives, and only then gives the go-ahead for me to take my plate.

I scrape the surface and use the last piece of toast to wipe the plate clean. I survived almost entirely on bread and cheese the three months I lived in Logan's basement. I thought staple foods like that no one would notice going missing. I may have had the odd piece of fruit that was on the turn, but staying hidden and safe was my main objective. Now, however, I eat anything and everything with gusto, but then Logan is an amazing cook. He takes the newspaper I folded away and irritatingly quickly fills in the missing answers on the crossword. He throws the pen down and leans back with his hands behind his head, a satisfied smugness plastered all over his handsome face.

"Smart-arse." I look at the words he's entered and roll my eyes that I didn't get them. They always look so obvious once you see them written down. He drains his coffee, and I pour him another from the pot on the table.

"Want to tell me about last night?"

"What do you mean? I had a nightmare. It's not the first; I doubt it'll be the last."

"I'm not talking about the nightmare. I'm talking about you getting up to paint. The picture was barely outlined yesterday, and now, it's complete. Which meant you were asleep in my arms for maybe half an hour? Something made you stay awake so long, and I know it wasn't my cock, so spill, little one, what's worrying you?" His hands are now wrapped around his coffee mug, fingers interlocked like he is praying to some Mayan coffee god, yet his focus is on me.

"Nothing, it's fine." He stops mid-sip. His dark eyes narrow, and he draws his lip in at the side. The only other movement is his slow, steady breathing. His eyes fix on mine, and it's all I can do not to cower. He hates when I lie, and I hate that he knows every time I do. "I'm sorry. Look, I'm probably just anxious about my job, maybe that's it."

"You don't have to work as a cleaner, Tia." His tone is filled with irritation at a conversation we've had a dozen times. He's so used to getting his way, I know he's really struggling with my stubbornness. It's been just him for so long, I don't think the word compromise is even in his vocabulary. I honestly think my refusal to do as he says is the bigger problem, not the job itself.

"I do." I hold his glare, and he instantly holds up his hands in surrender.

"Let me finish, you nutter. I meant you don't have to work there. I take it you knew it was *his* company when you applied, because I really didn't have you pegged as someone stupid." His tone is anything but playful.

"I did know, yes, and I'm not stupid," I snap, my arms crossing defensively.

"So this isn't some revenge thing?" he counters and leans forward, his expression dark and deadly serious. I swallow the thick lump in my throat. *I hate this.*

"No," I state with as much conviction as I can. I'm not lying, not technically.

"Because to anyone with a brain cell, it could look like you were walking into the lion's den in a Lady Gaga meat costume." He is pushing, and I have to fight not to cave under this level of intense scrutiny, but it's for the best. *I have to do this.*

"I'm not, and I would like you to give me some credit. I know what I'm doing." My voice catches, and I can't fathom why he's giving me such a grilling. If he knew the real reason, he'd probably support me. I just can't risk him. If I get caught, it's one thing, but if he's involved and goes down with me, it would destroy him. I won't let that happen.

"Good, because you would have to be seriously fucking deranged to start something with just under a year left on your probation…unless you did actually want to go back to jail," he warns, and I feel the chill in my bones at the very thought.

"No! I'm never going back," I state with absolute conviction, which for the time being, seems to placate him. He sits back in his chair, and the tension eases from his shoulders. His bare chest heaves with steady, deep breaths, and he gives me a slight, acknowledging nod.

I can't have him interfering, either, so I offer a little more information in a way that I hope will convince him to back right off.

I stand, pushing my chair back, and roughly snap up the plate from the table, my temper prickling my nerves. I drop the dishes in the sink with a clatter and spin to face him. He looks startled at my sudden and obvious mood swing. "This isn't just some revenge thing, okay? Yes, I'm curious, but I'm not fucking stupid, and as much as I appreciate your concern here, Logan, it has fuck all to do with you." I pinch out a tight smile that borders on nasty.

"Really?" he fires back.

"Yes really."

"Fine." He stands abruptly, sending the chair flying, glaring at me. The fierceness would be extremely intimidating, if it wasn't for the fact that he is still naked. He turns and starts to stride from the kitchen. His mighty fine arse is just a mild distraction from the heated exchange.

"Fine," I call out after him, and just as he reaches the door, I add, "The eggs were really good, by the way."

"I know." He turns. I can see the anger in his face, but it's already starting to soften. "Clean up that fucking mess you made."

Okay, maybe it hasn't started to soften.

CHAPTER THREE

Logan

"Fuck!" I punch the frame of the back door for the tenth time. My knuckles are spilt and bleeding, and I'm pretty sure I have a shit tonne of splinters digging in between the bones. My hand is a mass of throbbing pain, so it almost feels numb. My stomach is a knot so tight, a troop of scouts couldn't loosen that fucker. I hate this, hate feeling so fucking out of control, which is why I *never* do this, never test myself. I know exactly where it ends up, only this time, I have a witness to my meltdown. *One step forward threes steps fucking backwards.* I can hear her light footsteps as they tentatively traverse the long hallway from the kitchen to the rear entrance of the house.

I can't even open the fucking door to take in some of the fresh morning air; my hand cramped on the handle like it had set with rigor. The sweats then started, making it impossible to grip, even if I did have the balls to turn the handle, which I don't, because I'm a motherfucking pussy who hasn't stepped a foot outside this house for ten years. I can feel the droplets of sweat running down my back, and my hair is slick to my face where it touches. I'm dripping, and I hate that. Until Tia came into my life, I wouldn't have given a flying fuck never to leave this house again, but now…everything has changed.

"Jesus, Logan, what are you doing?" Her tiny hand reaches for my arm, and she pulls my clenched fist away from the door-frame. "We're going to need a new doorframe," she mutters and slips her t-shirt over her head. It's my shirt. I love it when she steals my clothes. They hang off her tiny frame like clothes on a horse, but I won't deny she looks fucking sexy in my stuff. My cock twitches with the hope that she's naked underneath. Shit out of luck on that score too. Today, she's wearing one of those cami-tops that hugs her tiny waist and skims her per-fect, round, pert tits. The thin straps are straining under the weight of those delicious curves. She's not skinny, but at five foot nothing, she is tiny against my six foot four height, and whereas she is trim and athletic, I have spent ten years building bulk and muscle. She looks fucking perfect, almost naked, her pale, flawless skin next to my deep tan and ink—what is it they say about opposites? My cock continues to twitch and swell. "What's wrong with you?" she huffs.

"I'm just letting off steam." I shrug.

"No, I get that you're mad at something or someone. What I mean is, your hand is cut to shit and you're getting a hard-on. Do you get off on pain or something?"

"Not this kind of pain, no, but you are, in fact, wearing the skimpiest fucking top known to man, and you have a great rack," I state flatly and don't hide my smirk when she flushes a beautiful shade of dark pink high on her cheeks.

"Oh…damn it, Logan." She wraps the shirt carefully over my bleeding hand and cradles it to her warm body. She turns and leads me like a wounded pup back to the kitchen. She pushes me to sit and then drapes a kitchen towel over my raging erec-tion, which now looks like a floral tepee in my lap. She coughs to hide her laugh, but her cheeks have turned a ball-aching deep red now. And it's really not helping that she keeps wetting her lips before sucking them into her mouth. *Oh, man.* I flex and squeeze my fist, splitting the skin farther just for some sort of distraction.

"You're gonna need some tweezers. I may have a splinter or two." I can feel the stabbing like shards of glass, and I was hitting that frame with all my strength. Those are going to be buried deep.

"Mind telling me what you were doing, aside from the obvious re-modelling." She nods and digs around in the first aid box for supplies, pours the water from the kettle into a small bowl, and places the items on the table beside me. Pulling her chair in front, she shuffles and places her knees in between my spread thighs. I close my legs around hers and feel the spark of fire hit my balls, like it does every time her skin brushes mine. More recently, however, there's been a warm hit in my chest too. Her long chestnut curls fall over one side of her face. She scoops the mass of hair over to the other side of her head and tries to tame it by tucking as much behind her ear as possible. Her pale green eyes search mine, and when I shake my head, her whole body deflates before I even utter a word. She knows what's coming.

"Nothing." I grit my teeth when she unwraps the blood-soaked t-shirt. Looking at the mess, I'm thinking it might not be splinters after all, that looks like bone sticking out on two of the knuckles.

"I liked that t-shirt." She scrunches it up and throws it over to the bin, hitting it at the perfect angle to slide through the flap.

"Nice shot, ace, and I have others I'm sure you'll steal to replace it." I chuckle, trying to lighten the mood, but she barely twists out a strained smile.

"Hmm." She lays a fresh towel on her lap and places the bowl of water on top. She gently submerges my right hand. The water instantly colours bright red as my hand continues to pour out blood. Damn! That stings like a motherfucker.

"Is that just water?" I grimace.

"Stop being a pussy; I put a little antiseptic in. Those are some deep cuts, and it's not like I can take you to the emergency room," she throws out, but before I can say anything, her eyes are wide with mortification.

"Low blow, T," I add even though I can see she already regrets her outburst.

"Oh God, Logan, I'm so sorry, really I am." She places her hand on my cheek. It's wet from the water and warm droplets trickle down my neck. She cups my face, and her eyes become glassy with tears, and that's not what I want.

"Forgiven." I turn my head and kiss the softness of her palm. She resumes washing my cuts, and after several long seconds of awkward silence, she huffs and straightens her back. Her face furrowed with concern and I'm guessing frustration.

"Damn it, Logan, you have to give me more than 'it's nothing.'" She sighs, and her eyes seem to double in size, looking right through me, searching for my murky soul, wide and pleading like a damn puppy dog.

I can't.

I shake my head and affix a dark, warning scowl I only pray she heeds. She takes a moment and swallows what must be a lump in her throat. Despite all our time together, I still make her tremble, though she must know I'd never hurt her. She shakes off her nerves and powers through regardless.

"Nuh-uh, you don't scare me." She narrows her eyes, and her voice waivers just a little, belying her assertion. I raise a brow because I have to admire her stubbornness or her stupidity. "You're not allowed to shut me out when I have to tell *all*. I'm damn well not allowed to give you the 'it's nothing,'" she declares, and if her hands weren't busy washing the blood from mine, I imagine they would be perched on her hips, a mix of sass and indignation to go with that sexy pout.

"My house, my rules," I counter flatly, shutting the conversation dead with my tone.

"You want to die of septicaemia? Because if I don't get those splinters out..." she threatens, and I scoff.

"Fine, I'll just call a doctor." I pull my hand from the bowl and shake the excess water and blood onto the floor.

"Do you want to call a doctor?" A little line appears just at the bridge of her nose when she frowns with concern, and her face looks suddenly sad. The question itself sounded more like a worried gasp, the way she rushed the words. I should know better than to push her.

"No," I offer softly and replace my hand in hers, which she then guides back into the water.

"Good." Her face instantly lights up when she smiles, even when it's tentative and only just curling the corners of her mouth.

She looks so damn pretty when she smiles.

We fall into a comfortable silence while she cleans the wounds and picks the splinters from my skin. Some are really deep, and she has to gouge at the flesh. She keeps apologising, but it isn't her who's an idiot with anger issues.

"I'm twenty nine years old this year and I haven't been outside this house in ten years, Tia." I break the silence, and what I chose to break it with surprises me much more than her. To her credit, her jaw doesn't drop or anything comical like that. She just tips her chin and replies in the softest voice.

"I know." She holds my gaze, her green eyes sparkling as they fill with tears. I've never done this with anyone, and I'm pretty sure she knows this.

"I mean, I've never wanted to, either. I haven't even been near the back door the whole time I've lived like this, and the front one you've seen how I've had it modified so it opens automatically. Any deliveries are just put straight inside the house. I never test myself because I know the goddamn answer, and I'm just angry that I tried today. That's all."

"Oh. " She pulls her lips inside her mouth until they disappear, and a tell-tale thin line is all that's left. She's literally biting back what she wants to say, and I don't blame her. I made it perfectly clear if she asked questions, she'd find herself sleeping on the street before the words left her mouth.

"You can ask me one question, but I'm not promising I'll answer it. I just won't kick you out, either." I smile but I can already feel the tension rising inside me. My shoulders stiffen, and my jaw clamps like a vise. She takes her time, and I can see the effort she's exerting to contain her excitement. Her breathing elevates, and her eyes get a little wider. I've never given her this option, and too late, I'm challenging that wisdom.

"Why?" She grins.

"I bet you think you're really smart don't you?" I sniff and let out a flat laugh, because as open-ended as that question is, she's only getting one answer.

"A li'l bit." She holds up her thumb and finger with the smallest gap. I open my mouth to speak, only to hesitate and then fall silent. She finishes wrapping gauze and a bandage around my knuckles. I still haven't said a thing.

"You don't have to tell me if its hard, Logan. We don't have to share all of our darkness." She places her hand lightly over mine but doesn't squeeze. The comfort and warmth just seeps in from her touch, her very presence.

"I want to tell you."

"Then you will, when you're ready. There's no rush, Logan. I'm not going anywhere, and you can tell me anytime you're comfortable. Right now, though, I think you're still angry and in pain. It's probably not the best time for a trip down memory lane. I know I'd definitely need alcohol for that journey if it was me, and it's way too early to be hitting the bottle. Besides, I'm working tonight so maybe a rain-check is best."

She offers a get-out without hesitation, and I know she must be dying to know why I'm like this. I drop my head to one side and stretch, letting out a loud crack first on one side and then on the other side of my neck, as the air pops and releases some of the tension.

"Another time, then."

"Yeah, Logan, another time." She leans forward and kisses my cheek. Her eyes lock with mine for a moment, and I get that hit to my chest again, tight and warm. "Would you like me to bring you a sandwich or something before I head off?" She clears the debris and puts the first aid box back in the cupboard.

"What time do you leave? I thought you were working nights." I nod toward the kitchen clock and her eyes follow mine. "It's still morning, T." She screws up her face in a cute grin and snickers.

"Yeah, I am working nights, but I have to take Maria's picture to get it framed, and I need to get some more supplies." She starts to rinse the dishes, and I can't keep my eyes off the way her arse jiggles as she rubs the plates clean. I cough to clear my throat and step in front of the chair as I push it under the table, mostly using it to hide my ever-present hard-on.

"I can get you those supplies online," I offer, shifting and cupping myself to ease the ache that has been building since she leaned forward in that skimpy top and started tending to my hand.

"No, I'm good. I like browsing, and the art shop is right next to the vintage bookstore. It's a musty old world utopia for a bookworm like me. I can lose days in there."

She flashes me the widest grin, and I stifle a groan. *Damn, she makes my balls ache with that sexy little smile.* She barely draws a breath. "I was going to head out around two, so if you want me to fix you something—I'm not cooking," she clarifies with a flash of panic on her face that makes me laugh. "Just a sandwich Logan; I wouldn't want you to risk more injury," she quips.

"You're so thoughtful," I retort, and she flicks some soapy suds my way.

"I like to think so."

"No sandwich, I'll get a takeout delivered later. We can share the leftovers for breakfast when you get back."

"Well, get Chinese then because cold curry is gross."

"And cold chow mien is better?" I scoff.

"You know it." She wrinkles her nose and blows me a sassy kiss.

"Thanks for this." I lift my bandaged hand, but she isn't looking.

"What?"

"Playing nursemaid." She just shrugs it off, so I add, "I might have to get you a uniform."

"Oh, you'd like that, I bet." She barks out a dirty laugh, and I turn to leave.

Under my breath I let the words fall. "You have no idea."

"Just maybe use the punching bag in the basement gym next time, less blood and mess," she calls out after me, and I stop just at the threshold to the hall.

"Right." I lean my shoulder against the doorframe, taking a moment before I leave. "Thank you for staying, Tia."

"Nowhere else I'd rather be, Logan." Her eyes meet mine, and I know she's so nearly mine...so damn close I can taste it. The only thing harder than waiting for her to come to her senses and let *us* happen is knowing what made her this way.

CHAPTER FOUR

Tia

"I'm heading out now, Logan," I call from the bottom of the stairs, my hand just about to pull the front door open.

"Wait! Come here before you leave." His deep voice booms from above me, and I let out a sigh, muttering something about lazy arse, and maybe how a please here and there wouldn't go amiss as I trudge back up the two flights of stairs and along the corridor to his sanctuary. I push the door to his office wide. He's standing with his back to me, facing a wall of screens. He has on some torn low slung jeans that hang off his hips, exposing the dimples on his lower back, just above the firm curve of his arse cheeks. Strange that, even though I've seen his butt a million times, with a little covering, he just looks so much more tempting. I can feel my cheeks burn when he coughs, and I look up to see his wry, knowing grin.

"When you've finished ogling my arse, I have some news." He snaps his fingers and points to his desk.

"I wasn't..." I blurt, flustered and burning right up from his accurate observation. "Shut up, what news?" He chuckles at my embarrassment and walks over to his massive antique oak desk that looks oddly right in a room filled with the most up-to-date technology and geek shit available. He picks up a small Post-it note and hands it to me. I read the numbers and frown.

"What do these mean?" I hand it back, and he shakes his head, like I've missed something crucial. It's just numbers that don't look nearly long enough to be a phone number.

"That's what Bernard got for your painting he just sold." He turns the little yellow piece of paper around in his long fingers and holds it a few centimetres from my nose. I squint and focus with much more interest.

"Seriously? I mean, really, you're not teasing? Because that wouldn't be funny." I take the paper again, not quite believing my eyes.

"I know it wouldn't," he replies flatly, and his brow furrows at my comment. "I'm not teasing. I said they'd sell. You just needed the right gallery to take a chance on you." He places his heavy arm over my shoulder and pulls me in for a side hug, pride now replacing the brief look of confusion.

"And the decimal is in the right place? It's really eight hundred not just eight pound right?" I feel this burst of excitement rip through me, and I start to bounce on my toes. His arm is slipping from my shoulders, since I can't seem to keep still.

"God, you're adorable! Yes, it's eight hundred pounds. That's after his commission. Even as a friend, he was never going to do it for love."

"Oh, god no, of course not, of course. Oh, wow, Logan, this is amazing. I might not have to go cleaning for much longer after all. I mean, if this works out, and it's not just a one-off."

His tone drops low. "That's what I was thinking." A disapproving rumble escapes his bare chest, and his dark eyes look so much more serious.

"I know you don't think I need to do this."

"I don't think, I know," he corrects.

I let out a breath of frustration. *Man, he's stubborn.* "But I do, I have to contribute. It's just not in me to be a taker. I feel so damn guilty that I've taken so much already." It's not my only reason, but it's the only one I can share.

He drops his jaw comically wide and rolls his eyes. "You're kidding, right?"

"Not at all. There's a huge imbalance here, Logan, and I want to even it out a bit," I add. I know I can't repay him for everything he's done, but that doesn't mean I don't want to try.

His voice softens. "The imbalance is on my end, Tia. You've made my life almost normal, and I never believed that would be possible." His eyes hold a sadness that feels like a sucker punch to my chest. I reach for him, my hand on his arm, his large flexed muscle feeling like concrete under my touch.

"Logan, you know, if we maybe talked…" And just like that his shield slams shut, and he breaks all contact. The warmth I felt in my fingertips vanishes, and he turns abruptly away from me, snapping with open hostility in his tone.

"I won't wait up."

"Right, okay. Well, thanks for this." I fold the paper with my newly earned fortune and slip it into my jacket pocket.

"Don't mention it."

"Okay, then, bye."

"Shut the door on your way out," he yells as I step over the threshold.

"Fuck," I mutter as I pull his door shut. *Every damn time.* I know I'm out of my depth with someone like Logan. He's so smart, and he's probably read everything ever printed on agoraphobia. If there was a way, if he really wanted to, I'm sure he'd conquer that demon. It's just I can't help thinking or hoping that, if it's something else, and maybe talking to me might fix whatever *it* is, even the slightest chance, then I'm going to keep trying.

Even if it stings like a bitch when he shuts down like that.

I grab my courier bag which is just large enough to fit Marias canvas and sling it across my body. Opening the front door, I skip down the cracked steps that lead down the path toward the street, where the weeds are winning the battle against the decaying concrete in this urban turf war. The sun is high, but April still clings to a chill and I wrap my scarf around my neck and button up my denim jacket. I actually wish I had my woolly hat with me, but looking around at people in shorts and summer dresses, I would feel a little conspicuous. Looking at them makes me shiver because I'm always cold. Even in a heat wave I would probably still have socks and a jumper stuffed in my bag, just in case.

Logan's house is elevated at the top of a long residential street, with only a few other similar properties. Several Edwardian town houses and Victorian mansions dot the tree lined road, mostly hidden behind tall hedges, secure iron railings and automatic gates. Logan's house has the least security features which is one of the reasons it was so easy to break into. It's also the most isolated considering we live on the edge of one of the most densely populated cities in Eurpoe.

The end of the street is a junction that leads to the main road and my nearest bus stop. The walk itself takes about half an hour and there are always buses every fifteen minutes throughout the day, which is another perk of living in the commuter belt of a big city. In the village I grew up in there was a bus in the morning and one in the evening. If I missed either, I was walking, not that I had anywhere to go but I frequently missed my bus home and cursed both living in the countryside having a mother that didn't drive.

It's a short bus ride into the heart of town from where we live, but it takes forever with the London traffic. When I finally arrive at my destination, I spend a good hour in the art supply shop. While I wait for them to frame my picture I wander the isles, mentally making up my wish list until I actually get that money from the sale of my painting in my account. I am so low on materials, I will probably blow half of it in here. I settle on buying some charcoal and a new sketchpad. I have a couple of hours to kill before I have to be at work, so I make my way to the park and settle down to people watch and sketch.

This is what I love about city parks. Any break in the cloud and they are teeming with people making the most of these small patches of nature in an over-populated city. Office workers on late lunches, parents with children, a football being kicked around in the distance, and tourists clearly taken by surprise judging by the quantity of clothes they are now wearing tied around their waists or draped over arms and shoulders.

Doesn't it always rain in London?

Only one thing is missing on this perfect afternoon, *one person.* I let out a heavy sigh, and in lieu of any tissues, wipe my charcoal-blackened hands on the grass. I fish out my phone and dial the only contact in my address book. When it goes direct to voicemail, I want to kick myself and head back home to apologise. He must be really mad with me to ignore my call, and really I should've kept my big mouth shut, especially after his little re-modelling on the back door this morning. *Damn it.* I drop a text with an apology but don't bother waiting on a reply. If anything is going to drive me crazy, it's waiting for a reply from Mr Stubborn.

The sun has started to set when I finally pack my things away and stand. Brushing the grass from my jeans, I stretch the cramp and dampness from my legs and begin the forty-minute walk into the heart of the business district.

The grey and glass buildings towering on every side seem to close in around me. The roads are lined with cars making their way home, but the pavements are empty. Looking up, the buildings are so tall they converge to such an extent that I can barely see the darkening sky. It feels every bit as oppressive as I can only imagine Logan must feel when faced with the great outdoors. My chest feels tight, and I get a chill in my bones that makes me shiver. I physically shake to try and alleviate the heavy feeling of being closed in. Normally, I'm not remotely claustrophobic. I lived in Logan's dark basement for weeks, but there is something eerie about the business district part of the city when it's void of humans.

I reach the office block where I have worked for the last few months and have another full body shiver, but this time it has nothing to do with the cold breeze funnelled into a sharp wind whipping between the buildings. This is a direct result of reading *his* family name in big silver letters over the main doors, Kruse Tower. It's a stunning building, forty-four floors of sleek shiny steel and mirrored glass. The surrounding buildings fade into the background next to this impressive feat of architecture and engineering. Not unlike meeting Atticus himself, I muse, letting out a flat humourless laugh. He wasn't always so impressive, not so much when we met as children, but around the time when he turned eighteen, there wasn't another man on the planet that could touch him for looks and presence.

I turn away from the main doors and make my way to the service entrance, swipe my card, and dump my stuff in my locker. The padlock hangs broken, and I haven't bothered to replace it. It's not like I have anything worth stealing. I slip into my not-so-sexy shapeless beige overalls on top of my clothes and, with the picture I painted of her granddaughter tucked under my arm, head off to find Maria. I catch my reflection in the floor-to-ceiling glass walkways and cringe, I look like some kind of cross between an inmate at a maximum security facility and a baked potato.

The staff room is deep in the bowels of the building. That is, the staff room for the caretakers, cleaners, and maintenance staff is buried down there. Several other staff rooms are spread over on other floors of the block, and of course, the executive lounge for board members and family is situated one level below the top floor office suites. The Kruse family has always liked to keep that line between 'them and us' absolutely visible. *As if I could ever forget.*

"There you are, sweet cheeks," Maria calls out as I come into view. I don't quite enter the room, but her seat is strategically placed to spot anyone approaching her domain. "I was just talking about you to Loretta here, telling her what a great artist you are and all. Didn't I say that she's wasted here, Loretta? I said there's no way you're a lifer." She chuckles, and Loretta is nodding in agreement, although I'm not sure she understands a word Maria is saying; she speaks so fast with a thick Caribbean accent.

"I feel like a lifer in this jumpsuit." I tug on the coarse material of my uniform. Even cinched at the waist, it has to be the most unflattering item of clothing ever designed, but then fashion probably wasn't high on its list of requisite functions.

"Hmm?" A deep frown forms on Maria's face, my attempt at humour flying neatly over her tightly curled hair. Her smooth dark skin barely has a single wrinkle, and I know she is the wrong side of fifty. I wish I had her genes. The only gifts my mother gave to me were childbearing hips and high blood pressure.

"Never mind." I wave off my joke rather than try to explain, which would be painful for everyone. "Thank you, though, you're very kind." I hold out the picture, which is in a simple paper bag, but now at least it is framed. "I did this for you. I know you took a risk taking me on, and I'm really grateful."

"Hush now, it wasn't a risk, a sweet girl like you. I only wish

I could've gotten you in sooner but still better late than never. "She smiles warmly and I wave off her regretful tone. Meeting Maria was necessary, getting this job was crucial. How long that took was irrelevant. Becoming good friends, however was a complete bonus."You may have had no references, but the second you sat next to me on that bus all that time ago I just knew and I *know* people. Why, I wouldn't have cleared your pass to access all floors if I had any doubt. I gave you the top floors straight off. Sweet cheeks, because I trust you. Besides, it's not like this is brain surgery, sugar; we're just the cleaners." She gives a hearty laugh and holds her hand out. "Now, what's this you got?" Maria takes the gift and is quick to tear apart the wrapping. Her face lights up, and her smile couldn't be any wider without the aid of surgery.

"Just a token." I shuffle, suddenly aware that Maria and Loretta are both staring at me.

"Oh, my Lord, girl, this is amazing. My sweet little Honour looks the spit of her dear mother, rest her soul. I can't believe you did this; you should have your work in one of those fancy galleries off St James," Maria gushes, and I get a pinch, a tingle of pressure behind my eyes when hers fill and burst with tears at the mention of her daughter.

"Actually, I sold my first piece today," I say to stop us both from having an emotional episode. "Not from one of those galleries in St James mind, but Logan's friend has one off King's Road. Anyway, I have officially moved up from starving artist, to very poor artist." I laugh lightly, but Maria doesn't join in. I add clarification because she is looking more concerned than amused. "At least I'm not homeless anymore."

"You're not really starving?" She takes my hand in hers, her face the picture of concern. I shake my head vigorously.

"No, no, and I have a roof over my head, but I'm still pretty broke. My hobby and would-be livelihood is super expensive."

I shrug. She seems to relax with my light tone and explanation of my situation.

"Let me pay you—" I hold up my hand to stop her, and I'm just as quick to interrupt.

"Oh, God, no, Maria. I didn't mean anything like that. No, all I meant was, I just went to the art shop today, and now I have a pretty long list of what I need. I'm going to need to sell a few more paintings to replenish my stocks, but then that's why I'm here." I sweep my open palm in a gesture to encompass the entire Tower.

"You know, there's a perfectly full store cupboard on the fifth floor that has enough office supplies to support all the schools in the city. I'm sure they wouldn't miss a few pens and pencils." She winks conspiratorially, but I can't help but stiffen at her remark.

"I'm sure they would mind, and no, I'm good, thank you." I don't mean to sound like a stuck-up arse, holier-than-thou, but this is a line I won't cross. My tone softens. "Despite what my record says, I'm not a thief, Maria."

"Oh, I know, honey, and it ain't really thieving; it's topping up on the shitty pay." She tips her head, and Loretta is quick to nod in agreement, but I step back a little and shake my head again. I don't want to cause offence, but I have more than my job on the line here.

"I'm pretty sure Kruse Corporation wouldn't see it like that."

"Suit yourself, sweet cheeks, but you're the only one that isn't on the take in this building," Maria scoffs.

"What do you mean?"

"They are all just as dirty as a dealer on the street. They just wear nicer suits," she says, but I'm not sure she's talking to me. She's looking intently at the picture I just gave her. Her statement has me intrigued though.

"You have proof of this, of course?" I probe.

"Nah, just a feeling." She looks over at me and my momentary interest vanishes with the realisation this is just more hearsay and gossip. *I'm not a fan of either.* "I know a bad'un when I see them, and I've met them all on that top floor. The mother is the worst, butter wouldn't melt, but that is one ice cold bitch." I snort out a flat laugh at that comment because *that* observation is spot on.

"I'm not going to argue that," I mutter under my breath.

"I've worked here so long it's only the golden pension I got with them that keeps me here. Trust me, that pot of gold at the end is worth it. I'm gonna be able to buy me a sweet retirement and pay for this little one's education." She looks fondly at the portrait and continues to explain. "I can't afford to leave, but I wouldn't even if I could. See, you have to work every day up to the end to get the bonus."

"Bonus?"

"Yeah, the company doubles your contribution just like that, but only if you work right up to the last day."

"Really? That seems really generous. I'm surprised they could afford to do that with every employee."

"Not many stay till the end, hunny. Not many stay longer than a few years." She lets out a bitter laugh, and Loretta nods with her friend's observation. I know she's telling the truth. They have the highest turnover of staff in the private banking sector. The money is good enough to attract the very best, but it's obviously not enough to keep them.

"Where do you want me?" I ask when she falls uncharacteristically silent.

"Actually, you're on the top floor. The big boss is transferring back from overseas and needs his office opened up, cleaned, and sparkling."

"Big boss?"

"Yes, the son is returning. He's been working out of the

Moscow office, and apparently, he's coming home for good. They are having some financial crisis, and he's the wonder boy that is going to solve all their problems."

"Is there anything you don't know, Maria?" I quip.

"No, I'm the eyes and ears of this place." She chuckles.

"Remind me to buy you a drink sometime. I'd love to know more." I pick up the keys to the store cupboard and turn to leave.

"I don't drink, but buy me a cake, and I'll tell you everything," she chuckles.

"Okay, you're on but your cakes are the best Maria, not sure any shop bought compete."

"Birthday cakes are my specialty but I love any cakes that I'm not making myself." She chuckles and pats the roundness of her midsection. I smile and ignore the inference to her weight, she's perfect. "You want me to do the whole of that floor when I'm done in his office?"

"Yes, honey, that would be great. Work your way down to the fortieth. I'll grab you around two in the morning for a break."

"Oh, I'd rather work through and leave early if that's okay? "I smile sweetly with my request because Maria really likes her break time to be a communal thing.

"You got a hot date?" She raises her pencilled in brow nice and high.

"Something like that, a hot date with some cold Chinese food," I scoff and wave my goodbye to the sound of her laughing.

The view from the top floor is breathtaking. The length of this office is floor-to-ceiling glass overlooking the Thames and beyond. On a clear, star-filled night like this, I swear I can almost see the coast. I step flush against the window and press my nose against the glass so even my peripheral vision is filled with this vista. I feel like I'm floating or about to fall. It scares the crap out of me, but I love it, too. It's like a test. Isn't the saying, *do something that scares you every day*? I laugh bitterly to myself at the irony. I've spent so many days terrified for my life, this is nothing, and it's also in *my* control.

I exhale through my nose, and the glass steams up. Stepping back, I draw a lazy doodle of a love heart with my finger, which slowly disappears as the mist warms on the glass. It's no longer visible, but in a certain light, the mark will show. I am about to wipe the window with my cloth and spray, removing any trace but stop myself. *He always had my heart.*

I turn and look at the now sparkling clean office of Acting President Atticus Kruse. I did a good job, although it wasn't difficult. It's a very clinical and sparsely furnished room. A large oval glass and oak desk at one end and two long white leather sofas at the other. There's a display cabinet and a side unit with a fridge. The tall shelving unit behind his desk is empty other than a lone bottle of his favourite whiskey. Other than that, there are no personal items to speak of. Maybe that will change, but at this moment, the room could belong to anyone. It certainly doesn't feel like it belongs to *him*. I shake my wayward thoughts away because none of that matters. Wistful recollections and trips down memory lane are for naïve love-struck teenagers, and I haven't been one of those in a long time. I lock the door to his office and begin cleaning the rest of the top floor and then the next and the next until, at five thirty in the morning, I drag my weary arse home.

The dawn breaks around four o'clock this time of year, and it's almost fully light by the time I hop off the night bus and make my way up our street. I reach the gate and find two women on the doorstep. They have their backs turned to me and are searching around in an oversized bag for something. They look immaculate from here. Slicked dark hair pulled back into matching ponytails and heels so high I'd need an airbag for safety if I were to attempt to wear anything remotely similar. One is wearing a full-length fake fur coat, while the other has on a neat fitted black leather biker jacket. Her skirt clings to her arse like a second skin and barely covers the bottom curve of her cheeks. Her stocking tops and suspenders are clearly visible. They haven't heard me approach, and I'm about to push by, but they start to whisper, so I freeze, my foot lifted and hovering mid step.

"That's a lot of money for doing nothing." I can hear the surprise in her tone, and her friend nods enthusiastically.

"Yeah, I actually wish he would touch us though…just once, you know?" She snickers.

"Just touch? Fuck that. No, no, I want his cock. I want to fuck him so bad, have his cock in me, not your dildo or strap on. I want him to join in for a change, not just watch us get it on." She pouts and I think my jaw just hit the pavement. *What the hell are they saying?*

"Yeah, me, too, it's a shame, you know, a waste. He's built down there; hell, he's built everywhere, but you just know he'd be soooo good." She giggles and sighs.

"Never thought I'd say it about a John, but I feel bad taking his money. You think he's gay?"

"No, Jade, I don't think he's gay. He's only been like this since she—Ow!"

"Shit!" Jade's head snaps round to face me, her bony elbow interrupting her friend by digging into her side.

"Ow, what the fuck, Lacy!" Jade rubs her ribs and follows her friend's startled glare. "Oh, shit!"

"What did you just say?" I step forward and keep my voice low. Sound travels, and it's too early for the everyday noises of a street waking up to cloak the conversation.

"Nothing, we said nothing." Jade snaps her lips shut, as if it isn't already too late for that.

"But you did." I offer a smile and raise my brow, hoping my jokey tone will endear her enough to clarify and expand on their conversation.

"Escort-client privileges, we're not allowed to say." She bites back with a spiteful twist in her glossy bright pink lips. *Apparently not.*

"I think that's only with doctors, lawyers, and priests, and I don't mean any disrespect by assuming your trade, since you are none of the above."

"Smarty arse, hmm? Must be why he likes you, since we're not allowed to speak and all. That must be what's different," Lacy butts in with equal disdain for my presence and questions.

"Not the only difference, I hope," I blurt and instantly shake my head by way of a retraction.

"You got a problem, bitch?" Jade steps up to me. I don't back down, but I'm not going to defend myself, either. It was a low blow. "Because as I see it, we're here providing a service he ain't getting, and if he ain't sharing the details with you…" She jabs her finger into my chest. I flinch but don't move. "…then I guess it's none of your fucking business, is it?" Her face is inches from mine, and I can see in her eyes the fire is hiding a little hurt. I let out a slow breath and try and make amends.

"You're right; it's none of my business. I'm actually sorry for the snide comment. I'm in no position to judge. I've just had a long night cleaning offices." She huffs, and her shoulders lose a little of their stiffness. She steps back and Lacy slides her arm through Jade's.

"On minimum wage, yeah, that would make me a grumpy bitch, too." Jade laughs, but it's hollow.

"Yeah, needs must, though, a girl's gotta' eat." I step past them and up to the front door. Jade calls after me.

"You need extra cash, we're always looking for new girls, and you're pretty enough." Her smile is genuine, and her face is a picture of excited anticipation. I fight off the grimace that is threatening and flash an apologetic smile.

"Oh, thank you, but I'm assuming sex would be involved, so that kind of counts me out," I quip, and Lacy leans over to whisper, only it's louder than her normal voice.

"Oh, that makes much more sense."

"What does?" I step back toward the girls, but they hurry through the gate.

"Nothing. For fuck's sake, Lacy, keep your mouth shut. This sweet gig will end if he finds out we've talked, okay?"

"Shit, can you just forget you saw us?" Jade pleads.

"Hardly, but I won't say anything, either. It's not my place," I offer, and Jade lets out a relieved breath and smiles. Lacy can't seem to help herself and speaks once more before Jade drags her away.

"Not what we've heard."

I am way too tired for this cryptic shit.

CHAPTER FIVE

Logan

Why do my balls still ache? Jade and Lacy acted their toned little arses off for me as I directed them in my own personal porn show. Even if I closed my eyes at the final moment and saw only emerald greens looking back at me, I still thought I came hard enough to give me a little reprieve, but no.

I hear the front door shut, and I get that twinge in the base of my spine and that ever-present throbbing in my balls that I know will only be sated by one thing. *Tia.*

It's my own damn fault; I should've made my move on our first drunken night together, when I knew she was interested, before she started putting up these barriers and shifting me into the fucking friend zone. I hadn't done all my checks, and I needed to be sure she wasn't playing me. I needed to be sure she was telling the truth. I needed to be sure she was *real*. She did tell me the truth. She just didn't tell me everything, and when I found out, I hated myself for being so damn good at my job. Hacking into her prison records and medical file exposed a world of pain I can only imagine and something I can't in good conscience add to, what with my own fucked up shit. Not unless she makes the first move.

She freezes in the doorway of the kitchen, unsure of my mood no doubt. I have laid out two plates, there's a shit tonne of Chinese food, and there's a pot of tea steeping. To me at least, it's pretty fucking obvious I am over her 'best intentions'.

"You said you weren't going to wait up," she says, her voice hesitant. I don't blame her, although I have a grip on my temper most of the time, she's seen me at my worst, and that's pretty fucking scary.

"I didn't wait up." I start to open up the take-out containers.

"Oh." Her shoulders drop, and I shouldn't take so much pleasure from her disappointment, but I'll take that and any other sign she throws my way that this is more than a 'just friends' deal.

"I haven't been to bed, but I didn't wait up for you. I was busy." I don't have to make it easy, though. I'm not pussy-whipped... yet.

"So I saw." She sniffs derisively, and I take that as a win, too. My face splits into a shit-eating grin until she snaps with open hostility.

"Did you give them breakfast, too?" I raise a brow, and her eyes narrow on mine. Heat and hurt hide behind those long lashes, and I'm desperate to explore the former and heal the latter. It wasn't always like this, but recently the tension, sexual and otherwise, between us seems to be escalating on a daily bases. *Something is going to give. I just hope it's her, to me.*

"Did they look like friends?" I ask, my tone softer, and I take the seat opposite.

"No, not exactly." She flops down into the seat, and I notice the dark circles under her eyes and how her skin looks so pale. She's exhausted. Now I feel like a complete shit, not for shutting her down earlier but for goading her now.

"Then you've answered your own question." I wink and start to dish up her favourites. She rests her head in her hands and rubs her temples. Her dark hair falls in long, loose curls like a curtain, covering her face until she draws in a deep breath and sweeps it back.

"I'm sorry, Logan." She holds my gaze, and all I want to do is sweep her into my arms.

"I know, Dodge, I know." I stand up and walk round the table. She looks up, startled, when I lift her into my arms and sit back down in her place. She lets out a peaceful sigh and relaxes into my hold, her head heavy on my chest, her eyelids starting to droop.

"Hey, you need to eat something." I kiss the top of her head and, with enormous effort, ignore the swelling in my boxer shorts when she lets out a heavenly moan.

"I think I'm too tired." She stifles a yawn but loses the battle to keep her eyes open.

"Then let me." I scoop some rice onto a spoon and press it against her lips. She opens her mouth and for the second time in as many seconds, I have to try and focus on anything other than that sound of ecstasy escaping her perfect lips. *Next stop, cold shower.*

I'm making some homemade soup, as I know the smell alone will rouse Tia from her self-inflicted coma. I carried her up to bed around six this morning, and it's now nearly five in the afternoon. I checked on her several times throughout the day, even held up a mirror against her mouth to check if she was still breathing at one point. I swear she hasn't moved a muscle in the whole eleven hours. She'll be starving when she wakes and probably grumpy too, having wasted the whole day asleep, and since she's an idiot who is due back at work again tonight.

Heavy footsteps thump slowly down the stairs, the carpet only just dulling the sound but setting the tone of her imminent arrival. She has a face like thunder when she appears, her hair wild and looking like it is trying to get as far away from her and her foul mood as possible. I hold up my hands in surrender before she even opens her mouth. She narrows her eyes and scowls like it's somehow my fault she's an idiot. I told her she didn't have to work, and she has an alternate income now, so there really is no reason to do these ridiculous shifts.

"I made soup." I blow on the spoon and take a final taste, perfect. My smile fades at her response.

"I don't have time."

"Yes, you do. I called you a taxi to give you a little more time, now sit." My tone brooks no argument, and I point sharply at her seat. Her shoulders sag, and she instantly loses her irritation.

"Oh, Logan, that's so kind." She slips into her seat, her eyes on mine.

"I know." Her face lights, and that smile is all kinds of infectious. I take the bowls from the warming oven, pour the soup, and top the fresh minestrone with some oversized, deep-fried croutons and do the same for mine. She pulls at the baguette on the table and takes a huge bite. Her cheeks swell as she struggles to contain her mouthful, her smile, and her thank you when I hand her the soup.

"Don't choke, I've ordered a taxi, not an ambulance," I quip.

"Funny." She swallows and sticks her nose into the rising steam, and her tummy makes an audible and timely growl. "God, I'm so hungry. Did I actually eat any breakfast? I don't remember." She picks one of the croutons off the top and plops it in whole, puffing heavily when she realises it's way too hot for that, her hand waving manically in front of her mouth.

"So hot, so hot!"

"Don't, you'll make me blush." I bite back a grin, and she scoffs.

"I'd pay to see that from the man who shamelessly struts round naked half the time."

"I'm not a fan of clothes. Nothing shameful about that."

"No, I guess. It just took a little getting used to."

"I'm wearing clothes now." I sweep my hand down my body, which is clad in a black fitted t-shirt and dark jeans.

"Yes, you are. Are you expecting company?" She holds my gaze, and I give a curt nod, but I'm not inclined to share the details. My plans changed, and it's her damn fault. I ignore her inquisitive glare and answer her question from earlier.

"You did eat some breakfast, I forced it down you before you passed out."

She hesitates but wisely chooses not to pry. "I thought that was a dream. Did you undress me too?" She arches a brow, and her lips purse into the cutest grin. Her cheeks start to colour, and my balls are instantly in fucking agony once more.

"Yes, and it was complete torture, so don't remind me." I shift in my seat, and she drops her eyes, her tone no longer playful.

"Don't tease."

"I'm not," I state with absolute honesty. She keeps her head down, and I let out a frustrated groan when she changes the subject. She powers on regardless.

"I made a list of all the art supplies I'm going to treat myself to when the cash from my painting hits my account."

"Nice deflection there, T." I tip my head to one side, raising a brow and holding her sheepish gaze. "I'd happily order on-line. I told you that."

"I want to pay my way, Logan. God, between you and Maria, you'd think I was destitute."

"Maria?" My spoon hovers just above the bowl.

"My boss from work. She said I could help myself to the

supplies in the store cupboard. She said no one would mind, probably not notice even." She scoffs, and I drop my spoon with enough force to make her jump. Her eyes go wide with surprise.

"Please tell me you're not so fucking stupid as to risk stealing with only twelve months left on your probation!" I grit out, my rage building with the tension in my shoulders and my white-knuckle fists.

"No! I'm not *that* fucking stupid!" she snaps back. She drops her spoon into her bowl and, placing both hands on the table, raises herself and pitches forward to meet my anger head-on. "Jeeze, a little fucking credit might be nice, Logan."

"Tia…" I reach over and cup the side of her face, the tenderness of my move disarming her anger and taking her completely by surprise. Her body reacts to my touch like I hoped it would. She leans into my palm and closes her eyes when I speak softly, the words catching in the back of my throat with their truth. "I can't lose you. I won't let you go back to jail." She nods, and I pull my hand away, adding when she opens her eyes to look at me, "I believe I would hate that more than you, sweetheart."

"I doubt that." She pulls her mouth into a soul-sad smile, and her eyes fill with tears.

"No, you're probably right." I agree, and since we are on this subject, I need to understand what is really going on in that head of hers, because not for a second do I buy that her new career choice and location is a coincidence, or that it has anything to do with her contributing to the household coffers. "So tell me again, Tia, that you working for *his* company has nothing to do with revenge, and remember: you're piss poor at lying." She stiffens, her back straight like I've just inserted a four-foot pole up her backside.

"You know a little faith would go a long way here, Logan."

"You have all my faith, T; you just have a shit tonne of my

concern, too." My tone is rising to match her irritation.

"I know what I'm doing, Logan." She stands and snatches up the bowl of soup. It's her turn to be pissed at me for overstepping a line that, between us, keeps shifting. I stand and catch up to her at the doorway, my hand resting on the small of her back. My fingertips ache to touch her skin. and they fist in frustration into the loose material of her sweater, preventing her from moving forward.

"I can't lose you, Tia." I repeat my words from earlier, and she lets out a heavy sigh.

"I'm not going anywhere."

"That's not what I meant." I stand flush to her back, her heat seeping across the damn material barriers between us. My other hand rests on her hip, and my fingers curl around her soft flesh. I pull her back against me, firmly fixing her body to mine.

"Logan, I can't. You don't want someone like me, and I won't risk us." Her voice breaks, and her body starts to tremble. I can hear her heart beating; it's so damn loud. I can feel her, like every nerve in her body is alive because of our connection. I drop my mouth to her neck, and she leans her head to let me get where I need to be, where she needs me.

"Us together is the only good thing in my life, Tia. I have nothing if I don't have us." My breath washes over her silky pale skin, and I can see the blood pulsing through the vein in her neck. I place my lips over the pulse point, and she sucks in a sharp breath. She holds it for blissfully long seconds, and I'm momentarily filled with hope.

"You're my best friend, Logan," she says, slowly letting out the breath she had been holding.

"Bullshit, I'm your only friend, and this is more than that, and you know it." I can't hide the frustration in my voice, and this has nothing to do with sex. I hate that she won't give us a chance, any chance. I know what's holding her back; still, she has to feel this in her bones; I know I sure as hell do. "You have to trust me on this, Tia."

"Like you trust me to help you, you mean?" She twists out of my hold, and man, my hand just twitches to spank that obstinate arse.

"Fuck, you're stubborn." My voice is a deep grumble, but I back off, for now.

"Must've rubbed off then. Now let me go. I have to get ready for work."

"We're not finished here, Tia," I call after her as she scurries up the stairs.

"We're not started either," she yells back. *Fuck!*

The doorbell rings just as Tia comes down the stairs, ready to leave. She offers me a tentative smile I can't quite read. Her eyes have this crinkle in the corners from her smile, but they keep darting to the floor and then the door. I am about to press the automatic open when Tia beats me to it, pulling the front door wide. Jade and Lacy are standing on the porch, arms linked and looking like any man's wet dream. Damn it! I flinch when Tia gasps.

"Back so soon?" Tia smiles sweetly, but her jaw is so tense, she's having to push the words through her clenched teeth. The girls enter, their wide eyes firing between me, Tia, and each other. Tia may have made herself clear where *we* stand, but I'm not done playing my hand, even if this is a particularly low blow.

"I have blue balls from hell, Tia, and I blame you," I bite back.

"It's okay, Logan, I blame me, too." Her eyes fill with tears, and she steps past the girls too quickly for me to stop her. *Fuck.*

I'd kick the door shut if I could get close enough, my anger coursing through me like a wildfire, burning my insides and needing an escape. I freeze at my own imaginary safe distance in the hall, nowhere near the door. I drag my hands through my hair, and from the bottom of my belly, let out a deep and frustrated howl. The echo of my torment bounces off the walls and up the stairwell.

"You want us to do the same as yesterday, sweetie?" Jade ventures after I fall silent. The only sound is my ragged breathing and my teeth grinding. I fish a wad of notes from my back pocket and hand it over to Jade.

"No, I want you to get the fuck out of my house."

CHAPTER SIX

Tia

I'm a mess by the time I get to work. My head is spinning, and my chest feels bruised from the inside. My heart hasn't stopped thumping like a rabbit in the headlights since Logan kissed my neck the way he did. I can't breathe when I think about it. I can still feel his touch like a brand on my skin. His firm, full lips were so soft and sensual, they were completely perfect. Sparks of electricity ignited and flashed across my skin from that single point of contact. All I could feel was him, in every fibre of my body, in every cell, in my *soul*. It was just him, and he knew it.

I ran; I know I did, but I felt that everything changed with that kiss, and I'm terrified. It's not like he hasn't touched me before. He's kissed my cheeks a million times, held me in his arms all night more often than I care to remember when I've awoken screaming from a nightmare.

This was so very different.

So tender, so intimate, so…raw.

I panicked and gave him my standard brush-off, only this time, when I reached my room, I had the biggest smile on my face. My cheeks were burning from the stretch. I was floating. I felt the shift, and for the first time in forever I wanted to do something about it. I cursed that I had to work and right up to opening the front door, I was tempted to call in sick. Then reality hit me with a sucker punch in the shape of Logan's evening entertainment. *How the hell am I going to compete with that?* I doubt I could open my legs without having a hideous spirit-crushing flashback.

Logan doesn't deserve that.

Even if, for a split second, I thought all he deserved was a kick in the balls for being such an insensitive arsehole and inviting them over in the first place, especially after *that* kiss. Still, it didn't even take a moment to realise why he did it. He's lashing out, frustrated, and his attempt to get some sort of jealous reaction would've been spot on, *if* I hadn't overheard the girls' conversation earlier. *He's not actually fucking them.* I don't know why that means so much, when I have no rights over his sex life, but it does.

This is such a fucked up mess for both of us. I need to sort my head out. We can't go on like this. I just don't know if I can give him what he wants. I don't think he really has any idea what he's letting himself in for.

Does he really want to learn what the T in my name really stands for?

I grab my bag from my locker, utterly exhausted and grateful that my shift is over. I stretch my neck out to one side, pain radiating all along my spine, and there's tightness in every muscle. My whole body is crying out for a long, hot soak in a deep bubble-filled bath. I let out a heavy pleasant sigh, thankful at least, that I won't have to work here for too much longer.

I hate lying to Logan, and my feelings may be all over the place, but if anything, that just solidifies my decision to keep him in the dark as being the right one. I need to keep him safe, but I have to do this. *I'm owed this payback.* I swipe my security card and push the heavy glass door, only the lock doesn't release. I swipe again, then rub the metallic strip of the card against my sweater when it doesn't work on the third attempt. Sometimes the friction helps, although not today. I turn at the sound of multiple heavy footsteps rushing toward me.

Security guards, lots of them.

My forehead is numb from resting the heavy weight of my head directly on the cold metal table. There is fuck all else to look at in this clinically bare box room, and after hours of staring at the blank wall, my head just needed the support. I'm so fucking tired that I don't move when I hear the door slide open or the hollow sound of solid footfalls echoing off the walls of the interrogation room. The Kruse security guards took me directly to the police officers waiting in the service yard. I was whisked away like a common criminal. *I'm nothing of the sort.*

I can almost picture a toxic cloud accompanying the now familiar stench of the detective's stale aftershave, which hangs so heavily in the air. It may even be a classy brand of scent for all I know, but it's been contaminated beyond anything remotely pleasant by this man's own noxious odour. I curse that I didn't draw in a breath when I heard the door click, and now it's too late. I lift my head and suck in a shallow breath through my mouth and prepare to answer the same damn questions in a slightly varied way for the umpteenth time. I've lost track of time, drifting in and out of sleep as I have; however, what I do know is, if they don't charge me soon, they'll have to let me go.

Getting caught was always a possibility, and oddly, for my plan to work the way I hoped, a necessity even, but the timing here is not of my own making, and I'm mentally kicking my own stupid arse that, once again, I am being accused of something I didn't do.

Detective Doyle is in his late fifties, and he wears every hard year of his life in the deep lines on his pallid, pock-marked face. His dark beady eyes could be black for the lack of colour, but given his fair thinning hair are probably blue. He sports a sneer rather than a smile, with thin lips pulled into a tight straight line, which look to be sticking to his nicotine-stained teeth. His light grey suit is fraying at the cuffs, and his cheap shoes have been repaired on more than one occasion. I'm not judging the man for his cheap clothes and style or lack thereof. I'm judging him for being thoroughly unpleasant and a creepy arsehole.

"So, Miss Parker, do you want to tell me why you stole from your employer?" His eyes drift from my file to my breasts and linger there. His lips curl with pleasure when I fold my arms across my chest.

"I haven't stolen anything," I state, keeping my tone level, but I can't hide how fucking bored I am. How many times do I have to answer the same question?

"Really?" He lifts my bag, which he brought with him this time and pulls it from the floor, tipping the contents onto the table. Small items like my keys, chewing gum, lip balm, and the odd penny scatter and roll along the surface, falling over the edge. I don't bother to try and catch anything. I am too busy staring at all the office stationery that *doesn't* belong to me, two pads of drawing paper, some inks, boxes of marker pens, pencils, and an expensive looking fountain pen. I close my eyes. This is bad; this is *really* bad. *Maria, fuck!*

"I didn't take those." I point to the items but I don't pick them up. I don't want to touch them.

"No, we can see that." Sarcasm drips from his ugly mouth, and his smile creeps from flat impassive to smug. My mind is racing. There is a knock on the mirrored glass behind me, and the detective scowls. He pushes back from the table, all his weight on the spindly metal legs of his chair, which screech their disapproval. The horrendous noise causes a pain in my head akin to an ice pick between my eyes, and my ears feel as though they are actually bleeding. He does that every single time. Motherfucker.

I try not to move when the door closes, even if I want to howl, scream, and get the fuck out of this room. *This can't be happening.* I can't go back to prison when I am so close to being free, totally free, safe and set up for life, getting back what is rightfully mine and making the son of a bitch and his family pay for a crime they *did* commit.

The door opens, and this time the scent that fills the room is so different, it's like I have been hit by a fucking freight train. Some smells are more powerful than photographs at conjuring up memories, freshly-cut grass after a thunderstorm, cooked spices wafting through open windows maybe, or in this instance, sunshine and whiskey drenches the small room, so much so I can't seem to breathe. The only sound is the blood pumping in my ears. The air is frozen in my lungs, and it feels as if we are both transfixed in a vacuum, where it's just *us*.

My eyes fall on the most beautiful man I ever loved, the *only* man I ever loved. He hasn't changed a bit. His eyes widen, and just for a moment, he looks like the little boy I grew up with. I get a high definition flashback recollection of pale cornflower blue eyes, filled with wonder and mischief. The crooked smile over perfect white teeth, dimples in his cheeks, that really only show when he smiles wide and wicked, and strands of ice-white hair flopping any which way. Not now, though. Today, his hair is cut and styled for serious business. The brief moment of lightness vanishes as quickly as it came, and his expression shifts to a blank canvas. Breathtakingly handsome, but with no emotion, and, if I hadn't witnessed that change myself, I would question whether he recognises me at all. It's obvious he does.

I do have to wonder why a few pens and a pad of paper have brought the Acting President of the Kruse Corporation down to the police station.

"Morbid curiosity," I say out loud.

"What?" His deep voice makes the hairs on my neck prickle. It's both familiar and strange. He has a subtle twang; he has picked up a little of an American accent, only I'm not sure which part of the States exactly. I don't know where he's lived all this time, but all those years is going to rub off somewhere along the line.

"I wondered what would bring you here, being a big important CEO and all. I can only think it was morbid curiosity. You saw my name and—"

"And what?" he snaps. The deep boom in the quiet of the room makes me jump.

"And nothing," I reply and hold his gaze. I can feel his anger radiating off him in waves, and as much as I thought about this moment a thousand times, I am struggling to keep my own rage in check. It's bubbling in my belly with a hairpin trigger, and unfortunately, he knows all my buttons.

"Where is it, princess?" His tone drops an octave, and he rolls my nickname around his tongue like he owns it.

"No nicknames, Atticus, we're not kids anymore, and you lost the right to call me that five years ago. This isn't some cute reunion." My jaw is clamped shut, but I manage to push the words out through gritted teeth.

"You're damn right it isn't, Tia." He slams his fists on the table, shaking the whole damn room with his fury. "Where is it?"

I frown and look at the table and then at the floor where the debris from his tantrum and Maria's haul is now lying. His eyes follow mine, but there seems to be no light dawning, so I point sharply to the supplies.

"Exhibit A, Atticus. There's your stuff."

"Cute. You think I give a shit about a few pens, Tia? I want to know where my fucking money is," he growls, his knuckles white as they grip the table. I hold the fierceness of his glare and match it with my own.

"What money?"

"The money that is missing from the company bank account, Tia, *that* money." He leans on his hands, his face inching closer to mine. I can smell the faint scent of whiskey, and on him, it always smelled so sweet, so heady. I swallow the lump in my throat, fighting off the images of our past that are bombarding me and making it really difficult to stay focused.

"I don't know what you're talking about."

"Don't lie to me. This isn't the first time you've been caught with your hand in the cookie jar," he sneers, and I scoff out a bitter laugh.

"Cookie jar, fucking cookie jar! You piece of shit, you've got some fucking nerve!" I stand up, and we are now just millimetres from each other, our noses practically touching. His eyes look like a crystal clear azure ocean this close up, and even filled with suspicion and a heavy mix of hatred, they are utterly mesmerising. "You make it sound like I got a slap on the wrist for being a naughty girl. I didn't steal shit from your family, and I got sent to jail for six years. Six. Fucking. Years. Atticus. Your family ruined my life, and you stood by and watched, you bastard." My voice cracks, but he is unmoved. He stiffens, and his reply is as cold as the look he levels on me.

"You only served three."

"For good behaviour, yes, but it still ruined my fucking life. How was university in the States, Cass?" The pitch in my voice rises, and I hate that I'm losing what little composure I had, but damn it, this is like the floodgates of years of pent-up emotion, pain, and ultimate betrayal unleashed.

"No nicknames, remember?" he snarls.

"Did you go to *all* the frat parties, Cass?" I fire back, ignoring his retort. "Fuck lots of lovely cheerleaders? Was Misty the best cheerleader girlfriend a jock like you could wish for? Was your first time a dream, Atticus? Was it? Because mine was a fucking nightmare." Tears flow onto my cheeks, taking us both by surprise, and I roughly dry them, thankful there are just a few when I can feel the tidal wave building. I won't give him the satisfaction.

"What are you talking about?" His voice softens, and that's worse. I shake my head and tighten my lips.

"Nothing, it doesn't matter." I draw in a steadying breath, and with enormous effort, I calm my tone before I continue. "I didn't steal then. I didn't steal this stuff here. And I haven't taken your money either, but it doesn't matter, does it? I have a record, and you didn't believe me back then, so why the fuck would you believe me now?"

"You're lying," he counters, and I almost laugh, but there is nothing funny about this situation.

"No, I'm not," I repeat.

"Yes. You. Are. Or have you forgotten, princess, I know you."

"You *knew* me," I correct and watch his face for any sign that my words mean anything to him. His jaw is ticking, and he purses his lips like he's thinking through some complicated math, but whether that problem has anything to do with how he feels about me, I'm clueless. I no more know this man in front of me than I do Detective Doyle.

"I want my fucking money back," he growls out slowly, fire and anger burning in his glare. He doesn't believe me. Well, no fucking surprise there.

"And I want my fucking life back, so I guess we are both shit out of luck, aren't we?" I snap, setting my jaw tight and tipping my head to one side in defiance.

"Oh, princess, you know I don't believe in luck." He pulls

away from me, and I feel his loss, the heat, the connection. For fuck's sake, what's wrong with me? After all that time, after *everything*, why do I feel anything at all? It must be that I'm in shock. That's all this is; I just wasn't expecting the draw, the pull, or whatever it is. I wasn't prepared for *him*, period. He affects me, and that's a worry I wasn't anticipating. I didn't think I would see him so soon, or at all, if I'm honest. I think I was hoping for not at all, and now I know why. For the second time today, I want to kick myself for being an idiot. Why should any of this come as a surprise? It's always been *him*.

He walks out of the room, and my hands grip the table to stop myself collapsing. I suck in a slow deep breath, trying to remain composed when I feel anything but. My head is a mess, racing with question after question.

What the hell was that? What the fuck am I going to do? I can't go back to jail.

What about Logan?

"Here and here." Atticus slides the piece of paper in front of me, pointing to two lines where I need to sign. This is it. It may be black ink in the pen, but I know damn well this is my blood on the paper. I scratch out my signature and grip the pen tight to stop myself using it as a weapon and end up having a murder charge added to my probation for Category 1 theft. I just made my deal with the devil, and I wonder, not for the first time, if the nightmare I keep waking from was actually a premonition. Atticus swiftly takes the papers from me, as if I might change my mind. If I could, I would. I racked my brain for three hours after the detective came in and offered me a choice of rock and a hard place. I couldn't come up with an alternative. This wasn't in my plan, but really, what choice did I have?

"I can't believe you've done this. You must have some serious sway and some high-ranking officials in your pockets to get this sort of deal. Is it even legal? Tell me this isn't really happening?" I stand and grab my bag from the chair. Atticus is holding the door for me to leave the room with him.

"Oh, it's really happening, princess, and I will only say this once: This was your choice." His face is impassive, and I can't fathom why he is doing this.

"I didn't have a choice, did I?"

"You could tell me where the money is," he clips, and I tighten my lips and shoot daggers his way. It's my stock response to that question. "Don't look so broken up, princess, I've just saved you from finishing your probation and some serious extra time inside. All you have to do is spend the next twelve months with me. It's not exactly a hardship. I live in the fucking penthouse at Number 1 Blackfriars."

"Stop calling me that. I don't give a flying fuck where you live. I do care that now, I have to live with *you,* and if you really believe you still know me, then you'd remember I've never cared about material shit," I fire at him, my eyes narrowing, and if I had heat vision, he would be a smouldering pile of ash right about now.

"Well, you took my money for some reason," he counters as I pause on the threshold, his tall frame towering over me. I tip my head to keep the eye contact. All the time I knew him, he never once scared me. *How times have changed.* I can feel my tummy tighten with something akin to fear, yet I won't give him the satisfaction of knowing just how terrified I really am.

"I didn't take your money," I repeat.

"Yes, so you've said. I'll have my pen back, please. Can't have you picked up on another theft charge before we've even left the station," he quips, and my jaw drops.

"Really? Jokes? This is so far from funny, it's unreal," I bite out, venom dripping from my tone. He leans down, and I have to arch away from him to keep the distance.

"This is as real as it gets, princess. For the next twelve months, you're mine, and I *will* get my money back." He holds my stare, his blue eyes darkening to the colour of a bottomless ocean. He searches my face, but his expression is unchanged, handsome with a hint of hatred. I struggle to see any sign of the man I used to love, not that it matters. He's not here for me; he's here for his money. He lets the door close, and I follow him along the corridor.

There is a Range Rover with blacked out windows and a suited driver waiting with the back door open. Atticus nods and steps aside to let me in. His hand hovers close to the base of my spine, but it doesn't touch. I can still feel the heat as if he did, though. *I'm in so much trouble.* I shuffle to the other side of the seat, as far as I can from Atticus, which is a challenge since his long legs spread wide, and he drapes his arm over the back, his fingertips just millimetres from me. I swallow the lump in my throat and turn to face him, shifting a little farther away as I do.

"I have to get my stuff, and I have no idea how I'm going to explain this to Logan."

"Logan is your cat?" His thick blond brows knit together, clearly troubled, but I doubt he's in a sharing mood.

"Not exactly."

"Boyfriend?" His jaw ticks, and his tone is clipped with irritation.

"It's complicated."

"I understand." He brushes off whatever *that* was, and he is once more a stony-faced statue. I can't begin to get a read of him at all. I sniff out a light laugh.

"I doubt that. I don't understand it myself." I can't help my smile when my minds drifts to all things Logan and *us*. I let out a heavy breath. "He's not going to be happy."

"He cares about you?"

"None of your fucking business," I snap, and he grins and

waves me down, my hackles clearly showing through all my layers of clothing.

"Calm yourself, I'm not prying. I meant, he cares enough about you that he wouldn't want to see you back in prison?" Atticus clarifies.

"No, he wouldn't want that."

"Well, then, he'll be fine," he states and turns away, his eyes fixed on the bustle of the city as we crawl our way out of town. Mine do the same, and I really hope I'm wrong when I mutter to myself,

"No, he won't."

CHAPTER SEVEN

Logan

I want to take it slow, but I've waited too damn long for this, and those little panting breaths are driving me fucking nuts. Her arms are stretched taut, high above her head, both her tiny hands are in one of mine, and my grip is tight. She's not going anywhere, but then, the way her eyes are burning into mine, I know she's exactly where she wants to be, *finally*.

"You ready, T?" My lips brush hers, and her whole body shivers. *God, that's the sexiest fucking thing.*

"I'm scared." She nibbles on her bottom lip, and I press mine over hers, pulling the soft flesh into my mouth and taking her troubles with it. I suck a little too hard, and she whimpers before I release it with a soft plop. I press another kiss at the corner of her mouth and smile. Her lips mirror mine and transform her face. She glows when her face lights like that, when she's truly happy.

"I've got you, you're mine, remember?" I whisper, and she falls.

"Then I'm more than ready." She releases her breath, and a sexy moan escapes the back of her throat. Before she can draw her next breath, my mouth is once more on hers. Our lips crash together with the urgency of months and months of pent-up lust and passion unleashed. *Damn, she tastes good.* My tongue traces the seam of her lips and dives inside, drinking in her flavour and taking everything she has to give. Her tongue, tentative at first, twists with mine, pulling me closer, until I fill her mouth and draw the very breath from her body. All-consuming, this kiss is so pure, when I break, it leaves us both breathless and wanting more.

I cup her chin and hold her face immobile, firm and posses-sive, *mine*. Her eyes lock onto me, her pupils so large there is no colour at all, just inky black pools to lose my soul in. It's like every part of her is opening for me, wide eyes, mouth gasping for air, and when my thigh slips between her legs, they fall to either side of me and melt like butter around my leg. I push my body against her, the heat from our connection incendiary, and collectively we have on way too many clothes. I need to feel that heat, naked and raw. I need to feel how wet she is for me, because she can damn well feel how hard I am for her.

"Keep your hands right there." I press them against the wall and let go, happy when she does exactly as I ask.

"What are you going to do?" she gasps, and I press my finger against her swollen lips.

"Shh, angel." I kiss where my finger was, and a low rumble from my chest accompanies my declaration. "I'm going to do *everything*."

"Oh." It's barely audible. If I hadn't been watching her mouth, I wouldn't know she had spoken at all, just laboured breaths and sexy-as-all-hell sighs.

"But first I'm going to peel these jeans from this beautiful body and taste you. I want you to come all over my tongue be-fore we f—" I stop myself, because as relaxed and sexy as she looks right now, she's gone. Only for a split second, but she's not with me, and I can't have that. I kiss her lips.

"Tia, stay with me. I'm not going to hurt you. I will never hurt you."

"I know, sorry." Her eyes glaze, and my thumb catches the first and, thankfully, only tear.

"And don't ever apologise. What I was going to say was, I want to taste you before I make love to you." She blinks and shakes her head.

"It's okay, you can say fuck, Logan. It's ok to say it. I just—" I interrupt before we lose this moment. She needs this as much as I do, I can see it in her eyes. It's like we have this demon surrounding us both, one she needs to slay, with my help, but either way, she's ready.

"Hey, I will say it when that's what we are going to do, but this isn't what we are doing, not by a long fucking long shot. This is me, making love to you, with this body and my soul. You're mine, Tia, but make no mistake, you own me just as much as I own you. And right now, I am going to worship your body, and we are going to make love until we both pass out."

"Sounds good." She giggles and then swallows the lump in her throat, her eyes darkening with lust and fire. I smile the biggest fucking smile known to man. I have her back.

"Fuck good, Tia, it doesn't get any better than this...this, this is heaven." I drop to my knees, and for the first time in my life, I say a silent prayer, *she's mine.*

I unhook the buttons on her jeans and peel them slowly down her toned legs, taking my sweet time, even if my mouth is literally watering at the sight. It's a battle. I want to rip the clothes from her body, shred them, and devour her, but that's not what she needs. She steps out of her jeans, and I plant a kiss on the cotton triangle at the apex of her thighs. Her tummy muscles clench, and she sucks in a breath. I keep my lips there, kissing and lightly nudging, until I feel her relax, and she lets out that breath she's holding. When one of her hands threads into my hair, tugging and gripping, I slide my fingers over the elastic and pull her panties to the floor.

Kissing her inner thigh at the top, I alternate until I am back where I started, but this time there is nothing to hinder, no barrier. I hook one of her legs over my shoulder and move forward so she is spread much wider. She's dripping wet and even with a little more hair down there than I'm used to, she is fucking perfect. I press my mouth against her soft folds and drag my tongue along her sweet wetness, drinking her in. I thought her mouth tasted like nothing else, but this here, this is intoxicating, a perfect mix of musky sweet and her.

I can't get enough.

Her hands are in my hair, and her fists are pulling me this way and that, her greedy little hips grind against my mouth, and I am just about ready to explode. My cock is straining to the max and is in absolute agony in my pants. I can feel she's letting go, and I am on cloud fucking nine that I'm taking her there. I slip one finger inside her tight little hole, and her muscles clamp down. She gasps, and I ease back a little.

"No, no, don't stop, more, Logan, I need more," she pants, her voice so squeaky and high pitched, I chuckle.

"Okay, angel, anything for you." I cover her clit with my lips, working it with my tongue as I slide two, then three fingers inside her. She's fucking tight, and that just makes my cock throb like a motherfucker behind my zipper. But this isn't about me... *yet.* I gently pump in and out, twisting a little and putting just the right amount of pressure when I turn my fingers and press her sweet spot. Her legs shake, and her fists pull at my hair so much it makes my eyes water, but I keep working her higher and higher.

"Oh! Oh, God, Loga...ah! ah! God, Oh, Lo—!" She loses any coherence somewhere between her declaration to God and saying my name over and over. Her hips buck against my mouth, and then every muscle in her body sets rigid. Time stands still as I watch the most amazing sight in the whole damn world: my girl, coming apart at my fingertips.

She slides down the wall supporting her back and into my waiting arms. I scoop her against my chest and carry her to my bed. She has the sexiest smile, and her cheeks are flushed with colour. I can't keep my eyes off her as I fumble with the buckle of my belt and kick my jeans to the floor. I crawl up her body, kissing patches of skin that take my fancy. All of it takes my fancy, so by the time my mouth is above hers, I can see she is once again a needy mess, and her body is writhing underneath mine, clearly desperate for some contact.

"Need something, angel?"

"Oh, God, Logan, you! I need you, now!" she groans, her hands at my shoulders, trying to pull me closer. My arms have locked my body above her, close, but obviously not close enough. I chuckle.

"I'll let you have that one, angel, but I'm not sure I'm a fan of sassy Tia. I like my women compliant."

"And I like my men mute, but we can't all get what we want, can we?" she quips and bites the sass back with a cute grin.

"I can, and I did," I state with absolute seriousness. She beams the brightest smile, but then frowns with frustration when her tugging on my shoulders has little impact on my position.

"Me, too; me, too. Now, please, Logan, I need you." she begs. Now, *that* I do like the sound of.

"As you wish." I lay my weight on her, lining up the tip of my cock at her entrance, and we both catch our breath when I push forward. Her whole body trembles, and I hover. It's killing me to be this close to heaven and stop, but I have to be certain she's sure.

"Tia?"

"I love you, Logan." She smiles, and her soft lips form the perfect 'o' when I sink into her. I hold her gaze, and I push deeper, sinking every inch, until she can't take anymore. My balls rest against her intimate centre. There's absolutely no space between us. Her legs lock around me, arms wrap around my back, and her hands spear into my hair as mine thread into her silky mane. We are and we move as one, sharing more than our next breath. This is everything, heaven, utopia. Whatever trite words are available for such a moment, they wholly fail to describe this feeling.

All I know is it's fucking perfect.

"Logan, Logan," she sighs my name, her sweet breath on my lips. "Logan! Logan!" Her voice is muffled, angry. Why the hell is she... *No, fuck, no!*

"Logan! Open the damn door I need to talk to you!" Tia bangs on my bedroom door, and her voice is now much clearer. Now I'm awake. Fuck, fuck, fuck, and double fuck!

"Fuck!" I curse into the pillow that I now have held over my face. I didn't want to let my frustration out full volume. It would wake the fucking dead and scare Tia. I pull myself out of bed and stomp over to the door. Flicking the lock, I pull it wide open.

"Jesus, Logan, erection!" She slaps her hand over her eyes, a little too late given her shocked observation.

"I was having a rather good dream, Tia. Get used to it, because trust me, this is not going down anytime soon." I was expecting her to laugh or curse or something, but her eyes fill with tears. "Tia, what the fuck! What's wrong?" I pull her to me and wrap my arms round her. She does this inverse bend thing trying to avoid crushing my cock, but I couldn't give a fuck about that, she looks so unbearably sad. She hugs me back as best she can, but all too quickly, her arms slip from mine, and she walks over to my bed. I grab a pair of boxer shorts and jump into them before sitting beside her. I take both her hands in mine. "Talk to me, T. Whose arse have I got to kick, virtually of course, unless you can invite them round." I try and nudge her into some sort of smile, but I'm getting nothing. I get a sick twist in my gut.

"Logan, I'm so sorry. It's not my fault." Fat tears burst onto her cheeks, and she rubs them dry before I can.

"What? What's not your fault? This isn't fucking funny, Tia. Tell me what's going on." My jaw fixes as worry and something worse begin to bubble deep inside.

"I have to leave here. I have to go and live with Atticus for a while." She could be holding a blade at my chest right now for the pain about to slice into me. I stand and spin to face her. My hands are shaking with rage, and I clench my fists to try and hide the level of my fury.

"Like fuck you do! I'd rather you went back to jail than live with that son of a bitch!" I yell.

"Would you? " Her soft tearful voice halts me dead.

"What? What do you mean would I?" I drop to kneel in front of her, clasping her hands in mine. Her head drops and then after a moment and a deep breath, she lifts her tear filled eyes to meet mine.

"I mean would you rather see me in prison, because that's what's at stake here. I either go and finish my probation with Atticus or I go back to jail and they add a bit more time on for bad behaviour." She sniffs back the tears, failing to stem the flow now that they have broken. I grab a tissue from the bedside table and help to dry her face. This is fucking killing me.

"I don't understand, Tia; you haven't been bad...have you?" I tip her chin high when she drops it. I need to see her face, need to look into her eyes.

"No, I haven't, but—"

"But…" I repeat after her when she falters.

"Look, it's kind of irrelevant now. It's a done deal, and unless you were serious about wanting me back in jail, this is really my only choice." She scrunches her eyes tight as if pain is coursing through her. I feel exactly the same.

"Humour me."

"What?"

"I don't care that it's a done deal, tell me what the fuck happened." She gives an imperceptible nod and lets out a heavy breath before she elaborates.

"My boss, Maria, put some art supplies I didn't know about in my bag. They caught me red-handed, leaving the building. I didn't know at the time why I was being taken away, but my bag was pretty much packed with Kruse office supplies."

"Tell them it was Maria," I state flatly and let out a derisive sniff. *Simple.*

"It's not that easy. She'll lose her job and she needs it. She needs that pension. That zero tolerance policy they have is not just an idle threat; she'd get jail time too. She was only trying to help. I'm not going to throw her under the bus, Logan."

"No, you're going to throw yourself, for fuck's sake." I drag my hand through my hair. I know from that look alone, I have a fat chance changing her mind, but it still doesn't make any sense. "I can't believe that arsehole is going to send you back to jail for lifting some office stationery."

"Well, that and a hundred million pounds," she mutters and rightly avoids all eye contact.

"What the what, now?"

"A hundred million pounds has gone missing, and he thinks I've stolen money from the company," she explains and my stomach drops, now I get it.

"I see."

"I see? That's what you say to that?" She pulls her hands

from mine, and her back is ramrod straight. "Not, 'oh, for fuck's sake, that's ridiculous, Tia, why would he think that'?"

"Why would he think that, T?" I paraphrase and take all the attitude out of her air quotation.

"I don't fucking know. You trust me, right?" she asks, and her voice catches. I don't hesitate.

"Of course." I cup her cheeks and hold her gaze. She's a dreadful liar, but I still trust her. She needs to hear that more than she needs this dumbass revenge. "So what now?"

"Now, I keep my head down and bide my time with Atticus for twelve months." She gives a light shrug.

"Twelve fucking months! I don't like it."

"I'm not over the moon, either, but I can't go back to prison, Logan."

"I know, T, I know… fuck!" I throw my head back and yell. The room falls silent, and when I feel calm enough, I ask the question I don't want to hear the answer to. "When do you have to go?"

"He's in the car outside. I said I had to pick up my stuff and tell you."

"You told him about me?"

"I told him nothing. This isn't a sweet reunion type deal, Logan. I have no intention of making this anything other than a living hell for him."

"Oh, I'd pay to see that." I can't quite make the smile work, and the humour in my joke falls flat.

"It's only a year." She reaches for my hand and squeezes a little comfort. It's not nearly enough.

"You'll be able to visit though?" I hate that our time is no longer *our* own.

"I don't know. I hope so." She shrugs, and I get a flash of unbearable rage igniting my blood. I fail to temper it and have to pull away. Snatching my hands back, I jump to my feet. My tone is hostile, and I practically snarl when I dismiss her comment.

"Fine, whatever. Do what you've got to do."

"Logan, don't be like this," she pleads, her soft words are a faux balm, they sting like a motherfucker right now.

"Like what, Tia, I said I can't lose you, and yet—"

"You haven't lost me, please, Logan, don't make this any harder." She is instantly at my side, her hand on my arm, her fingers resting on the curve of my bicep, and I can't stand it.

"This is fucking bullshit, Tia." I drag my hand through my hair and storm off, slamming the door to my en suite. "Fuck!"

Maybe forty minutes pass when there is a light knock on my bedroom door.

"Logan, can I come in?" I don't answer, several painfully long seconds pass when I hear her let out a sigh. "I have to go now. I'll try and visit soon. Take care of yourself, Logan." I wait until I hear her retreating footsteps. Skidding across the landing in my bare feet just as she opens the front door, I can see the man standing on the porch. I know it's him. I've done my background checks on her ex, and there is more than enough Google fodder on the Kruse family to fill a meaty dossier.

"Tia! Wait!" I yell and bound down the stairs.

"We have to leave, Tia. You've kept me waiting long enough." The arsehole speaks but wisely doesn't enter my home.

"I don't know, Atticus, have I kept you waiting six years?" she snaps and steps away from the door as I reach the bottom of the stairs.

"Logan." She turns to me, her tentative smile nearly breaks my fucking heart.

"Tia." I step flush against her, my arm sweeping around her waist, and I pull her up my body, her legs instinctively wrap my hips, and she grips tight. I support her weight in the palm of my hands, which fist the cheeks of her arse. Her breath catches, but before her lips can form a smile, my lips crash into hers. Her hands are in my hair, and I turn and slam her against the wall, chasing the depth of the kiss with my entire body. Her taste is so familiar, but then it wasn't so long ago I was drenched in her scent. Even if it was a dream, I still drank her in, just as I am now. Her tongue dances with mine, lips sucking, biting, teeth clashing, an urgency we both feel in our bones, and as much as I hate this, I take a little comfort that she feels the same, *finally*.

There is a cough behind me, and I let a deep disapproving growl escape as Tia breaks our kiss. She drops her forehead to mine, her eyes wide, and her smile even wider.

"What was that?" she exhales, her tone shocked and filled with awe.

"That was just the beginning."

PART 2

Tartarus Hall
Tia aged seven years old.

CHAPTER EIGHT

Tia

"Can't I stay here?" I actually grip the kitchen table as if rooting myself to the small piece of flimsy pine furniture will help my situation.

"No, sweetheart, you can't. Seven-year-old girls are not allowed to stay home alone even if you think you're all grown up. Mummy would get into serious trouble, and you'd be taken away from me." Her warning words send a panic to my heart, and my stomach rolls so much I get that watery liquid pool in my mouth, and I think I'm going to be sick. I don't know where I would be taken, but she says this as a warning whenever I'm naughty, so I think it will be a very bad place. Almost as bad as the place she wants to take me to today, but still I'd rather stay at home.

"I wouldn't tell, Mummy," I plead as she manhandles me into my coat, roughly tugging the woollen hat over my ears. She drops down to help me into my wellington boots, and my heart just drops at the inevitability of this day, like every day of my school holiday. *I hate it.*

"I know, sweetheart, but you can't stay here. You have to

come with Mummy to the Hall. You can bring a colouring book, and I'm baking cookies today." She tries to placate me with treats and even plants a soft kiss on my nose. I still don't want to go, but the cookies do sound good.

"Really?"

"Yes." She tugs me toward the door, and I fall into step right behind her.

"Is Cass going to be there?" I know the answer before she replies. If he was, we wouldn't be having this daily battle.

"No, sweetheart, he's still away at school."

"Doesn't his mummy love him?"

"Of course she does, why would you say that?" She stops at the door and spins to face me, shock and outrage on her face.

"She sent him away." I explain my summation of what seems to me a very obvious observation of the Cass situation. She shakes her head emphatically.

"No, no, darling, he went to boarding school. She hasn't sent him away, and yes, she loves him very much. That's why he's gone to the best school in England, because his mummy wants what's best for him," she adds with a strange sense of misplaced pride.

"Oh." I shrug because I really don't understand.

"And I want what's best for you, but we will have to wait for that day to come," she mutters as she opens the back door and we brave an icy February dawn

"Hmm?"

"Nothing sweetheart, come on, let's get moving. It might only be a short walk up the drive, but it snowed last night, and it's freezing, so no time to be dallying. I can't have you catching a cold."

"Okay, Mummy." She locks the back door, holds my mitten-covered hand, and tugs me the length of the drive.

I hate having to go with my mother when Cass isn't there, I know I'm not welcome. Mrs Kruse rarely comes downstairs to where my mother spends most of her time. However, when she does, she makes a point of ignoring me and looking down her nose at my mother. Not that my mother seems to notice or mind. She is so grateful for the job, she practically kisses the ground that snotty woman walks on. Working as housekeeper gives us free accommodation and security. The latter is of the upmost importance since Mum told me my dad left the day he found out I was more than just a bad case of stomach flu.

There are two drives to the main house, one from the main gatehouse where the head gardener lives and one at the rear of the property to our lodge. This gravel drive is lined with over-bearing oak trees. The branches hang low, and in the winter, they seem to reach out for you as you walk beneath them. I cling to my mother's hand and try to calm my overactive imag-ination. It's only about a half-mile walk, but to my little legs, it feels much longer. My skin is red raw under my sweatpants by the time we walk the distance in several feet of snow. Chilblains are my own personal hell. Tight swollen skin that prickles and feels like it's on fire the second we get inside. After a start to the day like that, I never get warm; even huddled next to the open fire in the kitchen trying to thaw out, I never manage to get toasty. I just defrost enough to not die of hypothermia.

It isn't just the sense that I'm not welcome, but the house itself is terrifying to most adults, let alone a child. It's a Gothic monstrosity. Some of the older parts were built in the twelfth century, although only the East tower resembles a typical Castle structure with battlements, arrow loops and a turret. It was re-named Tartarus Hall when it was extended and updated in the nineteenth century. It has hundreds of rooms spread over three stories. It sprawls in a hexagonal shape, has an East and West tower and five angled ranges, the sixth being open and giving the perfect view down to the gatehouse. Some of the rooms are enormous; the great hall, I think, is larger than our entire house, yet it has such small panes of heavily leaded windows that they barely let in any sunlight. The smaller rooms are worse, and with the thick velvet curtains always only partially drawn open, it feels like night time *all* the time.

The furniture and deep carpets are in keeping with a more modern period. Mrs Kruse kept some of the authentic pieces, but she isn't one to sacrifice luxury, style, or comfort in order to maintain authenticity or a more sympathetic interior to the period of the house.

The artwork, however, is an acquired taste and one that I hope I never acquire. In most of the reception rooms, the walls are dominated by the most horrendous oil paintings. Whole walls depicting some bloody battle or mythical underworld carnage, even the smaller portraits of Kruse ancestors sends an icy chill through my veins, if I was unfortunate enough to accidentally catch a glimpse.

My mother is the only housekeeper, and I am more than happy to stay in the kitchen and not keep her company on her rounds cleaning the rooms in rotation. She prefers it that way too, since I'm apparently always under her feet. The family employ some extra staff that come in to help for special occasions, like holidays and if they are having guests to stay. Extra waiting staff and Michelin starred chefs are brought in for those special events, but other than that, my mother takes care of the house and the meals when the family are in residence. It's more than a full-time job.

She told me once that old houses are special and need extra care, because they hold on to the secrets of whoever lived there, past, present, and future. This didn't help me to warm to the place. If anything, that makes it just a little creepier and as far as I am concerned, secures my spot by the fireplace in the kitchen until I am old enough to stay at home alone.

At that time I didn't realise Tartarus Hall was *very* special. I was unaware it had secret passageways, corridors, hidden staircases, or an attic that was a labyrinth from which you could access the entire house. I didn't know, and I didn't care. I was happy in the kitchen, either drawing at the table or curled up in the old saggy armchair by the fire, reading or more likely falling asleep from boredom.

Then I met Cass.

I'm not sure how I had missed him before that day. He was like a bolt of lightning entering the room. He rushed over to me and grabbed my hand. He yelled at my mother that he was taking me to find treasure, and we disappeared for the whole day.

He was eight years old, and I was five. It was the best day of my life.

Every day with Atticus is the best. Each school holiday after that day we were inseparable. He is like a force of nature, so much energy and spirit. He has so many stories his grandfather had told him that he wanted to share with me, it is like having my own personal walking, talking library. When I get tired, he pulls the cushions to the floor in whatever room we happened to find ourselves, and he makes a fort to protect us both. While I nap, he stands guard or sometimes falls asleep right beside me.

He is naughty too, opening up rooms that are forbidden and taking me beyond the boundary of the walled garden where I know I'm not allowed to go. I'd always pull to a standstill when he tried to drag me somewhere we shouldn't be, and I'd argue or shake my head. However, I wasn't so good at coming up with reasons why we shouldn't, not when he was so good with all the reasons why we should. The bottom line is I can't say no to him if I want to, and I knew in my heart, even then, I didn't want to deny him anything.

He showed me all the secrets of Tartarus Hall. At the time, I wasn't sure if knowing more helped or just made the place more terrifying. I soon learned it wasn't the house I needed to be afraid of.

I asked him at the time why he came for me that day, and he told me that I didn't look sick. He'd heard me laughing and wanted to play. I was confused, but he explained his mother had said I was sick and to stay away from me. She had said that every time he asked about me. We had lived in the lodge for over two years, and I'd been in his house a hundred times, and every time his mother had said I was sick and to stay away.

I wasn't allowed to have friends come over and play from school. Mrs Kruse didn't want the local children snooping, and my mother wasn't fond of other people's children. It was a grey and lonely childhood, and when Cass was home, my whole world ignited into a high definition adventure in glorious Technicolor.

I hear the sharp clicking heels of Mrs Kruse, and I curl up tighter into the armchair, not that she will acknowledge me, but I'd rather not be here at all. I camouflage myself with the cushions and a worn blanket that hangs over the back of the chair. Closing my eyes, I simply imagine myself anywhere but here.

"Margaret!" Her thick Swedish accent is highlighted by the sharp shrill of her voice as she calls out for my mother. "Margaret!"

"I'm in the pantry, Mrs Kruse, I won't be a moment," my mother replies with a bright breezy tone.

"Where's your daughter?" I can just picture her disdain; her thin, wrinkled nose turned up, as if having to mention my name at all would cause a nasty smell.

"Oh, I'm not sure, she was here a moment ago; maybe she's gone to the little girl's room. She knows not to wander the house, Mrs Kruse. She only ever ventures out of this kitchen if Atticus is here." My mother's detailed explanation sounds more like an apology.

"Yes, Atticus, that's what I want to talk to you about. He will be arriving home tomorrow." Mrs Kruse's haughty tone is clipped with irritation. Still, it takes all my effort to not squeal out with excitement. However, since my mother was also oblivious to my whereabouts, I'm more than happy to remain hidden. "I want you to keep your daughter away from him. He's a difficult child, and I would rather he didn't have friends like... well, they aren't suited to play together." She sniffs in a sharp breath, and her voice is sharp and harsh. I feel the sting of her words even if my mother doesn't.

"I understand," my mother agrees. I don't, and I don't understand why she isn't saying anything. I don't understand what 'suited' even means. Atticus is my best friend, and we have fun together. I simply can't fathom why she doesn't want me near her son, but that doesn't matter. I'm seven years old, and now I'm not going to be allowed to play with my one and only friend in the world. I can feel my eyes tear up, and my shoulders shake, trying to keep the sobbing silent. I definitely don't want to be discovered now, or ever, for all I cared.

My mother tells me the next day that I am to keep away from Atticus, even if that means I have to hide when he comes for me. When she tells me I'm not allowed to play with him, I don't ask why. I don't want to know her explanation, because it couldn't possibly hurt any less with her made-up excuse.

I hear his footsteps above the kitchen, racing down the corridor and clearly on his way to find me. My mother flashes me a worried look.

"He'll always come looking for me, Mum. If he wants to find me, he will." I shrug my shoulders, and she rushes over to me, helping me put my things back in my rucksack.

"No, no, he won't," she flusters, and I get a painful hit in my chest that she's ashamed of me, just like Mrs Kruse. She's so eager for me to be gone. "I'll tell him you're not here. I'll tell him you're staying with friends." She smiles brightly, but it looks pained. I wonder for a moment if she feels a fraction of my pain, but then the panic in her eyes as the footsteps get nearer makes me realise she's just worried for herself. She made a promise to Mrs Kruse, and she intends on keeping it, regardless of her own heartbroken daughter.

"Okay." I don't even feel bad that I should've told her he would know that was a lie. I want her to tell him exactly what she just told me she was going to say. He knows I have no friends, and he is going to know it's all a lie.

Above my mother's promise, above everything, I wanted him to come and find me.

I wanted Atticus.

I quickly pack up the rest of my stuff, my drawing book and pad, grab my pencils, and run up the servants' staircase to the attic.

Tears are streaming down my face by the time I reach the end of the attic in the West Wing of the house. The door had been locked for centuries, but Atticus had found the key, and it was my favourite place, apart from the kitchen. The eaves close in on both sides, and there is only one window. It is large and oval, and the panes of glass are arranged in an intricate pattern and are held in place by thick lines of lead. The sun casts an ethereal shadow when it hits and the mix of floating dust particles, light, and shadow make the room feel like another world.

A dense supporting beam sits just below the window and gives me the perfect hiding place, with the most amazing view.

From the doorway, I am invisible, yet I can see everything from where I lay, over the courtyard and right down the drive to the Gatehouse and lakes. On a clear day, the view stretches as far as the eye can see, far beyond the immaculate manicured lawns, rose garden, terraced flowerbeds, and ornamental ponds. It is the perfect vantage point to see over the hedges that are trimmed to artistic perfection and line the length of the drive with a menagerie of mystical creatures: Minotaur, mermaids, Hercules, and my favourite, Pegasus. I could draw this view all day.

My tummy wakes me with a loud rumble followed by a snicker. Only it's not *any* snicker. I lift my head up and peek over the beam.

Of course, it's Atticus.

"I didn't think you were ever going to wake up." He chuckles and crawls over from where he is setting up a picnic. He rests his arms on the beam and peers over at my sketches then back to me. His eyes fixed on mine. I rub the sleepy dust away and let out a long, slow yawn.

"How long have you been there?"

"I had to wait until Mother went out because I am supposed to be studying for some test to get into a school in the States, but I came to find you just as soon as she left. Why did your mother tell me you were with friends? I knew she was lying. You told me you don't have any friends." He doesn't draw a breath, firing questions and his own answers at me.

"I don't." I drop my gaze and give a light shrug. I bet he has lots of friends, although he never has anyone over to visit at the Hall, just like me.

"You have me," he states with misplaced conviction.

"Not any more." I sit up and turn to rest my back against the beam, pulling my legs up and tucking my knees beneath my chin. Atticus hops over and lands gracefully beside me. Our thighs are pressed together. He turns to face me, then follows my gaze out over his family's Estate.

"What are you talking about?"

"Your mother doesn't think we should play together," I say as a matter of fact, but I can't hide the sadness in my voice. The prickle of tears is already fighting behind my nose and welling in my eyes. I draw in a steadying breath. "She said you're a difficult child, and I'm not 'suited' to play with you." He sniffs out a flat laugh and agrees, in part.

"I can be difficult, but you're my only friend, too, Tia, and I *want* to play with you. I actually enjoy coming home now. I don't want you to hide from me, *ever*. I will speak to Mother." He brushes this situation off like it's of no consequence. My jaw drops at his confidence, and I have to physically snap it shut to reply.

"Atticus, don't, it's not worth it. My mother would kill me if she loses this job and your Mother was deadly serious." I shake my head at the thought of the trouble this could lead to. Letting out a heavy sigh, I add, "I think my mother agrees with your Mother anyway, so it's probably for the best."

"Do you know what having friends really means?" He ignores my concerns completely, barely registering that I have spoken at all when he voices his question.

"Not really,"

"It means I'm here for you, and I'll prove it," he states with absolute certainty. I'm kind of in awe of him, and a little bit scared, too. He has this dark look in his eyes, and his face no longer resembles a young boy; it's sincere, serious, and stern.

"Cass, I don't want you to get into trouble." I nudge him, and he puffs out a breath that just adds to his general dismissive attitude regarding my concerns.

"Tia, I think that's what the T in your name should stand

for. A capital T for maximum trouble." He laughs so much I have to join in; it's infectious. He jumps to his feet and offers his hand to help me to mine. "It's why we're best friends, Tia, you're *trouble* and I'm *difficult*; we're a perfect pair. Besides, we're more than friends, anyway. We're like this really small gang." He grins conspiratorially and leaps over the beam dragging me with him.

"A gang?" I stumble, but he catches me before I fall head first into the little carpet banquet he has prepared.

"Yep, and this gang is hungry. Want some lunch?" He stands proudly and sweeps his arm at the array of food he has laid out.

"I'm starving. What have you got?" I sit down cross-legged, and he does the same. With a flourish, he removes the cloth covering a small mound in the centre.

"I've got your favourite." Stacked high is a pile of triangle white bread sandwiches that I immediately recognise.

"Really? Didn't my mum ask why you wanted banana and sugar sandwiches?"

"She did, but in case you didn't know, I'm a really, really good liar." He tries to wink, but the two-lid scrunch thing he has mastered only makes me giggle. I fall quiet for a moment before I speak. He has a way of distracting me, but the underlying problem sits heavily in the pit of my stomach.

"I'm not sure that's a good thing, Cass." He narrows his eyes and takes a huge bite of the sandwich, chewing slowly, all the while keeping his eyes on me. He takes a sip from the juice carton and sets me straight.

"I like that I'm your only friend, Tia. It means you need me, and if I have to lie and cheat and steal to make sure I am here for you, then I don't care if it's right or wrong. It's just what I will do for *us*."

"I don't *need* you, Cass, it's just nicer with you here. This place is very boring when—" I can't help loving the way he said *us*, even if I'm not especially pleased that he seems to know how I really feel.

He interrupts. "It's okay, Tia, I need you too." I put the feeling down to hunger, but I'm pretty sure that is the first time I feel the swarm of butterflies riot inside my tummy.

CHAPTER NINE

Tia

aged 12

My first year of secondary school is the worst. I tried so hard to make friends. I know Cass said he was there for me, but he also wasn't. He transferred overseas to study in the States when he turned fourteen, and he doesn't always come home for the holidays. He sometimes spends time with his grandfather in New York, or the family goes skiing, or takes a beach vacations, or perhaps goes sailing. It doesn't really matter. It just means he isn't home; he isn't with me, and I am alone, and I've never felt so lonely.

My move to the big school was exciting at first. My primary school only had sixty children so changing to a school with over a thousand pupils, I felt confident I would make at least a few friends, and then perhaps I would have some sort of normal teenage social life. I had a few invitations to parties at the beginning of the year, but my mother doesn't drive, and we live so far from anywhere I can never get home afterwards. I'm not close enough with anyone in particular, not more than a forced lab partner status, and definitely not close enough to garner a sleepover invitation. Declining invitations so early on was social suicide and meant that, pretty quickly, I stopped getting asked altogether. Despite the potential of a much larger pool of possible friends, I am back to being cripplingly lonely and isolated.

It was easier after a while to keep to myself, a depressing self-fulfilling prophecy that means my life is in full pause mode until Cass returns. I know it isn't healthy, and with puberty kicking in big time at the age of twelve, it means when he does finally come home for the summer holidays, I am going to be an angry mass of raging hormones.

And I was.

"If you don't open the door, Tia Parker, I'm going to break it down!" Cass continues to thump his fist against my bedroom door. It's the seventh day in a row he's called, and this time he's managed to get all the way upstairs. He must've waited until my mother left, because I knew full well she wouldn't have let him in. Despite Mrs Kruse's abrupt U-turn regarding my suitability as a playmate when I was seven, my mother is ridiculously uncomfortable with our friendship and wants to maintain what she sees as our proper 'station'. She really doesn't like it when Cass calls at our house.

"Go away!" I call out, still lying on my bed but with my pillow pressed against my head because that banging has now given me a kicking headache.

"You can't still be sick, and even if you are, I never get sick, so just open the damn door." He pauses the thumping just long enough to be heard.

"Don't swear at me!"

"Damn isn't swearing!" His voice drops, and I can hear the smile in his tone. He sounds different though. There's a roughness that wasn't there only a few months ago. "Open the fucking door, Tia. That's swearing, and just so you know, I have enough food here to last the week. I'm camping outside your door until you let me in and tell me what the hell's going on."

"My mother won't like that," I argue.

"Your mother won't mind, trust me. I can do no wrong in that woman's eyes."

"Pff," I snort and kind of hate that he's right. His own mother may find him difficult, but mine adores him.

"You know the shit I had to go through to stay here all summer. I want to spend my summer with you, Tia, and you're being a brat."

"I'm a brat! You...you—" I yell but get flustered when my mouth fires off before my brain has secured a witty or more likely, snarky retort.

"Me, yes, what about me?" he goads, and he starts to chuckle. I get a strange mix of anger and hurt that he's laughing at me.

"Go away, Cass. I don't need you anymore," I state with as much conviction as I can, hating that my nose tingles with the lie. I squeeze my eyes shut and pray he doesn't hear when my voice catches on that last word. The silence is thick, and I can hear him let out a heavy sigh that matches my own.

"Well, I need you, Tia 'Trouble' Parker." He punctuates each word with a heavy hand banging loudly on my poor pine door. The hinges rattle and the poster of The Smiths loses at least two of the pins holding it in place. I think for a moment. He might just break through like he threatened, but he doesn't. The thumping stops, and I hear him slide down and slump to the floor.

I prop up on my elbows and stare at the door. I can picture his icy white hair falling into his impossibly perfect sapphire blue eyes as he hunches over, pulling his long legs up and most likely resting his head on his knees, plotting his next move. His blond brows are probably crinkled with irritation at not getting his way, not this time, at least. He has this calm seriousness about him that he maintains at all times, almost without exception. Oh, he has a temper that's akin to a mini apocalypse, but I have only seen it once, and although I'd never want to be on the receiving end, I did benefit in that instance. We both did. The ban his mother tried to enforce when I was seven was instantly retracted, and even at the age of ten he was more articulate and forceful at expressing his wishes than a fully-grown adult.

That aside, he also has some pretty devious ideas of how to get his own way too, which are much more fun; but he has the tools to argue his case when necessary and he can be *very* persuasive. He is very smart, and I can listen to him for days. Which is what it feels like I am doing now. He hasn't drawn breath for three hours straight, and I need to pee. *Man, he's stubborn.*

"I need to use the bathroom Atticus." I'm bouncing on the balls of my feet, because I've actually left it a little too late, and I'm now at the toe-curling uncomfortable stage.

"And?"

"And you need to leave, so I can pee." I rattle the door handle to give warning of my impending exit.

"Why? Don't you have a door on the bathroom?" he quips.

"Don't be an arse, just go home Cass. I don't want to see you. I'm not sick, I just—"

"Just what, Tia? Talk to me. I've missed you, please," he pleads, and I hate myself right now. Why don't I want to see him again? It's not his fault I'm a friendless freak.

"Damn it," I huff and drop my head to the door in defeat.

"Hey, don't swear." His tone is affronted with mock shock.

"Fuck off!"

"You kiss your mother with that mouth?" he retorts.

"I don't kiss anyone with this mouth," I mumble.

"Well, that's a crime right there."

"Cass, don't be mean."

"I'm not being mean, Tia," he replies with a stern tone, and I can just imagine the serious glare he would be giving me if the door wasn't in the way. "Now open the door." I can hear him move, shuffle to his feet, and my hand hovers on the handle, my fingers trembling. Why the hell am I nervous? *This is Cass, for goodness sake.* I swing the door wide, and my mouth goes dry, my breath just freezes halfway between my lungs and my throat.

He's so unbelievably beautiful. When did that happen?

It takes all my effort for my jaw not to drop open. He must be nearly six feet, towering above me and blocking the natural sunlight from the hall window with his frame. He might only be fifteen, but he is easily the best looking man I have ever seen, and he's not done growing yet. *Holy hell*, I swallow the lump and try and mask my awkwardness by coughing, not hugely subtle, and I doubt it's gone unnoticed. I can't stop staring. *Get a grip, Tia.*

It's just Cass. You're best friends, remember? The boy you played hide and seek with, made mud pies with, built forts and castles with? The boy you got lost with from dawn till dusk? Only he doesn't look like that boy anymore.

My heart feels like it's trying to replace the lump I just swallowed, or at the very least, it's trying to escape from my body that way. I'd be surprised if he can't hear it, it's beating so damn loudly. He rests his arm on the doorframe, exposing a small patch of smooth tanned skin over his bony hip. His jeans are hanging off his narrow waist, and the button-down white shirt he's wearing is a little too baggy for his slight frame; he's all skin and bone. I think all that energy from the mountain of food he eats must've gone straight to his height. My eyes seem to take too long working their way up his lanky body, because by the time they reach his, he has a huge knowing grin plastered wide and wicked on his face.

"Cat got your tongue?" He pulls his full soft bottom lip through his teeth. *Oh god.* My face must be able to generate its own electricity, it's radiating so much heat.

How do I know his lips are soft? I don't. Only looking at him now, I realise I have imagined many, many times that they are, and judging by that look on his smug face, he knows the exact same thing.

"Shut up!" I snap, mortified and flustered and I don't know what, but I barge past him, take two steps, and I'm in the bathroom opposite my bedroom. I spin and slam a new door in his face. The handle starts to shake, and the familiar pounding resumes. I quickly relieve myself for fear he will actually break down this much flimsier door.

"Aw, come on, Tia, I'm only teasing. God, I've missed you, your cute temper, and pouty mouth. Come on, Trouble, give me a hug?" he coaxes.

"No!"

"For fuck's sake, what have I done?" The thud is much louder, and I imagine his head dropping against the door with frustration. His tone is more perplexed than angry, but it's a fine line that I can't seem to help myself crossing.

"Stop swearing at me!" I bark.

"Stop being a pain in my arse, and tell me what's up." I was expecting a flare-up of biblical proportions, but his tone is filled with sweet concern. I forget completely why I was so filled with rage and now just feel hugely embarrassed for acting out.

"I…I…it's nothing." I open the door and try and shrug off my mood like I haven't made a big ol' fool of myself.

"Oh, that's all right, then." He grabs my hand and pulls me into the warmest hug. Strong arms wrap around my body, and I take all the time in the world, breathing him in, before I speak. I don't know what to say because I don't know what the hell is wrong with me.

"Cass." I tilt my head back, but he hasn't released his hold so I only meet his gaze when he drops his chin to look at me.

"Tell me, please," he implores. His crystal blue eyes glaze, and for a moment, he looks so tortured, as if I have already hurt him too much. I feel a deep ache in my chest, a similar pain I feel each day in his absence, but it is unbearable to me that I have caused him a fraction of that sadness.

"I missed you." It's all I can offer as way of an explanation. Luckily, it seems enough to lighten the darkness on his features and instantly lifts the mood that cloaked us both. His smile is brilliant, bright, and dazzling. It's both infectious and breathtaking, or maybe that's just the way he's looking at me. *I hope it's the latter.*

"And I'm here now." He plants a light kiss on my forehead that I feel tingle from where he touches me to the tip of my toes.

"But—" I want to at least try and explain my meltdown.

"But nothing, princess. The way I see it, you have two choices. One, we can fight and argue, or two, we can spend every possible minute together having the best summer before I have to go back to school. Your choice, Tia, but I have to tell you, choose your answer wisely." His arms drop their hold from around my body, only to hold my shoulders and pull my posture straight. Like he is trying to shake some sense into me. That is an almighty challenge from where I'm standing, as I'm still focused on the sudden loss of his body heat and how good his arms felt, how good I felt. It's my turn to shake myself

"That sounds like a threat." I drop my hip and arch an accusatory eyebrow.

"No, Tia, it sounds like a promise." He bends so we are almost nose-to-nose and definitely eye-to-eye. His deep voice rumbles from his chest, and I feel a flash of gooseflesh strike across my entire body. This is going to be an exhausting summer if my body is going to react like this every time he looks my way. He interrupts my wayward thoughts. "I want to spend my summer with you, and you want to spend your summer with me. There is nothing stopping us doing exactly what we want to do, so come on, Tia, what's it to be?"

"Do you always get what to want?"

"Without exception! Why?"

"God, you're an arrogant arse sometimes, you know that?"

"And it's taken you this long to come to this conclusion. And there was me thinking you were smart." He ruffles my hair, and my stomach drops at the easy switch to playmate, from something to nothing. *Oh, God, maybe this is nothing for him.* "Now come on, princess, we've wasted enough time. I have so much to do." He keeps hold of my shoulders and manoeuvres me back into my bedroom.

"What have you got to do?" I frown, watching him try and gather things that he thinks I am likely to need: swimming costume, flip-flops, sketch pad, and sunblock. He grabs my baseball hat and slips it on his head, tugging the peak low so I can barely see his eyes, which, in my book, is a crime. He steps toward me slowly, with a hint of menace, making the most of his new intimidating height. I match his advancing steps with a backward one of my own, his grin bordering on nefarious. My breath catches when I hit the wall with my back. His hands press flat either side of my head, and he dips low. With his next words, he makes my life a whole lot more complicated.

"I have to make you smile."

CHAPTER TEN

Atticus

I let Tia have a few days, and in fairness, I needed the time to get over my jet lag, but a whole week was crazy. I should've broken down the damn door on the third day and dragged her up to the Hall. I didn't believe for a second she was sick, but there's something going on, and I didn't give up summer camp and come all the way home to be shut out.

She looked so pretty when she finally opened the door, and if her eyes hadn't been so red and a little too swollen from recent tears, I would say she looked damn near perfect. Actually, she does look perfect; the sadness ghosting her complexion makes her all the more beautiful. Her hair has streaks lightened by the sunlight, and the deep chestnut colour is redder than the dark brown I remember. She has a few pimples, but somehow that just makes her look more *perfect*, her imperfections make her *more*. However, her deep emerald green eyes are going to be my downfall. The way she looks into my eyes, unwavering, soul-searching, as if reading my every thought and my darkest secrets, and I really can't have that. *I don't want to scare her away.*

She's mine, always has been, always will be.

Still, refusing to see me for seven days is a new tactic I wasn't anticipating, not from the weekly letters she wrote or the infrequent phone calls. Nevertheless, it seems that my most recent absence has let her forget *us,* and I need to remind her.

I pick up my rucksack with the day's supplies, and we head down to the boathouse. The sun is reaching its highest point, but I know we have all day and into the evening to cross the lake and chill. It is one of the perks of living on such a vast estate: there's always somewhere to go and get lost, and no one is going to worry, as apart from the odd insect bite, nothing bad happens here. We cut across the lawns at the back of the Hall, and I sprint off to get changed into some shorts and a t-shirt. It's too hot already, and I know I will be doing the lion's share of rowing. Tia has absolutely no co-ordination and as funny as it is spinning in circles and confusing the fish, I do actually have to check the island's wildfowl shelter. The river runs for about a mile before it widens into the lake, and it's a farther half-mile until you reach the island. It's part nature reserve, and I offered to check for any repair work that might be due. Colin, our old gamekeeper, is never one to turn down an extra pair of hands, and it makes a change from schoolwork or TV.

I run back to Tia and notice she's shed one more layer too. Her loose scoop-neck blouse is hanging off her shoulder, and her jeans shorts couldn't be any shorter. *Damn.* I guess we've both grown a little since Christmas. I take her bag, too, and slip my hand into hers. It's not the first time I've held her hand, yet it feels odd, natural and good, but strange at the same time. She seems happy enough, and even if she did try and tug it away, I have a pretty good grip. We fall into an easy silence, shoulders touching and perfectly in step, striding down the unmade part of the gravel drive that leads to the timber boarded boathouse.

We have a speed boat and some canoes, but I want to take

my time, so I untie the two-man rowing boat, and Tia hands me our supplies before stepping on board and taking the seat nowhere near the oars. I cast off and start to row us up-steam, setting a good pace and quickly working up a sweat in the midday summer heat. We are nearing the mouth of the river when I pull the oars off the water a little and catch my breath. Tia hands me a bottle of water, and after downing half, I pour some over my face to try and cool down. Her pink cheeks darken, and she averts her eyes when I catch her starring.

"You okay?"

"Yeah, I'm fine. It's hot. I think I'm catching too much sun." She rummages in her bag and pulls the sun block free. Smearing her face and any bare skin she can reach, she hands the tube of cream to me, but I shake my head.

"You wanna tell me what's really up?" I rest my elbows on the oars, keeping the tip just dipping in the water, but I'm able to link my fingers into a bridge I can rest my head on and hold her gaze.

"Where do you want me to start?" She sighs heavily, quirking her lips with a sad resignation that I don't quite understand.

"I want you to start with school, and then we can work our way to why this is all kinds of awkward between us now." I address at least one issue I am certain is causing her concern. The other, I am just taking a wild guess at.

"Oh my god! Cass!" She buries her head in her hands. *Yes! Nail on the head.* I decide to take pity on her, chuckling lightly, and probe the easier of the two topics.

"So what's so bad about school?"

"School's just school. It's fine." She always avoids eye contact when she's lying, that and she tucks her hands away, usually under her arm pits but this time under her bottom.

"Sure it is. Tell me another lie, Tia, and I'll capsize us," I state calmly, and her eyes widen with worry. Her hands quickly shift to grip the edge of the boat on both sides.

"You'd lose all the food." She's quick to argue, her eyes darting from the boat, over the distance to the riverbank, and back to me. My face is impassive, but she should know by now I don't make idle threats. "Cass, we'd have to go all the way back and get changed. You've rowed for ages upstream… you're not gonna capsize us. Stop being an arse." She rushes her justifications and lets out a nervous laugh, her bravado wavering when she see my smile. I drop the oars and pitch all my weight heavily to one side and then the other, flipping me, the boat, and her into the river.

"Oh, my God, Cass!" She screams in a gasp of horror, her arms flailing as she surfaces in a spectacular splash of water. She reaches for the overturned boat with one hand while slicking back her river-matted hair out of her face. The water is crystal clear and icy cold. The gentle current has the two of us, the boat, and all its contents drifting back the way we came. I swim to each side of the riverbank, grabbing any debris from our ruined picnic, trying to contain the flotsam as we glide back to the boathouse. My hair is much longer than normal and is heavy with water, I flick it clear of my face with a swift jerk of my head and flash my widest smile at Tia, who is still spluttering, gasping, and looking very much like a drowned rat.

"When are you going to learn, Tia, I don't take kindly to being told what I can and can't do?" I pull through the water to get closer. There is a flash of fear in her eyes, and her voice is pitched with panic.

"I can't touch the bottom, Cass!" she yells. Her arm is half on the belly of the boat but it's too slimy for her to grip onto the wood. She loses what hold she has and slips right underneath the surface. The boat drifts off, but Tia is still struggling to keep her head above the water. I can't see what the problem is, but from her impossibly wide eyes, I know there is a serious problem. The reeds must be wrapping around her legs. She hasn't moved an inch since she let go of the boat, and I'm still not close enough to help.

"Swim, Tia, you do know how to swim, or have you forgotten that too?" I shout out, my attempt at humour sounds more angry than I hoped but at least it masks what I'm really feeling, *fear*.

"Fuck, I can't... I can't move my legs...my foot's stuck, Cass!" she cries out, and then she's gone.

I don't know how we drifted so far apart, but with two long strokes through the water I am right where she is...*was*. All I can see is darkness below me. Sunlight bounces off the ripples as the surface settles where there's no more splashing. I dive under. The river's deep, thirty feet, maybe more, and swimming into the icy darkness, it feels much deeper, but it's clear, and I can see her. Her hair fans out with the swirling water, her skin has an ethereal pallor; her eyes are pitch black and wide with terror. The moment feels surreal, almost magical, the way the particles of light dance in slow motion and at the same time cloaked in darkness, calm and silent; so close to death I can feel it at my fingertips.

I grab her hand and use it to pull myself down her body. My hands feel their way down the leg that isn't moving. The other is still fruitlessly kicking. Her leg has a mass of reeds wrapping around her ankle and her foot seems to be wedged under something metal. I quickly pull the reeds free but her shoe is stuck. My fingers pull and tear at the laces, which just tighten. I yank the back of the trainer off her ankle, and her knee jolts past my head as she fights to get to the surface. I'm right with her, pushing her arse with the palm of my hand. We reach the surface, and I drag her to the riverbank. There's a part where it's not so high, and the edge has eroded to a dip low enough I can push her to safety. She flops down, not making a sound, and I am instantly on my hands and knees beside her. My lungs are burning, but the pain in my chest is fucking killing me. *No!*

I flip her on her back, she has mud from the bank smeared all over her face, down her arms, and her clothes are caked. She's not breathing; she's *still* not breathing. I clear her airway, tilt her head, and listen for any sign of breath escaping her mouth, nothing. She looks so damn pale. My hands are shaking when I place them on her chest, one over the other and pump. I can't remember what else I'm supposed to do. Do I breathe in her mouth or is that just something in the movies, fuck, why don't I know this? I pinch her nose and place my mouth over hers, blowing oxygen in three times, and when I release, she coughs. My head is so close I get a face full of river water, but that gut-wrenching, throat-clearing noise she's making is music to my ears. I pull her tight against my chest, and I have no intention of ever letting go.

"I'm okay, Cass. You can let go now." She lifts her head up and clears her throat, her mouth settling on a soft smile.

"Not likely, you scared the crap out of me. You stopped fucking breathing, Tia." My grip tightens around her. It's involuntary and entirely due to the fear still coursing through my bloodstream. I can feel her bones creak with the force of my hold.

"And I kinda can't breathe now." She groans and lets out a light mocking laugh.

"Oh, sorry." I jerk my arms to momentarily snap away at the notion I might be hurting her, but I can see that's not the case, so I quickly resume my position. Lifting my hand to lightly stroke her face, I close my eyes and relish the weight of her head when she leans into my touch, no longer a dead weight.

"So I really stopped breathing, hmm?" she whispers with a tremor in her voice.

"Yeah. I think your heart stopped for a moment too."

"My throat feels like I've swallowed the riverbed." She tries again to clear her throat, coughing from the bottom of her belly, purging whatever is left in her lungs. I gently rub her back until she finally draws in some clean, full breaths.

"You did," I quip, scooping a handful of mud from her neck and slopping it to the ground to highlight her observation.

"And my chest, it feels like I've been hit with an anvil." Her tiny fist clutches at her t-shirt, and she pulls at the material that's now see-through and slick that is stuck to her body.

"Or my fists trying to get your heart to beat." My jaw clench-es, forcing the painful words through my teeth. *It wasn't just her heart that stopped beating.*

"Shit!"

"Yeah." I keep stroking her face, smoothing her soaked, mat-ted hair out of the way. She's covered in mud and couldn't look more beautiful. "I'm so sorry, Tia."

"Yeah, all that food." She tries to joke, but I just can't.

"Not what I meant Tia. Fuck the food, you...you—" I suck in a deep slow breath, trying to fight off the rising anger, fear, and unbearable sense of being so close to the end. I physically shake myself and swallow the bile in my mouth. "I couldn't get your foot free."

"But you did, and you saved me." Her eyes bore into mine. They spring wet with tears, and she offers me the sweetest smile. She's so grateful, and I can't even look at her.

This is all my fault.

I close my eyes and drop my head. Her fingertips touch my cheek, and I squeeze my lids tighter. I can't get the thought of what might've happened out of my head. What I was so close to losing: this right here, this touch, her light, Tia, my soulmate, gone, and the pain is ripping me apart.

"Don't, Cass, I'm fine. You saved me." She has both her hands on my face, holding me until I meet her perfect emerald green eyes.

"I nearly—" I choke on my words, but she shakes her head and interrupts before I break.

"You saved me, Cass. I think that means I owe you." She tilts her head and quirks her lips into a teasing smile. I sniff and drop my head back, letting out a laugh filled with relief and more.

"What do you think you could possibly owe me?" I ask.

"My soul." Her fingers entwine with mine, and she pulls both our hands to her chest. "You have my heart, Cass. You saved my life. It seems only right I give you my soul, too." Her chest rises when she holds her breath, having laid herself bare before me. It's a staggeringly beautiful gesture that brings a sad smile to my lips.

"Not sure you should offer me that, Tia."

"Why not?" She exhales, her breath escaping in a sorrow-filled sound, her expression on the edge of breaking.

"Because I'm not the type of guy to decline such a gift."

"I don't want you to decline. I love you, Cass. Why would—" Her voice catches, high pitched and broken, but I stop her before she falls. I might be the devil my mother believes me to be, but I'm not a complete monster.

"Hey, hey, it's all right, princess. I love you, too." My words are an instant balm, and she physically softens against me, drawing into my lap and wrapping herself as tightly as she can around my body. Her little heart is hammering like caught prey.

Perfect, perhaps I am a monster after all.

We sit huddled together for endless minutes, but when she starts to shiver, I make to break the hold. Standing, I pull her to her feet. She rubs her arms, and her whole body is shaking.

"Come on, we better get home."

"Before I freeze to death, you mean?" Her teeth are chattering, but I'm not sure if it's residual adrenaline or the light breeze hitting her still-wet body.

"Don't even joke about that, Tia, it's too soon. That was fucking scary."

"I'm not joking, I can't stop shivering, and look, my t-shirt's still completely soaked through." She lifts the transparent material from her body, but she really didn't need to point it out. It's not like I hadn't noticed.

"Yeah, I did get that." I suppress my shit-eating grin and opt to look away from her cute bra. Tiny cartoon unicorns dance over the soft swell of her breasts and fail to hide her very perfect pointed nipples. *Shit, when did that happen?*

"Oh, my God, kill me now." She quickly crosses her arms. The chill she was feeling is replaced by obvious burning embarrassment that creeps across her skin like an adorable crimson shadow. I take pity and swiftly change the conversation.

"Can you stop with the death references? I think I've aged ten years." I nudge her but pull her back to my side, my arms hanging over her shoulders, as we start to walk back toward the house along the riverbank.

"That would make you like seventy then." She grins impishly, either pleased with the change of topic or her cute attempt to sass me. I frown and wait for her to elaborate.

"You're an old soul, Atticus Kruse. Some people have something about them that makes you think they've maybe been here before, you know, or at least their soul has, and I think you have an old soul. There's no way you could know what you know in your fifteen years, not even with the amount of studying you do at that fancy American school. It's not normal. So, yeah, I think you have an old soul, and if you've aged ten years today that would make you ancient." She sniffs and shrugs off her explanation.

"An old soul, I like that, old and wicked," I mutter.

"Hmm?"

"Nothing. Come on, let's get you home." I slip my hand into hers and pull her to keep up, but she stumbles. Her face loses all its colour, and a sheen of sweat covers her skin. I grab her arms to stop her from falling.

"Are you okay?"

"Just a little dizzy."

"Maybe you stay here, and I'll go and get the quad bike."

"No, don't leave me. I'll be fine. Let's walk slowly and maybe give me an arm to cling to?" She smiles shyly.

"I'll do better than that." I bend and lift her in my arms. Her legs dangle, and she rests her head against my chest. After a little way, I have to switch positions and carry her the rest of the way on my back. I'm uncharacteristically quiet, and after a little time, Tia decides to answer the question that nearly cost her life.

"I don't fit in at school. I don't have any friends. I thought secondary school would be more fun, but I'm not allowed any-one back here, and hanging out is kind of a reciprocal thing, and besides, I'm a bit odd." She rushes her words, but much of what she says, I already knew. It's very much a repeat of her primary school experience, just on a larger scale. I hate that that's her life, but there's nothing I can do and wound-licking isn't my style.

"You're very odd," I retort, and she snorts out a throaty laugh.

"Cheers, asshat. If this is you making me smile, please don't try and make me cry," she quips, flicking my earlobe with her fingertip.

"Ow, I'll never make you cry." I flinch away in case she tries to do the same with the other ear.

"You make me cry all the time." She says this softly and so quietly I know I wouldn't have heard it if her mouth wasn't so close to my ear. I shift her around to my front, and she slides down my body. The feel of her makes me forget what the hell she just said. However, the sadness in her eyes brings me back from my much more wayward thoughts.

"What? Tia, what are you talking about?"

"I'm sorry." She drops her head to her chest and lets out a heavy sigh. I tip her chin and wait for her to speak. She holds my gaze and starts to shift from one foot to the next under the intensity of my stare. I haven't said another word, and I won't until she speaks. She sighs, and her shoulders drop in defeat. "I didn't mean anything by that. I just miss you, and when you leave, I cry. I can't help it, but be under no illusion, you *do* make me cry." Her back straightens, and I can see she is trying to hold herself together. She's exposed so much today, I can only imagine how raw she must be feeling. I need to ease her pain and not just because she eases mine, but because I know I can.

"I can't help leaving, Tia. I have family obligations, but I promise I will never make you cry by my own hand." My thumb brushes her bottom lip, and her tongue darts out in its wake. "I promise. Cross my heart and hope to die."

I don't know when this thing between us changed exactly, but it has, and I have no intention of letting it change back. I dip enough so my mouth is a whisper from hers. Her body is trembling, and I hold my position to savour this moment. Her green eyes swirl with light and depths I can't wait to explore. Her hands rest on my hips, her fingers pressing and kneading my flesh, pulling my body to hers. She closes her eyes, and my lips press to hers, sweet softness and so much more, I feel it in every nerve. My hand lies against her neck, my fingertips holding her jaw lightly at an angle, the other hand holding her waist. She opens her mouth, tentative and welcoming. I know she hasn't done this before, and I wish I hadn't, because this is so fucking perfect. I know now with single-minded clarity that I want her. I want all my firsts to be with her. If they feel a fraction of how this feels, I know in my soul this is my own personal heaven, and I'm never letting her go.

My tongue traces the seam of her lips. She tastes of strawberry, and inside she's even sweeter. The way her tongue dances with mine, it's like we are the counterparts of a perfect puzzle piece; we just fit together. I am rock-hard in my shorts, and given that I'm three years older and we're both legally still too young for anything more, I break the kiss. I'm the old soul apparently, so I should at least act the part, even though it kills me. The smile on her face somewhat lessens the ache in my pants. She blows out a slow breath, her face on fire with heat and a lust, like me, she's failing to hide.

"Wow," she gasps.

"Told you I'd make you smile."

CHAPTER ELEVEN

Tia

Aged Fourteen

After that first kiss, it just got harder and harder each time
he came home. I mean, who has a first kiss like that?
There was no awkward nose bump, saliva leakage, or
clash of teeth. I could even breathe perfectly well if he hadn't
stolen the air straight from my lungs with his delicious blend
of tender and torrid. I didn't sleep that night thinking about
his perfect lips on mine. The rest of the summer holiday was a
tortuous mix of burgeoning sexual temptation and normalcy.

I think the normal bits were worse.

I don't have a mobile phone since my mother is some sort of
technological puritan. We have a landline, and that is for emer-
gencies. I am allowed a computer for schoolwork. However, the
internet connection is so slow a carrier pigeon would've been
more effective at reaching Cass during the school term. But
even if I was allowed to call him, the time difference is a killer. We write letters to each other, and it isn't nearly enough. *I
miss him.* It is as simple and as complicated as that. I feel I can't

breathe properly until he is home, like a part of me is missing, the best part. I only really feel alive when we are together. What makes it only just bearable is that I know he feels the same.

It's the school holidays just before my fifteenth birthday, and I'm in a particularly foul mood. My mother needs extra help opening up some of the rooms at the Hall. They have guests due to visit, and she doesn't know how long they are staying, and I just don't care. Cass isn't one of them. I never thought it was possible for me to be any more of a stroppy teenager, but I am testing that assumption to its limits today.

"Good Lord, girl, could you be any slower? A glacier moves faster than you do. What's got into you?" My mother is standing in the doorway, her hands on her hips, and her lips are pursed tight with obvious irritation. She gave me instructions to clean the solarium over an hour ago, and all I've managed to do is remove the dustsheets from all the furniture and dump them in a huge pile in the centre of the room.

I draw in a slow breath and bite my tongue. I try not to swear at my mother like some of the girls at school do; she doesn't deserve my attitude. Only I have particular trouble playing the amenable daughter on account of the fact that this is very much *her* life, not mine, and being the Kruse's skivvy is not *my* dream job.

"I will get it done, just leave me alone," I mumble and pull the last dustsheet from the daybed near the grand ornamental fireplace.

"I was hoping you'd get more than this room done, Miss-I'm-too-good-to-clean," she fires at me, and it smarts, her tone filled with anger.

"I never said I was too good to clean. I'm helping, aren't I?"

"Begrudgingly." She sniffs derisively, and I scowl, roughly screwing the large sheet into a tight bundle in my arms, clouds of dust billowing with every jerky fold of the material.

"I'm sorry I'm not ecstatic with my to-do list today, but please, let's not misinterpret this as some great favour bestowed on us that you seem to think it is," I snap and watch her jaw drop. I don't think I've ever answered my mother back.

"There you go, Miss high and mighty. " She tuts and rolls her eyes as if we've had this conversation a million times. We haven't, there's no point. We're never going to see eye to eye on this subject. "If you only knew the half of it…oh never mind, perhaps it's for the best, you don't deserve-" She rarely finishes her cryptic rant and today is no exception. As much as the un-answered questions use to plague me. The outbursts happen so infrequently and however vague and venomous I don't think she realises half of what she says most of the time.

She's never answered my questions and afterwards, she al-ways seems a little dazed, resignation hanging heavy from her slight frame. Worn weary by it all, I find I just don't care enough to pursue the obtuse comments she drops like an anvil. I close my eyes when she continues to preach, wishing I could lose my ears too. "I love this job, and the fact that you look down your nose doesn't exactly help. The Kruses have been very good to us."

"Mrs Kruse gets her pound of flesh from you, Mum," I snap and instantly regret it. I let out my breath slowly, trying to calm myself with each passing second. My voice softens because I know this argument is both energy-sapping and futile. "I'm sorry, Mum, I just don't see it as the two-way street you do, and I *never* look down my nose. That is definitely Mrs Kruse's pre-rogative." I shrug and try to lighten my comment with a joking tone. It's ineffective. She stiffens, and her voice has a harsh edge to it.

"Well, don't think for a moment that young Atticus thinks any different, despite what he may have told you. They keep themselves to themselves when it comes to the important things like family or marriage." She strikes hard and accurate. I feel the pain like a blade slicing through my flesh and bone, a direct hit.

"Jesus, Mother!" My hand grips the bundled sheet and pulls it tighter to my chest for protection. It's too late, and for a second, the agony feels so real, I wonder if I look down, will there be blood seeping through, colouring the white with my crimson? My voice catches when I try to reply. "Thanks. Like I don't know that. Like that hasn't been on my mind since the day he told me he loved me!"

"He told you that?" Her voice softens, and that's worse. I fight the prickle of tears at my lids and swallow down the sob that is stuck in my throat. I'm so desperate to hold myself together, to not break and be the foolish girl reflected in my mother's sad eyes.

This is different. We're different.

"Yes, when I was twelve and every day since."

"I'm so sorry, Tia." She walks up to me and falters when she is just an arm's length away. She places her hand awkwardly on my shoulder as if touching me causes her pain. I know it does. I look so much like my father. Every day I am just a reminder that the love of her life abandoned her with me. Today, though, I'm strangely grateful for her distance, because anything else would break me. "He's a good boy, Tia. Maybe he will be different."

"You believe that?" I curse myself the instant I let the hopeful words leave my lips. I should've known better. I do know better. Her reply is still a sucker punch all the same.

"No, I don't." She doesn't hold my gaze even as her words cut me open. There's nothing there, no motherly love or comfort, just a hard life of hurt and betrayal colouring her worldview so much, she can't bring herself to offer her only living relative some small amount of *hope.*

"What other room would you like me to do?" I turn away, cutting the conversation dead. It had pretty much died with her final nails, but just in case she wanted to add salt onto my gaping wound, I drop the sheet onto the mound and walk off to the adjoining room. She calls after me.

"Oh, the library needs a good clean. I understand whoever is coming likes to spend his days in the library."

"Fine, if there's nothing else, no other motherly words of comfort, I'll get on." I hear her quick steps on the polished hardwood floor scuttle to catch up to me. Her hand touches mine, but I pull it from her grasp, snatching it to my chest as though her touch scalds.

"No point lying to you, Tia. I could tell you all the things you think you want to hear, but what good does that do when it's all lies?" She steps over to stand in front of me, and her tone is anything but harsh; it's filled with kindness and heartfelt best intentions. "Despite what you think of me, I don't want you broken, Tia. I want you strong. You need to be." She tucks the long strands of hair falling across my face behind my ear and looks into my eyes. "This is my life, because it makes me happy, being in *this* house close to..." She hesitates and her voice catches, she physically shakes herself and her eyes soften for a moment as she takes in the grande room we are both standing in. It's only for a moment but for that fraction of time she looks truly happy, whatever memory just flashed in her mind, that's what I really I want to know.

"What? What was that mother? Why here? What's so special about Tartarus Hall?"

"No, not the Hall, well yes the Hall but also...Oh Tia it just doesn't matter now. This is my life, but I also had no choice. You do. All I'm saying is make sure it's you who makes the decisions, and that you're not waiting for someone to take that choice from you. Your time will come." She turns away, leaving me a little speechless, confused, and a lot heartbroken, for her and maybe a little for me.

I still couldn't tell where her loyalties lie, since she's rarely taken my side in any altercation. On the many occasions Atticus and I got into trouble, she would hand me over on a sacrificial silver platter to Mrs Kruse. However, this rare moment of warmth has taken the wind and anger out of my sails. It's the first time she's said anything remotely protective. I walk back to the main bedroom suite and slump down in the heap of dust cloths. Emotionally drained to the point of exhaustion, I try to process her solemn words of wisdom.

I think the problem is that I know she's right. I've had this deep-seated seed of doubt for so long I sometimes forget it's there, festering. Every now and then, though, it throbs and claws at my insides, growing and demanding my attention. Cass and I, we have such different lives, and even if we are soul mates like he says, is that enough? It's strange that, when he's here, I have no doubts, no reservations, not a single one. I feel together we're invincible, but that absence is so very hard. I can feel the tears trickle down my face, and I hate that I cave to these insecurities with absolutely no foundation, just because it's so damn easy to believe the bad stuff. I close my eyes and rest my head in the sheets. The silence of the room cloaks me like a warm blanket, and the last thing I see is light refracting off the deepest crystal blue eyes in the world, *so beautiful.*

"Hey, princess." His breath kisses the skin on my neck, and then I tingle from top to toe when his lips touch just below my ear.

"Cass," I sigh, moaning, and stretch out, twisting so I am facing him, and he is half hovering above my prone body. A sleepy smile stretches my face wide to almost splitting in two. I can't believe my eyes, so I reach up to touch his face. "You," I whisper, and it's his turn to mirror my face-splitting grin.

"Me." His eyes search my face, taking everything in, and I

can feel my cheeks get just a little hotter under his scrutiny. It's possible my eyes are still swollen from crying myself to sleep, but it's more likely the raw flush to my cheeks is causing the crinkle of curiosity to settle on his brow.

"It's really you? I was just—" I stop myself too late, and his lips quirk with knowing amusement.

"Yes?" He shifts so his weight is pressing me down, and he is able to keep eye contact as I try to evade his inquisition.

"Nothing." I shake my head vigorously, causing him to blurt out a deep throaty laugh.

"Oh, no, you don't. Come on, Tia, what were you just then… hmm?" he goads, running his nose lightly either side of mine before planting a delicate kiss on the end.

"Shut up."

"Tia, tell me, or I'll guess." He wiggles his brows wickedly, and I scrunch my eyes shut, willing the visual flashbacks of my dream to stop popping into my head and being so blatantly apparent on my mortified face.

"Oh, God," I groan.

"Oh, I don't think this conversation is one for Him, do you?" he teases and holds my gaze expectantly. I let out an exasperated breath and have to close my eyes again. *Ground, swallow me now.*

"Gah, I was dreaming about you," I blurt and try to wriggle out from under him. He slips to the side of my body and pulls me flush against his much larger frame. His mouth is once again just below my neck. I shiver as a slew of goosebumps dance where his breath touches.

"I got that much. I want specifics. Your face is this adorable pink, which really only happens when I catch you staring at my—"

"Cass!" I cry out, and he buries his face in my hair, chuckling. He pulls back and finishes his sentence.

"Cock."

"Oh, God!" I cover my eyes with my one free hand, but he picks it free and entwines his fingers, resting both our hands across my tummy.

"Really, Tia, let's keep Him out of this. Now tell me exactly what I was doing to this sexy little body." He rolls his hips gently against my bottom, and there is not an inch of him I can't feel in my core.

"You're not going to let this go, are you?"

"I'm really not, so come on, spill." I draw in a fortifying breath, and as always, give Cass exactly what he demands.

"I dreamt it was my first time...you know."

"*Our* first time, oh, yes, please. Now I really need to hear the details." He kisses the back of my neck all along my hairline, and my mouth goes dry. I squeeze my thighs together, because right there I am just melting.

"Please don't make me do this," I plead on a breathy whisper.

"Tia, we won't actually have sex until you're legal, so the least we can do is tell each other how we imagine it will be."

"Why? I mean, you know I want to, right?" I protest.

"Yes, my little love, I know that, but I'm eighteen, and you're fifteen. That's statutory rape. End of conversation," he states flatly.

"But I wouldn't—"

"I know, but it wouldn't be up to you," he interrupts my shocked reply.

"Who would know? I wouldn't tell, and you wouldn't tell, and unless there's cameras—"

"No, no cameras, but it's still a no, Tia. I won't risk it. I won't risk *us*. I can wait, and you can, too, but in the meantime, please continue with story time." He softens the sting of his refusal with a series of warm and tempting kisses along my jaw to my lips. "It's what I think about all the damn time. It would be nice to know what you dream it will be like."

"Really?"

"Absolutely." He's emphatic in his tone, and that alone obliterates any trace of rejection.

"Okay, well, we were in the attic, and there's a mass of cushions, like the fort we used to build, but piled together in the middle of the room," I begin, snuggling back into his embrace.

"I can do that."

"It was just a dream, Cass."

"I know, but dreams are your subconscious wishes. So if I can make your wishes a reality, I will. Now continue." I smile from the warm glow his words evoke inside me, radiating through every fibre and making my heart swell.

"It wasn't dark, but the light was fading. There were maybe a hundred candles flickering, and the sunlight still managed to hit particles of dust; the whole room seemed to sparkle. It was magical. I wasn't nervous, but my heart was beating hard, and you placed you hand right here to feel it." I point to the bottom of the v on my sweater just above my heart. "I don't remember what I was wearing, but you peeled the layers off, and I did the same. My fingers were moving so fast. You placed your hand over mine and told me there's no rush. We both laughed. My laugh sounded more nervous than yours." I turn to look up at him. He smiles wide and pulls me a little closer against his body. There's not a millimetre of space between us. *It's perfect.* He has one arm resting under my head, the other resting over my hip, his long fingers tracing the waistband of my jeans. He pops the first button, then the next until his hand is flat against my tummy. I'm acutely aware of his rock-hard erection pressing into the curve of my bottom. I swallow the lump in my throat and let out a whimper when his fingers stroke the edge of my panties.

"Carry on, Tia." His voice is hoarse, deeper somehow from

only a moment ago, and I take comfort in the fact that it sounds a little strained.

"Your hands were strong and sure, sweeping across my body, unhooking my bra, and then you...um, you had my breast in your hand."

"Like this."

"Oh, um, yes." I puff out a cooling breath. I can't help but arch into his touch. His hands are much larger than my soft round flesh in his palm. He squeezes gently and runs the pad of his thumb over my aching nipple. He can't see, but my eyes roll to the heavens at the feel of him on me. It's electric and sensual and all things delicious, and I want more. *I want it all.*

"Tia, what happened next?" His voice brings me back from my ultimate desire.

"You kissed me."

"I like kissing you."

"I like that, too. You kissed me for what felt like a lifetime."

"I could live with that." I can feel his lips smile against my neck, and I sigh out the words.

"So could I."

"Then?" he asks, clearing his throat with a sharp, deep cough.

"We kept kissing, but your hands moved down my body, and you lifted me in your arms and carried me to the bed."

"Mmm." He rocks his hips, pulling me against him, and I'm so damn hot, I feel like I have liquid fire pumping through my veins.

"You laid me down and crawled up my body. God, I want you so much," I groan, writhing against his body as much as I can at this angle.

"How much?"

"Heart and soul, Cass, remember?"

"Trust me, Tia, I'm never going to forget that," he states with absolutely certainty.

I let out a strangled whimper and attempt to finish my tale. "I...I opened my legs, and you felt so good between them. I hooked my ankles high around your waist, and I could feel you."

"Where?"

"I...I..."

"Here? Could you feel me here Tia?" With his question, his hand slides purposefully inside my panties, his bold fingers stroking along my soaking wet folds.

"Oh, oh Cass...yes, yes, please," I beg, and short sharp breaths escape with each word.

"Shh, tell me what happened next."

"You...you were inside me...Oh, God, Cass!" He slides two fingers inside me and pumps in and out, a perfect gentle rhythm that makes my toes curl. I can't breathe. Bright sparks of light dart behind my tightly-squeezed lids as he ignites something primal inside of me, an explosion at the base of my spine that rips through me with such power and speed, I quake. Only his strong embrace has me tethered to this world as I float on another plane, his sensual touch tenderly guiding me back to earth.

"Cass?" I turn in his arms. His eyes are wide with wonder, and he has the most amazing smile illuminating his face. He steals my breath away all over again.

"Wow, that was pretty fucking amazing, Tia. My balls ache like a bitch, but that was so worth it, having you come on my fingers like that. It was incredible; you're incredible."

"Oh, um, do you want me to...um."

"No, Tia, I mean my balls will still ache regardless. That problem will only be sated by one thing, and my right hand, or yours, for that matter, isn't going to cut it. Besides, I'm trying to be good here, and I know for a fact I won't be able to stop my-self if your hands are on me like that. So distract me from that please, and tell me what happened next?"

"Next?" I hesitate, because I'm pretty sure that's where the dream ended.

"Yeah." His expression doesn't reflect my thoughts, and then I remember.

"I cried."

"You cried?" He smiles, and I get an icy chill up my spine from nowhere, and just as quickly it's gone.

The back of his hand brushes my cheek, and his lips cover mine. It feels so good, I'd forget my name, let alone what the hell that was. I look into his eyes, hold the gaze as he holds me, and I whisper.

"You felt so good, Cass. I felt good, like I was whole, *fixed*. It was perfect." I can feel the tears now, bursting before I can blink them back. He catches a trickle with his thumb, wiping the skin dry before sucking it into his mouth.

"Yes, perfect." His voice is so low and gravelly I only know the words because I can read them on his lips. *He's perfect.*

CHAPTER TWELVE

Tia

"W hat are you doing here?" I twist in his arms and beam my brightest smile, relishing the feel of his body against mine and still burning up from what he just did. I can't believe he just did *that*. I opt for this question even if inner hussy is itching to ask when he might do *that* again.

"Um, my house, I live here."

"Barely." I sniff and wriggle out of his hold and shuffle up to sitting cross-legged.

He props his head on his hand, but his body is still gloriously stretched out on the mass of crumpled cloths.

"Ah, don't be like that, Tia, or I won't make you come again." He flashes a nefarious knowing grin, and I nigh on combust with the heat instantly hitting my cheeks.

"Cass!" My tone is more shocked with a heavy helping of embarrassment.

"What? Don't you want to come again?" His white blond locks fall over his piercing eyes, and he waggles his brow playfully. I may be blushing like a beacon, but when he says those words, I melt from the inside out.

"Um... I'll take the fifth on that one, please. Now, answer the question?" I bite my lips to stop the telling smile splitting my face. He knows, and the last thing his ego needs is more affirmation of how much he owns me.

"Not sure that applies to Brits, Tia," he quips and answers part of my question. "There's someone I want you to meet."

"Okay, but why are *you* back?"

"Always with the questions?" He chuckles. "I'm back because of my grandpa, and that's who I want you to come and meet."

"Oh."

"Come on, he's downstairs, probably grilling your mother." He jumps neatly to his feet, and I have to tilt my head back to keep the eye contact. Towering over me and peering into my eyes from this angle, I swear he is staring right through me. His features darken, and if I didn't know him better, I would question my safety, that look is so lethal. He holds his hand out to help me to my feet.

"Aren't you going to wash your hands?" I nod toward the en suite when I refuse to take the offered hand, and I wrinkle my nose at his reply.

"Absolutely not." He lifts his fingers to his face and sucks the middle two slowly into his mouth.

"Oh, God!" I cover my eyes, but that doesn't stop the sound of him enjoying every second of licking his fingers clean.

"What?" His tone is all innocence.

"Look at my face. What do you mean 'what?' I'm lit up like a super nova, and you're going to introduce me to your grandfather with—"

"Your scent all over my fingers." He takes a quick but mortifying sniff, and I just want the earth to open up and take me now. "I've cleaned them, Tia. I didn't have you pegged as a prude," he teases.

"I don't think you can level that label at me after what we just did," I scoff.

"No, you're right, and especially considering what else we plan to do." He steps closer, and with his hand around my waist, he pulls me flush to his hard body, his rock-hard body.

"Oh, God," I whimper.

"Him again." Cass sighs, rolling his eyes. He shakes his head, his tone lightly reprimanding. "Now, Tia, why is He getting all the credit when it's me doing all the work."

"You're the devil, you know that?" I put my hands flat on his chest and push him away, laughing at his brazenness.

"I believe I told you I was," he continues with the warning lilt to his voice.

"You're not the Devil, Atticus, but you are wicked." I point my own warning finger his way, which he grabs and uses to tug me closer.

"Tell yourself that if it gives you comfort, Tia. I have no doubt I will remind you of this conversation at some point in your future," he mutters, and I'm not sure I heard the last part at all, it was so softly spoken.

"Hmm? I didn't quite—" He shakes his head and interrupts.

"Come on, Tia. I want you to meet my second favourite person in the world." I hesitate to follow.

"I still have to finish cleaning this room. My mum will kill me if she comes back, and it's still not ready." I try to argue, but he brushes me off.

"She won't kill you, and I will help you later. Come on." He opens the door and stretches his arms for me to dip underneath. "He's the best; you're gonna love him."

"If he's anything like you, I'm sure I will." I snicker.

"Aw, Tia, you'll make me blush."

"I doubt that's even possible," I snark.

"You could be right." He shrugs, his expression not holding

the least trace of remorse. "I have no shame and a wicked mind hell bent on corrupting a certain young lady." He slides his hand into my jeans pocket and grabs my arse cheek with a squeeze that's a little too firm. I squeal and jump forward, his hand still staking its claim on my denim-clad flesh.

"You're not so *very* wicked Cass Kruse. After all, it's you who has drawn a very clear line regarding having sex with me, and I'm nearly sixteen. I'm only *just* underage."

"I've drawn a fuzzy line, and believe me, I intend on taking us as close to that as I can bear," he clarifies, and I feel the heat start to build when his eyes meet mine, if only for a brief moment.

He's keeping us both walking at a fair pace along the gallery from the guest wing to the main stairway. I have to skip a few strides to keep up.

"Torture us both, you mean."

"Precisely, but there's no pleasure without a little pain." His voice drops deep and low; it makes my skin prickle like millions of my hairs are charged live with electricity and are standing at full attention.

"You're a little wicked, aren't you?" I laugh, but I keep my voice in a hushed whisper, as we are now nearing the top of the grand stairway, which leads to the vast entrance hall, and anyone could be listening. Atticus stops, steps in front, and turns to face me, a move so abrupt, I crash into his chest. He barely moves, absorbing all my momentum into his large frame.

"I did warn you," he says, and I smile softly.

"You did, you really did, but since when does the heart ever listen to the head, hmm?"

"It's not your heart I'm after, Tia."

"You have my soul, Atticus, you always have."

"Good." His hands are under my arms, lifting me high enough so I can wrap my legs around his waist. He seems so much bigger in every respect, not just his height, but there's something else about him that's so changed. His mere presence, his assured demeanour and commanding tone, make me wonder if there's a single thing I could deny him if he asked. His lips cover mine in a rough, passionate, and deeply possessive manner that would make my knees weak and wobbly if I was standing. Breaking the kiss almost as quickly as he began, he grins wildly and drops me to my feet. I'm a little dazed until he grabs my hand. I do, however, stumble to catch up to his long purposeful strides the remainder of the distance to the library.

"Is your mother here?" I ask.

"You're funny. Like I would do that to you."

"Sorry, I just —" He doesn't let me finish; he never does when the subject is his mother, and he is always so quick to try and make me feel better.

"Really, you don't have to explain, Tia, and you certainly have nothing to apologise for. My mother is a bitch to you. She won't ever stop, either, but it's only because you mean so much to me. If it's any comfort, she avoids you as much as you avoid her. We're always together when I'm here, and she knows I will not stand by and let her treat you the way she does, and she's terrified of being exposed as the unbearable snob she is. It's not an ideal situation, but my only concern is keeping you protected, so I'm happy with her absence."

"I'm happy, too." My genuine smile is actually more filled with relief.

"My grandpa is nothing like her. He's my father's father. When my father died, Grandpa pretty much stepped in as my primary guardian. My mother was happy to hand me over, and when I'm not here, I'm with him. He's not a huge fan of my mother either, so I just know you two will hit it off." His enthusiasm and obvious affection are abundantly clear on his face, which seems to brighten with each step closer to the Library.

"He's your guardian?"

"Not in the legal sense, my mother wouldn't allow that, just the pastoral care. He's my go-to guy."

"Why have I never met him before now?"

"Well, like I say, he's not a huge fan of my mother, and he doesn't like to fly. His health has not been so great recently, and this is where he grew up, so he wanted to come home for..." He falters.

"Cass?" I squeeze his hand after his silence has stretched on too long, and his footsteps have come to a halt.

"I'm just gonna miss him, that's all." He gives me a tight smile that doesn't reach his crystal clear eyes, and the sadness in his quiet voice is painfully loud. I choose to ignore the portent of his weighted words.

"Then you'll have to come home more often." He's already drifted off too far, and I tug his hand to bring him back to me.

"I will, I promise." He nods, and I nudge into his side.

"Promise?"

"Come on." He pushes his shoulder against the massive carved dark oak door, which resists with an audible groan but slowly exposes the cavernous library.

The open fire is blazing, and the smell of burning kindling and damp wood is thick and heady. The soft glow from the fire mixes with the rich aroma and illuminates one side of the room. I've never seen the room like this. I'm a little stunned. For such a large room, it is transformed and looks both cosy and inviting. The walls are filled with books upon books, and there is a spiral staircase to a gallery housing more volumes. There are several freestanding bookshelves dotted around the room. A few high back chairs are scattered and there is seating built into each of the four imposing stained glass windows. There are three weathered chesterfield sofas arranged around the fireplace, and in the one facing us, there is an elderly man seated at one end. He is dressed in an immaculate three-piece tweed suit, has a full head of short white-grey hair, and has piercing blue eyes, although not quite the same shape as Atticus's, and these are now staring at me through half-rimmed gold glasses. His skin is pale, deeply wrinkled, and looks almost as worn as the aged leather of the cushion he's perched upon.

"Grandpa, this is her." Atticus practically drags me to the centre of the library, clearly over-excited, he spins me around like I'm a prima ballerina. I giggle when I come to a stop, and he sweeps me low into a dramatic and extremely romantic backward dip.

"Cass, you're being an arse." I chuckle and squeeze his waist in a grip-type of tickle that always makes him fold in half, too late to protect himself. We both laugh and stand. I nudge him playfully and turn back to face his Grandpa who raises a thick, bushy brow, his face a picture of puzzled amusement.

"Come a little closer, Tia. My eyesight isn't what it was." He closes the book he had open in his lap and motions me to move forward with an encouraging wave of his hand.

"Your eyesight is twenty-twenty, Grandpa." Atticus keeps hold of my hand, shakes his head, and winks at me. The old man lets out a hearty chuckle but pats the seat beside him all the same.

"You can't blame an old man for wanting a better look at the young lady that has my grandson's heart all locked up." I let go of Cass's hand and walk over to the sofa, and turning back, I smile.

"Ooh, this is where you get your charm from, then, Cass," I tease.

"You know it." He snorts and follows me but takes the seat opposite.

"It's really nice to meet you, Mr Kruse." I offer my hand

before I sit. He takes it in both of his and gently encourages me to sit a little closer beside him.

"Call me Oskar, my dear. Mr Kruse is much too formal for us." His kind eyes crinkle, and I get a warm burst in my chest, hearing the sincerity in his voice. I nod, and despite the awkwardness I feel calling any adult in this place by their first name, I push through, because this feels somewhat important to him.

"It's nice to meet you...Oskar."

"The pleasure is all mine." He keeps my hand captured. His hands are warm, impossibly soft, and very bony. "Once Atticus has gone back to the States I can tell you all of his compromising stories that will help you to keep him in line." Oskar winks at me conspiratorially.

"I doubt you have enough for a long weekend. Butter wouldn't melt in his mouth," I retort and Oskar chuckles.

"Oh, young lady, I have enough for the rest of his life." I laugh at Cass's strangled groan of embarrassment.

"Ah, you get your wicked side from your grandfather, too, then?" I observe the two men casting affectionate glances at one another. I've never seen Cass like this with anyone except me. It makes my heart swell that he has this type of relationship with someone else, and I'm a little jealous. No, jealous isn't right; I'm glad he has someone. I know how cold his mother is, and I love him so much, there's no way I'd wish my loneliness on anyone.

Still, I feel a little lost, he has so much more than me, when really, I *only* have him. *Does that make me jealous, selfish, or just an idiot?* My troubled thoughts are interrupted when Cass answers my question I'd forgotten I'd asked.

"Perhaps a little but I'm the new and improved model." He straightens his shoulders and puffs out his chest. His grandfather and I both roll our eyes.

"So Tia, you live in the Lodge, and your mother is the housekeeper?" Oskar inquires, and I hear Cass chuckle to himself. I look over, but he won't meet my eyes.

"Yes, that's right. We've lived here since I was three years old."

"And your mother worked for the family before that?"

"Um, no I don't think so. She came here because the job had accommodation. My mother became pregnant and had no job, her options were extremely limited." I don't know why I'm blurting all this out but the certainty of his tone and his question took me by surprise.

"I see, and Mrs Kraus took you both in, how very kind of her."

"My mother works very hard. I don't think there is a whole heap of benevolence underlying my mothers employment."

"Of that I'm sure and forgive me. I know your mother works extremely hard, I didn't mean anything by my comment. Now come, sit closer, I may have been joking about my eyesight, but my hearing is really dreadful." He pats the space right beside him on the sofa, and I hesitate. "Atticus, would you fetch us something to drink and perhaps some cookies. Tia and I have much to discuss."

"Grandpa." Cass's tone carries a note of bored petulance, which Oskar cuts dead.

"Did that sound like a request, son? I'm sorry if it did. It was very much an order," he snaps and the faint American accent is replaced by a much stronger Swedish clip to his tone.

"Of course, sir." Atticus stands, flashes a warm smile at us both, and in an overt display of huge respect he gives a sharp nod of obedience to his grandfather before exiting the room.

"Oh, I like you." I turn, and the tone of my voice fails to hide the awe.

"The feeling is quite mutual. Atticus is one of a kind and a dear boy, but give him an inch and he will—"

"Take a mile," I finish the well-known saying with a snicker of agreement.

"And more," Oskar adds. "He loves you very much, Tia," he says without pausing, and the candid nature of the topic takes me by surprise. My jaw drops a little; however, his kind expression instantly puts me at ease and endears me to reciprocate his openness.

"I love him, too, Oskar. I know we're young—"

"Age has very little to do with true love, Tia. I met Atticus's grandmother when I was in kindergarten. We were together for sixty years before she passed." His lips tighten, and I pause a moment before speaking. He takes that moment, then turns to face me when he is ready.

"You were married for sixty years?"

"No, I was married to another woman for ten years, but I was always *with* Atticus's grandmother." My face must be a picture of utter confusion because he lets out a deep belly laugh and pats my knee. "I think that's a story for another day, don't you? Tell me, do you often come with your mother to the Hall? I would hope you do." He switches the topic like the wind changes on a brisk winter day, and I feel a little whiplashed.

"I don't actually, Mr Kr...Oskar, not unless I can help it. It's not my favourite place, unless Cass is here." I shrug and pull my mouth into a thin, apologetic smile.

"Inga?" He nods with understanding.

"Who?"

"Atticus's mother."

"Her name is Inga?"

"Does my boy tell you anything?" He barks out a laugh, shaking his head, and I mirror his astonishment. Although, maybe it's not such a surprise, I never liked her, so I probably never asked.

"He told me all the stories you told him growing up. We

tended to skip over his family history," I reply.

"I understand." He tilts his head and his thick grey eyebrows knit together. His eyes seem to search my face with such scrutiny I wonder if I have something embarrassing stuck to my face. I even surreptitiously sweep my hand over my mouth just in case, but I can't feel anything. The silence is at the point of being excruciating when he speaks again.

"Your father is where exactly?"

"Um." I shift back, taken a little off guard with the question. It's not that I haven't answered that type of question before, but for some reason, with him asking, it feels just too personal.

"I'm sorry; it's none of my business. I understand he doesn't live at the Lodge, and I wondered if you remained in contact. Just a nosy old man. Forgive my impertinence."

"Oh no, that's fine." I shrug off the awkward feeling because it really doesn't matter. To me, my father is one subject I have no problem taking about, since there's nothing to tell.. "No, my father doesn't live with us."

"But he's alive?"

"Honestly, I have no idea. He left before I was born."

"I understand." He pats my hand as if he is sharing some unbearable loss on my behalf.

"Really, it's not anything I think about. It's his loss." I force a tight smile, hoping this subject is going to change or I might have to excuse myself and go and offer to help my mother with the cleaning. My father is not worth this wasted breath.

"Yes it is. Anyway Tia, I would very much like to change your mind regarding the house." I feel the tension in my face soften at the swift turn in the conversation, and my widening smile is evidence enough that I am happy to discuss anything else, even the Hall. "Tartarus Hall has been my family home since my great-great grandfather bought it from some very wealthy merchant fallen on hard times. He came over from

Sweden with his young bride and fell in love with the place. I'm very fond of her," He takes a slow look around this room, casting his eyes upward to the high vaulted ceiling and along each of the panelled walls; his eyes smiling with affection before returning his attention to me. "And I'm always grateful for the company," he adds and holds my gaze expectantly.

"I will visit, if you're sure, but I have to warn you, I'm a bit of a bookworm, so I usually just have my nose stuck in some novel, or I'm drawing in my sketch pad."

"Why do you think I'm in the library, my dear? We don't have to talk, in fact, an easy silence is one of my favourite things." He stares intently at me, and I get the feeling that, a little like his grandson, Oskar is used to getting exactly what he wants. Although, looking around the room and sitting beside this kind and inquisitive man, I can think of worse places to be.

"Then I'd love to keep you company." He beams a bright smile that I've may have seen before in a face not changed with time and one that is far too handsome.

"What has he got you agreeing to? Whatever you do, don't sign anything." Cass returns just as my mind has wandered his way. He's carrying a tray with the contents spilling with every step. I doubt there'll be a drop of coffee left in the cups by the time he places the tray on the low table.

"Your grandfather may have persuaded me to spend a little more time at the Hall when you're not here."

"Oh, I'm not sure that's such a good idea." He shuffles to sit next to me and flashes a wide-eyed warning look my way, which makes me laugh.

"Too late, young man, it's a done deal," Oskar states emphatically. I'm looking forward to the tales of Oskar Kruse, especially if they involve Atticus.

CHAPTER THIRTEEN

Tia

Three Months Later

"I'll pay you, Tia. I need the extra help and from someone who knows how Mrs Kruse likes things. You know how particular she can be," my mother pleads, and my heart sinks.

"Boy, do I," I mutter under my breath, the sarcasm heavy, but I endeavour to hide it all the same from my mother's over-sensitive ear. In my mother's eyes, the Kruse family can do no wrong. She has, over the years, elevated Mrs Kruse, in particular, to a platform so far above us mere mortals, it's a wonder she doesn't have a permanent crick in her neck. The Tartarus Hall annual Summer Gala is today, and my mother has been relentless all week in trying to enlist my help. I have attended this party with Cass in the past; however, he is still in the States, and I have been relegated to staff. I don't have a problem wait-ressing, working behind a bar, or cleaning even, but if there's one thing I hate, it's serving *that* woman. *If only I didn't need the money.*

"Can I stay in the kitchen?" I'm set to negotiate my terms in order to make this a tolerable experience for everyone.

"Oh, definitely." Mum exhales, nodding with a rare display of enthusiasm. On this occasion, I happen to share her relief. "You'll still have to wear the uniform, just in case you are needed elsewhere, and maybe tie your hair fully back so you don't confuse the guests. Some will no doubt have seen you at the Hall with Atticus, and that could be awkward." She gathers her bag, keys, and her jacket ready to leave for the Hall. I am still waiting for her to acknowledge how I might feel about that last comment. She rarely makes eye contact at the best of times; I'm not sure if she just can't stand to look at me, or if she is just uncomfortable with my relationship with the heir apparent.

"Not for me," I state. My confidence in this area unnerves my mother. Mrs Kruse may have tried to carve the line between them and us a long time ago, but Cass erased that, and I will not let her or my mother try and draw it back in, not even in pencil.

"No, but Mrs Kruse wouldn't want to be seen as—"

"As what?" I snap my interruption. This conversation never gets old. I swear my mother thinks that family shits gold. Who knows? They're rich enough, maybe they do. "A pompous snob that would rather hire her son's girlfriend than invite her to a social gathering? Yes, heaven forbid she should reveal her true colours."

"Any chance you could lose your voice for the day, too, young lady, as well as the attitude?" my mother fires back, and rather than rehash a very tired argument, I let it go. I'll never win. I just like to make sure she knows we're not on the same page when it comes to Mrs Kruse; we're not even in the same damn library.

"What time do you need me?"

"Come up at lunch time. You can clear the kitchen after the afternoon tea and help me prepare the evening meal."

"Great," I say to myself since my mother's jacket is just a blur of pink, disappearing as the back door slams shut.

I spend most of the afternoon washing up and refilling trays for the other temporary waitstaff to serve to the guests, which suits me fine. It's the evening I am dreading. Mrs Kruse has my mother and I dressed up like prudish French maids, and my hair is slicked back so smooth and severe, I barely recognise my reflection in the antique silver spoons I'm polishing. To top off my humiliation, I have to wear this stupid little frilly white cap, which perches precariously on my head. My feet are killing me in these damn court shoes, and I think I have managed to reach a whole new height of hatred for Mrs Kruse, since the temporary staff's attire is simply black shirts, skirts, and flat pumps.

"The table is all set, and the first course has been laid out," my mother mutters more to herself than anyone else, mentally crossing off her never-ending to-do list. "Tia, would you like to call the guests through to be seated." I really don't, but I give a tight nod and dry my hands down the front of my skirt.

"Tia, for goodness sake," she huffs, shaking her head with disappointment.

"My hands are clean, they're just wet. Don't worry, no one will notice. That is the general idea, I believe." My snide comment is either not heard or, more likely, ignored, and my mother clearly pretends I have said something entirely different.

"Oh, thank you, Tia, yes, would you hold the aperitifs for me? Make sure everyone has one as they pass through the great hall and into the orangery." She hands me a full tray of small crystal glasses filled with a bubbly something, and I follow her brisk steps to the orangery, a relatively recent addition to the house that's still older than Oskar's great-great grandfather. It was built in the late seventeenth century and has several very old citrus trees still in situ. It's by far the lightest room in the house with twenty-seven tall windows and pale stucco construction. Apart from the trees and plants, the furniture is sparse, some teak recliners and a table set for taking afternoon tea, but tonight, it has been transformed. Hundreds of candles edge the room, and fairy lights are interwoven in the vines and small potted trees transforming what, in the daytime, looks like the picture of a Queen Ann greenhouse into a rather magical room.

"Wow, it looks really lovely." I can't hide the awe in my voice. She really has excelled herself this year, not that my opinion seems to count, her response is evidence enough of that.

"And collect the empty glasses from the garden when your tray is empty," she adds, turns on her heel, and is gone before she can hear my reply.

"Sure."

I call the guests through and take my place by the doorway. My tray empties quickly, and I have to suppress a wry smile when one of Mrs Kruse's friends stops to chat. Mrs Kruse seems particularly irritated when I inform Lady Spencer that I had received my unconditional offer to study Fine Art at the London School of Art, and that Atticus's grandfather had been a huge help. I explain that's why I am working tonight; I need to save for the crippling student debts. She let out a raucous laugh, but in fairness, I think she thought I was joking. Mrs Kruse certainly doesn't find the interaction funny. My first win of the evening.

Once the guests are all seated, I slip out to collect the glasses from the garden. I have to walk the length of the wall to the maze at the very far end to collect the debris. The guests seem to have wandered the entire garden, far and wide, but I don't blame them. It is a staggeringly beautiful garden, fifteen acres all sectioned and cut up into various areas of interest, the maze being one. There's also an herb garden, an ornamental pond, a mini orchard, and Mrs Kruse's pride and joy, the award-winning rose garden.

I have to make several trips to ensure I have collected everything, the fading light making it a particular challenge, although I love the way the blooms seem to release more of their scent as the sun sinks in the sky. The aroma from the roses dominates the evening air with a sweet heady fragrance. Cass and I would often lie on the lawn nearest to the flowers, staring at the night sky and making plans. I think the smell just makes me miss him more.

"Tia!" my mother calls out.

"Coming!" I skip up the steps and walk around the side of the house to the entrance nearest the kitchen where my mother is yelling in a hushed manner that defeats the object of trying to remain unheard. Staff are supposed to be a little like children, seen and not heard.

"Take the water through, would you?" She hands me two large pitchers of iced water.

"Sure." I use my bottom to push the kitchen door open and walk toward the Orangery. The main dining room is better suited for entertaining large numbers like this, but this is a smaller gathering, and since it's a summer event, Mrs Kruse likes to open up the Orangery. Stepping into the hallway, however, I hear a low groan come from along the corridor. Whoever it is, he's in pain. I rush to where I can hear the noise more clearly and knock on the Water Closet door.

"Excuse me, is everything all right in there?"

"Tia, is that you?" His voice is strained but unmistakable.

"Oskar, are you okay?" I pull on the handle, but it's locked. Panic kicks up my heartbeat to a loud thumping in my chest. We have spent almost every day together since Cass left for the States, and we've grown extremely close. He's interesting, fun, and charming, but he's also very ill.

"Lord, no, I'm so embarrassed. I need…I need some help." He lets out a painful groan that makes my stomach turn.

"What's happened?"

"I feel like a fucking infant is what's happened. Oh, Lord, maybe you should get Mrs Kruse." His voice wobbles, and I hate the vulnerable intonation in his voice. I may have only known him a short time, but anyone who takes the time to look can see he is a proud, strong man, and this illness is eroding away at his very fibre.

"Of course, hold on." I rush down the hall to the Orangery. With my back to the edge of the doorframe, hidden from general view, I attempt to catch Mrs Kruse's attention. It takes a good few minutes, and I hate that all that time, Oskar is waiting. It doesn't take a brain surgeon to guess what's happened. His health is in steep decline, and the medication doesn't seem to be helping. He looked quite pale tonight, and I wasn't surprised when I noticed he didn't take his seat for the evening meal. I just assumed he had retired for the evening.

"What?" Mrs Kruse steps around the corner and grabs my arm, moving us both out of earshot.

"Oskar," I say, and her eyes narrow at my comfortable familiarity with using her father-in-law's first name. "He needs help. He's in the toilet, and I think he's been calling for some time," I explain. The urgency I feel has me edging toward Oskar as I speak, only she remains rooted.

"And what do you want me to do about it?" She stiffens, holding her nose a little too high and wrinkled with displeasure like I have created some foul odour.

"He's Cass's grandfather, your father-in-law. You know, he's *your* family, and he needs *your* help. I didn't think I needed to spell it out."

"I have guests." She waves her hand dismissively, and my

jaw just about hits the floor at her cold and callous tone. Her lips thin to almost invisible when she speaks with poorly veiled contempt. "Since you are so cosy with *Oskar*, why don't you help him out?" She snidely emphasises his name, but her petty jealously at my relationship with her father-in-law is wasted on me. I don't give a shit what she thinks. Unlike her, the only thing I care about right now is Oskar.

"He's sick." I'm incredulous that I have to state this and unbelievably naive to think it will make some difference.

"And he will still be sick in a few hours time when the guests leave. It's up to you how long he remains needing help."

"Forgive me for thinking you *actually* gave a fuck," I snap, rage making my blood boil and my fingertips twitch to slap that condescending malicious smile off her face.

"How dare—" Outrage colours her face bright red, but I don't allow her the satisfaction of finishing whatever she intended to say.

"Oh, I dare," I interrupt, my tone thick with disgust, and I level my best death glare at her shocked face. I spin on my heel and run back to Oskar.

"Hey, Oskar, I'm going to unlock the door from out here, but it's just me coming in, okay?" I slip the penknife from my pocket and twist the screwdriver attachment free.

"Oh, no, Tia, please don't. I can't bear the—"

"Too late." I turn the screw and loosen the escutcheon. I manage to ease the nib of the screwdriver though the gap, depressing the latch and opening the door slightly. I grab the edge of the heavy door with my fingertips before it snaps shut again and quickly step inside. The smell hits me like a brick, and I have fight the very real urge to gag. Oskar is crumpled over, resting his arms on his bare legs, his trousers in a very messy heap around his ankles on the floor, and when he does pull his face up so his eyes meet mine, his expression is one of utter mortification.

"Oh, Lord, don't ever get old, Tia, it's a wretched thing." He shakes his head, the weight of his helplessness so heavy, it's palpable. "The damn bowel cancer, Tia, it's the worst. I couldn't bring myself to have a bag fitted. I'm so sorry, but I've—" His voice catches, and I can't bear it. It's heartbreaking, but if I know him at all, and I think I do, he would hate pity more than the illness.

"Really, it's okay, Oskar. Shit happens." I keep my tone light and am rewarded with a genuine and surprised grin. He barks out a deep laugh, and I can see the tension leave his shoulders, and almost instantly, he begins to regain his former formidable persona.

"You're going to joke?" He raises a challenging brow.

"I think it's best, Oskar. No one likes to see a grown man cry," I quip.

"No, that would not do." His eyes widen with the horror of my suggestion, and then his face softens with a heartwarming smile, his expression a picture of relief and misplaced gratitude.

"Right. I'm going to run up to your rooms and get a change of clothes and some towels. I'm going to re-lock the door so no one comes in. The guests have just been served the first course so we have plenty of time." I smile to give him some reassurance that this is not a problem, which it isn't. He nods, and when he replies, I slip from the room.

"Very good."

I kick my shoes off once I have relocked the door, a trick Cass taught me years ago. There's not a room in this house I can't get into, or any other house, for that matter, if I put my mind to it. I rush silently up the stairs and gather what I need from Oskar's rooms. I pick up a few fresh towels and smaller handcloths. When I return, Oskar is fully naked from the waist down but his long dress shirt is preserving his modesty. The room stinks but we both do our best to ignore what must be a mortifying situation for such a proud man. It's not like this is on anyones' bucket list or anything, but I couldn't leave him like this, and if I'm honest, I couldn't leave him to that hateful bitch in the orangery.

I fill the sink with some hot water and liquid soap, and together we make the best of cleaning the considerable mess. There's actually more blood that anything else, and with a painful twist in my gut, it brings home how very sick he is. I may not have been told the specifics—Cass could barely bring himself to speak about it at all—but I know the cancer is terminal. It's why he came home. I've never been this close to death before. I have to fight the tears burning behind my eyelids. The last thing he needs is for me to break down.

It doesn't take long before he is fully dressed and looking just as distinguished and handsome as always.

"Thank you, Tia, I can't express—" He takes my hand. The one I would've used to brush off his statement.

"Please don't, Oskar. It's what friends are for."

"It's what family's for," he says, and I don't correct him, even though I am hardly one to champion the benefits of *family*. He lets my hand go and reaches for the door.

"I think it's best we don't leave the room together," I say quickly before he opens it. He tilts his head back to me and winks.

"Yes, we have to protect your reputation."

"See, you are ready for jokes." I snicker.

"So it would seem." He chuckles, and a relaxed smile softens the anguish that has been a permanent fixture since I discovered him.

"I'll stay here and give it a few minutes before coming out. I need to get rid of this." I motion to the pile of dirty towels and clothes.

"Of course. Please come to my room before you leave, Tia. There's something I've been meaning to give to you and now seems a very good time."

"You don't have to give me anything, Oskar, I didn't help because—" He shakes his head vigorously and interrupts.

"Oh, I know that, my dear, and I'm not giving it to you be- cause of tonight. Come to my room, and you will see that to be the case."

"Okay, I'll bring you up some cocoa, but it won't be for a while. I still have to help Mum," I add when he glances at his watch.

"I'll be awake. I rarely sleep as it is." He smiles once more and opens the door, disappearing shortly after I tell him that I'll be up as soon as I can.

Once he shuts the door, I gather up the soiled clothing and towels, hold my breath, and wait as long as I can bear before I open the door. I can hear voices in the hall so I hang back and pray they are not coming my way, no such luck. The footsteps get louder, and in a panic, I spin in my stocking feet, my ankle twists, and I collapse in a painful heap. The clothes and towels I had been holding at arms length, I instinctively pull close to protect my fall and succeed in covering my self almost head to toe in shit. I start to gag, the smell and feel of the raw waste sliding down my cheeks is too much. I fail to hold the rising bile in my throat back, my stomach violently contracts, and I throw up, all down my front. I don't even have time to dwell whether this could get any worse when I hear light giggling behind me. The sharper condescending voice of Mrs Kruse, however, cuts the laughter short.

"You!" she hisses, taking a step toward me but freezing when she sees the source of the mess I'm really in. Her nose rightly screws up, and her eyes look comically wide with horror. I slowly pull myself to stand, wincing when I put pressure on my foot. Without making eye contact, I gather the towels, not bothering with the whole, arms-length thing, kind of pointless now. I suck in some fortifying air through my mouth and flash a tight smile.

"Yes, me, Mrs Kruse, Oskar is fine, by the way. He's retired for the evening." I fix my gaze at her now and walk directly at her. I let out a humourless laugh when she practically throws herself against the wall in her desire to clear a path and get out of my way. *She's pathetic.* I keep my head high and make my way down the long corridor, past the kitchen to the laundry room.

"Where the hell have you been?" My mother shouts at me when I enter the kitchen after making the best of a head to toe body wash in the cast iron double sink in utility room. "And why is your hair all wet? Where's your uniform, you're not finished yet, young lady," she snaps.

"I am *so* finished, Mother. I'm going to make Oskar a cocoa, and then I'm going home." She pauses for a moment, and her brow furrows with confusion. The seriousness of my tone prevents her immediate retort, so I continue just to ensure I am fully understood. "Keep the money. If I have to look at that woman again, I won't be responsible for my actions. Trust me, you don't want that."

"Tia, what have you done?" she scolds, and her hands fly to her hips, her indignant posture adding to the accusatory tone.

"Of course it would be *my* fault." I laugh, a hollow flat sound that echoes off the flagstone floor and vaulted ceiling. "You know what Mother? Forget it, it doesn't matter. The sooner I'm out of here the better. You've always preferred the Kruse family to your own flesh and blood. At least with me gone, you won't have to pretend anymore."

"You ungrateful, spiteful, uncaring little bitch. Mrs Kruse is right about you, you're a bad seed, just like your father." Spittle flies from her mouth with the ferocity of the venomous words, which just roll off my skin like they have a hundred times before.

"And yet still not an insult, Mother. I would rather be like a man I've never known than be like you. Does that not tell you something about your distorted loyalties?" I hold her gaze, trying to see anything remotely maternal in her eyes. Affectionate and compassionate are hardly qualities I would have used when describing our relationship, yet even a benign neglect would be a welcome improvement. All I can see is an unhealthy mix of anger, hatred, and regret. She brushes past me without another word. I feel the weight like a millstone of something irrevocably lost, and I sag when I hear the door slam. *I'm so alone.*

I take a much-needed moment, then pull myself together because all I want to do is go home, curl up in my covers, and dream of Cass. One of *those* dreams would be perfect right about now. Still, I gave my word.

I use the servants' staircase at the back of the kitchen to avoid running into anyone and make my way to Oskar's quarters, a mug of steaming hot cocoa in hand.

Oskar is seated by a small open fire that is just in the final throes of life with softly glowing embers and barely a lick of a flame. One side of him is illuminated by a small standard lamp and the other by the warm glow of the dying fire. He turns when he hears me approach, his smile broad and strong, any shadow of his ordeal gone from his frame and features.

"I'm glad you came," he states, relief and pleasure lifting the smile on his face.

"I said I would." I shake my head that there was any doubt.

"Yes, I know, only I can understand if, well—" He falters, and I repeat my quip from earlier, which garners the same rueful smile as before.

"Shit happens, Oskar. Here's your cocoa." I hand him the mug, and he places it on the small table next to the folded newspaper he was reading when I came in.

"Yes, it does, Tia. You are a very dear girl. Atticus is a very lucky man."

"Thank you, I'm glad at least someone thinks so," I scoff lightly.

"Sit here, Tia, what do you mean?" He motions to the old high back chair facing him.

"Nothing. Same ol' same ol'." I sit in the chair, kick my shoes off, and pull my knees under me. He gives a slight nod. "Mother daughter issues."

"Family dynamics are often more complex than they appear, and unfortunately, you can't choose your family." His knowing smile stops only when he takes a sip of his drink.

"Ain't that the truth?" I sniff derisively.

"I have something for you. I have been meaning to give you this for some time, but I needed to make sure my Will was in order." He passes me a sheet of paper from a much larger document stacked on the floor by his feet. My eyes scan the page and fall on the part with my name. This is a section of bequests and my name is listed amongst others, all the others however have his family name. Mine stands out like a sore thumb.

"I don't understand." My voice catches because that isn't entirely true; I don't want to understand is more accurate.

"You know I'm dying, Tia?" It's a rhetorical question he states calmly, and it's like a direct hit to my chest. I crumple, and I can feel red-hot tears just brimming behind my lids.

"No, Oskar, please don't—" I choke on my words as I fight to contain the sob leaping from my chest.

"Hush, no need for nonsense. It's very simple, the chemo hasn't worked." He cuts me down, and I'm grateful. I don't want to break. With everything that's happened tonight, I'm not sure I could stop. "It is what it is, Tia. I've had a very good life. I have no complaints, but I do have some regrets that I intend to rectify. I need to make sure everything is in order." I manage to meet his gaze, but the tears blur my focus before I can blink them away. He reaches for my hand and squeezes some comfort before he continues. "I have no intention of going just yet, my dear child. However, I'm a stickler for the details, and as you will see, I have left something for you. I want to give it to you now. I have it recorded here, in case there is any dispute when I am passed." He points to the few lines with my name.

"Dispute?"

"Families never become quite so vile and loathsome as when they are fighting over a Last Will and Testament. I have made sure that won't happen. This is my final Will." I don't doubt that for a moment, and it chills me to the bone to think Mrs Kruse could stoop any lower than she did tonight. *Who am I kidding? Tip of the iceberg.*

I hand the sheet of paper back, and he replaces it carefully into the document on the floor.

"Okay." I wasn't expecting anything like this, and I'm not sure what else to say. We have become very close over the last few weeks, unexpectedly close, really. I find his company entertaining and genuine; he's very much like Cass, and I think in his absence, I am drawn to anything that makes me feel closer to him. Every day I find some excuse or other to visit, and I know Oskar wouldn't tolerate my company if he didn't enjoy the visits just as much as I do. He told me himself, he's too old to play nice for politeness sake.

"This was Atticus's grandmother's bracelet." He hands me a tatty red Cartier box, which squeaks when I open it. My stomach drops, and I start shaking my head, because I'm too speechless to tell him this is too much, *way* too much. It's the most gorgeous thing I've ever seen. A delicate art deco bracelet with so many diamonds my hands start to tremble with nerves that I'm holding the most expensive thing I ever have or am ever likely to hold. *It's so beautiful.*

"There are matching earrings and a ring. I very much expect Atticus will want to give you those himself, but this is from me." He beams at me, and I swear there is the twinkle of a much younger man in his eye. "It was the first piece I bought Aurora when I could draw money from my trust fund. She was so surprised. I'm afraid it might be a little dated for your tastes."

"Oh, God, no, Oskar. It's beautiful, perfect, but there's no way I can accept it." I reluctantly close the box and try to hand it back.

"Nonsense, it's mine to give, and I want you to have it." He tucks his hands under his legs like a child, and I snicker. "You'll offend me greatly if you refuse." I let out a sigh, and he grins, knowing I am unlikely to continue to object after that statement, but he adds to his argument all the same. "I can't very well take it with me. I won't let you refuse because I can't bear the thought of Mrs Kruse having any of the things I bought for the most wonderful lady in the world. It's only fitting that you have this, Tia. Let that be an end to it."

"I don't know what to say." I take another peek inside the box.

"Thank you will suffice." His tone is all satisfied and smug. Just like his grandson, Oskar always seems to get what he wants.

"Thank you." I close the lid and slip the box into my pocket.

"I'm sure you don't need me to tell you, but keep it safe. Its value is just over a quarter of a million pounds." Sipping his drink, he casually mentions a sum of money I can't fathom.

"Holy shit, Oskar!" My jaw drops. This may well be a trifling sum to the Kruse family, but in my world, money like that only ever comes from picking five numbers on the lottery.

"I think we've had more than enough of that for one evening." He raises a brow and lets out a deep chuckle.

CHAPTER FOURTEEN

Tia

One year later

"Tia?" His voice is pleading, but the hurt and anger is just tearing me up; I can't bring myself to speak just yet. The only sound is from his end of the line, background noise of God knows what. He hasn't been home in over a year, and now he's just told me he's not coming back for Christmas. He missed my birthday again, and all the plans we've been making for what seems like forever are proving to be more elusive than my nightly dreams. Dreams that feel so real, I often wake either in a hot sweaty mess or in a flood of tears.

"What?" I snap when the silence becomes too much. I opt for cold hard anger rather than letting the pain escape. I know it won't stop, if I release that floodgate. *I miss him so damn much.*

"Please don't be like that. I miss you so much, princess. I wish I could change things, I really do. It won't always be like this, I promise." His voice is softly coaxing me, but the tension is palpable, and his usual effective techniques at soothing me are having little to no effect.

"You know your promises mean shit to me right now, Cass! You promised you'd be here for me, you promised you'd never miss another birthday…you promised me…*us*." My voice wobbles, and I have to bite my mouth shut, grateful he can't see the silent tears now flowing down my cheeks.

"I'll make it up to you, Tia. Please, you have to trust that I will keep my promises one day." I can hear the anguish in his tone. It goes some way to placate me, knowing this is just as shitty for him as it is for me, but it's only marginal.

"When?" I manage to ask without audible evidence of my sorrowful state.

"Soon, just not right now. It's complicated, and I need you to trust me. I love you; that will never change."

"I don't understand, Cass. I don't see why you can't just come home for a few days." I rub my eyes dry.

"Do you trust me?" he asks, avoiding my question.

"Of course."

"It will get worse before it gets better, Tia, but when it does get better, it will all be worth it. You will be mine, and I will spend every day of the rest of my life making you happy and making up for *this*. I hate it as much as you do, believe me. That's a solemn promise. Just remember that this is not forever. *Us*, Tia, *us* is forever."

"I still don't understand." The sadness in my voice is so damn pathetic, I wish I could take it back.

"I know, but you trust me, and that's all that matters. Now tell me you love me." His tone switches from sweetly sincere to cocky arrogant, which actually makes me laugh

"Arsehole," I retort.

"Close, but I think you pronounced that wrong."

"I love you, you arsehole."

"Tia," His playful tone drops with the warning way he says

my name. I huff but comply.

"I love you, Cass."

"And I love you too, princess. You're mine forever, remember?"

"I seem to recall I made that promise at some point, yeah," I quip, breaking the first smile in this entire conversation.

"Good, because I'm going to hold you to it."

"I hate this long distance shit, Cass."

"Me, too, Tia, me, too. Look I don't have long before my next seminar. Tell me something else, because your heartbreak is cutting me up, and I can't go to class all shaken and glassy-eyed," he argues.

"You get glassy-eyed?" I snort at the ridiculous notion.

"Well, not exactly, but I hate that you're hurting, Tia. That fucking stings," he clarifies, and my heart clenches with the reflected pain I can hear in his voice.

"Yeah, it does. Not much to tell really. My art teacher thinks I should apply for a scholarship to study for my degree. She thinks with the unconditional offer from the Royal School of Art, I stand a really good chance, but I said I was thinking of taking the other offer. Do the business degree courses I had applied for, you know, study something that might actually make me employable." I sniff and shrug, although he can't see. My fingers twirl through the thick curled cord of the phone until the tips are a deep purple with no circulation.

"Your art teacher's right, Tia, you have a gift." Cass's voice brooks no argument, and I smile at his obvious pride in my artistic ability. "You know, Grandfather spoke to me about offering to pay for your tuition. You don't have to apply for a scholarship, Tia. If you want to go to art school, you don't need to worry about money."

"He did say something like that, and I'll tell you what I told him." I can feel my hackles rise, but I know the offer is kindly meant, so I keep the attitude out of my reply. "It's very sweet, but I'm not and never will be a charity case. *If* I accept a place, I'll pay my own way. I'm just not sure art is the smart choice, after all, you're not studying sports even though you have a gift with a bat." I counter his argument.

"I don't have a choice, Tia. I have an empire to run when I graduate, and baseball skills aren't going to secure the future of my family's company. Besides, my gift is nothing compared to yours. Look, just think about it, okay?" he asks, and as with many things, I find I am unable to deny him.

"I will."

"Good. Now, how's Grandpa?"

"You know I'm the only seventeen-year-old whose best friend is an eighty-three-year-old man." I snort, but the thought of Oskar brings a huge smile to my face.

"I bet he loves that." He chuckles.

"I do, too. He's great, Cass. He talks a lot about your father, and he's helped me with my University applications. And he is still whooping my arse at chess and poker. If I had any money, he would've cleaned me out a hundred times over by now. He's a devil."

"That he is." Cass laughs before asking one of the same questions he always does. "Have you been to any parties? It's your last year of school, so you should go to a few, maybe."

"Maybe." It's the first time I've given a different answer, but he's right. This is my last year. It's still not that simple, though. "I'm not great at mingling, Cass. You know that. And getting home is always such a pain."

"I know. Just maybe make the effort this year, or you'll be in for a hell of a shock when you get to Uni," he warns. He's quick to add, "Not that I want you getting drunk when I'm not there. I just hate the thought of you sitting around waiting."

"I didn't think I was. I don't need your pity, Cass, I need

you," I snap, irritated at his change in tone and his inaccurate assumption.

"Sorry, I didn't mean that, Tia. I hate that I can't make you happy, and I'm stupid enough to think encouraging you to get out will ease my conscience. Honestly, it would probably drive me crazy. This is hard for me, too, Tia. I comfort myself that this is a *temporary* hell, and it makes it just bearable." He pauses, letting his voice drop low, and his words drift over my tender heart, soothing and healing the hurt. "One day we'll be together, and I won't ever let you go."

"I'm not going to ask you to promise, but I very much like the sound of that," I reply.

"I have to go, princess. I love you. Whatever happens, remember that." He rushes his words, but they strike an uneasy chord.

"What do you mean, 'whatever happens'?" I challenge, but he brushes me off with a light laugh and sweet words.

"Nothing, Tia, I love you." Despite the churn in my tummy, I am quick to reply.

"I love you, too, Cass."

"Good." He ends the call before I can add anything else. The flat dial tone cuts through my muddled thoughts, and I find I'm left a little speechless, and I'm not exactly sure why.

I rest my heavy head on my knees. I slid to the floor when I took the call, and my bottom is now numb, and my back aches from leaning against the wall in our narrow hall. The phone receiver's still hanging limply in my hand. We must be the only people in the country that still have a landline with a corded phone receiver permanently attached high on the wall in the kitchen. The monotone sound of the dial tone is now drilling through my skull, and the pressure behind my eyes is building to a substantial headache. I drag myself to my feet and replace the receiver. The momentary respite from the ear-piercing noise is welcome, but the headache is in full swing, so the relief is brief. It's five o'clock. I rushed home from school to catch Atticus before his afternoon lectures, and now I'm not sure how I feel. The excitement of hearing his voice has been overshadowed by the depressing reality of this long distance relationship remaining just that for a few more months.

I let out a heavy sigh and decide to walk up to the Hall to do my homework. I used to hate being there when Atticus was away, but now, with Oskar to talk to, I draw a strange, familiar comfort from the place. With news of Cass's most recent extended absence, I need that connection more and more. I grab my thick woollen winter coat and wrap my scarf several times around my neck and up to my ears. Slipping my portfolio over my shoulder, I brave the icy wind once more. It's pitch black outside, and the road is deep with mud, slippery, and with the crumbling potholes, it's treacherous. I make my way toward the Hall trying to avoid the darker patches on the road where the puddles could be anything from a few inches to knee deep. The ancient trees lining the drive creak and groan with the force of the wind howling through them, and the bare branches cast an ominous shadow against the cloud covered night sky. I shiver, but not from the freezing temperature. I don't know why exactly, only I feel all kinds of unsettled since my phone call with Cass.

In the distance, the Hall blocks out the horizon as I approach, rising like an ancient monolith. However, rather than scaring me as it once did, I smile. Only one of the windows in the front elevation has the faintest glow from inside, the rest are lifelessly dark. Oskar is in the library. I walk around the side of the house to the rear entrance into one of the boot rooms. My mother will still be here somewhere, but I'm not here to see her, and she will head home when she's done without hunting me down. I shuck my outer layers, kick my boots near to the radiator, and make my way directly to the library.

"Hello, my dear, I wasn't expecting you today." Oskar looks up from his newspaper, folding it neatly, and beaming his brightest smile my way. I've no experience of what a grandparent is, or how they act. I never knew mine. My only knowledge comes from Oskar, and I struggle to imagine there is a kinder soul than his out there. I quickly fell in love with his generous nature and wicked sense of humour. I flatter myself that he feels the same, his face certainly expresses his pleasure every time I enter the room. I have also seen him with people he doesn't like, so I know he wouldn't welcome me if he didn't really want my company; he doesn't suffer fools.

"No, I know, I hope you don't mind. I'm a little out of sorts and thought I could finish my homework here tonight. I'll go before your nurse comes back to help you to bed." I slip my bag from over my shoulder and lay it on top of one of the free-standing bookcases. Oskar had an easel set up by one of the large windows for me to use, but I only need to work on some sketches tonight, and besides, the light is dreadful in this room this time of the year.

"Of course, you know you never need an excuse to come and visit. I'm not sure how many times I need to tell you that; you're family." The sincerity in his tone makes my nose tingle with the pressure of tears. I didn't come here to cry. I shake myself and change the subject. I knew I felt out of sorts, but what the hell has gotten into me?

"You're very kind, although I'm not sure Mrs Kruse shares your view." I set my supplies out on the sofa opposite him. "Can I get you a cup of tea before I set up?"

"Maybe something a little stronger?" He nods toward the cabinet with a tray of cut crystal decanters and glasses on the top.

"Sure, whiskey?" I walk over and check the brass labels for his favourite tipple.

"Now you're talking, you can help yourself, too," he teases, only this time I surprise him.

"You know I think I will, just don't tell my mother." I tap my nose at our little secret. His wide eyes crinkle with pleasure.

"Oh, I'm very good at keeping secrets, you can trust me." He mirrors my nose tap, chuckling as he does.

"I do trust you, Oskar."

"Good." He sounds just like Cass when he says that word, so commanding and certain. I actually pause with the decanter hovering over the glass. I take a steadying breath before I continue to pour us both two fingers of his finest whiskey. "So tell me, young lady, what's got you needing your first sip of my 'water of life'?"

"Cass," I reply without bothering to turn.

"Oh, he told you, did he? Finally, I don't know why he kept putting it off. You're a sensible girl; he needed to give you more credit." Oskar sounds relieved, and it just makes my heart sink that, to everyone else, this is just how things are, yet to me, this is a daily torture and unbearable heartache.

"Sensible or not, I still miss him." I offer with a wistfully sad smile. I take the drinks over to where he is always seated, one end of the low sofa near the open fireplace. The flames are blazing high, licking the sides of the chimney flue. The firewood most recently added to the stack pops and hisses from the dramatic change in temperature. I love that sound, almost as much as I adore the rich aroma of seasoned logs burning.

"I know, my dear, but it really won't be forever." He takes the glass of neat whiskey and motions for me to sit beside him, patting the sofa lightly. I climb on and tuck my legs beneath me. This looks very much like story time, and despite the mountain of work I have to do, this is just what I need and the very reason

I'm unexpectedly here tonight. I nurse my own crystal tumbler of amber liquid. The fumes assault my nose, so I'm a little hesitant to take my first sip just yet. "Let me tell you about Atticus's grandmother, Aurora." He swirls the liquid and inhales deeply, a tender smile momentarily smoothing the permanent crinkles and lines around his mouth. "She was the most beautiful girl I ever saw. She was an angel, and I knew when I saw her in kindergarten that I was going to marry her." I snicker but don't attempt to hide the wide smile that notion evokes. "You may laugh, Tia, but when you know, you just know, don't you agree?" He peers over the rim of his half moon glasses and knowingly raises his thick bushy brows. I nod and let out a resigned breath.

"I do. How could I put up with Cass's absence if I didn't feel that in my bones."

"Quite. Anyway, Aurora was the daughter of the village Rector, a very respectable family but not connected and not wealthy by any means. We were best friends growing up. I attended the local school because of her, and unofficially, she was my girlfriend. It would've been a huge scandal at the time for me to be dating someone like her, but once I turned eighteen, I was no longer under any obligation to hide my true feelings. We courted for three years officially before she was of age and I could formally propose. I was twenty-two and she was just eighteen. I'd never been so happy or so devastated as the day I was going to propose. As was right, I informed my father first as to my intentions to marry Aurora. He calmly informed me that he had other plans. My father wasn't someone you crossed, ever. It nearly broke my heart, and I know it broke Aurora's for many years. The men in our family have *responsibilities*.

"I was unaware that my family had arranged for me to marry the daughter of Lord and Lady Fitzwilliam. They were a very influential, political family, extremely well-connected, and my betrothal was crucial to the plans my father had for

Kruse's business expansion into Europe. I hated my father for this, and I told him I would never give Aurora up. He told me I didn't have to. I just had to maintain appearances for ten years, enough time to secure the company's future, then I would be free to marry whomever I chose. I had to have at least one son of course, but that goes without saying" *Does it?* Despite his warm smile, I feel an uncomfortably icy chill numb my veins. He takes a long sip of his whiskey, and I find I need to do the same. The fumes sting my eyes and burn the hair in my nose, warnings enough to caution my approach, but I take a large gulp regardless. The whiskey is like liquid fire in the back of my throat and scours its length with raw heat until I can feel it hit my stomach. I swallow back the cough that is fighting to embarrass me, making me splutter back up a bit of what I had managed to drink down. Clearing my throat, I ask for some clarification, because I'm more than struggling to understand what the hell I've just heard.

"You said you never left Aurora?"

"Indeed, I didn't. I couldn't." He shakes himself with the mere thought, and I sink deeper into my own dark pit of confusion. *This makes no sense, none.* He continues, "When I married Arabella Fitzwilliam and we were set to leave for the States, Aurora came with me."

"She was your mistress?" I can't hide the horror in my tone. This fairytale romance has taken the nastiest twist and has my nerves on edge, my stomach in tight knots, and my mouth pooling with so much saliva, I think Oskar's very expensive whiskey is about to make a surprise reappearance.

"No, Tia, she was never my mistress; she was my wife-in-waiting. I had obligations, and she understood." His clipped tone does nothing to quell my need for answers.

"Potato, po-tah-to… What about your wife?" I push on despite the fact his back has stiffened, and he is now regarding me through piercing narrowed eyes. His voice remains calm, and he is impassive when he further explains this unique situation.

"Arabella knew I never loved her. I never lied, and I was a fair husband. It helped that we didn't have children. Still, it was a difficult time for everyone concerned, but we muddled through. My wife filed for divorce on our tenth anniversary and was happily remarried to a Canadian chap until they both died. Aurora became my wife, and she fell pregnant instantly with Ole, Atticus's father. Ole never fell in love. His marriage to Inga was entirely for the benefit of the family in order to secure the name, our fortune and the bloodline. It is the Kruse way." He takes another sip from his glass, his tone has once again softened, and he falls silent, pensively staring off into the glowing embers of the dying fire. I'm not sure if the whiskey has made me pleasantly numb, but I think the edge has softened on my judgmental outrage. I take another large gulp of whiskey, though, just to be sure. Oskar turns to face me before he speaks, placing his glass on his small reading table beside him. "We never really spoke about the time before our wedding. It's like it happened to someone else. In life, Tia, we all have to do things we may not want, but as long as you stay true to your heart, you can never really go wrong." His bony hand reaches for mine, and I let him take it and hold it in both of his. His gentle smile eases some of the sadness I feel for his situation, but the anguish and anger that I thought was being subdued by alcohol rears its fiery head.

"But you didn't stay true to your heart, Oskar; you married another woman!" I pull my hand free, because there is no way I can reconcile my emotions with his view of the situation. "Aurora must've died that day."

"I hurt her, yes, but I was hurt, too." His voice catches, and it kills any rage I had building. He looks so fragile and broken that I hate myself for attacking him at all. This wasn't my fight, and I can see now the pain was very real for him, too. His eyes say it all, soul sad and full of regret. I take his hand this time.

"I'm sorry, Oskar. I didn't mean to upset you."

"I never left her Tia, and I never gave my heart to another. It always belonged to her. We just had to do what we had to do until we could be together. No one said true love was easy." He shrugs, and I can see the effort to do that is exhausting. He looks world-worn and weary.

"I guess times were very different back then. It just feels unbearably unjust, horrific actually." I sniff and let out a small laugh to lighten the solemn mood, which rests heavily on both our shoulders. Then I shiver when an icy chill hits my heart, my breath freezes in my throat, and I have to force the words out, because I don't want to give them the oxygen to be heard. *No!* "Why are you telling me this, Oskar?"

"Atticus's engagement to the senator's daughter. You said he told you."

The glass in my hand falls to the slate flagstone floor, breaking it into a million pieces, a little like my heart. "No, that must've slipped his mind," I mouth, not sure if the words are being spoken out loud or not. The fuzzy noise of rushing blood in my ears is all I can hear. "Would you excuse me?" I think I say that, too, only I can't be sure. I'm numb and yet consumed with unbearable agony ripping through me, decimating every plan, every hope, all our dreams destroyed by one sentence. I stand dazed, and silently walk from the room. I don't pick up my bag, or my coat, not even my shoes at the back door. I just walk out into the night, hoping the darkness will take away this pain.

CHAPTER FIFTEEN

Tia

"Mr Kruse was asking after you again today," my mother calls from the hall. I haven't ventured far from my bedroom in the last week, and I'm not likely to open the door for a chat, so she doesn't attempt to enter. "What should I tell him? It's not like you to not visit all week." I hear her pick up the tray from outside my door. "I wish you wouldn't waste this food, Tia." I wonder if there will come a time when she expresses more concern for me rather than the food bill. *I doubt it.* "Atticus called again yesterday. What am I supposed to tell him?" She huffs as if my bad manners are just the worst thing.

"To go to hell," I reply loud enough to avoid the need to repeat myself.

"Tia!" I can almost picture the outrage on my mother's face. She's probably looking over her shoulder, in case my words are heard by someone who matters.

"Mother, I don't care what you tell him, or Oskar, and I'll pay for the wasted food." She doesn't reply straight away, but I can hear her shuffling from foot to foot. "I have work to do."

"You can take some time off from your studies, Tia, and eat." It's the first time in forever my mother's tone actually exhibits concern, and I'm not sure if I find it a comfort or unnerving. It's so wholly out of character from her default emotion of anger or indifference that I opt for unnerving.

"My scholarship is dependent on straight A's and it's the only thing that's keeping me sane, getting away from this godforsaken place so, *no,* I can't take time off my studies," I state flatly.

"Suit yourself. It's what you're good at," she bites out, and I am comforted that this is much more like her. I know *this* woman. She stomps down the stairs, the cutlery clinking on the tray with every heavy footstep. Only a moment later, and I hear the back door slam. I let out a huge sigh when I hear the front gate scrape open and close over the gravel drive. She'll be gone up to the main house, or more likely to the new gamekeeper's farm; she at least has someone to vent to.

I feel bone-tired, and despite my study schedule, I collapse onto my bed. I tried to call Cass as soon as Oskar had revealed the ugly truth. When I couldn't reach him, my mind just started to slowly destroy me with what he could be doing, why he lied, why he didn't tell me. I couldn't stop thinking that I must mean so little to him to betray me like that.

I just felt too empty to function.

I know some people come out fighting, all vitriol and venom, but I just feel so completely devastated, I barely have the energy to open my eyes each morning. I keep telling myself time will heal, but I know it won't. He was my everything, and that's the thing about first loves—they don't just burn your heart, they brand your soul for all eternity.

I wake to the gentle knock at my door. I lift my pillow to cover my ears and squeeze the soft down tight enough to dull the sound. After a short time there is another knock, then another.

"Go away, Mum, please I don't want to fight. I just want to

be left alone, because actually that's what I'm really good at."
There's no answer, just another knock. I swing my legs over the
bed and stomp to the door. Swinging it wide, I am hit with a
sucker punch to end all punches.

Atticus.

God, he looks good. His icy blond hair looks almost white
and is a little longer than normal. His chin is low to his chest,
and he's looking up through his impossibly long lashes, thick
strands of his fringe partly obstructing the intensity of the dark
scowl. His hand rests on the top of the doorframe, and the position flexes the muscles in his arm. The old rock band t-shirt
he's wearing has ridden up, and I hate that my eyes snap to that
muscle on his tummy that seems to make me stupid, more stupid, that is.

"I need to explain," he states. His face is implacable, and his
tone sounds more irritated than contrite, and all the apathy I
felt about lashing out vanishes. I am filled with an instant and
insurmountable flash of rage that surges through every nerve,
travelling from my broken heart to my boot-covered foot.
From the perfect distance, I launch my leg high, connecting
my Doc Martin boot with his unprotected balls. He crumples
to the floor on impact, and a hollow ear-piercing yell fills my
tiny house. He falls, curled onto his side, gasping for breath and
cupping his hands between his legs. *Good!*

"You broke my heart, you piece of shit! What's there to explain?" I would slam the door, too, but he is writhing in agony
over the threshold.

"Tia…" He coughs, his voice a pained gravelly whisper. "Call
an ambulance." I scoff at the notion and fold my arms defensively. He may be in pain, but it's my heart that needs protecting.

"Pussy, I barely made contact." I sniff out a humourless
laugh.

"Please," he pleads, momentarily pulling his hands away from his crotch. I gasp. They are covered in blood, dripping, and the crotch of his light jeans is a deep crimson and the size of the patch just keeps getting bigger.

"Shit, Cass, what's wrong?" I drop to my knees, my hand hovering over his curled up body, not sure where to touch.

"Ambulance, please, Tia," he groans, and I spring to my feet, jump over his body and race down the stairs to the phone in the kitchen, my sweaty fingers flying over the buttons. I make the call and rush back, crouching down next to him, I ask again.

"What's wrong, Cass? I really didn't kick you that hard."

"You busted my stitches. I felt them pop, and I'm about to bleed out. It might be what I deserve, but I don't want to die before I can explain." His eyes meet mine, and despite the pain on his face, I can only see regret in his crystal blue eyes.

"I don't want you to die, period," I reply, tentatively stroking my fingers through his hair, scared to touch him, terrified of losing him.

I've never seen Cass look so pale. There was so much blood, and when he passed out in the ambulance, I very nearly died myself. I certainly didn't want to live without him. By the time we were discharged, I felt about as wretched as could be. He barely said two words at the hospital, but insisted I stay with him the entire time. Twelve hours later, and I couldn't be more relieved to be going home, together.

"I'm sorry," I say for the hundredth time. The taxi pulls away, and Cass takes my hand and leads me back into my house, silently up the stairs and only speaks once the bedroom door is closed and we are seated, facing each other, on my bed. I shift round until I am cross-legged, wringing my hands in my lap; his legs are splayed, and with good reason. Last week he had a baseball injury that nearly left him with just one testicle, but after emergency surgery he was set to make a full recovery, *was* being the operative word.

"They said it's going to be fine, Tia. They repaired the stitches, the blood made it look a lot worse, and at the moment, the painkillers are keeping the agony at bay. Well, the agony in my balls. My heart is not faring so well." We're holding hands, and he places my palm on his chest. I can feel the strong beat of his heart in my fingertips. I shake my head at the warm feeling that creates in my own chest. *It's all so wrong.*

"Your heart, Cass? I'm not the one engaged to another girl. How could you?" My mouth is too dry to shift the lump in my throat. All the moisture in my body seems to be poised right behind my eyelids.

"Let me explain, and then whatever you decide, I will respect. I've never lied to you, Tia, and I don't intend to start now."

"Omission of facts *is* lying, Cass."

"Please, Tia." He drops his head, and his tone isn't nearly as confident as it normally is. His eyes are pleading, and he grips my hand just a little too tight. *He's nervous.* I don't think I've ever seen him nervous.

"Fine." I nod, and he lets out a sigh filled with relief. He draws in a slow breath before he starts to speak, and then he says with absolutely certainty.

"I love you, Tia. I think that's the first thing that needs to be clarified. I want you more than my next breath, and I will have you as my wife, one day." His lips carve the perfect smile, and I have to force myself to believe anything could possibly be wrong when he looks like that and makes me feel the way he always does—cherished, loved, complete.

"But you—" I interrupt, and he quickly does the same.

"Nah-ah…my turn. You've expressed how you feel with your boot. It's my turn now." I bite my lips shut and nod. "I am to take over from my uncle as CEO on my twenty-fifth birthday, but there are strings attached. I have some placements to under-take, learn the ropes as it were, and there are some deals I have to secure. Misty is the only daughter of Senator Jameson. I'm not going to bore you with the intricacies of what's involved po-litically or financially with this connection, just that in agreeing to an engagement, I am fulfilling my obligations and securing the future of the Kruse Corporation, *globally*." He pauses to ad-just himself, wincing and drawing in a sharp breath. I take the distraction as an invitation to contribute my own musings on what he just said.

"Bullshit." I pull my hand from his, and he snatches it back, holding it firmly, and narrowing his eyes with warning. I may be a raging ball of hurt and jealousy, but he does have a very intimidating way about him when he's mad. I've just never been on the receiving end, and I damn well know I'm not this time. He's mad at himself. I can feel it radiating off him in waves. He kisses my fingertips as if to confirm my thoughts.

"It really isn't, Tia. However advanced society is, important deals are still made on the strength of family connections and personal relationships. It's an ugly truth but one that's kept the very rich very powerful for centuries. I know Grandpa told you his story, and mine is not much different." He shrugs lightly, and my rush of air escapes in an incredulous hollow laugh.

"Wrong! If you think for one moment I'm going to be your mistress while you play house with Miss-fucking-America, your expensive education has been wasted, because you are one thick idiot." The bravado in my tone falters when hot tears flow onto my cheek. I can't wipe them away because he won't release his hold. My voice catches, and I no longer try and hide my devastation. "I can't believe you're choosing to do this, Cass, after everything we'd planned." Large ugly sobs rip through my chest, and fat tears streak my face. He holds my gaze, his own eyes glassy, but he has a little more control. His hand presses to my cheek, and he catches the tears, smearing my skin dry, only for a split second before it is once more soaked with my heartbreak.

"I'm not choosing this, Tia. I have no choice. I will forfeit my place in the company and much more besides if *we* don't do this." I hear the emphasis on the we, but I fail to see how this is a joint decision when he is already firmly walking this path, with or without me.

"You wouldn't lose me," I argue, sucking back the sobs.

"I'm not going to lose you now. I said *we*, and I meant *we*. I need you to be on board, or I walk. I just want you to understand what that really means." He waits until I look up, his gaze searching mine.

I scoff. "I'm not on board, Cass. You're engaged,"

"In name only, and I promise there will be no wedding. Misty no more wants to marry me than I do her. She's in love with a musician, but she's struck the same deal with her family."

"This is nuts."

"This is how things work."

"In the dark ages."

"In the *now* ages. We will have a long engagement and once the few deals that are in play are finalised, we call it off. Her parents will be pissed, my mother will be pissed, but Misty and I will both get what we want." He states this as if it is a done deal. My head is a mess, my heart just misses him, and I can feel it pulling me toward this dark place. *It's all wrong.* Still, even my stupid heart needs some assurances.

"You don't love her," I mumble. He shakes his head like I've said something ridiculous when this whole situation is fucking ridiculous.

"I love you. There's only ever been you, Tia, always and forever, remember?" His hand spears around my neck, and he pulls me so we are forehead to forehead. His eyes are my undoing, they always are. I don't fall, I dive into them, and I'm so lost. I know with a sense of doomed inevitability, just like him, I have no choice.

"Heart and soul," I whisper. His lips press against mine with painful urgency. The tingle I feel whenever he touches me ignites a fiery path of prickles across my skin, and I struggle to breathe. He will be the death of me. He breaks the kiss and waits expectantly, knowing I have more questions.

"Have you had sex with her?" He raises a brow, and I can feel my jaw pulse with tension. My stomach rolls, not from the lack of food for once, but the sick feeling and bad taste this question has left in my mouth.

"No, she has her boyfriend for that, not me." He tilts his head in preparation for more questions.

"Have you had sex with anyone else?" I clearly don't know him as well as I thought I did, that I even have to ask this question. His face is a mix of hurt and confusion.

"How could you ask that, Tia? I said I would wait for you, and I never lied."

"You are engaged to another girl, Cass, and I've been legal for over a year. So excuse me if I think having sex with me may not have been a priority, since all evidence points to the fact that it's not." My cheeks heat with embarrassment and a little indignant rage.

"Trust me, you are my top priority, and making love with you for the first time is just about all I think of. It's certainly all I thought about on the flight over. Tia, I know I'm asking too much, but I need you, and I need your understanding. Not everything is as it seems, and I'm risking more than you know just being here now." His voice drops and the cold, serious tone makes me shiver.

"What do you mean you shouldn't be here?"

"I'm just not supposed to be here, that's all." He tries to

dismiss my concern, but I fix him with my unwavering stare. "I just have a lot going on in the States, and since you wouldn't take my calls, and Grandpa decided to *share* before I could tell you myself, I had no choice but to come. I had to clear the air... is it clear, Tia?"

"I don't know, Cass. I don't know what to believe," I answer honestly.

"Do you trust me?"

"Yes." It's always the same instant response; regardless of how confused I am right now, that is a constant.

"Then that's all that matters." He holds my gaze, and I see the truth in his eyes. He holds the contact for long seconds until he is satisfied I believe him, and I do. I hope that doesn't make me a fool. I swear it will be more than his balls he needs to worry about if it does.

"You've really not had sex? You must be the only twenty-year-old in college that hasn't." I sniff and let out a snicker that lifts the solemn intensity of the air weighing us both down.

"It has been mentioned." He barks out a deep laugh. "However, when I show pictures of you to those taking the piss, waiting is a no-brainer. And if you hadn't kicked me in the balls, trust me, we wouldn't be waiting one second more." He quirks a sad smile, and years and years of pent-up sexual frustration, temptation, and Atticus's imposed celibacy all turn around and bite me in my own arse. *My damn foot.*

"Oh, no!" My eyes dart to the heavily padded crotch of his blood soaked jeans and I just want to cry. "No, really?" It's a stupid question. Of course, really. He's in agony, and the last thing I want is our first time to be the stuff of nightmares.

"Yeah." His tone mirrors my own regret.

"Maybe you'll be better in a day or two?" I offer up some hope, but he shoots me down.

"Not going to help much. I have to leave tomorrow."

"No, Cass, please," I plead, and his face is the picture of remorse.

"I'm sorry, Tia, I can't stay."

"It's my last exam on Friday. I'm actually going out with others to celebrate. Can't you just stay until then?" I'm desperate to find a loophole, even if I can see in his face it's futile.

"If I could, princess, you know I would." He kisses my forehead, pressing his lips hard as if trying to brand my skin, savour my touch as much I need to do the same.

"This is so fucking hard, Cass, I hate the way I feel when you're not here." I bite my lip to stop it wobbling, and lower the pressure of the tears prickling behind my nose

"How about the way you feel when I *am* here." He shifts to his side and lies down on my bed, his feet dangling over the edge, and his large frame filling the single space. He pulls on my arm to lie beside him, and he turns to face me. His eyes pierce right through me, and I can feel myself burning up from the inside at the way his gaze is slowly devouring every part of my body.

"I don't remember that. It's been so long." The words are a barely audible whisper. His wicked smile is evidence enough he knows what he is doing to me. He draws in a deep breath through his nose. He can smell what he's doing to me, and too late I squeeze my legs together to quell the ache. *Oh, god.*

"Then let me remind you."

CHAPTER SIXTEEN

Tia

One Week after Cass's visit.
Friday

Are we ever going to see this boyfriend of yours?" Tiffany from my art class nudges me as we are pressed together, trying to get served at the local pub nearest to my school. Pretty much the whole of the year finished their final exams today, and we descended en masse to the Nags Head to celebrate. I smile wide and bright before I answer. I spoke to Cass last night and he gave me the best news ever.

"He's coming back next month, for good." I give a little bounce on my toes, because my body literally can't contain the excitement. We've spoken at length, every day since he came over, and last night he told me he had sorted everything and had renegotiated his 'situation'. He'd decided on the flight back that he wasn't prepared to put me though the whole engagement charade, not even for a pretend moment. To say I was relieved would've been an understatement of the century. Tiffany pouts and huffs. "That's no good. We've finished school now,

Tia. It's the summer holidays, work, and University. I'll never get to see him now."

"Yes, you will." Tiffany's boyfriend Carl leans over her shoulder having heard the best part of our conversation and offers his thoughts and suggestions. "When we collect the results in August, we'll all head back to his castle for a big ol' party, ain't that right, Tia?"

"Oh, yeah, sure! Mrs Kruse would love to open up her 'castle' to me and my friends, and it's not really a castle." I shrug, because Tartarus Hall is probably actually bigger than most castles.

"Aw, you called us your friends." Carl steps around Tiffany and hangs his heavy arm over my shoulder, pulling me in for a rough side-hug. He squeezes the breath from my lungs, it feels good, almost normal, and then his next comment reminds me I'm anything but. "We all thought you were allergic to friends."

"Um, no…I'm not like that." I can feel my cheeks flush with heat, where embarrassment is fighting with awkwardness. Fortunately, this time the general noise and crowd in the pub means no one is paying me any attention, and Tiffany interrupts before I have to answer further.

"Here, Tia, have a pint." She hands me a tall straight glass with a frothy white top. I start to shake my head, but she pushes the beer into my hand and scolds me with a lightly mocking tone.

"It's a village pub, Tia. It's practically in Middle Earth, we're so far from the cops, and besides, you're eighteen soon, and no one's going to tell." I smile and take a sip, foam coating my top lip.

"Thanks." I'm not sure I like the taste, but I like the feeling of being included. *That's a first.*

"That's pretty, is that from *him*?" She waggles her dark brows playfully, her brow-piercing catches the light as it bounces with her facial excitement. She lifts the long sleeve of my school blouse and tugs on my very precious bracelet.

"Oh, no, it's a gift from his grandfather, I'm only wearing it for the exams. Kind of hoping it's going to bring me luck. I need straight A's." I pull the sleeve back down to cover it, not wanting to draw any unwelcome attention, not that I think there are any thieves or muggers in my year, but I am far from knowing everyone here to make that judgment, and if Oskar taught me anything, it's a healthy distrust of everything.

"Well, if *you* can't get an A in Art, what hope do the rest of us have?" Tiffany groans and rolls her eyes with exasperation. She's an excellent seamstress and designer, and she will no doubt get an A in Fashion, but straight Art is not her forte.

"Come on, join me outside for a smoke." She tips her head toward the front door, and I follow where she clears a path through the crowd to the seating area out front. An excess of students have spilled out of the pub in search of some elbow room and fresh air. The latter is unlikely as the number of people smoking fills the small car park; a soft cloud seems to rest just above our heads, and there is an odd mix of aromas that I don't recognise as tobacco. Tiffany offers me a hand rolled cigarette and snickers when I raise my brow with suspicion. *Weed, really?*

"Just to take the edge off." She winks conspiratorially, and I am just about to brave my first puff of anything, when I freeze.

In the distance, I can hear the sirens, and the guilt of a crime not yet committed hits me, and I shake my head. Tiffany taps the end of her joint out in the nearest ashtray and pockets the evidence. As the convoy of cars screeches to a halt in the small pub car park I am also glad I don't actually have the pint of beer in my hand, although the number of officers would indicate a much more serious crime than underage drinking. There are three police cars and a blacked out Range

Rover that I recognise from the number plate as Mrs Kruse's car, *strange.*

"There she is!" Mrs Kruse points her finger directly at me, and the crowd of students gathered outside on this late afternoon all stop what they're doing and turn to face me. Tiffany's jaw drops, and she takes a step back like I am suddenly infectious. I shrug and shake my head with confusion. Stunned into silence, I manage to walk toward the police officer as he approaches. It's very obviously me he's after.

"Are you Tia Parker?" The officer flips his pocket book open and shut before I reply.

"Yes." I look over at Mrs Kruse who now is laughing lightly with one of the officers and what looks like a plain clothes detective. Her hand rests on his arm like they are more than familiar, and he is standing very much in her personal space, with a protective arm hovering close to her shoulders.

"Where did you get that?" He points to the bracelet peeking below my cuff. My other hand instantly flies to cover it.

"This?" I ask, although he can no longer see the piece of jewellery, as my hand is hiding it from view.

"It belongs to you?" His tone is disbelieving, and he smirks.

"Yes, of course." My affronted tone causes a knowing grin to distort his impassive face. He sniffs out and tuts, like he's just heard a tired joke for the hundredth time.

"Then may I ask where you bought it from?" He sounds so bored I wonder if he will even hear my reply so I speak very clearly, slowly, and just shy of shouting.

"I didn't buy it; it was a gift." I bite my lips into a tight line. His accusatory tone is like a slap to the face.

"There is no need to patronise me, Miss Parker. It's a simple question that doesn't require attitude," he retorts. I wasn't even trying for patronising. "That's a rather expensive *gift* for a housekeeper's daughter, wouldn't you say?" I don't like the way he emphasises the word gift, but I have to agree with the sentiment.

"Yes, it is, and that's why I was reluctant to accept it at first. However, Oskar insisted. May I ask what's this about?" I try to adjust my tone, but it has no effect. The officer steps forward, handcuffs in hand and spins me on the spot so I am facing away from him. He snatches my hands one at a time and secures the handcuffs behind my back.

"You're under arrest for the theft of *that* piece jewellery to start with, but from what Mrs Kruse claims, theft isn't the only crime we will be investigating." He pulls me away from the students silently staring at me, roughly leading me to the first police car.

"What the hell!" I struggle out from his hold and step away. I turn back to face him, rage boiling my blood and all I can see is red. I scream out. "Oskar gave this to me! I didn't steal shit! Ask him yourself if you don't believe me!" My voice is pitched with fury, and even to my own ears I sound more than a little hysterical, but this is ridiculous.

"He's dead." The police officer states, and I can feel all the blood drain from my body. Agony rushes through my veins as whatever blood remains chills to ice with this revelation.

"What?" I mouth out along with a silent sob that buckles me over. I raise my head to look over at Mrs Kruse for confirmation. Her face is plastered with a sneer that leaves me cold, sick, and devastated. She walks over to me, looking down her nose, and from her most favourite view, she speaks.

"You are a liar and a thief," she states as a matter of fact, then with a performance worthy of any Academy Award, she crushes her hand to her chest and wails, sobs bursting from her as she wobbles on her feet only to be steadied by the officers at her side. "You are very likely the reason my dear father-in-law passed away so unexpectedly last night." She buries her head in the chest of the plain clothes officer, only even from here I can see her lips tip in a cruel smile.

"Where were you last night, Miss...Miss?" I don't hear the rest of his questions. I close my eyes, my ears rush with blood, and I can feel myself falling, and I can't stop. I know I won't stop until I hit the very bottom. Until I'm in *Hell*.

PART 3

CHAPTER SEVENTEEN

Tia

Present Day

I can't stop sucking my swollen lips into my mouth. They tingle, and I can still taste Logan. I close my eyes because I want to savour him for as long as I can. I don't know when I'm going to see him again, and right now, my body is thrumming to learn what he meant when he said this was the beginning. The attraction and desire have always been there; I just felt I had too much to lose, and I wasn't sure that I wouldn't just freak at the first real intimate contact. I just didn't think my mind would ever let my body just *feel* without some sort of hideous recall. His touch was beyond intimate. That kiss was full-on feral and off the charts scorching hot. My body responded like it never has, well, not since…

"Penny for them?" Atticus's deep gravelly voice travels the length of the stretch limo. The silence was palpable but preferable to speaking. I don't trust myself when I can feel my emotions are already frayed, because this is Atticus and a riot of God knows what because of Logan. The limousine carrying us across the city is huge, and I am wedged on the opposite end of the bench from him. Atticus is lounging along the rear seat, his long legs stretched out, crossed at the ankles. His suit barely has a wrinkle, and the only concession to him being an off-duty CEO is that his navy silk tie is loose, and his top button is open. One arm rests along the back, and his long fingers are tapping out a beat that, when I close my eyes, I can feel my own heart is matching the steady rhythm.

I tucked myself at the farthest edge of the bench as soon as I got in, turned my back on Atticus, and have stared out of the window the entire time the car has crawled like a luxurious snail across the city. Taking me away from my home, my safety, from Logan. However, it's also taking me to where I need to be. He coughs too loudly and manages to infuse the sound with his obvious irritation. I snap my head around, narrow my gaze, and pinch my lips into a tight humourless smile.

"You sure, Atticus? Because according to the charges you brought against me, shouldn't you be asking for pounds, lots and lots of pounds?" He barks out a flat laugh and folds his lean body over so his elbows are resting on his knees, his fingertips pointed and pressed together under his chin. His crystal blue eyes couldn't be any darker and still retain their captivating co-lour, and I find myself struggling to swallow. All the time he holds my gaze with such intensity, I can feel my heart squeeze painfully with the memory of him, of *us*.

"You did always know how to make me laugh, Tia, but this isn't fucking funny." His harsh tone pulls me back to the stark reality, and his scowl just adds to the fury dancing across his features. His jaw is clenched, and he drags his hand roughly through his hair, pulling the ice blond strands free from his eyes, his gaze staring right through me when he speaks. "I could lose the company if—" He snaps his mouth shut just as I interrupt.

"No, you're damn right!" My voice is pitched high as, with

considerable effort, I try and calm my rocketing rage. It's bubbling in the pit of my stomach like molten acid, eroding my resolve from the inside, and I'm not sure how the hell I am going to last this car journey, let alone six months. I let out a calming breath, losing the hysterical edge but keeping all the animosity and hatred. "It isn't remotely funny, and I hope you do lose the company." I watch his eyes narrow and his back straighten. His lips curl slowly with misunderstanding, as if my words were an actual confession of the theft. He is so damn certain of my guilt, it turns my already fragile stomach. I sniff back an acrid laugh and continue to speak.

He slumps back when I fail to elaborate and perhaps give him what he was anticipating: a full confession. *As if.* "I hope you lose everything and more. Maybe losing something important to you will hit you as hard as losing six years of my life, my future, and losing *you*, hurt me." I internally curse and shake my head that I foolishly let that last part out. Not that I think he gives a shit, and I don't need to hide the truth from him, but it's still so damn raw. He didn't just hurt me with his betrayal, he destroyed me, and moreover, he made me who I am today. He needs to know the damage he's done, one way or my way. "But then you weren't mine to lose, were you?" My voice drops, and the silence once again cloaks the plush interior of the limousine. The purr of the engine ticking over is the only sound as the beast of a car rolls slowly to our destination. I manage to stop myself from scoffing when the smooth words fall from his perfect lips.

"I was always yours." His voice is barely audible, low and filled with torment. My heart jacks in my chest. It's so very desperate to hear those words that I want to tear it out with my bare hands. I smile with as much insincerity as I can muster and ask.

"How is Misty?" He reels in his seat like I have spit in his face; even from this distance my words were a direct and surprising hit.

"I don't know." He dips his eyes, for the first time breaking the contact and shifting with obvious awkwardness.

"Open marriage?" I tip my head with playful curiosity. Not that I'm particularly interested, though I do like that this is causing him some considerable discomfort.

"Divorced?" I probe, poking my finger in the sore spot and relishing the recoil. I have to shake myself again. *None of this matters.*

"You know what? I really don't care." I sniff.

"I don't believe that." His derisive tone matches the accusatory quirk of his pale brow.

"That's because you have an ego the size of Jupiter, but trust me, Atticus, *now you're just somebody that I used to know.*" I sing the lyric that should be a perfect fit for my situation, but, unnervingly, it sounds hollow to my own ears.

"Cute, now sing me another, how about "Money for Nothing", "Guilt". No, make that "Wicked Game", perhaps?"

He's quick with his list of suitable comebacks, but I'm losing what little fire I have. I can feel his nearness affecting me, and he was always so good at getting me to engage, even when I really didn't want to. Now it's no different, except this time, I can't risk engaging on any level; there's just too much at stake.

"Let's just get this next twelve months over with, so I can get back to my boyfriend," I reply, my tone a forced attempt to indicate that I'm bored with this conversation. I turn away from him, but he slides up the bench and lays his hand on my knee. I twist sharply at the contact. It feels like a high voltage jolt of electricity, and he removes his hand at my glare, but the damage is done. *Shit, this is bad.*

"You said he wasn't your boyfriend."

"He wasn't, but I think that kiss changed things, don't you?"

I try and shuffle farther away, only I am already squished as far from him as I can get. He's just so damn close, all I can feel is him. He might not be touching me, but there's not a cell in my body that doesn't feel him.

"You think one kiss would change things? Interesting." His eyes darken, and I can see his fingers tap out a pattern on his thigh, restless, for what I can't quite figure. Mercurial is the best fit for his gaze, which dramatically changes from a 'destroy the bitch' scowl, to a 'devour the bitch' incendiary stare.

"It wasn't just a kiss though, was it? It was *the* kiss." I drag my tongue over my bottom lip and can feel the tingle as fresh as if Logan's lips were still pressed to mine.

"Would one kiss change *us*, princess?" His voice drops to a low rumble, and he sounds like he's growling out the words. I can feel the hairs on my neck stand at attention. I just pray my prickly exterior is giving none of this away. The last thing he needs is more ammunition in his arsenal. I'm barely hanging on as it is. I clip out in my best curt tone.

"There is no *us*, Cass."

"There is only *us*, Tia." His retort is instant and sounds very much like a threat. I try and hide the effort it takes to swallow the thick feeling in my throat. He leans forward, his tall body looming perilously close, and instead of holding my ground, I panic and slide like water off the bench and scrabble to the other end of the car. He chuckles, a deep and throaty sound that helps me to regain my focus and a little of my anger. At this precise moment, I grab it like a lifeline.

"You know, Atticus, *if* I had your money, I would hand it over immediately, just so you could stop all this bullshit," I snap, straightening myself and pulling my satchel across my lap as some sort of barrier. His eyes follow the movement and crease with amusement. I don't know who I hate more right now— me for underestimating this whole reunion and not hiding my feelings, or him for just being *him*. I fix my eyes on his and steel myself to not blink.

Him, it's definitely him I hate more. "If you cared for me you never would've left me to rot. You showed your true self, Cass, and you bleed the Kruse family colours through and through. If you think pretending there is something inextricable between us…some soul deep connection you think I'm still yearning for, then you're an idiot and a bigger arsehole than I pegged you for. And don't misunderstand me, I think you're the fucking king when it comes to arseholes."

"You got one thing right, princess, I'm the fucking king, and I want my fucking crown jewels back," he states, deadly serious and with no emotion. His tone is perfectly calm, and his eyes are dark, deep pools of icy emptiness. I shiver and pull my satchel a little closer, my heart hammering so loudly in my chest, I swear it's the only thing one can hear in the silence of the car. He holds my gaze with such intensity, I know I'm dancing with the devil once more, balanced on a precipice. He broke me, betrayed me, but I can't escape the fact that when I look at him, I see the boy I loved with all my heart, soul deep and so sure… and *I wasn't expecting that.*

"This topic of conversation will never get boring, because the truth rarely does. I don't have your money." I ignore my troubling thoughts and repeat the sentence for the hundredth time.

"You're lying."

"Fine, I'm lying, but I still don't have your money," I quip.

"Now, we're getting somewhere."

"Oh, really?"

"Yes, in the space of this short journey you've admitted you're a liar, and that one kiss will change everything. Just imagine what I will coax from you in the coming months." He drags his bottom lip in between his teeth, and I want to shiver again. The sound of the stubble scratching sends a ripple of goosebumps across my skin. I clench my jaw tight and turn my head away, not trusting what will come out of my mouth next. It's bad enough I can't hide my physical reactions; the last thing I need is to let my unfiltered mouth off its leash.

"Probably wise not to answer, princess, I'd be pretty disappointed if you don't at the very least give me a challenge." He laughs, and I snap my head around to face him. I fire him a look that I wish could flay the skin from his bones like I'm silently willing. He has managed to push nearly all my buttons in the space of one car ride. Still, this journey has at least made one thing very clear. I need to keep my distance.

We cross the Thames over Blackfriars Bridge, and I peek up at the newly completed building, sleek and futuristic, juxtaposed next to the tired and dated Coat and Badge pub right on the water's edge. The limo pulls into the basement car park, and my heart kicks up a gear.

This is really happening.

Atticus goes to lift my case from the car but holds his hands up in surrender when I snap,

"Touch me or anything of mine, and I'll end you," I practically snarl and bare my teeth. Since indifference didn't work, attack seems to be my go-to tactic at keeping distance.

"Whoa! Nice over-reaction there, Tia. I was just going to carry your case because it looks heavy. I wasn't exactly sticking the tip inside somewhere not welcome, now, was I?" His tone is light and joking, his brows wiggle playfully, and I feel the urge to snicker. *Shit.*

"I'd like to see you try." I try to keep the hostility in my tone, but it fails because my mouth is being pulled in an involuntary grin. *Double shit.*

"Later. Let me show you to your room first. There's plenty

of time for fun...twelve months, in fact." He is out of the car before I can retort, not that I think I could do any more damage than I already have, *so much for hostile captive.* That remark and his utter arrogance has kind of left me speechless. I watch him stride off, his heavy footsteps echoing off the concrete cave of the underground car park.

"Would you like me to take that up for you, Miss?" That voice is so deep, it sounds like it's been put through one of those Darth Vader voice changers. I jump and spin round, half expecting to see James Earl Jones.

"Shit! Sorry, what? Oh, no, I'm fine. I didn't actually see you there." The man in question pulls together bushy, dark, and angry looking brows. He must be six feet tall and almost as wide. The seams on his chauffeur uniform are stretched to breaking with the size of bulk and muscle underneath, yet he was silent the whole time and standing right behind me. I place my hand on my heart, because it's hammering like a jackrabbit, and I'm not sure if it's from the fright of this stealthy giant or my most recent encounter with Cass. *Who am I kidding?* "You're really quiet for such a big guy."

"It's my job to stay in the shadows." A slow grimace spreads across his face, and I have to stop myself from stepping away. He's all kinds of terrifying, and I don't think he's even trying. In fact, I think the opposite. I force a friendly smile to try and encourage this softer side.

"Seen and not heard, hmm?" I ask in a light engaging tone; however, he stares back, searching my face and making me tremble for all the wrong reasons. My smile freezes on my face.

"You better move; Mr Kruse doesn't like to be kept waiting. You can't go up without him." He nods in the direction of the fading footsteps. "It's the forty-first floor, and the penthouse has the private lift, so you can't use it unless you are with him." I snort, and I know he isn't joking. Judging by the scowl he is boring right through me, if he has a sense of humour, it must be buried so deep inside the mountain of muscle it's just never going to see the light of day, at least not on my watch.

"Oh trust me, I'm in no rush." His brow arches high, and the break in his impassive expression makes me bold enough I venture another question. "What's your name?" Steely silence and narrow eyes are my answer, but I persevere. I know I'm on my own here, and I have a feeling I need to start making friends regardless of how impossible a task.

"I'm Tia."

"Oh, I know who you are." He snaps his jaw tight and I'm not sure how he could look scarier, but the flash of anger in his eyes brings a thick lump to my throat that won't budge no matter how much I swallow. I manage to choke out a shocked whisper.

"You do?"

"That was inappropriate." He instantly stiffens, his eyes wide and flicking over to where Cass had disappeared.

"It was intriguing, but not inappropriate. So he's mentioned me, then?" I shake my head and try to probe for more.

"Would you like me to take the case?" It's like some invisible steel doors have just slammed between us. His face is implacable, and I know this conversation is now dead. *Shame.*

"No, it's okay. Thanks anyway." I give a light shrug and let out a heavy breath. "You know, I feel a little nervous," I mutter, and I only realise I've said it out loud when he responds.

"That would make both of you, then."

CHAPTER EIGHTEEN

Atticus

The elevator doors close, and the silence is oppressive. *I hate this.* She looks so small in her oversized sweater, *his sweater.* My mind flashes with *that* kiss. I grind my teeth. I tighten my fists. And my chest heaves with the need to draw in a calming breath. I have no idea what he is to her, but he was definitely staking his claim, as clear as cocking his fucking leg. Her face is fixed forward, and her slight frame is rigid. Her long glossy hair is pulled away from her face, and her skin looks so damn soft, I have to wonder what her reaction would be if I just stroked her cheek with the back of my knuckle. My white-knuckle grip loosens with the thought, and my fingers twitch to sate the desperate craving of just one touch. I suppress a hollow laugh as my mind races forward to how that would play out. She'd probably break my fucking fingers off.

Honestly, I don't blame her. I fucked up on a biblical scale. I know this, and I will make sure in the next months I do everything in my power to make amends. I've never been afraid of a challenge, and this is a mother of a fucking mess, but I will do whatever it takes. I may not have orchestrated her incarceration, but still I'm ashamed to admit I unwittingly played an integral part.

I will unpick all the pieces, break her down, and get to the truth. I have to, if I am ever to have a hope of rebuilding *us*. That is something I knew I wanted more than any amount of money the moment I saw her in that interrogation cell, but I need the *whole* truth.

She was mine once, and I haven't had a happy moment since the day I let her go. It doesn't matter that I didn't have a choice. I doubt it will make a difference, but if I get the chance, I'd like to tell my side of the sorry tale.

I didn't realise how much that mistake haunted me until I saw her name on the report from my head of security last month. I haven't had a decent night's sleep in five years, and seeing her name, it hit me why. Regret runs so deep in my veins, it chokes any chance of peace.

This is my second chance.

Still, complicated doesn't begin to describe this situation. I don't know what her game is, but I don't think for a moment her working at my company headquarters is just a job to her. I believe it was very much a means to an end, and whether I have doubts about her actual involvement in the disappearing money or not, I need to find out what that 'end' is.

The lift opens, and I stretch my arm to allow her to exit first. She rolls her eyes like my ingrained manners offend her, although when I think, it's more likely *everything* I do will offend her. I'm okay with that. I have time to change her mind, and I feel from the narrow-eyed scowl she is currently levelling at me, I am going to need every minute of the next twelve months.

The lift opens directly into the large marble lobby of my apartment. Two separate habitable units used to make up this floor. I had them converted into one sizeable apartment, affording the best possible 360 view of the city. The floor-to-ceiling glass walls offer uninterrupted vistas everywhere you look. It's impressive, even if I do say so myself. Tia's footsteps falter as she rounds the corner, and I turn just in time to see her snap her jaw shut. Her wide eyes take in the spectacle that is London as the sun goes down. A million twinkling lights reflect on the calm Thames. Tower Bridge is in the distance, and all the other iconic buildings span the horizon from the dome of St. Paul's Cathedral, along the riverbank and all the way back toward the Houses of Parliament.

"You like?"

"I like the view."

"Right." I ignore the not so subtle inference in the answer. "The kitchen is over there, help yourself to anything, and this is the main living room. There is a smaller one through there, as well as my office which has fingerprint access, so don't go getting any ideas." I point down the corridor that leads to one side of the kitchen.

"Oh, the trust runs deep, I see." Her tone is thick with sarcasm, but not as hostile as before. I'll take that as an improvement.

"I'll trust you when you trust me," I retort with all seriousness.

"Oh, when hell freezes over, then," she snorts.

"Perhaps a little sooner, shall we?" I sniff with a light laugh and see the first quirk of her lips at my attempt to ease the tension. She follows me down the long corridor leading off of the main living room, which is effectively the second apartment, and where the master bedroom and the guest rooms are located. Opening one of the double doors to the first room, I once again urge her to lead the way. She fails to hide her smile this time, and however fleeting the glance, I feel the warmth like a burst of lava in my chest. It's gone a little too quickly, and the afterglow just makes me crave more, so much more. I find myself standing right beside her when I state the bloody obvious.

"This is your room."

"Right." She gives a sharp nod, but I can't get a read on her. Her face is impassive, and I wait for any other reaction. Even if her words weren't clipped, her posture is like stone. She's giving nothing away, and I know this room is drop dead stunning. It has the same view as mine, and is only just a tiny bit smaller.

"I had an easel set up in the corner over there." I point to the far side of the room and her eyes follow my finger. Her nose wrinkles, and a deep line troubles her brow.

"Why?"

"I want you to be comfortable and not bored. I assumed from the stolen supplies you still paint." I keep my tone level. I don't want to rile her any more than she already is. I can feel the animosity rolling off her in waves. I know it may take time, but I want her to make this her home. I need her to relax, break down her barriers, and trust me. However I look at it this, I know it's going to be a Herculean task to end all of his labours. Still, it's essential, because I know she's lying about something, and given her motivation, if not her history, I can't rule out that it could very well be about my missing money.

I have to tread carefully.

I move past her, my arm brushing against hers. She jolts, and I feel it too. I felt it the first time I laid eyes on her. Even after everything and all this time, what is firing between the two of us is just as raw, just as pure and potent. I'm counting on it being the same for her. That sliver of hope depends on the feeling I have, that those barriers she's erected are akin to the little boy's thumb in the dike.

"See, all you will need is here, and I can send out for more supplies." I open several of the drawers next to the easel that is fully stocked with everything she could possibly need.

"You think I'm going to paint while I'm here?" Her tone is just as incredulous as her expression.

"You always found it a great outlet, and if you don't trust yourself to express yourself with words, I don't want you bottling anything up. I want—"

She responds with a short sharp acrid laugh. "You think I will have trouble expressing myself, hmm?"

"You did attempt, albeit unsuccessfully, the silent treatment in the car. I just thought this would help. You don't have to paint. Really, it makes no difference to me." I stop talking when she drops her bag heavily and strides past me to the easel. She opens the top drawer and picks out something, a pencil or maybe a pastel chalk. No, it's too dark and squeaks against the paper, charcoal. She starts to sketch. A few quick sure strokes and then she drops the stick and rubs her hands down the front of her jeans. A stark middle finger is flipping me the bird from the pristine white drawing pad.

"Cute. Not quite what I meant, but it's a start." I hold her gaze, and we have this highly charged standoff. The mix of emotions is cloudy at best, but I know, on my part at least, dark desire and lust is rapidly rising to dominate anything else that might be trying to claim my focus. "I'll be in my office, if you need me." I turn, breaking the eye contact before I do something stupid. Just before the door seals shut, her softly spoken words slice me open and cleave straight to my heart.

"That ship sailed five years ago."

She hasn't left her room, and I know she must be starving by now. She declined any offer of dinner last night, left the sandwich I made, and ignored me completely when I made late night cocoa. Same with breakfast this morning. I cooked bacon, even though I never eat breakfast, but since the smell of fresh coffee did nothing to crack the seal on that door, I thought the aroma of sizzling bacon would do the trick, still nada. It's getting close to lunchtime when I hear the soft padding footsteps nearing the kitchen. Tia appears fully dressed with her tatty leather satchel slung across the shoulder.

"Going somewhere?" I arch my brow high.

"Yes." Her tone and expression are impassive.

"Care to elaborate?" I coax with a wry smile.

"No."

I snort a brief laugh in reply. "Then, in that case, request denied." I dip my eyes back to my laptop, closing down the conversation. She huffs, and although I don't look up, I can just imagine her hands flying to her hips in outrage at my dismissive response.

"I didn't request, asswipe; you're not my jailer," she snaps, and there is a definitive snarl-like quality to her tone.

"That's exactly what I am. Did you not read the papers you signed?" I scoff. Of course she didn't. She was so angry at the time that this was the best and only offer on the table, she would've signed regardless.

"This is effectively house arrest, Tia. The only concession is if *I* deem it important, *and* I'm with you. I have work to do, so request denied." I don't bother to meet her gaze, which I know will be shooting daggers right about now. Her voice is full of indignation and injustice when she replies.

"I want to see Logan, and I'm hungry. I need to eat!"

"I offered you breakfast." I wave a dismissive hand toward the stone cold plate of food on the side.

"I'm not eating anything you cook. It could be poisoned, for all I know." I slap my laptop shut at her dramatics and the ludicrous suggestion.

"It was a fucking bacon sandwich, Tia, and if I wanted you dead, trust me, you'd be dead," I snap, and I instantly regret the severity of my tone. Her eyes narrow, but she doesn't recoil like I thought she might. She is either really good at faking her genuine fear, or she isn't the scared little girl she once was.

"So I am in jail. The decor is just a little flashier." Her hip drops, one hand resting in a tight fist, and she purses her lips.

"It's only a jail if you continue to behave like a brat." My observation has her jaw dropping when she gasps.

"Brat!"

"Yes, brat, eat my damn food, and we'll talk about visitation."

"Sounding more and more like a prison, Atticus." Her rebuttal has lost the brattish tone, but her indignation is very much evident.

"Just test me a little more, Tia, and I'll chain you to the damn bed. Now eat!" I growl and push my half eaten tuna bagel toward her. She swings her satchel behind her and slides roughly onto the island stool opposite me. She snatches the bagel from the plate and scarfs down three large bites like a huge child. I stand and pour her a cup of tea. The china cup I bought for her has the word 'princess' printed in simple pale pink letters on the front, and when her eyes meet mine, they hold for a few precious seconds too long with shared recognition of something more.

"Thank you." The words float in the air like a white flag.

"You're very welcome." We sit silently while she finishes the rest of the bagel and sips her tea. "Would you like me to make you another?" Her plate is clean, and I doubt so much has changed that she no longer enjoys her food.

"No, thank you, but I would like to visit Logan." She shakes her head at my offer, and my stomach rolls at her request. It wasn't that I wasn't expecting it; I just wasn't expecting it so damn soon.

"I have work to do. It can wait " I take the plate and drop it in the sink. With the height of the drop, I'm surprised it doesn't shatter. The noise is loud, though, and she jumps.

"I left some of my stuff there," she offers with a slight shrug.

"Stuff?"

"Tampons." She holds my gaze, and, damn it, I look away.

"Right, yes, of course. Wait, nice try. Can't I just get those delivered?" She did that on purpose, and I have to credit the play.

"Yeah. Look, Cass, this is hard for me, but it will be doubly hard for him, and I want to make sure he's okay," I can't deny that I fucking hate that she cares like this. My shoulders tense, and I don't know how I manage to give a civil answer when I feel the rage building inside.

"Call him."

"He's not picking up." I can hear the genuine worry in her voice. *Fuck.*

"Fine, but I can't do this all the damn time, Tia. I have a business to run and a hundred million pounds to find." I throw this in her face, and she doesn't flinch; she never does. It's the one thing that made me doubt the coincidence of her appearance and my money's disappearance. Well, that, and the fact that I knew she was innocent five years ago.

"I can go on my own. You don't need to come." She tries a placatory smile on for size, and it looks all wrong. At this precise moment, it's a toss-up whether she hates me or this situation more. I don't flatter myself that it's the latter.

"Actually, I do," I state as a matter of fact, but I kill the smug expression before it pulls at the corner of my lips. After all, I'm thankful I have this kind of leverage over her, because I know I'm going to need every single favour banked if I'm to redress the balance of her affection. "So when you're there, impress upon your 'boyfriend' the importance of picking up his fucking phone." I make a point of air quoting the relationship, which I know is still very much up for clarification. "Because if you get tempted to visit unsupervised, there will be nothing I can do to keep that sweet arse of yours out of jail."

"I'll tell him." She gives a sharp nod. "Thank you, Atticus."

"I prefer when you call me Cass; you're the only one who ever did." My voice softens and her eyes flit to mine, locked for only a second before looking away.

"Thank you, Cass."

"Don't thank me just yet." I stand and pull the chunky chain platinum collar from my back pocket. I drop one end and swing it from my clasped fingers.

"What's that?" Her throat moves up and down with the effort of swallowing. My eyes follow the movement almost as closely as my cock, which twitches and swells with lust and longing. I clear my throat and my wayward mind.

"Your tracking device." I hold the actual part of the chain that carries the technology between my finger and thumb, the necklace part dangles on either side. The padlock clasp is possibly a little over the top, but I didn't have a great deal of time to source what I wanted, and this is much better than the standard issue ankle tag. "I should've put it on you last night, but since you didn't come out of your room, and you can't leave this apartment until I scan your fingerprint, I concluded you weren't a flight risk." Her expression shifts from adorably confused to horrendously outraged.

"That looks like a damn collar!" she yelps.

"It is." I fight the smile that is desperate to take control of my stoic features.

"I thought the device was some big black thing you wore on your ankle?"

"I thought this more suitable." I take each end and move close enough to tentatively hold it in front of her face. Her eyes are like saucers.

"I'm not a fucking dog, Cass!" She leans away but not far enough to stop me placing it around her neck.

"I never thought you were. It's a platinum chain, Tia. It will easily pass as a pretty choker, and only we need to know the truth." I pause before I clarify its significance.

"The truth?"

"That it is, in fact, a collar, so you don't forget what you are." My voice drops, and I ache from my balls to that yearning in my chest.

"A criminal?" Her voice waivers, and I shake my head, hold her gaze, and tell her the truth.

"No. For the next twelve months, Tia, the collar means, once more, you are *mine*." I secure the lock with a click that makes her jump. I slide my fingers under the cool metal and make sure there is sufficient space around her neck, that no skin is caught, and it's perfectly comfortable.

It looks good.

I suppress the grin that threatens, because her eyes are on fire, and I fear one spark will light the powder keg between us and not in a good way.

CHAPTER NINETEEN

Tia

I'm in so much trouble.

I might be fooling him with my cool and mostly hostile exterior, but I can feel the cracks in my resolute resolve beginning to widen. That damn snack he left for me last night nearly had me banging on his bedroom door to more than share my midnight feast of a stack of banana and sugar sandwiches, *my favourite.*

I admitted to myself, in the wee hours, that I might not be entirely prepared. Who am I kidding? I'm in no way near prepared. Not for him being nice, being the Cass I remember. Even being in the same damn room, my body betrays me, and I know full well he's acutely aware of every goosebump. I'm an idiot for thinking I had a handle on this, that I somehow I wouldn't remember everything he once was to me, that this wouldn't affect me, wouldn't knock me sideways and then some.

Truth is, I just don't know how to deal with Cass still being the man I loved, *my first love.*

I need some space to collect my wayward thoughts, together with some straight talking and maybe some not-so friendly advice to help me regain focus.

And I need Logan to finish what he started.

My head may be a mess, but my body is in a war zone, and it's clouding my judgment.

All night I tossed and turned, trying to separate what I feel from what I need to do. When I finally managed to close my eyes, all I could see was impossibly deep blue eyes staring into my soul, and when I woke up, all I could think about was Logan's kiss and how I want more, *much* more.

I know the right choice is to keep to the plan, but my body is on the ragged edge, and I'm afraid it's going to leap arse first into the wrong direction. If I can't trust *me*, there's only one person I can trust to help me make the right choice. The dial tone is cut when the call connects, and I quickly speak first.

"Ghost?"

"What the fuck, Star? I'm hanging up, and don't call me again unless it's from the fucking burner phone. Did I not teach you anything, you dumb bitch?" Her soft southern American accent sounds brutally harsh, just in case I didn't get that inference from her calling me a dumb bitch. The line goes dead, and I curse myself. She did teach me better, she taught me everything and more, and she is spot on about being dumb, but I'm desperate, too, another thing she will be mad about and will rightly tear me a new one next time we do speak. *Desperation makes smart people do stupid things, and stupid things get smart people caught.*

Cass's mood seems to darken the instant we cross the Blackfriars Bridge heading away from his home and toward Logan's. I wasn't lying when I said I wanted to see him, but that brief aborted call earlier is the real reason I need to return today. The burner phone is in my room, hidden along with some other essential supplies that I now know I need. I can pick almost any lock there thanks to the excellent tutelage from Ghost, but biometric entry requires some special materials if I'm to get the access I need to Atticus's office. It's the whole reason I knew seeing him again was inevitable. I have everything I need in place, and I thought I was prepared for every curve, fork, or spanner. I just wasn't prepared for *him*.

The limousine pulls alongside the curb outside Logan's house, and my hand is on the handle before the motion of the car has completely stopped.

"Wait!" Cass calls as I swing the door wide. He grabs my jacket to stop me from disappearing. I hold my position half in and half out of the car, turning my head when he speaks. "How long are you going to be?"

"Why? Would you like to come in?" I instantly regret my snide and snappy retort. That's the last thing I want, and Logan would definitely throw a shit fit if I show up with Cass in tow.

"You're funny, and I'll call your bluff one day, princess, so you can drop the attitude. I will be back in an hour, and I'm being generous." His jaw ticks wildly with this concession.

"An hour! Come on, that's no time at all!" I huff out with obvious exasperation.

"Exactly. *Mine,* remember?" He reaches his long fingers to flick the tiny padlock, which is surprisingly weighty when it thumps back against my throat.

"Please, Cass, give me *three* hours. I have stuff to do. I didn't realise I wouldn't have easy access to my things, so I need to think a little more about what I will need. I don't want to have to keep putting you out like this." I soften my tone. If only my plea didn't sound so disingenuous, he might buy the sentiment. His brow quirks high, and his full lips thin into a tight line, and I know that's not the case. I hold my breath, because from that look, I will be lucky if he gives me five fucking minutes.

"Two hours and not a minute more." I exhale the held breath with a rush of air and a wide genuine smile.

"Thank you."

"You will owe me for this, princess." He tugs me back into the car, catching me off balance, and I brace my fall with one hand on his lean muscular thigh and the other on his shoulder. His breath is warm and minty, millimetres from my lips. The invisible hairs on his skin seem to tangle with my own, he's so damn close. His piercing eyes bore into me. There is so much there in those swirling depths—history, longing, and lost love. My stomach drops fathoms into the deep, and I have to force myself to speak. It's a raw whisper.

"Really, Cass, what more can I give you that you haven't taken already?"

"Oh, I can think of one thing." My mouth dries, and a million prickles kiss my skin with the drop in his voice and the incendiary glare in his eyes. *Shit.*

"Two hours," I choke out and push off of him. The heat between us crackles and dies at the break in contact as I hightail it out of his car. My feet hit the pavement, and I would be surprised if Bolt himself would've beaten me to Logan's door. I'm so in over my head with the whole sexual tension thing. Why the fuck didn't I factor this in to my plan? *Oh, yes, because I'm a dumb bitch.*

There's no sound in the house when I enter the front door, and a quick look in the library and kitchen makes me think Logan is probably still asleep. Before he 'found' me in the basement, he was pretty much nocturnal, so I'm not surprised he has reverted to type, although it might just be a one-off. It has only been one day.

It feels so much longer.

I spring up the stairs two at a time on my tiptoes, taking

care to avoid the creaks. I'm on the clock, and I need to speak to Ghost before I deal with Logan. His office is on the second floor but both our bedrooms are on the first, opposite ends of the long corridor and the floorboards could wake the dead with a poorly placed foot. I hate this feeling of uncertainty, and if anyone is going to put me straight, it's her. I've never met anyone like her. Smart, brutally honest, and most likely a sociopath. She was my best friend for three years while we shared a cell, and if she was capable, I think she would say the same of me. She wouldn't take a bullet or anything, because she lacks even a smidgen of empathy, but she 'cares' in a way that I appreciate. Educated, resourceful, and a brilliant mind for revenge.

I click my bedroom door shut and press my ear to the solid oak to check I haven't disturbed Logan. Satisfied, I drop to my knees and roll the rug back enough to expose the floorboards. Pushing one end of the only one that is slightly discoloured, I lift it free. There is a small steel security box with a padlock, not unlike the one I currently have around my neck. The key is hidden in the joist of the flooring, a small section I carved out which is invisible to anyone who doesn't know it's there. I prise the wood out and the key falls into my palm. The box contains my passport, some cash, a copy of the Will, some sentimental crap I couldn't seem to throw away, and the burner phone.

I sit with my back against the door because if, for whatever reason, I can't hear footsteps, Logan is large enough that I will feel the vibrations. I do not need him to hear this conversation.

This shit is complicated enough without that.

"Better. What the fuck were you thinking, Star?" Ghost snaps, her tone still laden with irritation and anger.

"I'm sorry, I have a situation, and—" She interrupts before I can explain further.

"I know. Why the fuck are you staying with him? How the fuck did you manage to get arrested ahead of schedule? Please tell me you haven't fucked this up already?" She fires question after question without drawing breath.

"If you'd let me speak…"

"Star, there's more than just a little payback at stake here." Her tone shifts down a notch, but I can just picture her permanent scowl. Her brown eyes are so dark they always looked black, and her sharp fringe and severe bob haircut frame her pale pixie face with hard angles.

"I know."

"Talk to me."

"I'm a mess."

"That's a given, you might need to elaborate."

"Logan kissed me."

"He what?"

"Kissed me, I mean he *really* kissed me, knee-trembling type of kiss. He all but pissed around my legs, marking his territory in front of Atticus." My tongue swipes my bottom lip at the delicious memory.

"This is a problem," she mutters, and I'm not sure if it's a question. I feel her judgment, and verbal vomit rushes from my mouth in an attempt to make some sense of what I'm feeling.

"Yes, no…I don't know. Atticus makes me…he…I can't think straight, and my body…he made me banana sandwiches." I am flustered, and this is exactly why I need help. I'm not this person. I haven't been giddy like this since… Actually, I don't think I was *ever* giddy.

"Oh, bringing out the big guns." Her tone is snide, and her sharp laugh is without humour. "Just stop, Star. You need to keep focus."

"I know. It's just these feelings." I press my hand to my chest where the strong, rapid heartbeat is rattling more than my ribcage.

"What *feelings*?"

"The tingly, fuck-with-your-head-and-heart kind of feelings." I close my eyes and shake my head. Even if she can't see me, I know she can hear my desperation.

"For who?" I can't get a read on her impassive tone, but the fact that she's still talking gives me hope that I'm not a completely lost cause. We may be a dysfunctional partnership, but she's still my partner, and I need her eyes and ears.

"Both." My admission sounds more like a question. The silence stretches for long and excruciating minutes, and I know from experience she can keep this up for days, weeks even, and I just don't have the time. I am about to ask more specifically for some guidance when she speaks. Her cold clinical tone brooks no argument, and if I'm honest, I'm just grateful she hasn't hung up. If some people are closed off and need their privacy, Ghost is an island on a distant planet in another galaxy far, far and even farther away. I think her only exposure to, albeit historical, loving relationships, human emotions, and affection are what I told her about Atticus and me, which I only did to while away the tedious days inside jail.

"Don't go there with Atticus, Star. It's too dangerous. End of." She's vehement and abrupt with that assessment. I knew she wouldn't pussyfoot around me; however, she pauses slightly before she continues. "My advice, since I know that's why you called: if you can't keep your dick in your pants, for want of a better expression, fuck Logan. You said he staked his claim, right?"

"But I lied to him. What if he finds out our meeting wasn't a coincidence?"

"Trust is an issue with him for sure, but that's true regardless of if you fucked him or not. There's no reason why he would find out now after all this time. He's satisfied he knows enough and believe me, he checked you out thoroughly. He never would've let you stay if that wasn't the case." I don't bother to ask how she knows all this. It's a toss-up between Ghost and Logan who is the better cyber whizz, and I'm only as good as I am because I've learned from them both, even if, all along, Logan was an unwitting tutor. She finishes a mouthful of something before she speaks again.

"You can always hope that, spreading your legs for him after what you went through, he'd just about forgive anything"

"Jesus! I don't want his pity, Ghost."

"That's not what I meant." She cuts me dead then sighs heavily. Her voice is strained, and I can hear she's struggling with this conversation, far too many emotions for her particular brand of sociopathy. "Look, I guess you probably feel something for him, love or whatever, but it doesn't matter. At some point Star, sooner or later, you need to allow yourself to live, not just exist." Her words are forced, but it's still a comfort to hear them from her, even if I can also hear her teeth grind when I reply.

"I do love him Ghost, I...I want him like *that*. I just don't know if I can." I can feel the pinch of prickles behind my eyes. It's not the first time I've wanted this. It's just the first time I've thought about wanting *more*. It's *all* I've been thinking since that kiss, and that's the problem.

"If you say so. Just be honest with him about what happened, make sure you tell him *everything*. You need to get your head back in the game, and Logan isn't your problem." She sounds irritated, and for once, I wish I had a more modern phone with video calling so I could get a better read on her. "Think about it, that's not what's really affecting your focus. You've got Atticus stirring things up, no doubt playing on an unresolved history of sexual promise. Logan's just reacting to a new alpha in town; it's so clichéd it's almost comical. He stepped up like a big dumb dog in a pissing contest with that kiss. It's a game Tia." She sniffs derisively, and I get a twist in my gut that she might be right.

I'm so confused. "It's kind of pathetic." She laughs and I feel the lack of humour like a damp blanket over my burgeoning sparks of ill-timed lust and desire. She switches tack and makes my head spin with the speed of her U-turn. "Still, I don't discount that sexual tension is a potent distraction that you don't need. My advice? Try to be like me and take the feelings out of it. Be honest with him, and after everything is said, it will happen or not." I can almost see the curl of disdain in her lip as she forces the unpleasant notion from her mouth and rushes to finish the sentence. "…then scratch this itch and get back with the programme."

"Simple as that." I sniff and look up to the ceiling, silently seeking the strength I'm going to need to tell Logan what happened.

"If you think for a moment Logan doesn't know most if not everything that went down in jail you're a bigger, dumber bitch that I thought. He's one of the best hackers for a reason." It's a thought that had crossed my mind a time or two.

"So how come he doesn't know what I'm doing?" I pick nervously at the threads in the hole in my jeans, tugging them loose, which ensures that the rip is pretty much beyond repair. I can push my whole fist through the gap at the knee when my leg is stretched out on the floor.

"Because I'm a better hacker, and I'm covering your arse." Her tone is derisive enough that she doesn't need to add a 'duh', which would finish off her statement of the bloody obvious perfectly.

"And I love you for it."

"Yeah. You know, you really shouldn't." I smile at her stock response. "Look, I gotta go, anything else?"

"No, that's all, No wait, sorry, just one thing I almost forgot. He's got fingerprint security on his office door. The safe and his main hard drive will be in there. The one that isn't connected to the network and I can't access from his office in the Kruse building." I internally curse myself that I almost forgot this. For fuck's sake, if my head doesn't need clearing, my arse certainly needs kicking.

"Just one more thing, hmm?"

"I know, I know, head in the game. I'm all over it. Look, I can lift his print, but I will need you to check once I'm in, in case he has extra hidden security, either cameras or on his computer." I brush aside her sarcastic undertone.

"Just upload the code, and I'll clean every move you make."

"Thank you. I don't know what I'd do without you."

"Just remember that when you cash out," she reminds me, and I'm quick to nip that tired conversation in the bud.

"I'm just taking what's mine, Ghost, not a penny more." I can hear her huff, but she doesn't push it.

"Fine. One more thing, I shouldn't have to remind you, but since your head is all over the fucking place, I think it bears repeating. Nothing changes between us, right?" Her voice drops with deadly seriousness.

"Nothing changes. Why would it?" I resolutely reassure her.

"Just make sure you don't mention me to Logan." She repeats what she told me the day she gave me his address and just as forcefully. I didn't ask then. I didn't care, and I had no vested interest other than needing a roof and access to the best computer hardware outside of the CIA. However, with things up in the air between Logan and me, I feel compelled to ask.

"Why?"

"Because you'll never hear from me again if you do."

"Oh!" I gasp at the decidedly chilly declaration.

"And he'll kill you," she adds before the line goes dead.

"Ghost! Ghost!" I call out.

What the hell?

I stare at the phone like it will somehow make sense of what she just said. That emphatic tone I recognise, and my mind races with a million questions that I doubt I'll ever get the answers to. We left prison together; however, I haven't seen her since. If I hadn't spent every day for three years inside in the same damn cell, based on our current relationship status, I would struggle to believe she was real.

There's a reason she's called Ghost.

I empty out the drawing pencils from the container, into the bottom of the bag and place the phone in the tin case before I bury it under all the art materials inside my satchel. I roll the rug back over the floorboard and smooth it flat with my hands, pressing down to make sure there's no tell-tale bump. Pulling myself to stand, I am still bent over when the door crashes open, hits my arse, and sends me flying across the room. My arms fly out to prevent a head-on collision with the bed frame, but I'm not quick enough to soften the momentum, and I smash my nose on the knuckle of my right hand. I hear the crunch and see the stars before the pitch-black blanket drops, knocking me out cold.

Shooting pain, no, that's not right, a throbbing, mind-numbing pain pulls me conscious, and I groan.

"Hey." Flecks of onyx catch the light in his dark chocolate eyes, his thick brow has a deep furrow but softens into a relief-filled smile, which seems to mirror my own, but for different reasons.

"Hey," I reply, only I don't recognise my own voice. It sounds like I'm congested with the mother of all colds. "Ow!" My fingertips barely touch the unfamiliar object in the middle of my face, when pain blinds me. I wince, screw my eyes shut, and feel the tears trickle down my cheeks.

"Oh, babe, you're a little swollen, and it probably feels much bigger than it is, but I don't think it's broken. There's a lot of blood, though." He holds up a fist full of tissues and his t-shirt looks like he's taken a direct hit from a sawed off shotgun, at close range. I shuffle up my bed and glance down at my own sweater, *his sweater*. I wonder if he gave me a quick cuddle while I was unconscious because my front is a mirror image of his T-shirt. "Here, eat these, they'll help." He hands me a thick gooey piece of chocolate brownie.

"Blood sugar for the shock?"

"Something like that." He grins, and I wince again when my nose makes an involuntary attempt to wrinkle with confusion. "Eat."

"This is a hash brownie, isn't it? Don't you think an aspirin might be better?" I try and school my face to not make any facial expressions. It feels like I've been hit with a shovel.

"No, I don't, now eat." He takes the brownie from my hand and places it against my lips; his expression shifts from stern to scorching. I'm not sure of the medicinal capabilities of the cake, but I'm suddenly unaware of any pain, and my temperature is rocketing. I open my mouth and hold his gaze the entire time, from the first bite to licking my lips when it's finished.

"Logan," I breathe out, and for the first time, his name sounds like a plea on my lips.

"Trouble." A deep rumble accompanies the gravelly tone, and I shiver as every hair on my body stands alert and alive.

"What you said the other day…" I swallow the lump in my throat and feel my skin colour from the heat crawling up my neck to my face.

"Yes." His smile spreads slowly across his handsome face, wide, warm, and wicked. I'm melting, and I have to fight the urge to squirm and squeeze my legs together.

"What did you mean by it?"

"Us, Tia…I meant *us*." He growls out that last word with

such heat, and it feels like a branding iron over my heart. "I'm done pussy-footing around. I saw the way he looked at you. This isn't a pissing contest because I have no intention of losing. He wants you, and I'm not going to let that happen."

"He doesn't want—" Logan interrupts with a hollow laugh.

"I never took you for a fool, Tia, so don't start now." He grits out the words as if he's angry. There's passion, desire, and hunger in his eyes, yet his jaw is clenched to the point of pulsing, and tension is rigid in his broad, strong shoulders. "I want you like I've never wanted anything or anyone in my life, and this little situation you've got yourself into has forced my hand, but in all honesty, I shouldn't have waited so damn long." He wipes the pad of his thumb across my bottom lip, and my tongue chases the movement. He lets out an audible moan and closes his eyes like he's in pain, no, more like agony. I reach for his other hand and entwine my fingers with his. I don't want him to be in any doubt. Even if I'm scared shitless of the actual act, I know in my heart I want him just as much as he wants me. *Ghost was so wrong; this is real.*

"Tia, you need to tell me what you want. And just in case you think I'll buy the 'friend-zone' bullshit, let me remind you, friends don't kiss like we did, and friends don't grind their hot, sweet pussy against hard cocks like you did."

"And friends' hearts don't beat like this." I pull our joined hands to my chest so he can feel the strength of my heartbeat. "Logan, I…I." Dropping my gaze, I struggle to find the words. He eases the path with his softly secure and coaxing voice.

"Hey, this is me, Tia, you can tell me anything, *anything.*" He urges with such tenderness and sincerity that I feel it in my bones. *It's terrifying.*

"Sex changes things," I utter. He tips my chin up with a light touch, his playful grin easing my trepidation.

"Not always, but in our case, I fucking hope so. And let me

clarify: Great sex changes things; phenomenal sex changes *everything*. We will be the latter, just in case you were wondering." He chuckles, a sexy sound filled with promise. "I want you, Tia, I want *all* of you."

"I don't know how often I can get back here, Logan," I deflect, but he's unfazed.

"You have a phone and a laptop, Tia, I take it you are still allowed to use those?"

"Yes, but he has cameras" My excuse sounds feeble, and I know in my heart it's futile resisting the inevitable. I want *all* of him, too.

"Not while we're chatting, he won't. I'm not going to lie and say I'm over the moon with this living arrangement now that *this* is happening, but twelve months is nothing when we have a whole lifetime together, understand?" The heat that dances between us is stifling, all consuming and like a lit-touched paper, the path of the fire is already racing through my veins.

"So this is happening?" I fail to bite back the smile splitting my face in two.

"Damn right it is." He smoothly manages to lift me into his lap and sits with his back against my headboard. My knees are tucked up in between his spread legs, one strong arm is holding me firm and sure against his bare chest. He kisses the top of my head, and I tilt back to look up into his eyes.

"Talk to me, Tia." He leans over to the bedside table and fishes out some cotton wool from a steaming bowl of water. He squeezes it dry and starts to clean the dried blood from my face. He pauses and offers a tender smile that makes my heart ache. He nods, and I draw in a deep breath. I want everything with him. I don't know if it's possible but this, at least, is something that I need to face, *for* me and *with* him, because more than anything I want there to be an *us*.

"I was a virgin when I went to prison." I suck in a sharp

breath as the pain of what comes next pierces my walls and reopens the gaping wound that nearly destroyed me. "I wasn't when I came out." My voice catches with the surge of bile making me retch. The blood inside me seems to drain from my body, and I can feel that I'm shutting down, just like it used to. I close my eyes and feel the numbing ice in my veins. It's how I survived.

"Stay with me angel, stay with me. I've got you."

CHAPTER TWENTY

Logan

I knew she had been raped, even reading between the lines of the prison doctor's report, I knew it was brutal, but listening to her break in my arms, retelling her own personal hell, has gutted me. If I didn't already know the bitches were dead, I'd conquer my own demons and dig the fuckers back up just to kill them all over again. Death was a blessing they didn't deserve. I just hope when I reach hell, I can track the fuckers down and spend eternity making sure they suffer, like she suffered.

Three inmates trapped her for more than two hours where they tore into every part of her body with anything they could find, and when they finished, they beat the living shit out of her and left her for dead and in intensive care for six weeks. She never told a soul who it was and even now she didn't see the point in telling me. They died in jail, and that was the end.

I know who they were, how they died, and I'd like to shake the hand of the cook that dished up that deadly meal. Freak incident, my arse. Tia was still laid up in the infirmary at the time. Nevertheless, once she recovered, the rumour mill churned out that she had something to do with the deaths, which pretty much secured her safety for the rest of her time inside.

She may have recovered physically, but her body has trembled the whole time she's been talking, and she's so pale her skin looks almost translucent.

"I'm damaged, Logan, not just emotionally, you know. I don't know if I can even relax enough to…and, and…" She's gasping for air, rushing her words in a confused and garbled race to purge herself of this nonsense. "I had to have a hysterectomy. I can never have kids, Logan. There was so much stitching with all the internal injuries. I just don't want to start something that has no future. You're worth more than that." She crumbles in my arms, guttural sobs wrack her body, and I pull her in tight enough so there is just no space between us, and I can feel her bones creak. I press my lips into her soft hair and hum a soothing sound, since she won't be able to hear me above the tears, and what I have to say, she needs to hear. Several heartbreaking minutes pass, and I don't think she's nearly done.

"Shh, baby, shh." This is killing me. "You have no idea, do you?" I have to stop her torturing herself anyway I can.

"Hmm?"

"And there was me thinking you were smart." I very gently kiss the tip of her nose when she tilts back to look up at me. "I said you have no idea what you mean to me, but I'm going to take the blame on that one, because I obviously haven't made myself clear." I hold her gaze, puffy red eyes filled with pain and lashes soaked with tears. She stares right into me. "I love you, Tia. It really is that simple. If you love someone, it's the beginning, it's the end, and it's the all the in-betweens."

"Logan, I—"

"Nothing, Tia, there is nothing you can say to make me feel any differently."

"I hope that's true." Her voice catches, and I get a nasty twist in my gut.

"I'm not *him,* Tia." I grit out the words since I know that troubled, tortured look in her eyes has little to do with what she's just told me, and everything to do with that arsehole. "I know I'm more than a little fucked up with my own 'issues', but I am not *him,* and I will never leave you. Couldn't even if my life depended on it." I offer a fiendish smile and a light laugh at my attempt at a poor joke. "In our case, Tia, the only person that can leave is *you.* So you see, angel, it's my heart on the line here, and it belongs to you." My declaration makes her suck in a sharp breath and causes the corner of her lips to quirk into a shy smile.

"I love you, Logan. I'm just...I mean, I have...there's things I—" She struggles to articulate as I interrupt.

"You love me?"

"Yes." She purses her lips like I've asked the dumbest question, and I fucking love that.

"Then that's all that matters, everything else is just *stuff.*" I shrug and watch her confusion settle in a cute little frown.

"Stuff?"

"Just stuff. We're what matters, you and me." I target my finger directly over her heart and then on mine for emphasis.

"Extremely complicated stuff, Logan." She wraps her tiny fingers around mine and grips.

"No doubt. It's nothing we can't handle together, but you have to tell me everything. You have to keep me in your loop, Tia, and you have to trust me." Pulling my finger from her grip, I use it to tip her chin high so I am looking into her emerald green eyes, glistening darkly and still holding way too many tears.

"I do trust you." She holds the gaze for only a second before blinking. I would think that suspicious, breaking the contact so quickly, but I know that's not her 'tell' when she lies. Besides, what she just shared is more than enough to know she does, still…

"Prove it."

"I don't understand."

"You can tell me what you're really up to another time," I state without judgment or hesitation.

Her eyes widen just a fraction when I hit the mark. She really should know me by now but that's not important. For me, that just falls under the same heading as 'stuff'. As long as she doesn't land that sexy arse back in jail, it's not relevant. No, what I want for us is the only thing that matters.

"Tell me what I can do to make it better." She chews on her lip, absorbing my question, a sadness clouds her sparkle, and that's exactly what I want to take away.

I want to see her shine.

Her words are softly spoken and break my fucking heart.

"I don't want to remember my first time."

"I know." My whispered understanding makes her close her eyes and swallow back a sob. Her body straightens in my arms like she is physically trying to pull herself together. I wrap my arms around her, hoping she can absorb as little or as much of my strength as she needs. It's hers for the taking.

"I hate that they took that from me, Logan. It wasn't supposed to be like that, I'd waited, you know, and…" She sucks in a steadying breath, her jaw twitching with checked and righteous rage. "I was raped. I lost my virginity to monsters. My nightmares are filled with images I can't escape. Every time I feel I maybe want something more, because there have been times when I so wanted us out of the friend zone." She wipes the back of her hand across her face, flips her palms to roughly dry her cheeks. When her eyes meet mine, I nod and repeat, even if it can only ever be a half-truth.

"I know."

"But I can't. The images and feelings flash as high definition as if they are real time, Logan, and I just shut down. It's the only way I know how to survive. I'm so sorry." She turns away and drops her head to her chest. Her shoulders shake, and I can feel the devastation tearing her apart all over again.

"Look at me, angel." I shift slightly to the side, keeping her tight in my hold but making it easier for her to face me.

Her bottom lip is shaking, and it takes everything I have not to crush that pain away with my own lips. I wish it would, if only I could bear her burden. *If only.*

"Don't ever apologise, Tia. You did nothing wrong, nothing. You survived, you did." My hand cups the side of her face. Slow, fat tears trickle over my fingers, and I have to fight to speak. This is killing me. "Angel, you're unbelievably strong. I know...I know fuck all about what you went through, how that changed you, or how the hell you managed to piece yourself together. Only you know that, but what I do know is that you want something I want to give you." My other hand joins to frame her fragile looking face. Her pain continues to dampen her skin as she takes in each and every word like it's gospel. "The choice that was taken from you when you were raped is now yours to make again. You died that day, literally, your medical records state that your heart stopped for twenty-two seconds. Like it or not, the moment your heart began to beat again, you became who you are today. I happen to love who you are right now. I can't imagine you being any more perfect, but my point is that what happened to you, happened to the old you. The new you is this incredible woman with courage, sass, and the sexiest arse this side of Nirvana. This might be our first time, but the choice is yours if you want it to be your first time, too."

"Logan," Her voice is whispered awe, and a tender smile splits her face. "I want you to be my first time."

"I know." I can't help mirror her smile and wonder if her

chest also feels fit to burst.

"I'm still scared." She might express the sentiment with her words, but her whole body has shed its tension, and I feel like I could leap tall buildings that I did that.

"I know."

"You're a bit of a know-it-all, aren't you?" She snickers, a laugh that's light and easy, and the first splash of colour pinkens her cheeks.

"Want to know what else I know?" I crane my neck so I can breathe the words low and deep in her ear.

"What?"

"I know how I'm going to make you come six ways to Sunday."

She shudders and swipes her tongue over her perfectly soft lips. Her pupils are so large, I could dive sideways into their depths, and her breathing is laboured as I hold myself milli-metres from her. Our lips are just about to touch; the charge of electricity firing between the non-existent gap when she pulls back, a deep frown darkens her features.

"I don't have much time. Atticus only gave me two hours." Her tone is seriously pissed, and that eases some of the anger that instantly fills me at the mere mention of his name.

"Then we better not waste another second." It's not ideal, and not what I want for our first time. Still, the courage needed to tell me her tale means this is more than the right time. I'm not being dramatic when I say that it could be the only time. *I know too well that tomorrow is a gift not a guarantee.*

If I don't take it, when she knows how I feel, what would she think? I can't take the risk she might take me wanting a better time as a rejection. *Like I could deny her anything*, especially something I've wanted since the day I caught her hiding in my basement. If we wait, who's to say it might just be another three years before she feels ready and needs me. Which wouldn't be a problem if she wasn't spending the next twelve months with her fucking 'first love'.

No pressure, but this has to be the performance of my lifetime. I need to make her mine in every possible way. At this moment, I believe my need matches hers, just for different reasons.

I lift her to my side, smoothly lying her on her back with me on my side facing her. I place my hand on her chest over my blood-spattered sweatshirt and smile when I feel the strength of her pounding heartbeat beneath my fingertips, *just like mine*.

"How's your nose?"

"My nose?"

"The swelling doesn't look so bad. Does it still hurt?" Her puzzled expression is adorable, and I chuckle when I clarify.

"Last thing on my mind, funnily enough, Logan. Unless you plan on head-butting me, I think it's fine."

"Not my idea of foreplay, angel." Even I can hear the lust coating my words with a deeper gravelly undertone.

"So what *is* your idea of foreplay?" She wriggles a little closer, and I have to say I love the way her body just moulds to mine. Even with the barrier of her clothing, I know she's a perfect fit. One eyebrow rises high, and the teasing lilt to her playful question does things to my cock that the most seasoned professional would struggle to achieve, and I should know.

"Well, for one, we need to lose these." I tug her sweater up her body, and she lifts herself to help. I quickly hook the t-shirt over my head and dump the bundle of clothes unceremoniously on the floor. Then I peel her leggings from her hips and pull them down her long legs; all the time, I keep my eyes fixed in her. I had removed her shoes when she very briefly passed out before, and once I take her socks off, I stand at the side of the bed and lose the rest of my clothes, and my boxers. I squeeze the ache in my balls, because as impatient as they may be, I'm in no rush. I want to savour every moment of this, even if, thanks to that motherfucker, Atticus, we are on the clock.

I climb back onto the bed, and kneel at her feet. I lift them and place them in my lap. She props herself on her elbows and is about to speak, when I shake my head to silence her.

"Trust me?"

"Yes." She nods, letting the word escape with a burst of her held breath. Her cheeks are flushed rosy red, and her eyes are a wild green colour I've only ever seen in my dreams. *She's absolutely perfect and all mine.*

"Good." I start to massage and stroke, varying the pressure and hitting the points that I know will make her moan with pleasure. I smile each time I hit the jackpot. Her eyes close, and she releases a heavenly sigh as my thumb works the tension from her muscles the length of her leg to her hip.

I lightly trace my fingers along the outline of her white cotton panties. Her skin prickles with bumps in the wake of my touch. I move to her tummy, sliding my hands to her hips. Gripping tight, I kiss a path from her belly button back to the top of her panties. Pulling them slowly down her legs I exhale a heavy hot breath, and she shudders. I peek briefly to see her curious expression levelled directly at me.

"Something wrong, angel?"

"God, no... Just..." She hesitates, and her tone is almost apologetic. "You're so tender. I wasn't expecting...I mean...after *that* kiss, I assumed—" I chuckle my interruption.

"Oh, trust me. I want to tear into you and bury myself so deep we'd need the emergency services to extract me, but that's not what you need, even if it is what I want." I drag my bottom lip between my teeth, savouring the very faint taste of her skin. Her tongue swipes her own lips before she breathlessly pleads.

"I want you, Logan, the real you. I don't want special treatment."

"Why the fuck not?" I reel back onto my haunches for just a moment and fix my most serious glare at her. My voice drops, and I crawl back up her body, placing my hands either side of her head, hovering so we are nose-to-nose, and I am staring into her soul when I speak. "You *are* special. You're amazing and incredible and mine. Why the fuck wouldn't I want to make you feel every inch as perfect as you are"

"I didn't mean… I just want you to be happy." Her words are whispered, and I can hear the uncertainty as her breath washes sweetly over my mouth. My lips brush against hers, smiling as they do.

"I couldn't be more happy, Tia, trust me. This is what I want." I pepper kisses over her mouth, top, bottom, and at the corners of her lips until her wide smile forces me to reluctantly stop. I pull back so I can see her face completely, her eyes more specifically. Those emerald pools I have very much lost myself in a million times and now is no different. "Angel, your first time should be everything you ever dreamed. I consider it my honour and duty to deliver that dream. But believe me, most of the time when I look at you, I want to feral fuck the shit out of you, so enjoy this, Tia. It may be the only time I *do* take it slow." She lets out a dirty laugh at my softly spoken, coarsely delivered honesty.

"Oh, all right then, please continue. I like your kisses." She grins sheepishly.

"Wait till you feel my tongue." I pitch myself so I am hovering above her, my legs either side of hers, and I stroke my tongue from her collarbone to just below her ear. I clamp my lips around the lobe and suck. When I release the soft flesh and she stretches her neck in open invitation, I strike. I move my lips to grasp the skin on her neck, my teeth graze, and I bite down, sucking and drawing her blood to the surface. He may have placed some sort of collar around her neck but I'm making my mark on her skin. She cries out and arches against me, like she feels the connection in her soul. *Fucking perfect.*

"Are you marking me?" Her words come out in a breathless pant, and I reply without hesitation or remorse.

"Yes."

"Good." She smiles so brightly, the light strikes me clean through my chest, knocking the wind from my lungs. My mouth crashes to hers, and I fear my earlier assurances of taking it slow may, in fact, be moot. Her hands fly to my hair, fingers spearing in and grabbing thick handfuls. She's matching my passion with a fire I fucking love. We writhe against each other, pawing, clawing to get closer when she takes me completely by surprise, rolling me onto my back and climbing on top. Her lithe legs are straddling my waist, while her hot little core grinds against my rock-solid erection. She breaks the kiss and sits up and unclasps her bra, which falls to the side as she cups her breasts, something my fingers are just twitching to do. She rocks back and forth, all the time staring into my eyes with a scorching heat I really wasn't expecting. *Not the first time.*

"Something wrong, Logan?" She repeats my earlier question with a wry smile that makes me release a deep throaty laugh.

"Not a damn thing, angel, not a damn thing. You got this." I wink, but she takes my statement as a question when she answers.

"No, not really, but being with you, I feel all kinds of confident and sexy. I know you'd never hurt me, and that is…empowering." She gives a slow sensual roll of her hips, and I nearly come right there. I let out a deep groan, filled with pent-up desire. She's killing me all over again, and this time I would be happy to meet my end just like this.

"God, you're amazing, but if you keep doing that, angel, I'm going to shoot my load before we really get started."

"I was thinking the same thing, that I could come so easily with you just staring at me like you are right now, all hot and hungry."

"Oh, yeah?" I buck my hips nudging my painful erection along her heat, and she moans before clamping her lips tight. Her thighs begin to tremble, and she rests both hands flat on my chest, easing herself up and back, greedily repeating the movement I just made on her.

"Maybe not just by looking at you, then." She drops her head and peeks her sparkling eyes up at me through long, thick lashes.

"Good, because my cock does not like the sound of that." I swallow thickly, my voice dry and rough with need.

"No? What does your cock like the sound of?" She squeals and bursts out in a fit of giggles when, in one swift move, I flip us both and pin her to the bed, my frame securing hers. Her arms are stretched above her head, and my cock lies heavily against the apex of her thighs.

"Think I mentioned being buried so deep inside, we need a team of miners to dig him out?" I dip my eyes to where we are so very nearly joined.

"Team of miners, hmm?"

"Figure of speech." I hold her gaze for long seconds as the playful banter sizzles under the incendiary glare firing between us. "Tia, just in case you thought this was a negotiation, I need to clarify: I don't play well with others, and I won't share."

"I've seen you play with others." Her tone holds no accusation, and in part, it's the truth. Only this is more than a little different, and she needs to know that.

"You've seen me with people I don't give a fuck about, not the same. Not even in the same ball park, Tia. Scratching an itch and making love with the woman I *love*? Not the same.

Understand?" My tone brooks no discussion, and I couldn't make myself clearer if I had the words tattooed across my chest.

"Yes." Her response is emphatic, and her tone is devoid of any hesitation; however, I feel the need to clarify even further.

"You don't have to worry the same about me, either, not now, not ever again. Something I'll explain, but not right now."

"Okay." She nods and grins, her eyes dipping down to where our bodies are pressed together, and a faint whimper escapes the back of her throat. Her cheeks are sporting the deepest red hue, the subtle undulations of her body and all her eager non-verbal cues are heard loud and clear. *She wants me as much as I want her.*

CHAPTER TWENTY-ONE

Tia

I drop my head onto the pillow with a frustrated sigh when he shifts again and moves his weighty cock farther away from where I really need it. I can't believe I'm so desperate for this. I was like a switch he flicked with his precious, insightful words and tender loving touch. Every time I feel I am drifting to a dark place, he seems to know, and with a carefully placed stroke of his fingers or brush of his lips, he tethers me to now. He's incredible and mine, and I want this more than my next breath.

My impatience seems to amuse him.

I can feel his smile against my inner thigh as he works his mouth from one side to the next, inching seriously close to my core. *Oh god I want him so badly.*

"Please, Logan, please." I don't know what I'm begging for exactly, because I'm not sure I can take much more of this erotic torture.

"I know." He lets out a breath that hits me, and I want to scream in frustration, but his tongue follows the cool air and silences me with unbelievable sensation shooting through my entire body.

Oh, my God!

His lips suck and pull at the tender flesh, and his tongue has this perfect pressure sweeping long strokes from just near my clit to my entrance. I know I'm dripping, and from the rumble of moans coming from deep in his chest, he loves every drop. He slips two fingers inside me, and my hips buck instantly. His other hand rests on my tummy, firmly holding me in place. There's no escaping this onslaught of unbelievable pleasure, but it's too much. My core contracts greedily, grabbing at his fingers, which he pumps into me as I am seized with a tidal wave of ecstasy. My climax hits, and he just keeps pushing me on and on, pressing my clit, rubbing a light circling motion with the pad of his thumb. Before my body has stopped pulsing, he continues to pump and rub, building the pressure once more. This time, I scream loudly, with shock and wonder. I'm seeing stars, bright flashes of light before my tightly shut lids.

"You're so beautiful, Tia." He draws his lips between his teeth; his chin is soaked, and he is smiling like the proverbial cat, with my cream all over his face.

He holds my heated stare, his chest is heaving and matching my own ragged breathing.

"I need to go and get a condom." I grab his hand as he is about to lift himself from the bed.

"You don't, I can't get pregnant remember?"

"I know, but it's not just about that, is it?" He tilts his head with the unspoken list of other possibilities.

"Logan, I know you haven't been fucking the hookers, so unless there is someone else—" I start to explain the non-issue here, but he interrupts me.

"How do you know that?"

"Do you want to have this conversation now, because—" Once more he interrupts, shaking his head and this crazy interlude from his thoughts.

"Fuck, no, just…never mind." His eyes settle on mine with a glare so hungry it makes my tummy flutter. "So no condom. You're sure?"

"Absolutely." My enthusiastic nod causes his killer smile to burst onto his face.

"You got it." His voice drops to a toe-curling deep and husky tone. He smoothly pushes my legs wide, and I love the feel of his strong hands pressing my thighs to the point of a painful stretch. He positions the head of his enormous cock against my slick folds and rubs, spreading my wetness along his shaft. My eyes must be wide with worry, but I'd take worry about his mammoth cock fitting over the flashbacks any day.

"Tia, I've tried to make this easy, making you come like that, but this might still hurt a little. We'll take it slow." His voice sounds ragged, and I can see tiny droplets of sweat beaded at his temples. The softness in his eyes and the concern in his voice has me flashing him an encouraging and tender smile. However, the lump in my throat prevents me from actually speaking. "Okay, angel?" I nod. He keeps his eyes on mine the entire time as he pushes slowly into me. My body contracts at the intrusion, but it's not so bad. He pushes farther, and the feeling of fullness and stretching is wonderful, no pain, *no comparison*. He groans when he changes the angle and rolls his hips. Oh, good God, that feels amazing.

"Oh, ah, yes, Logan!" I cry out. His slow, steady thrusts drive into me, yet I can feel his reticence, his hesitation, and his loving intentions. It's absolute heaven, and I want more. "Do you think you could go deeper?" I want every bit of him. He laughs and moans with desire.

"Yes, Tia, I can definitely do that." Groaning a guttural sound, he plunges deep.

"Ahh, fuck!" I yell, and he freezes. "No, ahh, that was meant in a good way. Don't stop, please, please, don't stop."

"You sure Tia? You're really fucking tight. I don't want to hurt you."

"Only holding back would hurt me Logan. I need this; I need *you*." He briefly closes his eyes in understanding, and when he opens them, I know I'm going to get exactly what I want. *Yes*.

He pulls back and plunges again, deep, hard, and it's utterly fantastic. He thrusts and pumps into me, shaking my body, pulling me, riding me with a wildness I match with my own body. My fingers move from tugging his silky hair to clawing at the taut muscles on his back as they flex with every pound into me. I wrap my legs around his waist, and he grabs my arse cheeks and pulls me tighter against him, closer against each thrust. The exquisite deep sensation I feel, as his cock rubs and touches sensitive tissue deep inside, takes my breath away. My body takes over and starts the unstoppable climb to ecstasy. I feel Logan shift, and he starts to pump faster into me, chasing his own release.

"Tia, come with me!" The urgency in his voice has my body spiralling.

"Yes, yes, Logan. Ahhhh!" I scream. Every nerve ending seems to ignite and explode, all the air gets sucked from my lungs, and muscles I didn't know I had contract and pulse, riding this tsunami of a climax. Logan keeps us locked in an embrace that holds me floating on an orgasm high that is never going to end. *Bliss*.

"Fuck!" His hips jerk with an involuntary spasm when I finally draw a breath and regain some of my senses. His hot heavy body covers mine, and we lie, two sweaty bodies, entwined and exhausted.

"Logan." I stroke patterns on his bare chest, my finger tracing the spattering of dark hair, soft and sexy.

"Hmm?"

"Thank you." His eyes snap to mine when I tilt up to look at him. The frown that darkens his face I was expecting, but I still needed to say it.

"You know, 'thank yous' are right up there with apologies, totally unnecessary and kinda piss me off. Like I was doing some sort of favour. You're not a charity case, Tia; I'm the fucking lucky one." Irritation is thick with the clipped words and snappy tone.

"You know I didn't mean it like that. It just...that was amazing, and—" I exhale softly, not finishing what I was about to say because I'm a little lost for words. I feel so damn good. He sighs.

"I know, angel."

"That was a perfect 'first' time Logan."

"It was, wasn't it?" He grins when I look up. I snort a laugh.

"God, could you be any more arrogant?"

"Easily." He rolls half his heavy body back onto mine, his cockiness giving way to heartfelt sincerity. "I'm glad, Tia. That's all I wanted." His kisses the top of my head, and I swear I couldn't feel more cherished, and with his next question I couldn't feel more wanted. "Now, how about round two?"

"Round two?" I blurt out an incredulous laugh. "I can't feel my legs, Logan, how am I supposed to walk?"

"I'd rather you didn't, then I could keep you here." His playfulness has a sombre undertone.

"And that would have me visiting one of Her Majesty's hotels before nightfall." I point out the stark reality of my house arrest.

"Fuck, I hate this Tia. I hope you know what you're doing?"

"I do. I didn't *take* the money, Logan."

"I know, but it's still missing, and for some reason, you're playing along." I push up at this statement, shock almost making my jaw hit the floor.

"How did you know?"

"Please, Tia, don't insult me. Just tell me." He rolls his eyes, and I almost join him. Ghost did say he was *that* good. She also said I was a dumb bitch, which I have no intention of proving for the second time today.

"I can't. I mean, I will…one day," I add as a sop that I hope will do for now.

"Let's just hope it's not from across the table in a visitation room."

"Now who's being insulting?" I cross my arms in a defensive move, which only makes his eyes widen at the sudden plumpness of my breasts. I huff when he shrugs lightly, then he makes my heart hurt.

"I can't lose you, Tia." His words hit with a force that leaves me winded. The pain swirls deep in his dark chocolate eyes, and I hate that I can't give him the comfort he needs. *Not yet.*

"You won't."

"And Atticus?" The name cools the room, as if Cass himself has just walked through the door and brought the north wind with him.

"What about him?"

"You're playing with fire, Tia. He's not the boy you grew up with." I swing my legs over the edge of the bed and stand abruptly. I shiver with the loss of our joined body heat, as my crossed arms do little to abate the chill.

"I'm well aware of that, Logan," I bite since his tone is tinged with condescension, which has my hackles rising.

"I don't like it." His jaw is clenched so tight his lips barely move when he speaks.

"And I'm over the fucking moon?" I snap. "It's a necessary evil." I let out a heavy breath and soften my tone. "I have no intention of going back to jail, Logan, and I'd rather not spend what precious minutes I have here, talking about *him*."

"Well, we agree on something, at least." He grabs my hand

and roughly pulls me back to the bed. Rolling our bodies until he is positioned perfectly on top, his erection steely-hard and in the perfect place.

"What are you doing?" My legs twitch to make him more comfortable, but I'm not sure we should start something now.

"You said we don't have much time, so round two is going to be fast feral fucking." He states this as a matter of fact, which makes my whole body prickle with desire.

"Oh, goody."

I'm waiting by Logan's desk, looking at the numerous screens with no particular focus. We held each other for as long as possible, but the minutes have caught up with me, and by the huffing and puffing coming from Logan, he's just as pleased about my imminent departure as I am. Not.

"Put these in your room and anywhere you spend any time." He places several small pinhole spy cameras into my open palm.

"These are tiny." I pick one up between my thumb and fore-finger. It's about the size of a ten pence.

"That's the idea. He might notice a huge fucking camera or the sudden appearance of a sculpture on his bookshelf. These can be fitted to any picture frame, smoke detector, or light fit-ting and are pretty hard to spot unless you know where to look. Which he might, since he thinks you've stolen three hundred million, so be smart." He taps his temple. The possible insult, however, is lost at the figure he's just thrown out there. *What the hell?*

"Three hundred!? It's only a hundred, Logan." As if that makes it better. It's still a stupid amount of money.

"No, Tia, three hundred million has gone from their balance sheet." I try to swallow the dry lump choking my throat. My voice is a husky whisper when I co manage to speak.

"Atticus only said a hundred, do you think he knows about

the rest?"

"I don't know. Is he a dumbass?" Logan quips, but I'm in too much shock to laugh.

"How did you—?" He cuts me off with his response.

"I'll tell you one day." He raises a challenging brow, repeating my equally frustrating response to him earlier, and I have to concede.

"Touché! Well-played Logan."

"This isn't a game, damn it, Tia!" he roars. Stepping flush against me, his strong hands grip the tops of my arms, holding me fast and rendering me speechless. His anger rages behind his wild eyes until he shakes some sense back into himself and softens his grip. "Tia, I love you. I hate that I can't protect you because I can't fucking go outside, but I will die trying to keep you safe in any other way I can." I reach to touch his face, and the pain in his tortured expression almost breaks my heart. He leans into my cupped palm, and I try and ease his mind as best I can.

"This has never been a game. This is my life, Logan, and what you've just said is exactly the same for me. It's about protection. If I end up in jail, it will be on my own. I won't take you with me."

"That's not going to happen," he growls. His face is stern, and the words sound as deadly as they are serious. He pulls me into a breath restricting bear hug, and I gasp for air when he releases me.

"Agreed," I respond with a firm nod. He holds me rigid until he has taken all the time he needs to explore every part of me with his searching eyes.

"When can you come back?" he finally asks when we both hear the horn of the car outside.

"I don't know." I hold his face in my palms, rising up onto my toes to kiss the tight line of his lips. "I love you, and you have to trust me right back, Logan, or this won't work."

"I know. I don't have to like it, though." He leads me from the room and silently down the stairs. I turn when we reach the bottom.

"Take care, Logan."

"Same goes for you, angel." His lips soften this time, and I don't know how I pull away when his strong arms hold me just a little too tight. He releases the embrace, and I leave him standing at his safe distance from the front door. When I click it shut, my heart shatters at the hollow sound of his pain when he cries out to the empty house.

"Fuck!"

CHAPTER TWENTY-TWO

Tia

I barely look at Cass when I get in the car. I feel so fucking awful, leaving Logan like that, after *that*. I couldn't hate Cass more right now, and I think the best thing is to just keep my distance. I feel utterly spent, physically exhausted, and emotionally drained. I twist in my seat, and I have my back to him. I rest my weary head on the window only to jump back when it starts to automatically open.

"You smell like sex," Cass states when I turn to face him for an explanation. His nose is wrinkled with distaste, but his eyes flash with something else, not anger or disgust, which his tone might suggest.

He looks hurt.

My tummy tightens with knots, and I just don't know what to say. I know this is none of his business, and, yes, I do want to hurt him in some ways, but not like this. This wasn't the plan. I just wanted to stop my body making stupid choices, and the way it reacts around him, it was inevitable.

So why do I actually feel sick that it might have worked?

The wind whips through the car with a burst of fresh spring

air that lifts my hair and swirls it around, covering my face, and thankfully filling the car with enough noise to drown out the awkward silence until we reach his place.

The short journey in the lift to Cass's apartment is excruciating. The impassive tone of his accusation in the car is long gone, and all I feel is pain radiating off him in waves, from his slumped shoulders to the drawn tension in his face when he does bother to lift his head. We reach the penthouse level, and he leaves me standing in the lift. I watch him disappear along the corridor and into his office. I drop my head back against the wall, and sighing, I slide down to the floor. Pulling my legs up, I huddle in and hold that position, trying to draw some comfort from within.

What the fuck am I doing? I should be on cloud fucking nine after that time with Logan, and yet I can't get past that look of *loss* in Cass's eyes.

Why should he care now, when he didn't care when it mattered, when I needed him?

The doors close, and that's when I realise I'm stuck. *Shit.*

I scrabble through my bag for my phone but there's no signal. Centre of the capital city and I have no frickin' signal. I look for the panel with the emergency phone but there isn't one. There's a screen with fingerprint activation, which is fucking stupid. There has to be a way to call for help without needing a fucking fingerprint. I start to shout, but after several frustrating minutes, I give up and slide back to the floor.

My arse is so numb, I've pretty much lost all feeling from below the waist. Whatever misplaced guilt I may have felt evaporated after the first hour of boredom and realising that Cass either hadn't checked on me or more likely didn't give a shit where I was. If maintenance finds me, it will be a blessing because right now if it's Cass, well, he better be sporting some serious sort of protective clothing because it's more than harsh language I want to throw his way.

I've run out of insults to hurl as over the past few hours I've been through the alphabet several times and may have made up a few new ones, and I really need to pee. The doors glide open, and I am so grateful I forget every angry threat, every foul-mouthed tirade, everything actually, except my bladder. I push past a confused-looking Cass and dart to the bathroom.

Cass is in the kitchen, and my stomach rumbles so loudly, it announces my presence before I turn the corner.

"What were you doing in the lift?" He doesn't look up from the black coffee he's nursing between his fingers.

"Oh, just chilling," I retort without humour. He frowns, but just shrugs, and I can feel my blood boil.

"I could've died in there, Cass, and all you can do is shrug?" I snap, my voice pitched with indignation.

"A little dramatic, don't you think? It's not like I knew you were joking, Tia. For all I know, you could've just wanted to sit in a lift." He laughs at first, but his features darken when he adds, "I don't *know* you at all, remember?"

"What are you, twelve? I'm serious; I couldn't get out." He stands abruptly, the kitchen stool teetering on its rim before settling back with a clank of stainless steel on marble.

"Yes, you could." He stomps past me, grabbing my wrist and tugging me along behind him. I have to run to keep up with his normal stride. He swipes his finger to open the door and stares openly at the same screen I'm staring at as if it now magically holds all the answers.

It's still the same screen that says 'fingerprint here'.

"And?"

"What do you mean, and? All you had to do was swipe your finger. You may have thought you were stuck, but you weren't.

Your fingerprint is in the system for all the exits of the apartment and the building. That's just standard safety, Tia, and even if it wasn't, all you had to do was press your finger to access the concierge to get you out." His elevated tone is exasperated and full of disbelief. I snap my jaw shut and have the grace to look a little sheepish when he takes my finger and presses it on the screen, which then lights up with an array of options, open doors being the first.

"Oh, I didn't realise."

"Clearly had other things on your mind." He glares at me, a look that is more searching than hurt, and I have to wonder if he is already over me having sex with Logan.

I go to step past him and his arm slams across the doorway, halting my escape. I look up his towering frame, deep blue eyes smouldering down at me, and I catch my breath. I am about to challenge that assumption when he growls out, "It should've been *me.*" The deep timbre of his voice just adds to the raw urgency and desperation in the words. I start to shake my head when he pushes me back into the lift, slamming my back against the wall. His lips crash to mine, and I let it happen.

I don't just let it, I crave it, every touch filled with primal need matches something deep inside me, and as much as I know it's wrong, he's wrong, I can't fight the passion that lights my soul when he devours me like he is right now. His fingers fist my hair, gripping and pulling to the point of pain. I cry out into his mouth, and he just pushes deeper. His tongue dives and takes the very breath from my lungs. His body is so hard against mine, I can feel every cut muscle pressing and grinding against me. I can feel him everywhere.

My heart is racing and aching, and before I fall any farther, I push him away. Despite his obvious strength, he moves with the lightest of my touches, and only his forehead is still connected, leaning heavily against mine as he draws in ragged breaths, which match my own. *Fuck!*

If I could speak, I'm not sure what I would say, but I can see the torment in his eyes, and I know for a fact that they also mirror my own. He pulls back only to brush my now swollen lip with his thumb.

"It should've been me," he whispers, turns, and walks away. The sliding lift doors closing off his retreating image before I realise it, he's gone, and I'm once more alone in the damn lift.

The next day it is like that kiss never happened. I didn't sleep at all, and the more I thought about it through the night, the angrier I got. By the time the first rays of sunlight creep into my room, I am up and storming my way to Cass's bedroom. I'm just about to bang the shit out of the door, when I notice a thin sliver of light from beneath his office door. *Jeeze, does he never sleep?* I walk the remainder of the long corridor and strike three hard bangs with my fist, followed by another three until the door flies open. A soft glow illuminates him from the side and casts a darkly sinister shadow over his face. His eyes look inky black and hollow. I take a step back when he looms forward and into the full light of the corridor.

He's silent, and the way he is staring right through me almost makes me forget what the hell I wanted to say. Almost.

"You've got some fucking nerve saying those things and kissing me like that." I straighten my back and try to make the most of my five-foot frame. It's laughable that I even try when he looks as intimidating as he does, but I know power doesn't come from size, it comes from intent, and in that I'm an unquantifiable entity.

"You didn't like the kiss?" He stretches his arms up and leans on the doorframe, his t-shirt rising high and his boxers hanging low. The distraction is not what I need, and the effort is considerable, when all my eyes want to do is drink in that blond happy trail. I suppress a sigh and power through.

"Not the fucking point, Cass." I cross my arms when I feel my nipples tighten.

"So you did like the kiss?" He notices. Of course he notices.

"You're right." I'm irritated my body is the equivalent of a sex-starved runaway train, but I haven't come to play.

"About the kiss? So you did enjoy the kiss." His smug arrogance is momentary.

"It should've been you, but it wasn't, and you know why?" His eyes narrow, and I can see the emotions dance behind his eyes when my voice catches. I dig my fingernails hard into my palm to give me something to focus on. I need to get this out there. This isn't a game for me, and he has never played fair. Now it's my turn.

"Because you left me to rot in prison where my first time was at the hands of three mental lesbians with a penchant for ramming objects into tiny holes. So I happen to agree with you... it should've been you, but it wasn't, and now I'm with someone who won't ever let me down, won't ever lie to me, and won't ever hurt me like you did. So back the fuck off with whatever you *think* we have." I poke my finger hard against his pec and jab to make my next point. "Because, trust me, Cass, it's more likely that I *have* stolen your money than I am to have feelings for you. And as I've said before, I don't have your fucking money." I'm impressed I kept my tone level when I finish my speech. My heart feels like it's trying to escape through my ribcage, I drop my hand, and they would both be trembling if they weren't now in tight fists.

"I didn't know." He pushes out the words through his clenched jaw, and I snap back my reply with venom.

"What, you didn't get the t-shirt?"

"Tia, please...I didn't know." He reaches for me but pulls back before he makes contact. He looks unsure, and the pleading tone in his softly spoken words starts to weaken what strength I have.

"I was raped Cass, tortured for hours, beaten to a pulp and left to die. I can never have children because of what they did and the fact you didn't know any of that is fucking irrelevant. Because you *did* know I was in jail, and you *did* know I was innocent?"

"I didn't know the truth Tia. I'm sorry, I'm so fucking sorry." He holds my shoulders as the only option in my rigid frame, but from the pain in his eyes it looks like he couldn't *not* touch me. His fingers press hard enough to bruise.

"Yeah, Cass, me too." I turn and walk away, softly repeating the redundant sentiment. How can my heart thump so hard and break at the same time? I didn't think there was anything left to break.

The next day is the same, like the kiss never happened, but Cass's cocky, confident air is more subdued, and actually, that makes this harder rather than easier. It was easier when I knew he didn't care. It was easier to make myself numb, to focus and finish what I'd started.

I decide to retreat mostly to my room, keep my distance, and do my time. It's not the first time I've had to do this, but it will be the last.

The week passes, and we seem to move like ghosts, silent and hollow. I avoid him, and he avoids me. There are moments of life when he brushes past me or says something that makes my heart ache from a memory we shared, but I push it aside. I talk to Logan every night and that helps. I have asked if I can visit again, but Cass isn't going to let that happen any time soon. I think my revelation shook him, but it hasn't softened his demeanour, and I am going to need to try something else if I am going to get my way. I also need access to his office, which despite lifting his fingerprint, is going to be impossible if he doesn't leave the apartment sometime soon.

I decide to break the silence over late morning coffee.

"Don't you ever need to go in to work?"

"I am working here, location is irrelevant." He barely looks up from his laptop.

"Really? Because I thought a big CEO would have to show his face at some point." I keep my tone casual but he raises a suspicious brow all the same.

"I would normally spend more time in the main offices, only I have this special 'project' that needs my undivided attention." He fixes me briefly with his icy blues.

"Cute," I flash a tight smile, and instead of falling silent, he continues to talk.

"Besides, Mother has the day-to-day covered."

"Wow, she's really that involved. I always thought it was just an on-paper title." I knew she took over when Cass's father died. It was very controversial, and Cass's grandfather, Oskar, hated the idea. He tried to fight it, but he lost the backing of the board. It was a long time ago, but I do remember Oskar sharing the details, and we both shared our hatred of Inga, Cass's mother.

"Hmm, she had you fooled, too, did she?" Cass quips.

"No, she underestimated me, but I was never fooled."

"Good, she won't always be in charge. She has always held the power, though, even if I didn't appreciate how much," he says wistfully, and the tone alone piques my interest. "Still, things change."

"Vague much?" I've done my research. If Oskar taught me anything, it's to always check your sources. *Information is the lock, and truth is the key; only with both do you have real power.*

"I could say the same," he counters, and I shrug lightly.

"Ah, but I'm an open book, Cass, you know all there is to know." I sweep my hands along the smooth granite countertop, leaving them wide and open. It is a gesture of a truce rather than of a complete surrender.

"I thought so. Even when you said I didn't, I didn't believe you, but now, I'm not so sure. I didn't know about—" His voice catches, and he doesn't need to say another word. I can see the tortured pain etched in his face. I know it's low, but I strike when I think I have the best chance to get what I want, and with pain and regret swirling like a storm in his eyes, I happen to think I stand a very good chance.

"I want to visit Logan, for a whole day and night."

"No." His response is instant. I didn't even finish the last word.

Why the hell I thought I could manipulate him, when I never could in the past, is beyond me. Still, desperate times…

If I'm to get to see Logan and gain Cass's trust enough for him to leave me in his apartment alone, I need to give him something he wants.

"Please, Cass, please, I'm begging." The words slip from my mouth in a breathy plea.

"Hmm, if only," he scoffs and, just when I think he's going to refuse, he stops and stares at me. I can almost see the wheels turning. My tummy drops when his lips curl in a wolfish smile. "I'll let you visit, but I want something in return."

"I don't have your—"

He interrupts, and I'm shocked it's not for his standard request of the return of his stolen money. "I want to take you home next weekend," he declares.

I hate that my heart jolts at the same time my stomach clenches.

"Home?"

"Tartarus Hall. I want to spend the weekend with you there, just you and me. I want to leave all this behind and—"

I interrupt, shaking my head emphatically. "You know that's

not possible, Cass." I soften the words, because he sounds almost desperate for this break from reality, because that's what he's suggesting. A weekend where we could step back in time or maybe not step back at all, but where it's just me and him. He's delusional, because that suggestion is simply a fantasy too far.

"Just one weekend, and you can have your visit. I'll take you over tomorrow and pick you up the following night. I want to prove to you I'm not the devil in this scenario, Tia, and I can only do that if we go back to where it all started."

"Oh really, Atticus, are you sure about that? Because I believe I made my deal with the devil a long time ago, and his eyes look an awful lot like yours." I hold his unwavering gaze. "You have your deal, but I'm not sure what going back will prove."

"It will prove you belong to me."

CHAPTER TWENTY-THREE

Atticus

She spins on her heel and disappears back to her room. It takes all my strength not to storm after her and…and what? Hold her? Shake her? Make her mine again, when I know full well I don't deserve her? I thrust my hand across the surface of the kitchen counter sending my plate and coffee cup careening across the room, splintering into a mess of broken pieces when it crashes to the floor. It's a mess; everything's a mess.

My shoes crush the pieces further when I walk from the room. I have to get out of here. I need to clear my head. The fury, confusion, and unbearable pain are tearing me up, and I can't see past Tia in prison, *innocent*.

I grab my jacket and keys and head toward the lift. My finger pauses for a moment over the button, and I give a cautious glance over my shoulder toward Tia's room. Some playlist 'to hang yourself by' is now blaring, and it actually make me smile. She always loved to lose herself to some seriously depressing shit, but I know it always seemed to help, in some sort of reverse psychological way. I press my fingerprint over the call button and the doors instantly glide open. I only need an hour, maybe two.

I'm about to step into the underground garage but change my mind. I need fresh air, not the A/C, and this time of day, the traffic will be at a standstill. I doubt I'd get above 8 klicks per hour, and I can walk quicker than that. The air is sticky warm and has a density to it that you only get in an overpopulated city filled with fumes, smells, and a million sweaty bodies just existing. I've adapted to city life, but my heart will always be in the country, specifically Tartarus Hall. If I ever manage to get the shit sorted with Kraus Corp, I can quit the city for good. It's only part of my plan, but it's a start, as is getting Tia back there, first for a weekend and then for good.

I draw in a deep breath once I reach the brow of the Blackfriars Bridge. The light breeze carries enough freshness from the river that I don't feel the need to cough my lungs up. I'm exaggerating, the city isn't that bad. The oppressive heat of the long summer days makes it worse, that and the weight of my mistakes. I drop my head, as a heavy cloud of regret descends, and I recall with high definition the conversation that changed my life.

"She did what?" I drop the pen in my hand. My mother has brought some documents for me to sign. She rarely visits me, even when she is in the States. She prefers to keep her distance, especially since I was arrested. I got caught with Misty's brother in his car running a stop sign. That wasn't such a big deal, but the illegal firearms and half a kilo of cocaine he had stashed in the trunk were. It's still up in the air whether I'm going to get charged at all. I didn't know about his haul. Still, anyone with a brain cell would say the same.

My uncle hired the best lawyer, but since I have dual citizenship and two passports, the courts thought it was best that they keep them. The whole thing is a fucking nightmare, dragging out and making it almost impossible to get home, almost. Once Tia's exams are finished, I will tell her everything, but she needs to focus, and usually, I like being a distraction, but not like this. I stare at my mother's twisted expression. I think she's trying to look sad. If her face wasn't so frozen, she might pull off mild concern, but since her lips have a cruel smirk, I know she's relishing this moment.

"She stole your great-grandmother's diamond bracelet and had the audacity to claim Oskar had given it to her. Even said he had it written specifically in his Will." She tuts at the silly notion, derision coating each work like treacle.

"He may have given it to her, Mother. He was very fond of her. I believe he loved her like one of his own, so it's not beyond the realm of possibility that this is just a misunderstanding." I keep my tone level, even if I can feel the rage bubbling in my gut. Sometimes it feels as if my mother has hated Tia long before she was even born. It's wholly disproportionate and pisses me off at every turn.

"Your signature is on the Will, Atticus. Did it have her name anywhere?" She tips her head and gives a sly, knowing smile. My jaw twitches with tension, and my fingers slowly curl into tight fists. Her eyes dip and widen with worry.

"No, no it didn't. This is a mistake. She wouldn't do this. I know her." The edge in my voice makes her step back and then, with obvious effort, she walks toward me and places her trembling hand on my shoulder.

"Darling, she's not the same. Money changes people. Atticus, my love, I'm so sorry." Her voice is saccharin sweet and just as sickly.

"Please mother, don't feign compassion. Tia is nothing like you. It's one of the reasons I love her." I stand and her hand falls from my shoulder. She steps back as I brush past. I need some distance. Taking a bottle of water from the cooler, I take a long pull before I fix her with my own icy glare. "We both know money is the only thing that holds your interest. Cruelty runs through your veins, and I have no idea what makes that stone heart of yours beat, but it isn't fucking love."

"This family. This family is what keeps my heart beating, and I will do whatever it takes to protect what's mine." Her words are punctuated by her palm hitting the hollow shell of her chest for emphasis.

"Whatever, hmm?" I raise my own knowing brow, but it does nothing to settle the turmoil churning up my insides.

"You know what I mean." She sniffs dismissively.

"I wish I didn't." I watch her lips pull into an impassive tight line. "She didn't take the bracelet, Mother. I need to see her. I have to sort this out."

"And how are you going to do that, my darling? You have no passport, and until the investigation is quashed, you can't leave the country." She shakes her head lightly but wisely keeps her distance because her words aren't what I want to hear right now.

"I did before. I'll be careful."

"You were reckless, and if you are caught, you'll be in jail too. No, I won't allow it. You're uncle will sort the misunderstanding, but it will take time."

I curse, dragging a fretful hand through my hair as I feel the helplessness of my position begin to grip every part of me. My chest feels tight, blood rushes in my ears, and I swear my vision is tinged with a red mist.

"Tia doesn't have time. She needs me."

"Does she?"

"What's that supposed to mean?"

"She...look, it's not important. Trust me, Atticus, you can't help her." My mother turns away, only to spin back when I yell.

"Tell me!"

"Fine, look…" She's flustered, reaching into her bag and fishing around for something. She pulls a slim envelope and cautiously hands it to me, then steps back and around the other side of the table as if she needs a physical barrier. I feel a chill sweep my skin, and I have to shake the desire to rip more than the envelope to pieces. I open it and pull the papers free. My mother's toxic words choke the air. "I was concerned about her influence over your grandfather, and I hired a private investigator to follow her. It took some time, but he took these pictures and there are transcripts of some of her conversations."

There are several photographs of Tia and a boy, a classmate, judging by the location. All are in and around her school, outside her art block and one outside the local pub. She told me she didn't have friends, not real friends and certainly not anyone close. This guy is more than close.

He has his arm around her waist and shoulder in several of the pictures, and the way she's looking into his eyes is like a sucker punch to my chest. I've seen that look; I live for that look. I draw in a shaking breath, and my fingers are actually trembling when I slip the last photograph to the top. This one damn near tears my heart right out. He has her face cupped, lips smashed together.

"I want the actual recordings. I want to hear them myself." I force the words through a jaw so tightly clamped, I feel like my teeth are about to crack. My eyes quickly scan the pages, the words are blurring with betrayal.

"I will see if I still have them, but the point is she was cheating on you with this local boy and plotting to steal from us. What more evidence do you need?" She's quick to dismiss my request with her own forgone conclusion.

"I need to see to the girl I've loved for most of my life, that's what I need!" I yell, and she jumps only to steady her self when my voice waivers.

"*Atticus, you have your own problems to deal with: the investigation and your engagement. Let me handle this little mess.*" *She softens her voice and steps toward me like you would a dangerous animal, a wounded dangerous animal.*

"*I told you there isn't going to be an engagement.*" *I drop the papers and photographs on the table, my hands braced on the table for support. My head hangs over the array of images and words that are destroying me.*

"*That was before Tia broke your heart and stole from your family. Do you really want to throw everything away now?*"

"*I…I don't believe any of this. I need to see her.*" *I shake my head and let the tears blurring my vision fall.*

I never saw her. I couldn't leave the country, and in all honesty, after looking at those pictures a million times, reading the transcripts, I was so damn angry I couldn't see past the betrayal. My pride was battered, and my heart was fucking broken.

I wrote to her, and she never replied, which I took it as a tacit admission of her guilt. Why else wouldn't she answer my questions? Why didn't she call? She fucking owed me an explanation, and I got nothing. I loved her so much, and hated her so much more. Still, when the trial came, I didn't want her to go to prison. I offered a statement in her defence. It didn't help. I had done all I could, and then I walked away.

Two years ago, I found out the *truth*. It was too late, far too fucking late. She was already out on parole, gone off the grid. Then, out of the blue, she shows up on the Kruse payroll, just as millions of pounds disappears. I don't believe in coincidences, and I do believe in motive. And the only thing I could see in that police cell was my second chance. Besides, what's another hundred million?

I rest my palms on the handrail of the bridge and watch a glass top river cruiser full of tourists chug up the river and vanish beneath me and out toward the eastern docks and the Millennium Dome and Thames barrier. The muffled sound of the recorded commentary mingles with the constant mid level white noise of passing traffic and pedestrians. I try to clear my head of all the possibilities and focus on one thing at a time. My only problem is I can't focus on anything other than her and that is a big fucking problem. I know if I was her, the first chance I got I would be hell bent on revenge, but she was never like me, *was* being the operative word. I glance at my watch, and although it's only been maybe fifteen minutes, I push off the railing and start to walk back to the apartment. It was stupid to leave her alone. I should've known better; I do know better. I pick up my pace to a light jog, my long strides eating up the distance until I am taking some calming breaths in the lift.

The doors open, and I release my held breath and actually chuckle from relief. The music is still blaring and looking at the mess still on the kitchen floor I doubt Tia even knew I'd left.

I walk to my office door and quickly check the entry system for any breach and relax a little more when my suspicions are quashed at no sign of forced entry.

I turn when the music gets louder. Tia's head pokes around the open crack of the door.

"What would you like for dinner?" I ask, closing my office door behind me and searching her face for any sign of…what? Guilt? I almost laugh out loud. There's only one person who should be wearing that cap, and she isn't standing before me. Tia gives a noncommittal shrug and is about to shut the door.

"Homemade pizza?" I offer and watch her freeze. The memory hits just as hard as I hoped. Her knuckles whiten on the edge of the door, and she briefly closes her eyes. When she looks back at me, a tentative smile ghosts her perfect lips, and I have to fight my own smile to avoid scaring her away. Yes!

"I'd really like that, Cass." Her soft voice is like a balm and a shot of pure electricity at the same time. My heart jolts. She steps into the corridor, glancing over her shoulder before padding silently toward the kitchen. *We always made pizza together. Always.*

CHAPTER TWENTY-FOUR

Tia

"L ogan!" I call out as I slam the front door and walk to the bottom of the sweeping staircase. I tried to call his cell phone and the landline, but he wasn't picking up, and I have a riot of nervous knots in my tummy that something might be wrong. I don't know why. It's not like he always picks up when I call. It's just things are shifting and changing so fast, I can't help the rising levels of anxiety. I fucking hate anxiety. I take one step on the first rung and scream with shock when I find myself lifted high into the air. Logan spins me mid-air and catches my hips, only to drop me over his shoulder with a groan-inducing thud. He slaps his large hand on my arse and heads off, taking the stairs two at a time and winding me with every step.

"Logan, what the hell! Put. Me. Down!" I grunt with each stride, clenching my tummy to brace and at the same time trying to breathe. I attempt to gain some stability on his naked arse, which although it is mighty fine and firm, doesn't give me much to hold on to. Not like a pair of sweatpants, jeans, or even some boxer briefs might.

"All in good time, angel, all in good time." This time, he lifts the hem of my skirt and starts to nibble the soft flesh at the top of my thigh right around to the curve of my cheek. I drop my head and let out a tortured moan. *Oh, that mouth.* The stubble on his face must at least be a whole week gone from the feel of the long soft hairs. *God, I bet he looks feral packing a full beard.* He leans back briefly and tilts his weight, kicking the door to my bedroom flying. I'm so wet right now, he's probably got a damp patch on his shoulder. I squeal when he drops me from shoulder height onto the soft bouncy bed. I am just about to burst into a fit of giggles when his eyes scorch the humour right out of me. He doesn't look feral; he looks *lethal.*

Deep chocolate coloured eyes swirl and shimmer with flecks of gold and onyx and bore right through me. Searing heat courses through my veins like he has ignited an inferno inside me with just that look. I'm burning up, and when my eyes trail the length of his body, I swear I'm going to combust. His broad chest heaves with deep steady breaths, and each perfectly sculpted muscle on his abdomen ripples with the movement. His strong arms and muscular thighs could be carved from golden granite, they look so solid. Ultimate perfection. The icing for me is the spattering of dark hair in the perfect happy trail. Not that my eyes needed guiding to the goal, not when his impressive rock solid erection is all but dominating this sexy-as-all-hell view.

He reaches under my skirt and rips my panties down my legs in one smooth move, taking my pumps off at the same time.

"Spread your legs, baby." The words rumble from deep in his chest and sound like he's been chewing on gravel all night. My skin instantly prickles with a million goosebumps. I pull my knees up and out, watching his eyes darken as I slowly obey his command.

"Wider," he growls. The word is a soft whisper, though, and I smile at the way his cock twitches every time I move. "Show me how wet you are for me." *Holy shit!* That is the sexiest thing I've ever heard, and I'm pretty sure he can now see exactly how wet I am. Pretty sure I'm dripping on my bedcovers. "God, you're beautiful." He exhales, and I melt. I love the way his filthy words can make my jaw drop, just as much as those sweet ones make my heart swell.

"Touch yourself."

"What?"

"I know from the colour of your cheeks you heard me just fine, angel. Do I really need to repeat myself?" He palms his cock, and I can see from the tension in his jaw that this is causing him some sort of agony. I don't know if I'm feeling mortified at the thought of such a private act or so turned on I can't get my hand there quick enough. I opt for a slow hand, as that seems to make Logan stiffen in all the right places. I lightly trace my finger down the centre of my body, over my skirt, which is gathered at my waist, and I hesitate, only for a second, when I reach my tiny landing strip of hair. I shiver and suck in a sharp breath. My back arches a little with anticipation. I watch his eyes widen as I slide two fingers along my slick, wet centre. I tilt my hips and push into the bed with the ripple of pleasure washing over my body at my light touch.

"How do you taste?"

"How do I...oh." I let out the last word with an elongated sigh and an understanding tone. My mouth is dry, and wetting my lips makes him swallow thickly. His eyes are hawklike on my every move, raking over every inch of my body. He's definitely enjoying the show. I push my fingers in a little deeper before pulling them out and lifting them to my mouth.

"Good girl." His skin seems to glow with perspiration, and the raw lust and desire radiating off him is intoxicating. It's empowering, *I'm doing that to him.* "Holy fucking shit, Tia." His groan is a guttural, manly sound that makes my tummy do flips and makes my toes curl.

"Here, I saved some." I hold my wet fingers out, and he swoops to devour them, scraping any trace of me off with his teeth.

"Needs a little salt." His eyes flash with a sexy mix of deviance and mischief. He stalks up my body, licking and nipping anywhere there's a soft piece of flesh he can get between his teeth. Even through my clothes, I can feel his incendiary touch. He holds his body millimetres from mine, his heavy cock resting at my aching entrance. I whimper at the nearness, and he grins.

"I've never wanted anyone like I want you, Tia. You're *everything,* you know that?" His words tumble from his perfect mouth, and the sincerity and truth hit me hard. I feel winded all over again.

"I feel the same, Logan. I love you." I place my hand on his cheek, then tuck the hair that's falling across his face behind his ear. It's the only time I don't like the length of his hair, when it's covering his handsome face. His eyes flash with something I wish I didn't recognise—*worry.* But about what exactly, I couldn't guess. At this point in time, there are just too many variables.

"We'll see."

"Whaaa...oh ...ah, God, yes!" Any rational thoughts of concern regarding his vagueness are gone the second he drives into me. Powerful precision, perfectly aimed to distract me, no doubt, but it works. I can't breathe, let alone think straight. He's everywhere, moving inside me, filling every part of me. His hands caress and tease, skimming my body and leaving a wake of heated prickles. He pulls my body this way and that; we roll and tumble, grasping at each other. He tears my clothes from my body with an urgency that borders on aggressive, and I'm just trying to get to as much of him as is physically possible. I want everything he has to give. *I want him.*

He rolls onto his back, and I take a moment to catch my breath and sit up when he breaks the kiss. My hands rest on his chest, and his hands settle on my aching, heavy breasts, his thumbs working the tingly pointy parts like a pro.

"Ride me, baby, take what you need, and give me what I want."

"What you want?"

"Your pleasure…I want all your pleasure. I want you to come so hard on my cock that I can't help myself from exploding inside you. I want you full of me, now, tomorrow, *always*." He couldn't be clearer if he was burning my skin with a branding iron. The primal need to mark me as his runs deep and strong, like a life force, through him. I can see it in his eyes and feel it in his every touch, so what did he mean when he said, 'we'll see'? The thought is barely there a second when it's forced from my head with a shooting bolt of pleasure.

"Oh, oh, God, Logan that's so deep!" Logan sits up and pulls me down onto his cock with a jerk. He's buried so deep, even as he holds us completely immobile, I can feel every twitch, every pump of blood through the thick veins throbbing inside me.

"Stay with me, Tia." His voice is strained and husky. I couldn't be anywhere else if I wanted, and I don't want to be. I want *him.*

"I am, every inch of you." I grind and secure my arms under his so I am holding his shoulders from the back, locked and ready. I start to roll my hips, and the movement flows up through my body like a gentle wave lapping the shore. We writhe together. It's almost instant, the first spark of pleasure igniting at the base of my spine. I can't move fast since we're anchored so tightly together, and he's in control of the hold and gripping me to him like I am some sort of lifeline.

Still, the depth of penetration and pressure is so fucking perfect, I start to tremble with the impending climax as it starts to take hold of every nerve ending in my body. Flashes of pure pleasure rip up the length of my spine, shooting an explosion through me like New Year's Eve fireworks on the Thames; igniting every cell and where all I see are bright lights, shooting stars and I quake to the thunderous tremors consuming every part of me . My body takes over, climbing higher and higher.

"Look at me, angel." My eyes fly open; I'm more than a little dazed from my high and I didn't realise I had them so tightly shut. The slickness from my climax is worked and spread from where we're connected and is now it's on the tip of his finger between my arse cheeks, swirling in a pleasant motion. I feel the pressure pushing inside my back hole, a single digit. I clench down, which feels all kinds of strange and good. "Relax, baby, feel me, feel all of me." He works his finger inside, pressing against the tight ring of muscles and against his cock. It's too much.

"Oh, fuck!" I cry out, as every muscle in my body seizes, and I gasp in a silent scream of unbelievable ecstasy. Logan's other hand moves to my hips since I am frozen in some sort of euphoric catatonic state. My vision is hazy, but I can see him looking into my eyes the whole time he continues to move my body where he needs, chasing his release.

"God, Tia, you feel so fucking amazing." I feel his warm pants on my lips like a caress just before he crashes his mouth to mine. I swallow the groan of pleasure he releases into my mouth, smiling against his soft lips as he pulls us both to lie back on the bed in a sated heap of tangled limbs and sweaty bodies.

We lay entwined, my leg resting over his hip, his cock still pretty sizeable and solid, considering I can still feel how much he came running down my thigh. He hasn't opened his eyes in twenty minutes. He's not asleep, I've slept with him as a friend many, many times, so I know when he's just resting, and this is one of those times. I haven't taken my eyes from his peaceful face. He's so beautiful, inside and out. I can't for the life of me think why Ghost would say what she said. The notion that Logan would kill me is ridiculous. It would be funny if it wasn't so unnerving coming from her. How could she possibly make a claim like that? Based on what? She doesn't know him. I've lived with him, and there is not an ounce of killer in this gentle giant. He might be a little damaged, but who am I to judge that? And it's not a problem, not for me, not for us.

Even if it was, we're together now, and we'll handle anything, *together*.

Ghost may be a lot of things, but I know she wouldn't shack me up with a murderer just because he has really, really good wifi.

Still, I hate that she has me doubting. I trust her more than anyone, mostly because she couldn't lie if her life depended on it. She told me in our very first conversation that telling the whole truth was a particular personality trait or flaw in her case. It was all part and parcel of her type of autism. It's how we ended up serving time together, not because of her autism but because she confessed to her crime. Regardless of every other problem she has, that she has my back. It's not that I don't trust Logan, I do; it's just different. Ghost knows everything.

"Whatever you're doing, Tia, I think you're in over your head." His deep voice breaks the quiet of our shallow breathing, and I suck in a gulp of air with the surprise.

"Oh, ye of little faith, thanks." I pitch up on one elbow, keeping my tone lightly joking. I'm surprised, though, by the deadly serious expression on his face.

"It's not about faith. It's about knowing who you're dealing with."

"I do." I hold his gaze with just as much seriousness.

"Really? So you know about the ghost accounts and the dodgy Russian business partners your ex is hooked up with? Seriously, Tia, this isn't some fucking game." I sit up, gathering the sheet to cover myself as I do.

"I'm well aware this isn't a game." I keep my voice level and calm, despite my rising irritation at his condescending tone. However, his flippancy has pushed me too far.

"Couldn't you just cut the guy's clothes to shreds?" His derision is thick and ugly.

"He's not some cheating ex, Logan," I snap and drag the whole sheet off the bed as I stand. I start to gather my clothes. Logan regards me with a raised brow but makes no move to stop me. "Atticus's family set me up and stole my life. I can't ever go back and be *that* girl, the one with a *real* future all her own. I can't be the girl with unicorns in her dreams because I have monsters, real fucking monsters, Logan. I can't have a normal life, because I'm not that girl, anymore. I will *always* be a thief and a criminal because of *him*. He could've saved me any time he wanted, and the son of a bitch is going to pay." I roughly pull my cami top over my head and slip my arms quickly into my cardigan, wrapping it around my waist crossing over the soft wooden fabric with my folded arms. My light, tightly knit coat of armour.

"I want you out," he states flatly, and I let out a heavy sigh when I can see the genuine worry in the dark lines crinkled on his forehead and the trace of sadness in his eyes.

"Sorry, Logan, but that's not your call. I'll be out when I'm out and not before." I deliberately keep my voice soft, because I know my words are resolute. His face fixes with a steely cold look, all hard dark edges and fury. I barely recognise him with the change in his expression; it's so altered. I add a half-hearted shrug to try and ease the rising tension.

This is not how I wanted to spend our short time together.

"Look, I'm sorry, Logan, but honestly, if you weren't such a super-snooper you wouldn't even know. I would do my time, get what's mine, and come home. You'd be none the wiser." A dark cloud seems to descend in the room, whipping up a terrifying storm around Logan as he slowly rises from the bed. He grabs the towel draped over the end of the bed and wraps it around his waist. *Shit, this must be serious if Logan is covering up.*

"So lying is the answer?" He towers over me, but I hold my ground. It's like the room gets smaller, and the temperature drops. I don't like the distant look in his eyes. I've never seen that look before. *What the hell just happened?*

"I didn't say lying. You just go looking for trouble, and I said I know what I'm doing." I reach for his hand, but he pulls it from my fingertips, lifts his arm, and brushes the dark strands from his face.

"This only works if there's trust, Tia." His tone matches the recent icy temperature drop. I shake my head in confusion.

"I know," I offer, but it sounds like a plea.

"Do you?" He dips to maintain eye contact when I make an involuntary attempt to break the gaze. *Shit.*

"Yes."

"And you trust me?"

"I do." I don't hesitate, but my stomach drops from a sense of foreboding I can't fathom.

"And there's nothing you can't tell me?" His eyes narrow, and it takes everything I have not to cave under the intensity of his scrutinising glare.

"I can't tell you this. It's the only thing, Logan, and you have to believe me, it's for the best." I snatch his hand and hold it in mind.

"The only thing, hmm?" He grabs my jaw and twists my head so I am only a centimetre from him. The hold is firm and a little painful. I don't flinch, I can barely breathe, and my heart would be beating like a jack-hammer if it hadn't plummeted to the floor.

"Yes." I mouth out the words.

"Just so we're both clear here, *angel*…" He grits out the words and my nickname like it is causing him physical pain. I know where this is going, and I just can't…I can't stop it, even as I can see the looming train wreck before me. *Don't do this, Logan.* I try to shake my head and stop the inevitable from playing out; his grip is just too tight. "This would be the perfect time to come clean about *anything*. Anything you think might *destroy us*, given what you know about me, and how fucking important trust is to someone like me. You understand what I'm saying here, Tia, right?" He yells the last few words, fury and rage emblazoned across his face, anger rolling like a tidal wave from him and crashing full force against me.

"Right, I do." I can feel my voice breaking with the untold truth he's so desperate to hear. All I can hear is Ghost's threat and words of warning. My gut is in knots, and I don't know what to do. I don't know who to trust. I fight the pinch of tears behind my eyes, blinking away the ones already clouding my vision.

Even if I could give him what he wants, what happens then? Ghost would be gone, my plan dies, and according to Ghost, so do I, so what choice do I really have? I have to believe the one person who can't lie, the one person who proved herself when she poisoned those bitches that raped me. I snap my head out of his grasp and try to dismiss the dramatics with an accusation of my own. I can only guess at what he's asking, and I can't for the life of me, think how he would've found out. I have to bluff this out. It's my only choice.

"I don't understand why you're getting so angry."

He tilts his head and pauses, intently searching my face. His eyes flick to my twitching fingers that are itching to tug at the hair on my neck and a cruel smile transforms his face to something heartbreaking.

"This, Tia, *this* is why I'm so fucking angry." He holds up the bus ticket on which Ghost scrawled Logan's address and his real name,Logan Beckett It was the only time we met up after I was released. It was the beginning. "How the fuck did you get my details? Who gave you this address?"

"I can't tell you that." My shoulders drop, and I dip my eyes away from all the hurt and betrayal I can see. Fat tears start to fall, and I just fucking hate myself right now.

"Get out." It takes a moment to realise he said those words out loud. It takes a whole minute for the devastation to take hold. The silence is deafening, and my hands fly to my ears to stop the unbearable noise. I shake my head and frantic desperation takes over.

"Logan, please don't." I grab his arms and he pulls back like my touch is toxic, flaying the skin from his bones.

"Get the fuck out of my house!" He yells so loud in my face the tears stop falling from pure fear alone. I've never seen him so angry, so hurt. He picks up my bag and thrusts it into my chest. I stumble back and whisper words that I know are too little too late.

"You said you loved me, Logan!"

"If anyone should know that loving someone isn't enough sometimes, Tia, it's you."

I shake my head at the finality and bitterness of his tone.

"I'm so sorry."

"I'm not. At least I know what the T really stands for... *Traitor.*" I don't know what hurts more, the look of betrayal on his face or those last words spoken as he walks casually from my room. I crumple to the floor in absolute agony, my chest imploding, and all I feel is loss, utter, heartbreaking loss. I can't contain the pain. Loud ugly sobs escape my gaping mouth, masking the heavy sound of his retreating footsteps. *What have I done?*

CHAPTER TWENTY-FIVE

Tia

"**A**re you okay?" Cass speaks, breaking the silence. Barely five minutes have passed since I slammed the car door shut and retreated into my shell after shattering two hearts with my choice. The tender concern in his voice is just what I don't need. Fat tears burst onto my cheek, and I fail to wipe them away quickly enough to avoid detection. The sleek Aston DB9 swerves into the coach parking along the Embankment, and I jolt with the force of the break. "Jesus, princess, what happened? Did he hurt you? The motherfu—"

I suck back a sob-filled interruption. "Not like that, Cass, no." Sniffing back the tears, I try to downplay my desolation, but it's futile. My heart feels so damn heavy I can barely breathe; it's crushing my lungs. In spite of myself, the troubled expression plastered on Cass's face has me trying to ease his concern. "I…I'm fine."

"Yes, I can see that, what with all the tears." The sarcasm falls flat since his tone is thick with worry.

"I'll survive," I reply. His clenched jaw jumps at the impassive delivery of my apt statement.

"I can see that, too." His hand hovers with uncertainty, his fingers poised to stroke my face. Our eyes meet, and whatever passes between us is enough to allay his reticence at my possible reaction.

I close my eyes at the contact, so familiar and strange at the same time.

My tummy tightens, and I feel a warm glow of forgotten embers rekindling inside of me, something unique to him and something I haven't felt in a very long time. I lean into his touch, because, right now, I feel so broken I need this comfort, even if it's wrong, even if I know it won't last. Logan doesn't want me, not now. He can't trust me, and I know he'll never forgive me, but I need *this,* so bad.

"Talk to me, Tia, what happened?"

"I can't do that, and I certainly can't do it with *you.*" I pull sharply from his hold like his touch suddenly scolds my skin.

"Who else then, Tia? Who do you need to help you? Who can I take you to?" His retort doesn't sound remotely harsh. If anything, it's more pleading, but my blood is boiling with a mix of unbearable hurt and resignation to the truth.

"No one, Cass! I have no one. Is that what you want to hear? Does that make you happy?" My voice is high-pitched and a little unstable. I take a calming breath because I am so close to a meltdown I can feel it all the way from my trembling fingertips to my pounding heart.

"You have me," he states this with such sincerity I'm almost speechless. Almost.

"Phew, well, isn't that just a fucking relief." I choke out a bitter laugh, turning fully in my seat to face him. The shocked look of hurt on his face pulls me up short, and I let out a heavy breath. My voice softens from hysterical harpy to something more akin to how I'm truly feeling, beaten down and devastated. "Just drive, Cass."

Atticus shifts back in his seat and fixes his stony glare on the road ahead. He slams his foot to the floor, the engine roars like it's in pain, and he pulls from a stand-still with enough G-force to pin me immobile deep into the soft leather bucket seat. He eases off the acceleration just enough to screech a U-turn in the road, giving me whiplash and making me scream out like a little girl. He is sporting a killer grin, which should make me mad, but just like always, he has me at the very least, distracted.

We cross the river and head out of the city. It takes a few roundabouts for me to realise we aren't just heading back to the apartment via a different route, and he still hasn't told me where we're going. We hit the motorway, and my stomach churns enough for me to have to ask the question I hope I don't already know the answer to.

"Where are we going Cass?"

"Home." *Shit.*

The hairs on the back of my neck tingle as we reach the edge of the village. We pass the bus stop I used to stand at everyday to get the school bus, and for some reason I take a double look. Like I expect to see my former self just standing there, waiting.

I let out a hollow laugh at the irony.

I spent so much of my life just *waiting*, waiting for *him*.

The village shop is closed, and the lights of the one and only pub burn with a dirty orange tint from the lead latticed windows. The sound of hearty laughter breaks the quiet of a country night like this, tables full of both young and old spill out into the car park.

My window is fully down, and the balmy wind filters through my fingers as we crawl past, and once again I strain to see if I can spot a familiar face.

I don't.

It may have been where I grew up, but I rarely mingled. I was an outcast, and the only place that felt like home was Tartarus Hall. And then only when I was with Cass.

These feelings I had acknowledged but managed to keep at arms length, if not completely at bay, are rolling in like an unstoppable stormy wave. As much as I grew to love this place at one time, this is the last place on earth I need to be right now.

Cass swings the car to a skid turn on the gravel drive, only to slow to a crawl as we pass my old home. The Gate House is dark. Even in the fading light of the evening, I can see the thick dust on the windows. I know no one moved in after my mother died. It's probably been empty for the whole five years.

"I thought you would've gone to her funeral." I can feel his eyes on me; however, I continue to stare out the front window. The trees that line the drive are heavy with summer foliage, the canopy so dense I can't see a single star in the sky. The car has crawled to a halt, and I turn because he's clearly expecting an answer from the weight of the silence.

"I was tempted to go and say goodbye, but I was on kitchen duty, and you get access to the fridge on those days, so you know…"

"That's harsh, Tia," he reprimands, and I narrow my eyes in response to his judgment.

"Really, because I thought testifying against your only daughter was fucking harsh." He stiffens at my reply and gives a curt nod, which I take as either shutting the conversation down or accepting my reason. Either way, I don't really care.

It's done, and I wouldn't change it.

Another item for the list of evidence that the girl he loved no longer exists. Hopefully, it will start to sink in.

"Have you been back at all?" He presses his foot down, and we speed up the drive.

"I came back when I got out. I haven't been back since then, no point."

"I didn't know. Was there someone to let you into the place, or did you just go to the gatehouse?" He turns briefly to face me. I keep my eyes ahead for fear he will see the truth. He was always so good at that, and I know I've held my own so far. I can't risk that changing now.

"I collected my stuff from the Lodge and had a bit of a look around the Hall." I nod toward the looming gothic structure blocking the horizon.

"This place is mostly always locked up. You were lucky to come when there was someone here." he adds and raises a quizzical brow. I bite my lip and just give a flat smile in response. Not sure what telling him that I broke in would accomplish, except maybe adding one more thing to that list.

"I come back all the time." He puts a little more force on the pedal and the car leaps forward, eating up the distance. The house rises like a monolith or, given what died here, a mausoleum.

"Really?"

"Yes, it was the only time I was ever happy." He glances my way, and even in the darkness, I can see the depth of the truth he holds in his eyes.

"Yeah, me, too," I reply, but the rough sound of braking car tires on gravel swallows up the softly spoken words and my own truth.

"Come on, we'll need to open up the place a bit. I was planning on doing this next weekend so not everything is set up." We both stare up at the building that holds so many memories and so many secrets.

"Set up?"

"Clean up a bit, let some fresh air in, that sort of thing, and the supplies will be mostly frozen until I can go the shop in the morning." He quirks his lips apologetically.

"And clothes?" I ask. He drops his head and holds my gaze.

"Oh, I'm not sure we're going to be needing those." The deep timbre of his voice sends a shivers up my spine, and the serious intent in his tone makes me shift in my seat. He notices, but opens the car door and is out before I can feign nonchalance and scoff at his misplaced arrogance. Despite what signals my traitorous body is firing off, he needs to remember I'm heart-broken, not stupid.

He rounds the back of the car, and I get out my side. Lifting what looks like my overnight bag from the trunk of the car, he walks my way, stepping right up close and very personal. I have to tilt my head to maintain the eye contact, and it takes every-thing to stand my ground and not step back when he not only invades my space but dominates it. "Clothing is definitely op-tional inside the Hall but you will need what I've packed, since I thought we'd get some walking done while we're here, and I don't really want anyone else seeing what's mine." His body seems to cloak mine. I place my hand on his chest to steady myself.

"I'm not yours, Cass." I can hear the quaver in my voice, and judging by the instant smile striking his face like a slap, he can too.

"I think you'll find you will *always* be mine, princess." He slings the two bags over one shoulder takes my hand in a firm, no-argument grip. I run to catch up with his long strides, jump-ing two at a time up the main stone steps to the front doors.

Fishing a set of keys from his jacket, he starts to sort through the weighty bundle. Picking out the longest black-pitted iron key, he unlocks the door, and I am hit with a tsunami-sized wave of nostalgia and so much more.

We shouldn't be here.

He steps across the threshold, but I find myself rooted to the spot. It suddenly feels like crossing that line is more than just entering the building. "I've got you, princess. I won't let anything happen to you."

"It's not me I'm worried about," I mutter as my eyes take in my former playground.

"Tia, you look like you've seen a ghost." He cups my face in both hands, and the thump of the bags on the floor brings my focus to the two crystal blues staring right through me. I have to physically shake the sensations assaulting me.

"Felt one, more like, and not *a* ghost, *our* ghosts." I pull his hands away from my face. "I don't know what you're expecting, Cass, but I'm not the same girl I was back then. She died, and she's never coming back." I squeeze his hands to try and soften my stark revelation, and I am surprised when, unfazed, he squeezes me right back, adding his own blend of comfort with the hold.

"We'll see about that. Come on, let's light up the fires." He tugs me forward, and I let out a relief-filled sniff and weak laugh.

"There's really no one here?" I ask, looking over my shoulder at the portraits, hanging from the main gallery and lining the corridors, vacant eyes everywhere. I smile; they stopped being scary the moment I met Cass's mother. An ancient oil painting ceased to hold any horror when faced with pure evil.

"No, just you and me." He flashes a nefarious grin and winks before pulling me along beside him, explaining as we delve deeper into the house. "I keep Tartarus dormant and when I come back I just open up the rooms I need. Mother never visits." He keeps hold of my hand as he leads me down the long corridor toward the heart of the house. "A team of cleaners come in monthly for maintenance so there shouldn't be too many cobwebs and obviously Angus the Groundkeeper is still full time."

He pushes the heavy oak door wide and pushes the whole bank of switches up. The lights flicker and dim before settling in to give a soft glow to the cavernous kitchen. The flagstone floor and thick walls keep the room chilled all year round, and the Aga keeps it from freezing in the winter, but it's clearly not been turned on in months. I shiver and pull my hand from Cass's to rub the goosebumps from my skin.

"There should be hot water if you want to take a shower. I'll get the fire started in here and the Aga lit, so I can fix us something to eat." He walks directly to the open fireplace and places several of the dried logs stacked at the side in the centre of the grill. He fishes a lighter from his pocket and clicks the flame alive with one flick of his thumb. The fibres of the wood start to crackle but I know from experience he's going to be there for a while without some decent kindling.

"Luckily I'm not very hungry, then, because that Aga will take hours to get up to temperature," I scoff.

"Hmm, good point, and I'm fucking starving." He continues to hold the flame steady, and much to my irritation, the log starts to take. It glows, and flames lick the side, grabbing hold and lighting the grin on his smug face. He turns to me, and I get a flash of the boy, the arrogant, confident, and utterly insufferable boy I adored. I suck in a sharp breath, thankful the log spits and crackles loud and timely enough to mask my...my what, I'm not sure, but whatever it is, I know he doesn't need to see or hear it. He brushes his hands together, pleased with one item on his to-do list done. "I'll hunt and gather something to eat that doesn't need cooking for me now, and something I can cook for both of us for later. Why don't you go and put the bags in my room and let me know if you think the room needs heat and I'll bring up some logs. I didn't intend heating the whole house, just light some fires where we're likely to be."

"I'll probably need one in the guest room," I add as he starts to open cupboards he's clearly never opened in search of food. My mother kept all the dry goods in the pantry and the freezers are out in the back storeroom, although it does make me smile watching him go through all the cutlery drawers and saucepan cupboards.

"Guest room?" He uncurls his long lean body from stooping low and looks genuinely confused. It's an unaccustomed look for him and disarmingly cute.

"I'm not sleeping with you, Cass. This house has what, fifty bedrooms? And you honestly thought I was going to share." I sniff, shaking my head with light humour at his presumption.

"I wasn't intending on sleeping," he drawls, and despite the flutter of excitement and kick in my heartbeat, I remain incredulous, on the outside at least.

"Jeeze, you're unbelievable," I huff. My hands fly to my hips in disbelief, and he flashes a new look I haven't experienced before, sheepish. He looks so young, all I see before me is the man the boy I loved turned into.

I'm in so much trouble.

"I'm teasing, Tia. Really, I have no expectations. I have hopes, but I just want some time to talk and we used to do lots of talking at night, if you remember?"

"I remember," I whisper, and his smile widens. I can feel the threads of our long lost connection like a complex web weaving me closer to him, pulling me toward my fate, *our* fate. I turn before I do something I regret. Cursing myself, I walk back toward the main staircase. My head is spinning with a litany of words that, if I could be honest with myself for a moment, would not be as shocking as they feel.

Who am I fooling exactly?
Nothing like delaying the inevitable, Tia?
*This is Cass; it's always been **him**.*
Fuck!

I gave up on the hot water ever reaching a decent temperature to ease my aching limbs and made do with a flash cold shower, just to get the scent of Logan from my skin. It didn't feel right, bringing him here, and right now, I just can't think about that part of my mess. *One fuck up at a time, Tia, one at a time, and speaking of...*

"Hey!" Cass peeks around the bedroom door, concern and trepidation evident on his handsome face. I don't know how long I've been sitting on his old bed, but it's pitch dark outside, and where I wasn't hungry before, now I'm famished. He kicks the door wide, and holding a tray, backs into the room. Sweet smelling tomatoes fill the room and my tummy loudly groans its approval and neglect.

"Hopefully, that noise will accept the fact all I have is tomato soup to offer." He smiles and takes a seat beside me, placing the tray on the bed between us.

"What, no banana and sugar sandwiches?" I quip.

"Oh, I'm saving those for later. I have a feeling I'm going to need my A-game." He winks playfully, and I have this sinking feeling in the pit of my belly. I have been so sure of myself, my plan...everything, and now I'm drifting, and I hate that he just might be my anchor.

"I don't want to play this game, Cass."

"I am very aware of that, Tia." His voice drops to a deadly serious tone, and I swear the temperature in this chilly room has just dropped to sub zero. "You want the fire on?"

"No, I mean, it's fine; I'm not that cold." I shake my head, my hair is still damp, and limp tendrils whip against my cheeks with the enthusiasm of the move. His blond brow knits thicker with an intense frown, and I visibly shiver, yet I know inside, I'm just beginning to burn.

"Here, eat this, it will warm you up until I can." He holds the spoon to his lips, gently blowing the steam away before offering it to me. I open my mouth and watch as his throat bobs slowly with the effort to swallow. His eyes darken to impossibly deep, icy pools. My body temperature is rocketing with every spoonful of soup he feeds me. Why the hell am I letting him?

Because you're broken and raw, and it feels nice to have someone take care of you, idiot, and it's not someone, it's Cass.

"Are you going to tell me what happened today?" He scrapes the last spoonful for me and places the bowl down.

"I'm really not." I drop my gaze and hear him sigh heavily. I get a twist in my chest at the snide tone of my retort. He's being so nice, and I know that look of concern is heartfelt. I can see he cares. I just have to decide whether it's really too late, when he's trying so hard, and I can already feel my shaky walls begin to crumble. Tiny pockets of dust flow to the ground like an arid waterfall, taking larger pieces of my defences with it.

I match his sigh of frustration with my own, only mine is filled with sadness. "All I can say is when I've done my time with you, I will be looking for a new home." I shuffle back and pull my legs up, my knees tucked beneath my chin, and my arms wrapped tightly around my shins.

"Logan kicked you out? Why?" His wide eyes match the shocked inflection of his voice.

"It's complicated."

"Well, if he's smart, he'll have followed you here and will be knocking down my door any moment." I know he's really trying here, because the words of comfort are at odds with the tension in his voice.

"Unlikely." My lips barely curve with the effort to smile. Atticus shakes his head, dismissing my assessment with a comforting hand on my knee.

"I would be stunned if he didn't, Tia. I saw the way he looked at you. I should know, I've seen that look in the mirror every damn day." I have to drop my gaze when I see the honesty in his eyes. I can feel the prickle of tears, and screwing my eyes shut, I have to physically shake them away. I let out a slow breath once the threat has passed and look up.

"He's agoraphobic Cass, he hasn't stepped out side his house for ten years. The last time was for his parents funeral."

"Why?"

"I don't think it's a why kind of deal. He won't talk about it. He just said the next morning he couldn't get anywhere near the door. He tried and it just got worse until he stopped trying. But even if he wasn't, he won't be coming after me." I'm not given to dramatics, never was, and this time, Cass gives an acknowledging nod, holding my gaze to make sure. I don't waiver. I know Logan. He won't forgive me, and I don't blame him. The silence doesn't hang for long when Cass breaks it.

"I'm sorry."

"No, you're not," I scoff, and he has the decency to flash an apologetic smile.

"True, but I am sorry you're hurting."

"I've had worse," I fire back, and he winces. His next apology is much more sincere.

"I'm sorry."

"I know." I believe him. I have for a little while, even if it changes very little, it's still good to know He pulls one of my hands free and entwines our fingers, and I let him.

"How did you meet him, if he's agoraphobic I mean?"

"I broke into his house and slept in his basement until he found me."

"What?" The shock on his face is almost comical.

"I didn't have anywhere else to go." I can't hide the irritation in my voice. It's not like I had several family homes around the globe I could pick and choose from.

"You could've—" He starts to speak, but I cut him down, biting out my interruption.

"What, Cass? What could I have done? Called you? Written

one more of the hundreds of unanswered letters? Gone back to the Lodge house? I had no options, none. I was living on the street, and Logan took me in. He saved me, and I betrayed him." I suck back the rising sob and halt it before it takes hold.

"I never got any letters Tia." He states this as a matter of fact, and I believe this one too.

"I'm not surprised." I sniff and let out a hollow, humourless laugh. "It really doesn't matter does it? Your mother had her reasons for what she did, and you believed them."

"It might've made a big fucking difference." The muscle in his jaw bounces with a thinly veiled fury his eyes fail to hide.

"Did you know I was in jail?" I counter, and he closes his eyes with the pain of that single question.

"Yes." He nods but keeps his eyes closed.

"Then it doesn't make a fucking difference," I say, although the fire has left my belly. I'm so exhausted. I don't want this fight anymore.

"No, I guess it doesn't," he admits softly and looks into my eyes once more. The look alone quells what is left of the fiery rage inside me. I can't change the past and neither can he. "How did you betray Logan?"

I shake my head. "It doesn't matter, all that matters is he will never see me again, and I have to live with that, along with all the other shitty paths my life has taken. I have to walk them alone, and I'm so sick of being knee deep in shit." My voice pitches high and a little hysterical.

"Hey, hey. It's all right; it will all be okay. I promise." His other hand wraps around the back of my neck, and he holds me firm, tethering me to him when our eyes connect. I feel calm and unsettled at the same time.

"Do me one favour, would you?"

"Anything."

"Don't fucking make promises you can't keep." He pulls his

hands away when my caustic tone does the trick.

"What do you know about him?" He straightens his back to his full height, and I can see the torment play out across his features. There is tension in his jaw, narrowed eyes, and his knuckles are white from the iron-fisted grip he's got going on, but I'm confused why.

"Who? Logan?"

"Yes."

"Enough." I don't like the challenge in his tone. I hope my curt replies will end this topic of conversation. Logan is not part of this equation, and I want to keep it that way.

"Really? I know you were desperate, Tia, I just didn't think that would mean you'd shack up with a murderer." His flippant remark is like a slap across my face; I feel the pain and shock tear through me.

What the hell?

"What are you talking about? He's not a—" I falter as my mind races to a very recent conversation, and Ghost's words ring in my head and make my stomach drop. That can't be true; she wouldn't send me there if he was a murderer. Besides I checked him out. I shake my head at my own naïveté, I checked out one of the best hackers in the country, *yeah, right.*

"His parents died in suspicious circumstances, Tia. They were both young and healthy, and they both had heart attacks on the same night. His sister's body was never found, and he spent six months in a mental hospital before being released. And there are no records of any of this." He reaches for my hand, but I pull right out of his reach, pressing myself against the headboard. Not because I don't want him to touch me, but because I do. He's like this familiar comforting blanket that I crave with my soul, to wrap around my breaking body and take this pain away.

"How did you find this out then?" My words are softly

spoken, and even I can hear the break in my voice.

"I have sources, Tia, and when someone is important, I find out the truth," he adds, and I blurt out a bitter, hollow laugh filled with vitriol. It's enough to break the spell and help me see straight. It's the first time in this whole damn evening, but better late than too late.

"Oh, that's fucking rich! You knew the truth, and yet you left me to rot in jail!"

"I know."

"You know? That's all I get?" I'm incredulous at his stony-faced delivery.

"I'll make it up to you," he adds, but the impassive tone is like lighting a powder keg. I explode.

"How? How the fuck do you give me back three years of my life? How do you give me back the girl that died in jail? How do you do that, Cass?"

He swipes the tray to the floor, sending the dishes flying and breaking on impact with a loud crescendo. He grabs my shoulders and pulls my body to his, crashing his lips to mine with painful urgency. Salty tears flow freely down my face, pooling in the creases where our lips are joined. I push against a wall of muscle and then pull back. We break apart, and I suck in a large gulp of air, gather my one thought, and draw my hand back, clench my fist, and punch him square on his chiselled jaw. My knuckles crunch and pain shoots up the bones in my arm. His head snaps to the right. He massages the side of his face, but the grin that creeps across his face makes me think he's more impressed than hurt.

"Kissing me changes nothing, Cass, and unless you've got a magic dick, neither will having sex, so fuck off and leave me alone."

I stand and run for the door, and my hand shakes as I try to grasp the iron handle. The door flies open with the strength of my pull, and I hit the corridor with a flat out sprint. The need to get free is instinctual. I keep going, turning corners, running, breathless and frantic to get away, to get some distance, and to find a safe sanctuary in this mansion.

I reach the farthest part of the house and the secret staircase. I'm not surprised I'm here. It's like I was on autopilot. It's where I always went when I needed to get away and my first port of call when I needed to feel safe. It was *our* place to hide. I climb the narrow stairs, squeezing at the turns because I'm so much bigger now. The door is stiff and creaks when I slowly push it open.

Oh, shit, I mutter out loud, when I realise exactly how much trouble I'm really in.

A thousand candles flicker, and shadows dance across the open space bouncing off the fort of pillows stacked in the centre of the room.

It's magical. It's perfect, and I repeat to myself, *Oh, shit.* Only it's not to myself.

Strong hands hold my shoulders from behind, and he presses his body firmly to mine. I melt at his touch as the raw heat from his body puts a million candles to shame.

CHAPTER TWENTY-SIX

Tia

He turns me slowly in his arms. I'm surprised my feet move at all. My head is a mess. My emotions are all over the damn place. All I can hear is blood rushing so loudly in my ears, it feels like I'm wearing noise-muffling headphones. My heart is pounding like a rapid-fire machine gun on steroids, and I don't have a drop of moisture in my mouth. Any spare liquid is pooling right between my legs.

"I love you, Tia. I always have, and I *always* will." His crystal blue eyes reflect a hundred flames, swaying with the faintest swirl of air.

He's so close, I feel him everywhere; tiny hairs all over my body stand to attention, and the manly smell filling my nostrils is intoxicating. I sway with the heady scent. I'm utterly mesmerised by the intensity of the look he is levelling at me. I don't know what reserves I'm running on right now, but as lines of defence go, this feels very much like 'game over'.

"I fucked up so badly, Tia, I know I did, and if you'll give me a chance, I will make it right." I can hear the heartbreak and desperation in his voice.

"Cass…" I try to respond, but I know from the heavy sigh that escapes, I am struggling to recall anything other than how much I loved this man, how much I love him still.

"Please don't say no." He jumps in with more heart-melting weapons in his arsenal.

He was always so good with words.

"We were supposed to happen, Tia. You know it. I know it, and if you're honest with yourself for one goddamned second, you'll feel it in your soul." He takes my hand and places it over his heart. It's beating just as fiercely as his declaration. "Just like I feel it in mine." His voice softens to a barely audible whisper. "We're meant to be together, Tia, always. Remember?"

"That's the problem, Cass, I remember everything, every word, every touch, every promise you made to me." He nods and takes the hits. "You told me you loved me once before, Cass, so I know it means jack-shit." I don't shout, because I don't feel any anger racing through me. I just feel unbearably sad. I don't know how we come back from that. Despite his best efforts, we're just not the same people.

"I fucked up, Tia, but I never stopped loving you." He speaks with such raw honesty, I feel my heart breaking and healing at the same time. *Maybe*? "You have to give *us* a chance. I know you, Tia. The old you is still in there, and the new you isn't so very different. Everyone deserves a second chance, and you'll regret it if you don't give us our chance. Aren't you tired of regretting things you have the power to change? I know I am." He tips my chin high so I can no longer avoid eye contact. His thumb brushes my lips, and sparks crackle under his loving touch. "It's always been us, Tia. What are you afraid of?"

"Everything."

"You've never been afraid of me, princess." His touch is light and tender. *I have nothing left.*

"I am now." My voice doesn't sound like my own, and he

gives me a knowing smile that feels very much like a deal already signed and sealed.

"And why is that?" His nose brushes against mine, his warm breath flooding my senses with its sweet intoxicating aroma.

"Because I want you so bad, I can't think straight." A stray tear bursts from my eye and trickles down my cheek. He catches it on the pad of his thumb and sucks it into his mouth. I swallow the thick lump blocking my throat before I speak. "You cloud my mind."

"Tonight is about us, just *us,* okay?"

"Convenient." I try to look away, but he dips to keep the contact. I can see in his eyes he's just as afraid, for different reasons I'm sure, but we're both balancing on a knife edge here, fragile and precarious.

"Necessary. I want you Tia, and unless you tell me to stop, this is happening. I've been waiting my whole damn life for this, and I can't wait a moment longer." His hand threads around the back of my neck, and he pulls me flush against him, I hadn't noticed that I had begun to edge away, but he did.

"Cass," I gasp. I know I've lost the ability to think straight, and now I'm simply struggling to breathe.

"Yes?"

I open my mouth again, but there is no sound. I don't trust myself to speak.

"You said the problem was that you remember everything?" he reminds me and I nod.

"I do." I'm crumbling.

"Well, do you remember you loved me once?"

"I do." I don't know what's holding me together as my resolve is in tatters and my knees weaken.

"And do you remember how fiercely I loved you back?"

"Yes." I mouth the reply, not sure if I'm still making audible sounds. His next words tell me that I am, for now.

"Good, because for me that hasn't changed." He dips and lifts me smoothly into his arms, his eyes burning with such desire, I feel dizzy. If he didn't have me cosseted in his strong embrace, I would be a puddle on the floor. I didn't notice in the soft light, but the fort of pillows surrounds a deep mattress with sheets and more pillows. He carefully steps over the 'wall' and reverently lays me down. He holds his body half off, half over mine, supporting all his weight on one side.

"Tell me now, Tia, if you want me to stop." His voice is gravelly and strained. As calm as he seems, he can't hide this, and it gives me a little comfort that he is struggling just as much as I am. *Inevitable.*

"I don't want you to stop." I exhale, and my lips curl upward in a freeing smile. It feels good, right up to the moment he crushes it from my face.

It's not like we haven't kissed before, or maybe it is, because this feels so different. His tongue entwines with mine, controlling the movement and demanding my compliance. The friction of the soft tissue sends a wave of tingles that start at the contact and fire off in every direction across my skin. His hand cups the back of my neck, and his fingers spear into my hair, moving my head to gain better access, as if he can't quite get enough. He groans into my mouth when he drops his weight onto my body, and I sigh. His erection feels like burning steel against my thigh, and I want only hook my leg over his arse and grind against the massive bulge.

He smiles against my mouth, and I do the same, and when he pulls back, I can see the joy crinkling his eyes. He looks so young, I wonder for a magical moment if we did manage to time travel after all, and right now we are just where we were supposed to be. I want that so much. tears fall from the corner of my eyes, and I can't wipe them away quick enough. I hate that I want that to be true when I know wishes change nothing, *nothing*.

"Don't, Tia, please, baby, please don't cry." He peppers my face with kisses so soft and tender that more tears fall. His fingers dry the stray tears his lips fail to catch.

"This won't change a thing, Cass, and I hate that we lost our moment. It fucking hurts." I suck back the rising sob, because I know if I let it out, it will consume us both.

"It's unbearable." He drops his forehead to mine, looking at me through long lashes that frame soul sad eyes, which breaks my fucking heart all over again. "This though...*this* changes everything." The truth in his words holds me captive, and I can't even draw a breath to respond. He speaks after the longest time of just staring into me. "I'll spend every day for the rest of my life making it up to you, Tia. I promise." I squeeze my eyes shut, but I can't shake my head; his hand still holds it firmly.

"I told you not to—" I whisper my objection, but his interruption is emphatic.

"I promise." It's not an idle threat; it's a declaration, and I *so* want to believe.

His mouth covers mine, swallowing any remaining resistance and consuming me with such passion and urgency, in this moment at least, I am completely his, and *I want to be.*

His hands sweep every part of my body, loosening and removing clothes as they go. Mine do the same, and when we are both fully naked, I gasp at the sight.

He's like an angel. The soft glow of the flickering flames lights the curves and the lines of muscles on his arms, across his chest and abdomen. Ripples of solid muscle flex and contract with each laboured breath, and when I peek down between our bodies, I whimper. His thick cock, too hard to be lying heavily, just bobs between us and is too damn tempting for me not to tilt my hips and close the gap. He hooks my thigh over his, and his large hand presses my arse cheek so my liquid core slides against his length. He controls the speed and pressure of this unbelievably erotic grind perfectly. I close my eyes at the utter bliss assaulting my senses. Sparks sizzle, and my greedy body pushes against him for more contact, more pressure, more pace…more cock.

"Cass," I plead against his mouth. My fingernails bite into the rock solid muscle of his fine arse with little effect.

"Something you want, princess?"

"Don't tease me, Cass. I've waited too long for this," I unashamedly plead.

"I have no intention of teasing you, baby, well, not this time." His deep kiss makes my toes curl, and he draws back so slowly, sucking in my bottom lip, that I have to question whether the teasing comment was in fact a lie. This is torture.

He presses the tip of his cock right at my entrance. My eyes drift shut, and my whole body thrums with anticipation.

"Look at me, princess." His deep voice rumbles with his warm breath across my lips. His glare is so incendiary, I feel the burn in my soul. "I want to see you when I do this."

"Oh, my god!" I gasp out in between little pants as he inches inside of me, filling every bit of space and deliciously stretching me until I am full of him. He nudges just a little more, and I suck in a sharp breath filled with pain and pleasure, mostly pleasure.

He secures his arm tightly around my waist and rolls us, so he is on his back, and then he sits and pulls me back down, firmly back in place, impaled. I wrap my legs around his waist, and he opens his legs to allow me to drop fully onto him. His large hands support my arse and hold me firm. His eyes are fixed on mine, and we're nose-to-nose, lip-to-lip, with ragged breaths mingling, just absorbing each other and this perfect moment.

But it's not perfect. I wish it was, but there's so much wrong with us, with me… and Logan. God what the hell am I doing?

"Stop, stop thinking, Tia, just feel." His hands move and massage my round flesh, pulling my body onto his, making me ride his cock and meet his deep, nerve-tingling thrusts.

"Ahh." I throw my head back in ecstasy as my shaky moral compass is shattered with the here and now.

"Look at me, Tia." His voice is strained, and I can feel him swell inside me, enough to make my eyes water. "Jesus, you feel amazing. I want you to come with me."

"Not gonna be able to control that one, Cass. I'm not that good." I start to laugh, but stop when my tummy muscles contract, and a shot of pain makes me freeze mid-breath. He chuckles and jerks his hips to hit that perfect spot, and I shudder with pleasure.

"Oh, princess, you are so much better than good. You're fucking perfect." He brings one hand around to where we're joined and skims his thumb over my clit, and I jolt from the shock of his touch. I feel the spark at the base of my spine, igniting an almighty burst of electricity that fires every nerve alive. He keeps the right amount of pressure, avoiding a direct hit, but building insurmountable pleasure in small circles that match the impossibly deep penetration of his cock. This combination, coupled with the gentle roll of his hips, and the way he is just staring right into me I know I'm in the arms of an angel, seconds away from heaven.

"Cass, I…I…"

"I know, baby, I can feel you squeezing like crazy, just let go. I'm right with you…all…the…way." His fingers grip my arse so hard the imprint will last for days. He moves his arm up and around my waist, wrapping me in an embrace so tight, there's no space for air. His lips consume mine, his tongue stealing the last of my breath as my climax grips us both, climbing so high only his strong hold has us tethered to earth. I can no longer keep my eyes open, and I bury my head in his neck as shuddering vibrations wrack my body, uncontrollable and violent tremors shaking us both. I cling to him as he wrings out the very last of my climax from my weak body, filling me with his own release.

CHAPTER TWENTY-SEVEN

Tia

I have been walking for hours, and my legs ache almost as much as my heart. My calf muscles scream with each step, and I must have blisters the size of saucers, yet nothing hurts as much as seeing Cass in the distance. The Hall dominates the horizon, but I can see him like the day isn't fading, and he is generating his own light.

He's standing on the gate of the walled garden looking out across the parkland. He spots me, drops to the ground, and hits it running. My stomach plummets even as my heart kicks up a few extra beats. I woke just before dawn, snuck out from under Cass's heavy arm, and left him dead to the world. It's dusk now.

I had to get out.

I'm a mess.

I needed to wander through my past to try and figure out what I'm doing with my future. These fields and paths, I must have walked a thousand times, a lifetime ago. This was my childhood, and although they might be a little overgrown in places, I would know them blindfolded. I sat under the tree Cass carved our names in until my arse was numb, hoping for some sort of divine intervention, but I guess you have to believe to get that sort of help.

I'm so conflicted. I know I didn't steal that bracelet, and other than in the police cell, Cass hasn't mentioned that part of my past. He's certainly intimated as much that he knows the truth, but he's never told me why. I guess I didn't actually ask, even if I know why. To me, it didn't matter, the net result is the same, and he obviously didn't love me enough to stand up when I needed him. I'd convinced myself nothing he said would make a difference, so I just didn't care, only now...now, I just don't know.

I wish I had my burner phone.

I really could use some Ghost advice to help me see straight, because all I can see is a confusing swirl of piercing blues that make my soul burn and warm chocolate eyes that make my heart weep.

"Where the hell have you been? Fuck, Tia, I nearly called the police." He skids to a stop and isn't remotely breathless despite the near full half mile he's just run. His eyes checking up and down, settle on mine, and are filled with concern and relief.

"Oh, I don't think that's a good idea." I sniff out a hollow laugh that falls ominously silent between us.

"No?" His tone is cautious, and the instant tension is palpable. I can feel that my wall is now at full strength.

"We need to talk." I straighten and go to walk past, when he steps to block my path.

"So talk." I feel I should step back. He's on a slight incline, and it makes his body seem that much bigger, more imposing, and his scowl makes me falter. I draw in a fortifying breath and tip my chin. He doesn't scare me. Well, he scares me a little, but I'm not the one in danger here, so I square myself and talk.

"What if I told you I found your money, but I'm not giving

it back?" I cross my arms at the chill flashing across my body when his eyes narrow to icy slits.

"I'd say you're not a thief, Tia, so don't start now." His jaw jumps with the tension, and his voice is tempered anger I can only see because his knuckles are pure white.

"You see, that's really interesting, Cass, because why would you say that?" I soften my voice and my defensive stance, dropping one hip and tapping the corner of my mouth like I'm pondering the same question I just posed.

"I know you," he states flatly, and I smile with apparent pleasure.

"You have one chance to tell me why, Cass, so choose your next words wisely," I advise.

"Princess." He reaches and I let him stroke his finger along my jaw. I don't respond even if the hairs on my neck might spark to life at his touch; he can't see that thankfully.

"Not your princess, Cass. Tell me why I'm not a thief," I retort and watch as he pulls his hand back like I've bitten him.

"I need that fucking money, Tia. You don't understand," he snaps, and I scoff out loud.

"Really? I don't understand that it's really *three* hundred million missing or that your mother has been gambling with the company's pension fund? Or that you owe a small fortune to some very nasty Russians? Or that your mother has racked up debt you can't possibly repay in ten lifetimes?" He remains impassive. "Which bit of that don't I understand?" His eyes widen briefly, until, just as quickly, he checks himself. He steps closer, and I stand my ground.

"It wasn't my money to begin with." His cool breath brushes over my face, and his icy glare freezes my heart.

"What?" I respond. I must look the picture of confusion at the curve ball of a conversation change.

"I'm sorry." He holds my questioning gaze and steps one

foot away.

"For what bit, Cass?" I ask, too distracted to notice his change in stance, and I'm an idiot for not recognising the need for distance.

"For this." He steps closer and wraps a strong arm around my waist, imprisoning me with the strength of the hold. His lips smash against mine, and then he bites my neck. No wait, he can't be doing that, he's still kissing me. It must be a sting, not a bite. He pulls back, and I see the needle in his hand. Where did that come from? I feel the rush of air hit my lungs as I fight to breathe, then a sudden, woozy, swirling, heavy darkness and then…nothing.

End of Book 1

ACKNOWLEDGEMENTS

Gah…this just gets scarier and scarier with each book. Just because I'm a worrier and I know I will miss someone, by complete accident, but I will. So i'll apologies now and know that you are supposed to be in this bit…yes you!

A huge thank you Shannon Boltin, my wonderful PA, Nicole, Nese, Caroline, Alison, and Sarah who tirelessly promote and pimp me to all and sundry and I know Facebook doesn't make it easy.I am and will be forever in your debt because I literally would not be visible in the ocean of Indie authors if it wasn't for you ladies.

Joan Readsalot, sorry to lose you but ever grateful for all you've done. My other Beta readers, Jane Kennedy, Sarah Tandy (you get another mention here :)), and Katie Fezer-Sedan thank you so much for your invaluable input into making Wicked Little Games what it has turned out to be…hopefully good. My street team, especially, Amanda , Gaynor, Jenny and Melissa(s), Lisa, Charlotte, Susan, Kellee, Mandy, Belle and Lynne..But really all my street team, my new members…I love you ladies…you totally rock!

My ever expanding review team and I'm not going to name you because Amazon will hunt you down and remove all your hard and valuable work...but you know who you are and I FLOVE you.

Saya my wonderful editor, and Maggie Truelove and Jane (again)...words fail me...I am so grateful for your grammar ocd...I can't even. Stacey at Champagne formats I just hope I got this clean before it came to you...I can't count how many time my work needs ...just a tweak ;) and Judi at CLP for my glorious cover...You ladies are the foundation.

Extra help came this time from Simon Maughan for some useful and very thorough legal knowledge...googles good but a real lawyer is much better.

My Divas...most of you I've already mentioned and I know I'm taking my life in my hands giving this an extra section but, Patty, Penny, Donette, Karen, Leanne and Steffy <3

Bloggers: Claire, Steph, Vicki and Vivienne at Romance Readers Retreat, Jo Booklover, Jesey at Schmexy Girl, Michelle, Yaya and Grace Afterdark Book lovers, Mel and Gayle Bloggers from Down Under, Tanya and Sharon from mom's Secret Book Blog, Rachel and Jo from Hourglass..., Gitte and Jenny from Totally Booked, Ana Ives and Bri Partin(I know you're not bloggers but you are a champion of the book world all the same), I am super grateful to you guys. Other authors...because this is a community in every sense and I have drawn inspiration and guidance from many many talented people but here's a few and in no particular order...Jana Aston, T.M Frazier, Pam Godwin, Alice Raine, always Jodi Ellen Malpas, M Never, Stylo Fantome, JL Perry, Kitty French, Donna Alam, LP Lovell, Stevie Cole,

Leslie Jones, Skye Warren, Mandi Beck, CJ Roberts, Audrey Carlan, Aleatha Romig, Jana Aston, and JA Huss…Don't get me wrong most of these people wouldn't know me if I sat on their face but they have affected me in a positive way and for that I am thankful.

I would also like to thank my bestie..Kymme because in all honestly there would be no books if it wasn't for her, for all the swag making for the signings…I'm gonna take you to Vegas if I ever get asked lol… I love you to the moon and back.

My family…again are quietly supportive…proud I think and certainly happy about the money!

But mostly, I'd like to thank you, for choosing to buy my book and taking the time to read it—a huge, I mean really huge, thank you, you will never know how incredibly grateful and honoured I am that you have and I would be even more so if you are kind enough to **leave a review** on Amazon or Goodreads.Please… please…oh and please :)

The People who make it all happen.

Dee Palmer—Author

Website—www.deepalmerwriter.com

Follow me here
FB Reader Group -The Chosen Ones

www.facebook.com/groups/902682753154708

and here for exclusive nibbles
Book + Main Bites

Editor—Ekatarina Sayanova—Red Quill Editing

Formatter—Champagne Book Design,
www.champagebookdesign.com

Cover Design Judi Perkins at Concierge Literary Promotions

OTHER BOOKS BY AUTHOR

THE CHOICES TRILOGY
Never a Choice
Always a Choice
The Only Choice

Never a Choice 1.5—A Choices Novella

Ethan's Fall

Disgrace

Disgraceful

Grace

Wanted

ABOUT THE AUTHOR

Dee Palmer lives just outside of London with her husband and (slightly embarrassed) children. Her passion is writing sexy steamy romance stories that will scorch the pages right off your kindle and are guaranteed to make your heart pound. She loves an HEA but isn't afraid to put her readers through the ringer before she delivers.

When not at her desk she can be found either fannying around on Facebook or with her nose stuck in her Kindle. Once in a while when the lights are down she might be spotted about town searching for the best French martinis and throwing some dubious shapes on the dance floor.

Why not join my Member's Lounge and be the first to learn of new releases, freebies and extras include a FREE book library

Click here for the to join: Member's Lounge:
http://eepurl.com/biZ6g1

Where it all began…Bonus Book
Bethany's story starts right here with *Never a Choice*

Stalk me On
Facebook: www.facebook.com/DEEPALMERWRITER
Twitter: twitter.com/deepalmerwriter
Book + Main: bookandmainbites.com/users/110
Instagram: www.instagram.com/deepalmerwriter

Join my reader group…it's not all books, I have giveaways on Fridays and never a day goes by without some sexy shenanigans
/www.facebook.com/groups/902682753154708

If you haven't already signed up to my newsletter now is a good time. I don't spam but you are the first to learn of new releases, freebies and extras
Click here for my: Newsletter:
landing.mailerlite.com/webforms/landing/m6r3y4

Never *a* Choice

The Choices Trilogy, Book One

Prologue

Four Years Ago

"You're an idiot!" John jerks me further up his back to get a bit more comfortable, and I grip a little tighter with my thighs to prevent me slipping back down before he repeats. "You're an idiot for working with a busted ankle tonight."

"Says the idiot carrying me half a mile home at one in the morning." I kiss the soft hairs on the back of his neck and smile against his warm skin. He smells of fresh cut wood and mint from a recent shower.

"It's bad enough you have to work on a school night, but you needed to rest. It looks like a freaking balloon now." He lifts my leg, but the dim street lamp fails to highlight his argument as my ankle is covered by my jeans and hidden in the shadow of the dark night. He's not really mad. he's never really mad, and he sighs as I rest my chin on his shoulder and my arms hug him just a little tighter.

"I need to work and it looks worse than it is." He grumbles under his breath and continues to walk me home -- well, carry me home. He meets me each night I work late at the local pub. It's a small village pub, and I do a little cooking in the evening, serve food, and help behind the bar. It's not strictly legal, but I'm not likely to tell; I need the extra money and the late nights pay better. It's the only thing John and I ever argue about, I won't take his money and he thinks Kit, my sister, should contribute more. He gets no argument from me there, but he works just as hard. His money is going toward a place of his own because his Dad has given him notice to quit like some troublesome tenant. He needs every penny and at least I still have a home. He shifts again and I can feel the tension in his shoulders. This is the second time he has carried me today. The first was when the injury happened, when I decided to throw myself off the eight foot stone wall.

For the last seven years when my mum was happy enough to let me wander a little further afield, John and I would do just that. Miles and miles of footpaths and bridleways, fields, riverbanks, and woodlands we explored together, and I only ever had the vaguest sense of where we were. I was always in a state of constant surprise that we had managed to find our way home. John would tell me I shouldn't really leave the house without a ball of string tied to my front door, but I didn't need the string. I had John, who always knew where we were and where we were going. He had given me a leg up so I could grab the top of the wall, and using his shoulders I just manage to pitch myself up and sit on the top. He told me to wait, not to jump, and that he still loved me even though I had hopped off and twisted my ankle so bad he had to carry me home. After nearly three miles across the fields he also told me I was a dumb-ass.

For the second time in less than twenty-four hours, John carefully lowered me to my feet by the back door. The house is quiet but my mum has left the kitchen light on, which filters a warm glow across his soft dark features. He is frowning, and I know it has nothing to do with how much his back is probably hurting. "I hate that you have to work. Boo. I hate it might affect your studies." He is holding my gaze, his eyes serious and pained.

"I know, but it won't, I won't let it. I know how important-" I don't finish because he huffs in frustration. I reach my hand to his cheek, his smooth skin hidden beneath his evening stubble. I try to ease his tension and get a smile from his lips by covering them with my own. I am bolder with him now and the tender touch is quickly consumed with pent up passion that is slowly destroying me and driving me insane. I turned sixteen at the end of the summer, it's nearly Christmas and he is almost seventeen. I kind of thought he would be just as eager as me to experience each other in the way we had promised. I had the briefest meltdown when I thought that at best he had the patience of a saint, or at worst he just didn't think of me that way. I was very wrong on both counts and he assured me he thought of me like that every second of every day, but he wanted to wait. He wanted to make sure I was ready and not just because I had reached a legal age, and I know he knew I *was*, but he also wanted it to be perfect. He had saved his wages over the months and had bought the raw materials to fashion a unique promise ring. A smooth band of silver looped in a heart, which was beautifully distorted to look like the symbol for infinity, and had two shiny blue stones set where the metal crossed. He gave this to me on my birthday, his promise to me, and I was ready to give myself to him as my promise to him. This weekend he was moving into his own place and had a special day planned. With no expense spared he promised, but said we would play the rest by ear, adding that he'd had enough self-restraint to last him a lifetime.

He groans against my lips, and I can feel his smile against my mouth as he pushes my shoulder back trying to break away, but I stretch my neck to try and keep the sweet contact a little longer. I let out a heavy sigh and mourn the loss of warmth when he finally succeeds with the separation.

"I'll meet you after college tomorrow, now go get some sleep so you can study hard." He kisses me once more, but with tight lips. It's a definitive dismissal, and I pout, but he laughs and shakes his head at his own personal struggle to leave.

"I can't wait for the weekend," I whisper and grin when I hear him draw in a sharp breath.

He flashes his bright white smile, "Why? What's happening…Ow!" He grips his ribs as I retrieve my finger from jabbing it in his side.

"You're an idiot!" I try to hold my narrowed eyed scowl but end up laughing with him. He steps back to me, his body all hard heat and muscle. He cups my face, and his mint fresh breath kisses my skin when he whispers back, "Me, too," and with one last kiss he starts to walk backwards down the path.

"I saved for this because although I know it's just for one day, I want it to be special. I want to treat you like a princess." His eyes are darker now because his face is in the shadow of moonlight, but I can feel his fire.

"It better not be just for one day." I choose to misinterpret his meaning and am rewarded with a deep laugh as he chooses to misinterpret me.

"Well, in that case, I'm gonna need a second and third job, princess." He quips.

"Dumb-ass," I call after him. It's not about the money. He treats me like a princess every day, but I'll wait for him, because as crazy as I might think it is, it's important to him. It was the worst choice.

Chapter One

Today

"Oh, good God, Bets, what are you wearing?" Sofia practically screams at me as she bounds into my bedroom only to freeze with a look of complete horror on her face.

"What?" I ask with genuine surprise as I look down at my ensemble.

"I'm supposed to be a 'mature student' remember?"

Sofia has been my best friend since college. She sat next to me at the induction meeting and within five minutes of break time I knew everything. She told me she had recently moved to the area, had four brothers, many, many more cousins, and worked in one of her family's restaurants. She loved dancing, loved drinking more, though, and she had a small angel tattooed on her butt that would have her shipped to the mountains of Italy if her father was ever to find out. We were both aged sixteen starting college, and since John had decided not to go the college route, I was grateful she decided we would be friends. I had only known her four years, but the events of that time irrevocably changed my life, and Sofia, her brother, and her family were my lifeline, and I couldn't repay their kindness if I had a thousand lifetimes. I immediately liked her openness and quickly fell in love with her energy for life, her confidence, but above all her honesty. This is why I had asked for her assistance in creating the 'appropriate' first impression for my first day at University.

"Well, yes, but mature doesn't mean dead. I'm pretty sure my Aunt was wearing the same outfit when she was buried, and that was eight years ago! You haven't been digging, have you?" Sofia giggles, but abruptly stops when she sees my expression has quickly changed from confused to worried, and that really wasn't what she had intended with her little joke.

"Besides," she gently adds, "'technically' a mature student is defined as aged twenty five and over, remember, and what age are you supposed to be?"

"Twenty five, or so it says on my recently doctored and scanned birth certificate." I smile as I wave the documents I have to take for registration today. I can't think of a time when I thought I would be thankful to my sister. In fact, I can't think of her at all without grinding my teeth to the point of inducing a mind-numbing headache, which is why I don't think of her at all. I have not thought about her for years, not since the day she died. She didn't die, but she was dead to me. She'd wanted a clean slate; hers was dirty, I was sure of it, not just her reputation, her juvenile record for theft and drug dealing, but I always just got the sense she was hiding more. I gave up caring what that was when she stole all the money from the sale of our home and left me to pick up the tab for our mother's on-going health care. Our mum was diagnosed with Alzheimer's when I was fourteen, but she'd deteriorated rapidly, and when I was sixteen,

Kit and I made the decision to sell the house. I had found a nice care facility, the sale would mostly pay for, and between us we could make up the rest. Kit had Power of Attorney and ultimately had access to the money. She'd talked about starting afresh, rewriting her life, and I didn't understand why that was important at the time. I never believed she meant a fresh start away from me. I was staying with Sofia for a couple of months while Kit stayed at her boyfriend Dick's flat. She said it would take a while to sort out her new life and find somewhere we could both live. She just disappeared one day, and shortly after that I got notification from the care-home that the next quarterly payment was due, which was when I knew, really knew, what she had done. Sofia's family helped me with a full time job and sorting a payment plan with the nursing home. I couldn't move my mum into state care after seeing that she was settled and happy. I could still do my A-levels at night school, it would just take a little longer. I wasn't giving up on my education. The promise I made may haunt me because of what I'd lost, but it keeps me focused. "Ok, I may have overdone the age thing."

"Ya think?" mumbles Sofia.

"Let me change, just wait a moment." I try to spin quickly, only managing to jerk and squeak on my flat, square, crepe-heeled shoes. Really, what was I thinking? I return moments later.

"Oooo, yes, that's much better." Sarcasm dripping from every slowly uttered word. "An amorphous blob is exactly the right way to go." She raises her perfectly shaped eyebrows and I sigh. Damn those judgmental eyebrows! I slump on the edge and fall into the one and only armchair. I am actually feeling a little lost, and Sofia seems to know this, as she quickly has me in her tight embrace, squeezing the very uncertainty out of me.

"Bets, you have always been 'mature', regardless of the clothes you wear, I'm afraid, 'an Old Soul'. Remember that's what Mama has always called you? So how about you forget this," she says, waving her arms erratically around the array of clothes I'm wearing and have dropped in a heap. "Just wear something you are going to be happy in, comfortable, more confident, and more you?"

The uncertainty I am feeling right now and the knots I have in my stomach aren't me. I know I con't reach the dizzying heights of super confident Sofia, but I have had to assert myself from time to time, and I'm not shy. I don't have hang-ups and insecurities, because frankly, I don't have the time to care. I don't want a relationship other than my friends, and everything I have gained in my life is down to my own abilities and hard work. I'd like to say I wouldn't want it any other way, but I'm not a masochist, and I'm not an idiot. But I am definitely floundering here. I am uncomfortable with the fact that I'm pretending to be an age I'm not in order to study for a degree I want. It has to be part-time because I can't afford to not work full time. I'm uncomfortable with living illegally above the restaurant, a commercial property with no permission for residential use. Sofia's family is so sweet to let me live here, but this is a risk for them. The benefit of additional security, which I afford, could easily be performed by a decent alarm system

"Bethany Edith Thorne!" Sofia scolds, interrupting me from my inner flagellation. I hate it when she uses my middle name, it means she's losing her not-so-famous patience. I exhale despondently, and I bury my head in my hands.

"This just isn't you, Bets. I'm your best friend and I don't understand why you're trying to hide who you are. You're bright and confident, and you've got a cracking bod under all that shit!

I mean killer curves. You know it's not just your sparkling personality that has the boys lining up, right?" She's sitting directly in front of me now, daring me to break eye contact. She knows I'm not happy with the direction this conversation is heading, but before I can challenge her, she interrupts. "Brothers, I know, they are all like brothers. This is me, sweetie. I know how you feel and I know why you feel like that. I understand, I do, and I can see you're shutting down, so I won't push, but you know I want to, right?" She nudges my leg, and I give a weak grin. "Just don't hide." She whispers.

I smile with a bit more life and give a sharp nod of determination. "All right. All right, then!" I leap from the chair, lifting the gloom that had descended, forcing Sofia to fall on her butt.

"Give me five minutes." I call over my shoulder as I leave the room once more.

"Your last chance, Miss, or I'll dress you myself. I've got hot pants, boob tube, and high heels with your name on them!" she half threatens.

Well, okay, so I shouldn't want to hide, just stay under the radar, maybe, blend in, and I'm thinking six inch heals clip-clopping across the cobbles of the Quad would not aid this objective. So third time lucky, I emerge.

I've settled on my soft and worn pale blue Levis rolled up with my favourite red lace-up pumps, a fitted plain white T and my dark green, short, leather jacket, and striped cotton scarf wrapped loosely several times around my neck. My wavy dark chestnut hair is scooped into a loosely manageable knot, and my make-up is barely there, with some mascara and a splash of nude lip gloss.

"Beautiful butterfly, beautiful butterfly." Sofia beams and I lightly punch her on the arm for taking the piss, but I know I'm good to go.

"I'll want all the deets later...so call me?" Sofia's hug is getting a little emotional and tight.

"Stop! You're making me nervous and I don't need to call. I'll see you later. I'm working the late shift."

"I thought you would take tonight off at least, you know, just in case you hook up?" She teases.

"Bye Sofs." I leave. She has a key, and she can lock up.

I tend to walk everywhere, but today I'm running late and don't want to spend the rest of the day sweaty from rushing. All the same, it's a shame to get the tube when London is in midst of Autumn, and there has been no wind severe enough to strip the trees bare. It's my favourite season, and the only time of year when you really notice the sheer number of trees around the city, which are now golden bronze and fiery copper.

The campus itself is spread over a few locations across the city, but the oldest and main part is the Quad, a cobbled courtyard surrounded on three sides by early nineteenth century buildings. They may no longer dominate the skyline as they once had but they are imposing nonetheless. I pass the Gate House and make my way through the crowds of students to the Student Information Center. My main objective today, aside from the actual registration, is to work out how I can fit my part-time degree into a full-time timetable without raising suspicion. I need to double up on the part-time units in whatever way my work timetable will accommodate. I really don't want this degree to take the typical eight years, when I know I can do it in three. As I see it, I just have to approach each subject tutor individually and get them to accept me taking their extra lessons in addition to the lessons I'm actually assigned and just hope they don't compare notes. Simple.

I move slowly down the corridors, which have notice boards brimming with information on either side. Course and lecture information, clubs and interests, jobs and welfare; every food group is represented. I quickly scan the boards. Not that I will be 'joining-in' anytime soon, since free time is a luxury I haven't had in a while. I'm naturally drawn to the jobs and opportunities board, and am surprised and intrigued by a simple small flyer pinned and fighting for space. Call center, flexible late night hours, excellent pay. Not a huge amount of information, but I tear off one of the strips with the contact number and slip it in my jacket pocket.

I head toward the library with all my course information and stacks of flyers, which have been pressed into my hands as I've wandered, trying to get a feel for where I am and where I need to be. I would always gravitate toward the library, regardless. I can't live without my Kindle, but really there is no comparison to finding yourself lost in a room with shelves stacked high, soft chairs scattered, and quiet secluded corners surrounded by tombs of literature. Especially seductive if the building is as old as this; it's like a warm blanket of knowledge waiting to unfurl around me. I find one of the silent areas and a comfy seat, sinking down I take my notebook and pencil from my bag and start to doodle as my mind drifts. The shapes my pencil makes are repeating patterns of tightly bunched ears of corn, and the image makes me smile.

It was late August, and I had agreed to open my exam results with John in the hayfield. I had waited for the postman, and when he arrived, I took the letter addressed to me, a blanket, some provisions, and a notepad, then made my way to the hayfield. I walked through the churchyard and into the field, which was full of dozing Friesians, and guide to the field recently harvested for wheat. The farmer had baled and stacked the straw into several large blocks, and I couldn't see from the ground which one John would be on. He wasn't going to make it easy by leaving any clues or answering me when I called. I know he was there; he was always there before me.

I walked around three of the stacks and couldn't even see any tell-tale flattened footprints or bent stubble, the only thing I could do was climb and look from the top. I called again.

"You know a gentleman wouldn't let me climb all the way up there, especially when I've brought food!" It was a semi-whine, but I knew questioning his manners would get a response.

"Low blow, Boo, you're no fun, you know?" He peeks his head over the edge of the stack I'm directly next to, and I smile at his pout. His dark hair is flopping into his warm chocolate eyes.

"Yeah, I know, but you'd feel bad making me haul my arse up the wrong stack, and you know it." I sling my bag over my shoulder, tie the blanket around my waist and start to climb the straw bales. Poking my fingers and toes in hard to get purchase, I manage to grip and climb while John has his hand dangling for me to take as soon as I can reach it.

We sit cross-legged, knee to knee on my blanket with our letters in our hands. We both rip the envelopes at the same time, and I stare at mine in shock.

"Well, I've got what I need, how did you do, Boo?" He takes the letter from me.

"Bloody hell, Boo!" He leaps forward and knocks me onto my back. "You're a freaking genius!" He laughs, but I'm still in shock, I got nine As and one C in PE. I hated PE. He rolls to his side and grabs my notebook. "Right, we need a plan, you know you can do anything with these, Bets, I mean it; you could be anything you want to be."

I smiled at him and he looked so happy for me. He didn't care about his results at all; they were enough, and that was that. But for me, he was, well, he just looked so proud. "Well, it gets me into college, but let's not go crazy. It's not like I won the lottery!" I nudge him but he pitches up on one elbow and looks stern.

"No. No, it's not. That's just money. Money you can lose, money can be taken away. This, this is yours; this gives you choices and no one can take that away from you." He holds my gaze, "I mean it, Bets. It's really important to give yourself choices in what you do with your life, you can be anything you want to be." He leant in and kissed my cheek. "You are already everything to me, but this," he takes the letter, "this is for you." He looks deep into my eyes. "You have to promise me, Bethany, you'll do this. Whatever it takes, you have to give yourself choices. Promise?" He looks so serious, and he's used my real name.

"I promise."

Confirming with a nod he looks relieved and flops back down beside me. "What did you bring me to eat, wench?"

I laugh at him, and when I look at the faces staring at me, I realize I have laughed out loud in the library, but I also notice the curious looks, and I can feel my wet face. I quickly wipe the tears with my sleeve. I am always shaken when I remember, but at the same time I don't want to forget. I get back to sorting through all the information in my overstuffed bag. I spend the next hour sorting through the timetables and think I can juggle a few seminars and double dip a few units to get the extra credits I'm going to need. It looks like there will only be a few gaps in the four days I have to attend, which will suit my working hours at the restaurant perfectly. I'm starting to feel a little more confident I can pull this off.

There is an informal gathering for the new mature students

in one of the basement classrooms, an opportunity to meet with fellow students and current students to get an insight, that sort of thing. I thought I should pop my head in, so I pack my bag and make my way back to the Quad.

I lean my entire body against the reluctant fire door to the classroom and the sprinkling of people inside turn my way. God,,I hate these things. It's not that I find making friends particularly difficult, it's just that I find these forced situations excruciating. I take in those in the room as I make my way to the safety of the coffee table. I am not sure if they are all mature students, or if there are Lecturers here, too, but I am by far the youngest, feeling that my first choice of outfit wouldn't have been misplaced, after all. There are some dodgy double denim combinations, some corduroy, I'm thinking Lecturer, and a few leather jackets, which belong to much younger men. The women seem to fare a little better and are dressed in either pant suit and blouse outfits or thick woollen type matching skirt and jacket. Being slightly thankful that I really don't have time to socialize, I start to fix myself a drink with purpose and confidence I'm not really feeling. A double espresso would be welcome, but I'll settle for the crappy instant coffee from the dripping silver canteen style dispenser.

"Don't look so scared, Bethany, they are all in the same boat and just as eager to make friends, I'm sure." A kind gentleman's voice speaks directly behind me.

I turn with my coffee in hand to see Mr. Wilson, my course leader, smiling at me. His wrinkled face gives way to more wrinkles, if that was possible. Mr. Wilson is in his early sixties with wavy grey hair and dark grey eyes which are framed by square, black-rimmed glasses that perch on the indent in his nose indicating many years of use. He wears a worn dark green tweed three-piece suit, a bright shirt, and an even brighter bow tie. I understand he was a formidable businessman in his youth, having built and sold several companies. Now, however, he is firmly entrenched in academia.

I couldn't apply for the undergraduate through the normal channel. Although my actual grades were good enough, the dates and ages on the documents would conflict and might have been flagged up as suspicious. I am too young and they would insist I take the full-time degree route. Instead, I had to fill out a departmental application form, have a general entrance exam, interview, and a date of birth stating I was in fact twenty-five. Mr. Wilson was, at the time, quick to put me at my ease at my interview earlier in the year, and we have exchanged a number of emails since I accepted my placement. He is the least intimidating academic I have come across, and I am thankful he seems to have taken me under his wing.

"Oh I'm sure." I return his smile. "Actually, I'm really glad you are here. I was hoping I could confirm my timetable amendments and just make sure I'm getting the most from what's on offer?"

"Yes, yes, of course, my dear. I said at the interview we would accommodate as best we can, and you were quite explicit in your requirements. I promised at the time I would help, and I wouldn't have offered you a place if I felt you wouldn't take every opportunity on offer, or if we couldn't fulfill our promise." He gently squeezes my hand as if to reinforce his sentiment.

"That's very kind, later in the week, maybe?"

"You have my email, my dear, anytime." He leans past me and picks up a handful of biscuits, which he tries to balance on the saucer holding his tea.

He doesn't seem to have any compulsion to mix and as I

have a full cup in my hand I am a little reluctant to navigate the room. So we remain standing together at the edge of the gathering, and he begins to munch noisily on his biscuits. The room has started to fill, and like many basement classrooms, it feels a little stuffy, but the noise level has risen from awkward silence to gentle hum. A number of Mr. Wilson's colleagues have come over and it is clear he is well liked and respected. He kindly introduces me as some will be my Lecturers, and I try to commit their faces and names to memory, but it's hopeless until they leave, and Mr. Wilson fills me in with some inappropriate piece of information that makes me laugh out loud and will definitely make it easier to remember them.

Ms. Stephens was a Karaoke queen, Mr. Philips nearly drove away with his newborn baby in his car seat on the roof of the car after several weeks of interrupted nights, and I was lucky not to spit my coffee all over him when he revealed Mr. Peters, from finance, nearly didn't get married last year, because there was a fight as to who would wear the wedding dress! I can feel my eyes start to water as he turns a wicked grin my way.

I look over toward the still closed door as I feel a cool wave of fresh air flow over me and a rush of goosebumps prickle my skin. Before me, Mr. Wilsons' eyes widen as he fixes his gaze directly above my head. I can't seem to move.

"Daniel! How simply wonderful of you to join us, I didn't expect you to accept my invitation to this little gathering, but I'm so pleased you could make the time," Mr. Wilson gushes.

Wow! I can't help but smile, this man is too sweet and obviously a little in awe of whomever is standing behind me.

"I didn't, and I don't." The deep voice growls his response.

"That's rude!" My hand immediately flies to my mouth as I realize I did in fact say that out loud. My shoulders tense, and I try to sink into myself as I notice the instant evaporation of Mr. Wilsons' smile. I would like to think that his change in demeanour is a result of the rude man behind me, but I can't help feel it is because of my inappropriate contribution.

I give a tight smile and try to apologise as I mouth, "I'm sorry," to Mr. Wilson. I straighten my back and turn sharply only to have my field of vision blocked by a wall of chest encased in a black, fitted suit jacket over a crisp white shirt. I lower my eyes taking in his smart well- fitted jeans, large thighs, and shiny black boots. I drag my eyes up. This feels like it's taking forever. I'm hoping it's only seconds, especially as my gaze lingers a little too long at his crotch.

Christ! Move your eyes, Bets! I do, up and up. .He is standing really close. My breath hitches when I take in the fierceness of the stare his eyes are giving mine. They are a 'divers dream' ocean colour blue, deep blue, with even deeper flecks. He narrows them slightly, and I see a tiny twitch in his jaw. He is intense. I can feel the anger radiating in waves. I am only guessing it's anger from the few words he has spoken.

"I need the keys to your office, Jack. You did say I would have access?" Curt and to the point, but his question has me confused, as he hasn't taken his eyes from mine.

"I'm sorry, Sir?" I'm generally confused.

"Accepted." He gives a flicker of a grin.

"Errr?"

"Yes, yes." Mr. Wilson interrupts. "Of course, Daniel, I have a set in my briefcase." He pauses to see if he is being acknowledged in any way. He isn't. Mr. Wilson continues, "Allow me to introduce..." He sounds flustered, but I interrupt.

"Mr. Wilson." I turn away from the unfathomable tension that's starting to build between this man and me. "Don't bother, really, I should try and meet some of the others here... Well, those who do want to be here, at least. You've been wonderful so far, but I better brave this myself and leave you to help this--" I can't help but pause, knowing it's rude, "--man sort the keys so he can get on his way." I go to move off and find I am again blocked by that large chest I can now smell it's so close. Fresh with spice and something exotic and a surge of heat returns like taking a direct hit in the chest.

"Jack, please continue... allow you to introduce?" I am again looking into his eyes as they briefly flick toward Mr. Wilson for encouragement only to return their fix to mine. I'm trying to swallow, and I am hoping the slight tremble I am experiencing now is not visible. With slightly less enthusiasm Mr. Wilson continues;

"Daniel, allow me to introduce one of our mature students starting with us part-time this semester...Bethany Thorne. Bethany, this is Daniel Stone. He is a respected and very successful businessman, and also a 'Friend of the University'. Daniel has kindly offered his valuable time to give a series of lectures for our entrepreneurs'...we are very lucky." Mr. Wilson seems genuinely thrilled and his smile is infectious.

"Mature?" Daniel raises an eyebrow, but his intense gaze doesn't break contact with mine.

"Friend?" I challenge. I'm trying to be brave and counter his question. It's not working. His obvious query removes the smile from my face, and I look nervously at my hands, which are now gripped together. I reach to tuck my hair behind my ear and tug gently at the nape, feeling the skin lift and pinch as I do.

"I'm twenty-five," I venture boldly, more bold than I'm feeling at any rate. "Yes, twenty-five. I'm twenty-five." Smooth, Bets, really smooth. I risk a glance up toward his face. His dark eyes crinkle as his grin transforms to a full on, breath-taking smile. He is possibly the most stunning man I have ever seen, and he can't be the most important man in the room, yet I feel the power and command like a force holding me rooted to the spot.

"Really?" He leans in further and I can feel his breath on my neck. I feel my face flush instantly. I must be seven shades of red right now, and I know my heart is pumping so hard, it might just succeed in escaping my chest via my ribcage. I try to swallow but manage only to make a whimper leave my dry throat. I lick my parched lips and notice his eyes fix on the slight movement. Christ, Bets! Get a grip. You'll be swishing your hair and swooning any minute now. He lifts my hair away from my neck, an impossibly intimate gesture, which does nothing to quell the raging heat building between my legs. I am only thankful that Mr. Wilson seems to be distracted from this very intense exchange.

"Interesting, Miss Thorne, now why are you lying?" His voice is rich and luxurious like velvet caressing my skin.

Shit! I don't say this out loud, but I'm screaming it to myself, and I make a sharp intake of breath, which has drawn Mr. Wilson's attention back to me. I try to take a step back and notice a number of eyes focused on our little exchange, just what I need. So much for staying under the radar, and it doesn't help that Mr. Stone has neatly mirrored my retreat keeping the intimate distance between us.

"I'm not, I mean, I don't know what you mean…" I fumble quietly hoping Mr. Wilson is catching none of this.

"Oh Miss Thorne, you most definitely are, but what puzzles me is why? But I do love a good puzzle." His tone is pure temptation.

"Well." I recover. "This has been delightful and as charming as you are…" I leave the statement unfinished as I turn my back, effectively blanking Mr. Stone and take hold of Mr. Wilson's hand. He looks a little confused, and I'm thinking, *join the club!*

"Thank you, Mr. Wilson, so much for this opportunity, I really am so grateful, Sir."

"Bethany, there is no need for 'Sir' please. I don't mind if you call me Jack."

"I'll be more comfortable with Mr. Wilson, Mr. Wilson." I smile.

"And I would be more comfortable with Sir." I freeze as his hands grasp my shoulders and his lips are again brushing my ear. I pray to God no one else can hear, because they can sure as shit see my face flame once more. "In fact… I insist." He gives a gentle laugh. I shift slightly to try and ease the pressure in my groin.

"I have to get to work. My shift starts soon!" I rush to announce it, as if this revelation will save me from this excruciating encounter. It's not a lie, but I could have stayed a little longer if I wanted; I don't. I step away and feel the sudden loss of heat. I have to lean awkwardly around an immovable Daniel Stone to place my coffee cup down. Only when I am safely on the other side do I release the breath I had been holding. I risk a look back into the room through the small window in the door. There are several groups of people now, but undoubtedly most eyes are fixed on the mountain of a man next to Mr. Wilson. His eyes are, however, undeniably fixed on me.

"So?" Sofia leaves a long dramatic pause. "How was your first day? Did you make any friends? Did the other children play nice?" She is carrying a bottle of white wine and two glasses from downstairs and flops into the armchair opposite me. I am curled up in a ball wrapped head to toe in a blankie.

"Pour first." I instruct, pointing at the empty glasses.

"It couldn't have been that bad; you didn't even have any lectures, did you?" She passes me a very full glass.

"Urghhh." I take a large gulp, this is not going to touch the sides. "I think I've been rumbled."

Sofia laughs then stops. "You're serious? How?"

"Some guy at the gathering, a 'Friend of the University' they've roped into giving some free lectures, flat out told me I was lying in front of my course leader."

"What? Oh my God, Bets. What did you do? What did Mr. What's-His-Name say?"

"Mr. Wilson, well, he didn't say anything, he didn't actually hear, this guy whispered it in my ear." I get a shiver as I say this, like I can still feel his breath skim my skin. I can feel my face heat, and I quickly down the rest of my glass.

"Oh my... Miss Thorne, I do believe you're blushing." She giggles.

"I know! What is that about? Some random hot guy whispers in my ear and I light up like a red light district. They all swear like sailors in the kitchen, and the topics they share, well, it's no holds barred most of the time and not a hint of colour!" I am just as shocked.

"Hot guy?" She hums with excitement.

"Oh yes." I swallow. "Did I not mention that he was off the charts, hot as hell? And he knows, I don't know what he knows, but he knows I'm lying." I'm frowning now and waving to get more wine. Sofia leans forward and tops up my glass. I take a smaller sip this time. "Oh God, I can't lose this place, Sofs." I drop my head in my one free hand.

"Random guy, you say, so he is not on the staff?" She muses.

"No." I like where she's going with her thinking.

"And you didn't confirm he was right?"

"No."

"And your Mr. What's-His-Name didn't hear?" Her lips begin to curl in a reassuring way.

"Mr. Wilson, and no." I mirror her pleasing smile.

"So then there is nothing to actually worry about, nothing material has changed here, so don't worry. Nothing will come of this, I promise, other than me laughing at you for actually blushing over some 'random hot guy.'" She moves to sit next to me and nudges my arm, not quite spilling my drink. I think about what she's said.

"You are right, he's not staff and not a student. I probably won't even see him again." I take a satisfying sip to drain my glass.

Chapter Two

I wish I had a bath. I stand under the less than powerful staff shower at the rear of the kitchens and attempt to dodge the range of temperatures, which fluctuate from skin flaying hot to freeze-your-nipples-clean-off cold. In fact, I think I would sell my soul for the luxury of a roll top bath with deep hot water and endless silken bubbles; throw in some candles and I wouldn't even put up a fight. I squeal as I'm blasted with a final spurt of ice water as I turn the tap off and step onto the slatted wooden tray, which in the winter prevents my feet from freezing directly onto the concrete floor. I wrap myself in my large fluffy towel, slowly open and peep around the door. The corridor is empty, and I'm pretty sure I am early enough to brave the mad dash upstairs without the other employees catching a flash of flesh. This fact alone is the reason I am always awake at five in the morning. A brutal and mortifying lesson learned the hard way, and even though I cringe at the recollection, I am ever thankful no phone camera was at hand at the time.

I have lived here for two years. My sister's disappearance kind of left me homeless, and my temporary month-long stay at Sofia's turned into two years until I was eighteen. Sofia's family took me in. They have a large town house in a fabulous part of London, and although they clearly have money, they are really down to earth; so friendly and welcoming. The house was always full. Full with friends and family, of wonderful aromas and of love. I dated Sofia's twin brother, Marco, for a short time, not my smartest move, but he was funny, smart and persistent. He didn't cover himself in glory when I found out he had been bragging about me to some friends. He was a little shocked when I didn't take the opportunity to shame him and deny it all when I had the chance. I had my reasons and laughed it off, even gave him a high score when pushed for details. Sofia was not so kind and tore into him in private. She was the only one I ever told about John and completely understood why I was the way I was, but she was protective of me all the same. This, in itself, could have made my move into the family home awkward, but I have a talent for turning fragile relationships into strong friendships. Next to Sofia, Marco is my best friend.

Marco works in the Knightsbridge restaurant with me while Sofia is studying a food and wine diploma at an exclusive private school in central London. She is happy to live at home, forgoing the student experience for the utter luxury her five star home offers. She also chose not to work in the family restaurants, opting instead to work at a private members club, learning the hospitality and event side of catering. As the only girl, she is spoiled and indulged, and could have so easily become a proper princess. She can spend money like there is no tomorrow, but she is generous, too, and she works really hard.

I knew I was welcome to stay as long as I needed, but the house was full and sharing a bed with the human starfish meant I never slept all that well. Even though Sofia's father kept on about not leaving me to "wander the streets," I started to look for a room as soon as I turned eighteen. Realistically, sleeping on the streets wasn't going to happen, I could afford a room, it just wouldn't be pretty, and it might be a little out toward the sticks. However, one Sunday I was wiping down at the end of my shift and getting ready to leave, when Sofia's father took me upstairs. He wanted to show me what his boys had been working on. The confusion on my face must have been a picture as he laughed and led the way. Above the restaurant were two small box rooms, which were too inconvenient to use for extra storage for the restaurant so had been relegated to a dumping ground for dying furniture and dead kitchen equipment.

I stood on the threshold and was completely overwhelmed; I couldn't take a step further when I saw what they had done for me. Sofia leapt from behind an armchair shouting, "Surprise!" That was the understatement of the year. I had no idea this was all happening above my head. The room had been cleared and painted a warm honey white. The threadbare patchy carpet had been removed and the wide wooden plank flooring had been stripped and polished. Two large chocolate and charcoal coloured rugs almost covered the entire floor, but you could still see the rich polished wood around the edge.

In the far corner below the window, a book lamp illuminated a small white desk with a high backed wooden chair tucked beneath it. In the centre of the room was a two-seater sofa with a huge, fluffy, cream-coloured throw, which was hiding a rather hideous seventies style geometric pattern. Next to that was a faded and battered leather armchair, which I recognised from Marco's bedroom. It was a much loved piece of furniture and very comfortable. The permanent indent in the seat cushion was a testament to that. Sofia had obviously been raiding my storage boxes and sixth form art portfolio case, as the walls now held two of my abstract landscapes. She'd had them mounted and framed. There was also a silver framed picture of my mum when she was my age on the coffee table and a cork notice board above the desk declaring, 'Welcome to Your New Home ☺' in the form of a colourful homemade poster.

Sofia came toward me and grabbed my hand, excited to show me all the improvements. There was a corner unit, which acted like a kitchenette with a single ring hob, kettle, and toaster. To be fair, there was a much larger kitchen downstairs if I was ever feeling more adventurous than tea and toast. Behind that was a separate toilet and sink; next to those, two smaller store cupboards had been knocked into one to provide a perfect sized bedroom. The queen sized futon bed dominated the tiny space and Sofia had hung white fairy lights all along the headboard. It looked magical. It was perfect. My new home was perfect! I was speechless and about to turn, when I noticed a tiny framed picture beside the bed. It is the follow on picture of the one I always keep in my purse. It is the photo of me and John, my soul mate and best friend since I was five years old. It was taken on my sixteenth birthday. It was my fault he never made it to seventeen. It was my fault he was murdered.

I couldn't stop the tears that had been building since I stood on the threshold. I let out a sob and was quickly muffled to silence by tight embraces from Sofia and her father. I had decided a long time ago that crying accomplished little other than huge, puffy, red eyes and a snotty nose. So I reigned in the breath-stealing sobs I could feel bubbling under the surface, which I knew I was capable of in private, and gave a light laugh to lift the mood. After all, I was genuinely over the moon with my new pad. I thanked them again and again. The grand tour took no more than five minutes and after seeing how truly happy they had made me, Sofia and her father left for the evening. I was able to wallow in the solitude of my new home, because although I am often lonely, I am rarely alone. It was bliss.

I work a split shift on Mondays, so having confirmed my timetable amendments with a quick email to Mr. Wilson, I head down to the kitchen. I am capable of turning my hand to most jobs in and around the restaurant, and Sofia's eldest brother Anthony, Jr., who runs this restaurant, is pretty flexible where I work. He prefers me front of house, and I don't flatter myself that I would ever be let loose cooking, but I can prepare vegetables and wash up like a pro. Besides, I am happiest in the kitchen. The pressure can be intense, and the language can be blue, but I like the banter and buzz that comes from working in a predominately dominant male environment. The guys never make any concessions for me being there, and they certainly don't censure their language or the topics up for discussion. Frankly, what I didn't learn in biology, I more than made up for in that kitchen. They would happily enlighten me, giving me tips and tricks, which would make a hardened professional blush but just made me laugh.

I prepped vegetables all morning; one of the specials today was zucchini fritters, which meant mountains of shredded courgettes. It's the only way to eat such a dull vegetable and the way Joe cooks them; they are light, crisp, and melt in your mouth. I had a taster as I finished work and headed upstairs to change. I planned to go to the library to make a start on my reading. I can't afford to buy all the course books, but reading them in the library is no hardship. As I put my jacket on, I dig in the pocket and pull out a crumpled piece of paper with the contact details I took from the job board, the one with the very vague but intriguing information. I decide to give the number a call, It was worth that to at least establish some details. I sit on the arm of my chair and punch the numbers.

The call is answered, "Late Night Calls…let me help you?" The voice is slow and sultry, and the question threw me. I couldn't speak.

"Come on sweetie, don't be shy," The voice encouraged. I'm pretty sure it was a female voice, but it was low, so I couldn't be hundred percent certain.

"Right, sorry." I stumbled, "I got your details form the jobs board at my University, you know about flexible hours, extra cash… um, could I speak to someone about that?" I definitely sounded like I have the wrong number and am just about to hang up.

"Oh, sure thing, sweetie, I'll just put you through to Mags, she'll sort you out. Bye!" Her bright voice is cut off abruptly, and my call is clicked over and put through before I could thank her. This gives me enough time to compose myself, maybe not sound like such a moron.

"Hello?" I ventured tentatively as the line goes silent.

"Hello, my darling, what can I do for you today?" Her voice was equally low, and I wonder if that is a job requirement or maybe just something in the water.

"I was calling about the job, but to be honest I don't really know what the job is, where it is, or, well, any of the details, really, so that would be a good place to start?" I try to come across as professional as possible, my voice a little lower than normal.

"Don't you just have the sexiest voice?" Mags says, ignoring my actual question.

"Urgg?" She can't see my confusion, but my eloquent noise must make that clear.

"Well, not when you grunt like that, you don't." She laughs a deep throaty sound, which still sounds inviting but not mean.

"Oh!" I am shocked, and given I work in the kitchen below, that is saying something.

"Yes 'Oh'. Now *that* I can work with." She laughs lightly this time. "I am going to say right off, I will be able to offer you something, but I think we should meet, despite my type of business, I really prefer to do this sort of thing face to face. Can you come by at three this afternoon? We are quiet then, and we can go over everything and start your training." She is super friendly and can't hide her enthusiasm.

"Training?" Pretty sure my 'sexy' tone had been replaced with pure panic.

"I know I'm getting ahead of myself, but I know people, and I have a good feeling about you. What is your name darling?" she encourages.

"My real name?" I ask, and she laughs out.

"Yes, darling, your real name." She is still laughing but I can't take offense. She makes me smile.

"Bethany." I tell her.

"Take my details down, Bethany, and I'll see you at three." The light laughter is gone, and this is purely business. Her tone shifts, and she gives me everything I will need to meet her later.

After ending the call I am a little dazed. I now have a pretty good idea what "Late Night Calls" is, and yet I still agreed to meet with Mags. More interesting still is that I am actually a little excited about it.

The door to the Late Night Calls office was unnamed, and I

almost missed it, nestled between the arches behind Waterloo station. I knew the pub to the left, The Hole in the Wall, but I had no idea there was office space too. I was half right; it wasn't really office space at all. I press the buzzer and the intercom lights up.

"Please come on up, Bethany." The same voice from earlier has lost a little of its sultriness with the accompanying crackle.

I climb the narrow stairs and tentatively open the only door on the landing. The room is more like a hotel lobby, luxurious and welcoming, a complete contrast to the slightly grimy exterior and not like any office I know.

"Hello, Bethany." The girl behind a small reception desk smiles. "I'm Susan, and Mags is just on the phone." She points to a closed door behind her. "She won't be long... they never are." She giggles.

"Please take a seat, and make yourself at home." She gestures to the seating area, which resembles an adult playpen without the bars. I could choose from a large corner sofa, which takes up most of the room, or alternately, I could perhaps romp on the oversized cushions piled high on a faux fur rug. As no one can get up from those things with a modicum of dignity intact, I decided not to risk the lure of their softness and opt for the safety of the sofa. I sit on the edge, which is apt because I am on edge. I smile at Susan, who has returned to flicking through, what looks from here, like a lads' magazine.

"No frowning, darling, you'll get wrinkles." Mags, I assume, enters the room with a dramatic swish emphasised by the flow of her chiffon three-quarter length bright pink jacket. She must be in her sixties and is immaculate. Her make-up is a little heavy around the eyes, and she has the brightest pink lipstick on. Her hair is cut in a sharp grey blonde bob, and her tailored suit and silk blouse perfectly fit her shapely curves. She's wearing six inch gold Louboutins, and I know this because they are Sofia's favourite, not because I am lucky enough to own a pair. After taking me in carefully, she sits beside me and sighs.

"Well, you are just as sexy as your voice. Pity we don't do video calls." She pauses. "Yet." Her smile is warm, and she gives a light laugh. I don't know why, but I find myself grinning back. She is warm and friendly, and I am about to be a huge waste of her time. I'm thinking it's going to take a maximum of five minutes for her to conclude I am wholly unsuited to provide the type of service Late Night Calls offers. She squeezes my knee, her eyes soften and she looks intently into mine. I think that might be a record for interviews, not even five minutes, and I can feel a 'Don't call us' heading my way. "Come on into my office; let's give you a test run!" This woman has managed to shock me twice in the same day. She grabs my hand and practically hauls me across the room into her office and closes the door before I can change my mind. "Darling, don't look so nervous. You know what we do, yes?" She raises her perfectly drawn on eyebrow at her query.

"Yes, Miss," I quietly reply. She raises both eyebrows in surprise and almost imperceptibly utters, "interesting," under her breath.

"Well, I will tell you the whys and wherefores, we will have a little trial and go from there." She is very encouraging, and her face is alight with misplaced enthusiasm.

"Yes, Miss." I hesitate and suck in a shallow breath. "I'll try".

"I run an exclusive service." Mags continues proudly. "Top service, top quality, and top price." She grins. "You work the hours you want, though I would like a minimum of one hour per day, I provide the phone and calls are directed through my switchboard. This protects you *and* the client. You can work wherever you like, you can come here if that suits, and you can earn up to a hundred pounds an hour if you can keep them on the phone that long." She chuckles and I'm starting to wish I was up to the task. She continues, "...or more if you provide one of the speciality services." As the obvious horror on my face must show, she quickly adds, "Oh, darling, I don't mean *that* sort of service. I'm no Madam, although I've been called worse." She laughs again. "I just mean we have dedicated lines, which cater to specific tastes." She pauses and eyes me carefully. "Any questions?"

I am actually speechless, another indication of my unsuitability for a job totally reliant on speech.

"All right, then, let me hear your audition piece?" She fixes me with her expectant kind eyes.

"Oh." I breathe. "Well, I'm not sure." I hesitate and can feel my face flush.

Sensing my extreme discomfort, Mags smiles and hands me her phone. "Use this as a prop if it helps. Imagine it's an actual call; all you have to do is imagine." She is sweet and encouraging, but I am so out of my depth. I look at the phone in my shaking hand, sigh, and hand it back to her. "Listen, why don't I let you listen to a few calls first, a few samples as it were, once the initial shock is over, I'm sure you'll get the idea...what do you think?" She places her hand over mine but doesn't take the phone back.

I am not given to running at the first sign of a challenge, even if I am so very far from my comfort zone and have no idea why she is being so kind, but I don't want to disappoint her.

"Yes, Miss, that's very kind. I'll do that." I am too embarrassed to raise my eyes to meet hers at this point, so she takes the phone, presses a few numbers and hands it back to me.

I am thankful she leaves the room as I put the phone to my ear and begin to listen to the sample calls. It turns out I wouldn't need that much imagination, as the calls give me vivid flashbacks to many a conversation in the kitchen. The descriptions are full on, and the details are explicit, extremely explicit. It isn't that I doubted my imagination or my ability to be detailed in my descriptions, but my actual lack of sexual experience is undoubtedly going to be a deal breaker here, and I know it. Still, as my face continues to flush, I continue to listen. The last call starts.

"*I've got your big hard cock in my hand--*" the breathy voice began "*--can you feel my tight fist? I'm gonna pump you hard. I'm gonna pump you into my hot wet mouth... mmmmm.*"

I can hear the caller's deep inhaling breath.

"*You're so hard against my tongue; it's hot and wet and I'm licking around the head and all the way down. I can feel your veins throbbing as I lap and lick it; it's like velvet over iron and tastes so good I can't get enough. Ahh, I can feel your rock hard cock twitching in my fist, I think I'm going to lick you all the way down to your balls. Mmmm, I'm cupping your balls with my other hand, and I'm fucking you with my fist, but I want more. Are you going to give me more?*" She pauses and breathes loudly. I'm shifting in my seat, more than a little uncomfortable, as she continues.

"*I am going to take your big hard cock and push it between my tight swollen lips, and take you deep, deep in my throat, and you're going to fuck my mouth, yes?*"

"*Mmmm... yeah, that's right.*" The deep rasping reply of the caller was the first real indication there was someone on the receiving end of this call.

"*Fuck my mouth, and make me swallow.*" She gives a long drawn out satisfied moan. The line goes dead.

"Wow!" I say as Mags returns. If I thought I was red before, I must look like I'm about to haemorrhage.

"The endings are always a little abrupt, but they are paying by the minute, so what do you expect, really?" I am hoping that's a rhetorical question because all powers of speech have deserted me. She hands me a glass of water, which I gratefully accept.

"I'd love to be that confident. I mean she seemed to really…" I'm struggling to articulate full sentences now, another stellar example of my ineptitude for this role. "And she was in control, assertive. I don't think I would be able to…you know…but-"

Interrupting, Mags states, "You're a virgin." She smiles warmly.

"Well, yes, to this sort of thing." I attempt to qualify her statement.

"No, darling, I mean you are a virgin; you've never had sex." It was no longer a question; it was a statement of fact. "It doesn't matter, you know," she continues.

"Umm, not to presume to tell you your business, but I would think that was kind of important, if not *the* most important part." I frown as she shakes her head at my incorrect conclusion.

"Don't get me wrong, it *is* unusual in this business, but you are not 'an innocent', or if you were, you would have run a mile as soon as you realised what we did, and you certainly wouldn't have been able to endure a whole sample call. So despite the adorable colour in your cheeks, you are still here. You have a great voice and a good imagination, I assume?" She raises a questioning eyebrow to which I nod my reply. "And you're a submissive!" My eyes widen. "Quite perfect." She adds.

I laugh out loud. Wow, that couldn't be further from the truth. I don't remember a time when I didn't make every decision myself. There is no one to tell me what to do, not that I would let them, and I kick arse at Krav Maga each week with Marco. Does that sound submissive? I know she has made a mistake, but I like her, and I find I can't be affronted by her misguided character assessment.

"Darling," she soothes, "I know people, I read people, and I can read you like an ABC or should I say D/s." She chuckles. "You are all, 'Yes, Miss. No, Miss', without a hint of irony." She seems so pleased with herself I almost hate to disillusion her.

"I was being polite." I point out.

"Yes, you were, but there's more, trust me, and what a wonderful way to explore this "worldview", through the safety of your telephone." She was being genuine and I can't take offense, even if she is way off the mark.

"Look, I have a proposal: take your time, think it over, and do some research, but remember to clear your browser history!" She laughs at her own joke. "I would like to take you on as a submissive for one of the premium lines. There will obviously be some artistic license, you won't be a to-the-letter submissive, after all, can't very well hold a conversation over the phone if you're gagged." Again she seems to find herself hilarious. I take another sip of water and give a very nervous laugh, trying to share her carefree attitude to the whole other world crashing into mine. "If you agree we will start you off one hour each night. From midnight onwards tends to be busiest. It's completely anonymous and completely safe, no one needs to know. You look like a girl who can keep a secret?" She looks directly at me. She is either the master of the understatement or she really can read people.

"I can, I do and I will… but are you sure?" I hold her gaze. Her lips twitch into a smooth smile, and she merely raises her brow, sweeping her knowledgeable gaze around her immaculate office and over her expensively clothed body, finally resting her eyes on her diamond laden fingers, the final piece of evidence of her good decisions.

"Here, take this phone, if you decide it's a no, then you can drop it back, but if we are good to go. it will save me a courier."

"Thank you. And thank you for your time Miss, sorry… Mags, just a few days?" I tell her.

"I'll be waiting." She was grinning as I left her office.

I have an email from Mr. Wilson waiting when I arrived home. It was an urgent message to come to his office after class tomorrow. Crap.

WANTED

WIFE ~~FOR~~ 4 NAVY SEAL**S**

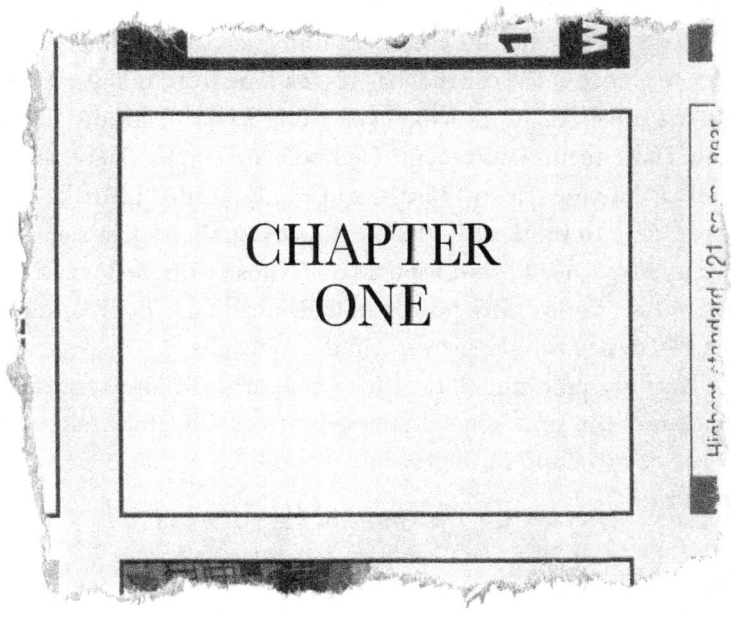

CHAPTER ONE

"Jesus, Finn, you sure you're not emigrating?" Hope laughs out a dirty throaty sound, as she struggles with the last of my suitcases. Stacking the final piece on the back seat on top of the mobile mountain, which pretty much contains my life or what was my *pathetic* life. I flash a tight smile, which sticks to my teeth, and a punch of guilt hits me in the gut, which I clearly fail to hide in my expression. "Finn?" I can hear the wobble in my best friend's voice, her tone pitched with genuine concern.

"No, I'm not emigrating." I make a show of rolling my eyes at her dramatics, even as I mumble 'probably' under my breath so as not to be accused of lying outright, if all *does* go well. "One month is a long time. I need a lot of shit."

"There's a lot and then there's *all* your shit. I should know, since you've been camped on my sofa for the last three months. My flat looks like it's been burgled, it's so bare. I think the only thing you haven't packed is Dolly here." She pats the soft-top roof of my ancient Citrëon 2CV.

"I would take her if I could." I tilt my head and cast an affectionate glance at the car that has rescued me from many a disaster, the most recent, moving everything I own from my home with Dave to the aforementioned sofa in Hope's flat. Luckily Dolly is like the frickin' Tardis, and I only needed to make one trip. Come to think of it, that isn't lucky at all, it's just sad. I'm twenty-six years old, and I spent ten of those with the love of my life, yet all my worldly possessions fit inside a 4-door, antique car, which has wildlife growing in the footwells.

"It's only a month; I'll take good care of her." Hope's face fails to achieve the smile she's desperately trying for, and I take that as my cue to jump in the car and avoid eye contact. *I'm such a coward.*

We chat for a while, and the car falls silent. Hope reaches over and her bony hand grips mine, which is clutching the steering wheel. Her eyes are glazing again, and I try, with enormous effort, to swallow the lump in my throat, but it won't budge.

"I'm going to miss you so much," she tells me for the umpteenth time. "Do you really have to go? He could be a psycho." I twist my hand in hers so our fingers are now threaded.

"He could be, but he isn't," I reassure her.

"I still think you're crazy." She states this with certainty but no judgment.

There are many reasons she has been my best friend since primary school. For a start, she's the keeper of all my secrets. The morning after every sleepover since my early teens, she would take delight in embarrassing me, regurgitating every word I spilt throughout the night when I talked in my sleep. The worst of all habits, in my opinion, because there was nothing I could do to stop myself, and I was, by all accounts, shamelessly honest and open. I bought a dreamcatcher, which seemed to help. Nevertheless, in the end, I begged her not to keep me talking. I asked her to wake me or even add a gag as a preferable alternative to sneaking a peek inside my subconscious. She told me I was a spoilsport but agreed, because above everything else, she always has my back. Even if she doesn't agree with my choices, she's undoubtedly my one-woman cheerleader, crossing everything she has and wishing me all the luck in the world without so much as a twitch of a judgmental brow.

"No. Crazy would be giving Dave another chance to humiliate me and waste another God knows how many more years of my life." My laugh is rightly humorless and filled with contempt.

"Yeah, that would be crazy. But the States? Do you really have to go all that way to find *one* decent guy?" I choke back a cough and feel my cheeks burn with the truth and lie I'm about to serve.

"Orange County, California, and yes, it would seem so." Not technically a black lie, it's vague enough. And if my damn cheeks aren't flashing like a fucking beacon, I might get away with it.

"What *aren't* you telling me, Finn?" Hope shifts in her seat, and her tone is deadly serious. *Dammit.*

Now I could lie, but she would know. If we lived in the Dark Ages, she would've been burnt at the stake years ago; it's kind of spooky, her witchy ways. But the truth? If I tell her the actual truth, she's likely to grab the wheel from my hands and flip a one-eighty in the middle of the motorway, rush hour traffic be damned, and probably end poor Dolly in the process. So, I have to give her something meaty, the truth, but not quite the *whole truth* and maybe a little bit of, *nothing but the truth.*

"He's asked me to marry him." I think that counts as meaty, and I try for a casual delivery with my level tone, though I don't think it matters.

"What the fuck, Finn?" she hollers, causing my shoulders to shoot up to protect my ears because my hands are occupied.

"Are you out of your fucking mind? You've 'known' "—she exaggerates her air quotes and lays the sarcasm on thick with her condescending tone—"him for what, three months? And now, you're going to marry the dude?"

"I didn't say I *was* going to marry him. That's what this month is about. It's a trial." My words are stark in the silence of the car. They sound ridiculous when spoken out loud. Who does this? What sane, normal woman would? She's right; it's nuts. I'm out of my fucking mind. Which is why none of that matters.

I'm a crazy woman, and three months ago, I said, "Fuck it." *I* made this decision, and I'm not backing out.

"Oh, well, that's all right, then." The sarcasm is like treacle now, and her tone is tinged with bitter disbelief and disappointment.

This is not how I wanted today to go. I fix my mouth tight shut for fear of saying something I can't take back. The tension is palpable, and I cringe when Billy Idol's "White Wedding" crackles through the retro radio hanging from a makeshift hammock under the dashboard. *Perfect.*

We reach the airport and Hope helps me load my cases onto the trolley. She still hasn't said a word. I hand her the keys to Dolly and go to walk away. She's double parked, so I know she has to get going. She grabs the sleeve of my denim jacket and pulls me into her tiny, surprisingly strong hold.

"Wow, the gym's been paying off for you, too. You hug like a heavyweight." I groan under her hold.

"Or like I might never see my best friend again." Her soft words hit me hard.

"Hope…" I sigh and return her embrace with a gentle heartfelt squeeze around her shoulders, her head resting against my neck. I feel her body shudder with the first gasp of a sob. It's enough to make my nose tingle, and a slew of big fat tears fall onto my cheek.

"But it's true. That might be the case." She sniffs, sloppy wet sounds she doesn't try to hide.

"No, it's not true." I pull back and hold her gaze with mine, her dark green eyes fill with tears, matching my own. I blink to try and keep focus.

"Stay, Finn...please," she mutters, her fat lip wobbling.

She's killing me. "I can't, Hope." I shake my head, and the heaviness in my heart, the sadness I feel is a fraction of the sorrow I have endured, and she knows this. "I wasted ten years of my life with a man who had no intention of marrying me, H, and he even took delight in humiliating me about the fact in front of all my friends. He made me feel utterly worthless, and now..." I stutter and draw in a fortifying breath. "I have these men, and one of them promised to marry me. I get to choose... me, I—" I clamp my mouth shut at my apocalyptic fuck-up.

"Men?" she snaps.

"Man, I meant man." I wave my hand to dismiss my seemingly silly mistake,

"You said *men*," Hope corrects and then gasps. "Finn you didn't answer *that* advert?" Her hands fly to her mouth, eyes like saucers, and we both suck in a shocked breath.

"I...I..." I can't construct a sentence. She steps up to me and interrupts so I don't have to. *I wish she didn't.*

"That's who you've been talking to so secretively these last three months every spare minute. That's what all this gym shit you've been dragging me to morning, noon, and night for the last three months has been all about. It's because you need to be fit enough to take on four guys?" She stares at me, and her mouth is open so wide it's comical, but I'm not laughing. I'm waiting for the scream, the howl of judgment to rain down on my slutty arse. I draw in a breath and brace.

"Yes." I tip my chin, and time comes to a halt...and remains still as I frown at my friend, the statue. Her wide emerald eyes are fixed and focused, though I'm not sure on what. I wave my hand in front of her face, but she doesn't flinch. *Is it possible to be catatonic standing up?*

"Hope? Are you okay? You're kind of freaking me out." I look around to see if anyone else is observing my friend's weird behavior, but no one is paying us any attention. Well, other than the parking officer who is scowling between Dolly and the No Waiting sign. "Hope!" I hiss a little loud, and she blinks and gives a full body shudder, regaining her senses.

"Four guys?" she asks with a degree of awe in her tone.

I hesitate before answering.

"Yes."

"At one time?" She arches a brow, and her lips begin to curl into a wicked smirk.

"Not necessarily. We haven't actually gone over the logistics," I reply, a little straight-laced given the topic, after all, we're hardly in a secret-sharing environment.

"But they wanted a twenty-year-old?"

Her incredulous face pisses me off, and I place my hands on my hips and tip my chin, my tone a little on the defensive side. "Well, they got a *mid-to-late* twenty-year-old, who has worked her arse off to knock the last several years off her clock…literally." I straighten my back and subtly tighten my tummy in lieu of drawing in an obvious slimming breath.

"Oh babe, you do. You look smoking hot; don't worry about that." She pats my arms and flashes her best friend a reassuring smile. "No. You need to worry more about the fact you don't have enough holes, because, babe, that's something you can't fix at the gym." She bites her lip to hold in her trademark filthy laugh, but I crack first and she's quick to follow. She throws her head back, full-on belly aching, dirty laughter falling from her lips, eyes streaming, shaking her head. "Oh my God, you're going to be kept busy around the cock." She doubles over at her own joke and waves me down because I think she has another gem. "They're in the Forces right? They're going to want everything to run like clockwork."

"Okaaaay, then, are we finished?" I pat her back as she attempts to regain her composure.

"Sorry. So sorry…too tempting. You're right, you have a flight to catch. The cock is ticking. No time to be *dicking* around now." She snorts with another laugh.

"Hope." I sigh.

"Look, Finn. I still think you're batshit insane, but if you have to go crazy, at least you'll have lots of nuts to keep you company." She pulls me in for a final hug, and I can see she's genuinely smiling. Her face is a little wet from her tears, but her expression doesn't hold any anxiousness or tension. There's a little worry, which is understandable. *Maybe I should've told her sooner.* "I want you to promise to do one thing for me." She clears her throat; her tone is soft but serious.

"What's that?" I wait with bated breath for her to tell me what she'll need from me to ease her mind, and will it be anything within my power. She hesitates a moment before her shoulders start to shake.

"Pictures…I want *lots* of pictures." She snickers some more.

"I'm gone. I'll call you when I land." I turn on my heel and start to push the half-ton trolley away from my best—annoying—friend.

"With pictures!" she calls after me.

"Sure, with pictures." I turn my back to the trolley so I'm facing her while pushing the beast up the ramp.

"You go, girl. Take one for the team! Oh wait, no. Take *four* with the team!" She shouts with the volume of a crowd control foghorn over the entire departures drop-off area. I cringe, but raise my hand to wave her off. Her own hands are flapping at me like a crazy person before she sinks into the car. The parking officer has finally lost his patience and points for her to leave or get towed. *Dolly wouldn't survive a tow with all that manhandling.* I watch the cream and raspberry car filter into the traffic and disappear. *Shit, I hope I'm in better shape than Dolly when it comes to being manhandled.*

CHAPTER TWO

Four Months Ago

"You can't be here when he gets home, Hope. It will kind of ruin the surprise." I slam the oven door shut, having checked the chicken is doing whatever it's supposed to do in the oven, when I'm not allowed to drench it in a decadent cream sauce or rich wine gravy. The best I can manage within my boyfriend's tight 'health freak' guidelines is a light pan fry to give it some color, and then steam the little fella in the oven to try and keep it tender and juicy. Dave owns an elite gym in the West End of London with a superstar clientele, and appearance has become a bit of a focus for him. I guess it always has been, but I'm more conscious of it now, perhaps, since it's become less important to me.

"Oh, don't worry about that," she says, with enough horror in her tone to convince me she isn't joking. "I don't want to be here when you start dry humping your man as soon as he gets in the door."

"That wasn't the surprise I was going for." I narrow my eyes and stick my tongue out at her disturbed expression.

"But sex is…I mean it's why, under that coat you look like you're auditioning for the *Rocky Horror Picture Show*." She leans over and pulls the lapels of my Mac wide open. I squeal and re-tighten the loose material, cinching it firmly at the waist. I take a quick peek myself, because now I'm filled with panic.

"What? You're kidding right?" I laugh nervously, searching her implacable face for any signs she's joking. "I was hoping for agent provocateur seductress, not transvestite."

She rolls her eyes, tutting and shaking her head with a light admonishing smile.

"I'm kidding, Finn. Jeez, you're easy to tease when you're strung out or frustrated." She snickers, a deep, filthy, wicked laugh, and reaches for my hand to offer some genuine comfort. I'm all over the place with uncertainty and zero confidence. "You look fucking hot under the Mac. Is that part of the get up? He's into the whole flashing-in-public thing?" She takes another sip of my wine despite having declined her own glass, and has proceeded to drink nearly all of mine.

"Hardly. No, I was hoping we could go for a quick drink, and this might turn him on. I mean I'm practically naked under here." I hate sounding tentative about this, but I'm more than a little out of my comfort zone.

"Shit, Finn. You could wear a used bin liner, and you'd turn most men on. What makes Dave so special you're worried it won't? Does he have a golden dick or something?"

"No. I just…" I hesitate as I struggle to articulate feelings I don't really understand myself. "He's my best friend, Hope, apart from you, obviously."

"That's a given. Continue." She beams a smile which crinkles her bright green eyes and widens her even brighter painted red lips. Her wild, glorious red hair is slicked back in a severe bun, practical for work but a little harsh for her soft pixie features.

"Sometimes I feel that's *all* I am. I don't know when it happened but I worry we've slipped from lovers to mates, and I miss feeling…wanted…desired, you know?"

"Um… Only ever one-night stands over here, so not really." She gives an unapologetic shrug. I didn't really expect her to understand. Her longest relationship is with me. She was with me when, underage and out looking for fun, we snuck into club. We ran straight into Dave and his mates. In borrowed heels and the tightest dress this side of indecent, I literally fell on my arse at his feet. He owned me from that night on. I never stood a chance. I fell for him and didn't look back. I do have my doubts about Hope, on the other hand. I don't think she'd fall if she was hit with a fucking freight train.

"We've been together for a long time, Hope, and I think he's a little bored. So I thought I'd spice things up a bit."

"And is he making the same effort?" She purses her lips in an effort to temper her underlying objections. She does this a lot when we talk about Dave, however, this time, she's very wrong.

"I think he's going to do more than that." I rush out the words with a surprised blurt of excitement, which seems to pique her interest.

"Oh really? What?" She leans in closer to me, her face mirroring my smile.

"I think he's going to propose to me on Saturday." I drop my mouth in mock shock. Well, not mock since I am shocked.

"Why Saturday?" Her face is unchanged. No more excitement, no less either; however, she looks a little skeptical.

"It's his birthday, and he's been really secretive. It's not like him. I normally organize everything we do socially, but this time, he's called all our friends, booked a private room at the new club on the high street. He's even sorted the caterers. Every time I offer to help he says he's got it covered, and all he wants from me is to say, '*Yes*'." I clap my hands together in a rapid-fire mini applause.

"Fuck!" Now that tone *is* utter shock.

"I know." I giggle and bounce on my toes. "Honestly, Hope, all this time I thought he was going off me. I know he loves me, but he really hasn't shown much interest *sexually* for ages."

Hope wrinkles her nose with distaste. "Eww…Do we have to? I can't help having a visual when you talk details." She sticks two fingers down her throat as if her tone isn't enough for me to get the level of her abhorrence.

"I'm serious." I flick the end of the tea towel and catch her with an impressive snap on her arm. She yelps and scowls, and I ignore the fiery stare. "I've been really busy at work, and I haven't been to the gym in like forever. This"—I grab my squidgy midriff and then shift my hands to my size D-cups—"is not the body he signed up for."

"What? The body from when you were sixteen, you mean? Well, no fucking shit, Sherlock. Whose body is? Listen very carefully. You are fucking hot, any size you choose to be, so don't give me that shit. Has he actually said that, because I will cut him—"

"No! No, he hasn't." I wave her down as she brandishes a spoon as if it was a mighty blade of body-shaming retribution. "He wouldn't say anything like that. But, I know image is important to him, so I'm sure it's in the back of his mind, and I can't help thinking—"

"The proof of the pudding is in the eating, and if he isn't eating…" She wiggles her finger in the general direction of my crotch.

"Exactly." I sigh. "I honestly don't remember the last time he did *that*." I mouth the last word silently.

"Too many carbs?" She lets loose an unladylike snort, and I blurt out a laugh. I love that about her; she always makes me feel better. "So the big seduction thing is a preemptive thank you...a timely reminder of how fucking lucky he is?"

"I hope so."

"You know I fucking hate this about you? No, not *you*. I hate how he makes you doubt yourself. I don't get the whole marriage thing, but I know it's important to you and he does too. So the fact he's kept you waiting all these years chips away at your self-esteem and you're all, 'Maybe I'm not attractive to him anymore. Or maybe he sees me as just a friend'. It's billy bollocks. You fucking rock, and he's damn lucky to have you. There are hundreds of guys who would think the same as me. You happen to have fallen in love with a bit of a dick." She holds her hands up to signal the end of her little speech and draws in one more breath. "I'm not judging, just stating fact."

"It's complicated." I shrug off her tirade, because I have heard it before, and it stings because it's true.

"No, it's simple, although I'm jumping down from my soapbox because, he may be a dick, but he's *your* dick, and you are the only one who matters in the equation. Your happiness and you've wanted that white dress since we used to play dress-up when we were kids." She steps around the kitchen island to my side and wraps her arm around my waist.

"I still love to dress-up." I snicker, looking down at my kinky ensemble.

"The outfits have become a little dirtier—a little more leather than lace."

Hope wiggles her brow.

"And at least I fit into the heels." I lift up my leg to showcase my most spectacular shoes.

"Killer heels, and if they don't seal the deal, I don't know what will. I can guarantee it won't be that meal you're cooking."

"It's his favorite." I try to sound offended and defend my efforts, but she's right. *Again.*

"Bollocks. That's no one's favorite: steamed chicken, brown rice, and broccoli. Oh God, I'm going to gag." She starts retching, and I push her away then walk over to the hob to make sure as bland as this meal is, it's at the very least perfectly cooked. "Okay, I'm going to be off. Do you want me to meet you for lunch tomorrow? I'm working at the spa round the corner. I could pop in." She slips her bag over her shoulder, then grabs her keys and phone from the counter.

"Depends on whether you're coming to see me for lunch or coming to fuck my boss." I point an accusatory wooden spoon her way, and she boldly returns my stare with no shame, a fiery spark in her eyes.

"Well, he is *very* fuckable."

"Hope…" I warn.

"Fine! Lunch." She holds her palms flat in an act of supplication. "I promise no fucking. Maybe a quick handjob, but definitely no fucking."

So much for supplication.

She grabs her coat from the kitchen stool and makes to run from the room. Not that I could catch her with my skyscraper slingback stilettos.

"See you tomorrow. I can tell you all about it," I call after her.

"Please don't. I've only just stopped gagging from the food." She pops her head round the door, her shoulders jerking and her cheeks puffed out holding in pretend vomit.

"Out!" I point my finger and give my dismissal in a firm and final tone.

"Love ya', Finn." Her reply is delivered sing-song, which always leaves me with a smile.

CHAPTER THREE

"Hmm...something smells good, RP, what's the occasion?" Dave walks into the kitchen dropping his gym bag and briefcase. His near-black hair is still damp from the shower he would've taken before he left the gym. He is religious with his workouts, and I have to admit he looks damn good because of it. He's not overly tall, five foot eleven. I'm five foot five, so he's tall enough. He has wide shoulders, trim, narrow waist. His thighs are kind of weird now though, bulging and distorted with muscle mass, it makes finding jeans that fit a challenge. Every muscle from his tanned nose to his pedicured toes is toned to perfection, if a little bulky for my taste. I felt he reached perfection a few years ago, but apparently, that wasn't perfect enough. His face is bright with a wide smile, and his jacket strains at the seams when he draws in a deep breath through his nose, capturing the aroma of the meal I have tried so desperately hard to make interesting. He strides straight past me to the fridge, grabs a bottle of water, and peers over my shoulder at the pans simmering. He ruffles my hair that I had artfully fashioned into a messy bun. I thought at the time, *It is amazing how much effort is required to look effortless.* "Why have you got your coat on, if we're eating in?"

"I thought we could go out for a quick drink before dinner?" I give him a genuine, shy smile as I feel a surge of nervousness start to grip my tummy.

"Have I missed an anniversary or something?" He frowns, taking in the fact my face has little make-up and my coat isn't all I'm wearing.

"No, I thought we could try something a little *different*." I twist around so I'm now facing him, and with a boldness that surprises both me and him, I drag my leg up his thigh. The gap in the front of my coat widens and falls back, exposing my long leg, stocking, and suspender. I press the spike of my heel against his butt, impressed I can, one, get my leg up that high and, two, maintain my balance.

"You want to go out like that?" His derisive tone is as harsh as a slap in the face, but his mocking laugh is worse.

"Well, For a start, I'd quite like you to maybe not laugh at the suggestion." I slip my leg back down. I don't want to sound hurt or angry, or this evening will be a non-starter.

On the other hand, right now, I can't ignore the real pain from the slice of rejection that cut deep with his response.

"I'm not laughing. I'm a little surprised, is all. This isn't like you, RP—"

"Could you maybe not call me RP tonight?" I watch as more bemusement twists his features.

"Why? You know I don't mean anything by it. It's a nickname." I can see he's struggling to understand, but I don't want to go into details. I want a bit of fun and *a lot* of intimacy.

"I know. Just maybe not tonight." I try and keep my plea lighthearted but earnest, because it really is a shitty nickname.

"Fine. You're acting really weird, Finn. Are you on your period?"

"Oh, my God!" I hold my breath and count silently to ten, thanking all that's holy I don't have a knife at hand.

"Sorry. Clearly not, although…" His accusation hangs in the air like a noose swinging silently in the gallows, along with the remainder of my surprise evening.

"Jesus, Dave." My voice catches with an equal mix of fury and emotion.

"What? What have I done?" His tone has switched from confused to inflammatory with a tinge of aggression. "I walk in and, bam, you're acting all weird, wanting to have sex and go outside with me, while looking like a stripper."

"I'm weird for wanting sex?" I take a step back and cross my arms tight around my waist, covering as much of myself as I can. I still feel more than naked, utterly vulnerable.

"That's not what I said." He lets out a heavy sigh, his hands deep in his pockets, and he shifts uncomfortably from one foot to the other. "Look, can we start this again, and maybe you can talk to me and tell me what the hell's going on?" His tone softens, and I think that's worse. I get an intense prickle at the bridge of my nose, and I have to blink to stop the tears from welling. *I won't fucking cry.* I shake myself and straighten, pulling myself together.

"Fine, but I'm going to need a drink." I grab my empty glass and the bottle of white wine from the cooler.

"Really, RP? You know that's like a meal in itself. Do you have any idea of how many cal—" He wisely snaps his big, fat mouth shut as I spin to face him with thunder, and possibly murder in my eyes.

"If you say calories, I swear to God, Dave, this bottle is going where the sun don't shine, and it's not going in narrow end first." I wave my weapon of choice at his startled face. The only words playing in my head are Hope telling me I fell in love with a bit of a dick. I pour a large glass of wine, making a childish point to fill it to the top, slurping from the lip of the glass before I can lift it. I watch Dave intently as he nervously draws small sips from his bottled water.

"Do you love me, Dave?" I hold his gaze as his eyes widen with worry.

"Is this a trick question?"

"It really isn't." I let out a sigh, feeling the warmth of the alcohol hit my bloodstream, calming me some. This conversation feels a little weightier than I was anticipating. *I wasn't expecting much conversation at all.*

"Then yes, of course I love you. You're my best friend, my little RP. Well, not so little."

"Really, Dave? Is that seriously the problem here? That I've gained some weight?" I take another gulp.

"I was joking, and I never said that." He has a look of mock hurt blazing across his face that I could make such an accusation.

"We hardly ever have sex, so there has to be some reason."

"I love you, Finn. I'm not going to lie and say you are at your most beautiful now, because I personally think you'll look more gorgeous when you lose a little weight." He tips his head like that will soften the shallow, passive-aggressive insult.

"Just like I think you are most handsome when you're not so bumpy with all those gross muscles." I counter in all seriousness.

"No, but joking aside, Finn…" He barely gives my insult any recognition, and he certainly thinks it was a joke. "…you're a very beautiful woman, and I'm a lucky guy." He steps forward and sweeps his arms around me, pulling me close and holding me tight. *This is all I wanted, to be held…well, held and some cock. I'll take being embraced over indifference.*

"And the sex?" I push, because, actually, I would *really* like some cock. I think I've healed over.

"I guess I've just had a lot on at work, and I know this might come as a shock, but guys don't think about sex every five minutes." He laughs out loud and playfully taps me on the nose. I'm not entirely convinced, but he holds my gaze, and I do see the love in his dark hazel eyes. It's always been him, even if he can be a bit of a dick.

"So, we're good?" I ask and grind a little against his erection, which is most definitely just as keen as I am.

"We're more than good, Finn. You are my perfect woman, and on Saturday, I'm going to prove it."

"Saturday?" I ask, hoping for more, then not. I'm all tingly with the anticipation, and I kind of like the feeling.

"Nuh-uh. I'm not saying another thing." He kisses the tip of my nose, then my cheek. His lips brush mine, and as soon as I open my mouth to take a little more, he withdraws everything. His heat and his body. I sag from the loss, but he takes my hand. "Come here." He pulls me over to the kitchen island and slides his hands over my shoulders, squeezing the tense muscles and massaging with just the right amount of pressure to make me moan. What am I saying? I'm so horny a gust of wind would make me moan.

"I'm starving," he declares, and all ministrations cease. I tip my head up to meet his gaze. He has a relaxed smile, and I sigh, a little defeated but only a slight amount. I still have Saturday.

"So, do you want your dinner now?" My hope that he wants to give me more flatlines with his answer.

"Yes! Then you can give me a blowjob, how about that?" *Talk about throwing the dog a bone.*

CPSIA information can be obtained
at www.ICGtesting.com
Printed in the USA
LVOW03s1504150318
569990LV00001B/111/P